Fools & Heroes

Tales of the Dungeon Crawlers

Volume 2

Matthew Phillion

Fools & Heroes
Tales of the Dungeon Crawlers
Volume 2

Lost Continuity Press

Contact:

theindestructiblesbook@gmail.com

www.theindestructiblesbook.com

April 2023

Printed in the United States of America

© 2023 Matthew Phillion

Originally published as:

The Tomb of the Maker – July 2020
Splitting the Party – July 2021

Printed in the United States of America

ISBN: 9850132-1-4
ISBN-13: 979-8-9850132-1-4

First Edition: © Matthew Phillion / Lost Continuity Press

Cover Design by Sterling Arts and Design:
http://www.sterlingartsanddesign.com

Dedication

To everyone who has sat around a table with me telling stories. May we all find as much adventure in life as we do in our imaginations.

From the Author

Here we are, back in Revery. And much like any RPG party, the gang has found that maybe all that random adventuring at the beginning actually leads somewhere—and that they may need to step up and be big damned heroes.

The Dungeon Crawlers started off as an experiment in improvisational storytelling, much like a real tabletop game. The plan was to build upon each smaller story and see where it all leads. And in Book 4, *the Tomb of the Maker*, it leads to some dark and dangerous places. You've probably guessed by the name of Book 5 contained within these pages, *Splitting the Party*, just how risky Revery has become for our heroes.

Thanks for accompanying me along this weird road. I'm curious to see where our gang of misfits ends up, and if they can leave Revery better than they found it. Or, in the end, if they can leave at all.

So… who wants to roll for initiative?

Matthew Phillion
Salem, Massachusetts
April, 2023

Book 4:
The Tomb of the Maker

Prologue: Atrocity

Jack listened to the wind, and the wind spoke back.

The longer he and his friends remained here in Revery, the less he felt like himself. Jack had been a quintessential city boy back in the real world. The closest he came to camping was yard work. He had no affinity for the outdoors, and he certainly wasn't a hunter or tracker unless hunting for takeout menus or being able to track down the nearest coffee shop counted for something.

But on the night they began their game, when selecting classes to play and roles to become, he chose the ranger, called himself "Raven," and rolled the dice. And when he woke up here in this strange, if strangely familiar, place, a ranger he became. He saw tracks in the mud, noticed broken branches, strands of fur, little hints indicating where a creature might have passed through the forest around the small town they'd come to call home for a little while.

This is what he did here, as if being a ranger in the game compelled him to be a ranger in truth, patrolling just beyond the borders of their home, watching for danger, looking for signs of threats. And threats he found. He and his companions had driven off goblins and bandits, a manticore once, other creatures out of mythology or folklore that lurked on the edges of this world, waiting for a victim.

He sensed more than heard movement in the brush to his left. Silence, the wolf that had become his companion in this world, trotted to his side, bits of leaves and pine needles stuck to his fur. The wolf and the ranger locked eyes, that silent, unbreakable bond between them both disconcerting and comforting to Jack. There was a purity in the connection between them Jack had never experienced before, as if the wolf were an extension of himself. He couldn't put rational, real world reason behind it, but he felt safer knowing Silence was nearby.

The wolf turned and trotted back into the forest. Jack followed, bow in hand. The bow, carved with hints of dragon imagery and humming with arcane energy, was a gift from an undead hunter, one of the ghoulish beings he and his companions had encountered no more than a month ago. The ghoul had betrayed his kin, who had, not long before, devoured an entire village. More monsters, Jack thought. Revery keeps pushing us toward monsters. It felt intentional. Uncomfortable.

The smell hit Jack first. Blood and the filthy stink of spilled guts, a greasy stench of burned leather, wood, and flesh. He nocked an arrow and followed Silence into a clearing.

He found an orc camp, ransacked, littered with bodies and debris. The corpses were all orcs, big bruisers with skin of green or gray. Most of the bodies were headless, scattered and sprawled throughout the camp, some still clutching the weapons they died wielding.

He found their heads soon enough.

A dozen orc heads had been stuffed onto pikes, long, makeshift spears that appeared to be of orcish origin. Their oft-scarred, tattooed faces were twisted and warped, yellowed tusks jutting out from drooping mouths.

Jack expected to find the orcs out here. He'd seen their tracks for several days, and found signs they were preparing to raid the town. His plan, his hope, had been to locate their camp and return with his adventuring companions to either negotiate with them if they were willing, or drive them off if not.

Clearly, someone else found them first. And they'd slaughtered them.

Orcs in Revery, Jack learned over the past few weeks, were not uniformly evil as they were in other stories. They had a nomadic society, and many turned to raiding or pillaging out of desperation.

Any orc encampment set up this close to a human settlement possibly had plans to cause harm.

But Jack had simply hoped to scare them off, or maybe bargain with them. They'd had luck before with a gaggle of goblins with a bit of diplomacy, sending Tobias and his bardic talents in to convince the goblins it wasn't worth the blood they'd spill to attack the town. Jack himself had more than once on his patrols encountered orc hunting parties and parlayed peacefully. Talking didn't always work, but that was what the others were for, Eriko with her daggers, Tamsin with her spells, Cordelia with her mighty axe, and Morgan to keep them all safe. But none of Jack's friends had gone so far down the rabbit hole that death and war were their first choice. There was no joy in slaughtering goblins, but there was a bit of fun in chasing them off.

But he'd thought the orcs would bring more trouble, so he tracked them alone with caution and stealth.

And someone else had made quick, bloody work of the whole tribe.

Jack puttered curiously around the camp, looking for signs of what might have done this. The wounds on the orcs were made by blades, he could tell. This was a melee, not a monster. And the heads on spikes. This was a humiliation. Orcs, he knew, were capable of brutality, but they had a code, a simple one, but predictable: they did not defile those who fought well.

This had a playful horror to it.

It's something men would do, Jack knew, his stomach twisting. Only humans were this gleefully callous.

He searched the orc tents and their simple packs and gear. Little had been taken. Food left to rot. Weapons left to rust. This wasn't done for profit, he sensed. And he'd been patrolling the town long enough to know there were no other warriors acting as guardians of this place. A personal vendetta? He wondered. A rival tribe?

Jack reached down and scratched Silence behind the ear. The wolf leaned in affectionately. He looked at the dead orc faces staring back at him. They died afraid. Their fear was plain to read in their final expressions.

Frightened monsters, Jack thought. And whatever did this could not be far.

Soundlessly, he turned and darted back into the forest, taking care to hide his tracks, to leave no sign of his passing or where he headed. And he hoped whatever killed the orcs was not a more skillful tracker than he was.

Chapter 1: Settling in

"We're getting too comfortable here," Cordelia said, shaking Tobias out of a daydream.

He'd been thinking about home more and more lately, but not in a good way. The bard, who went by the fictional name of Oberon the Blue in this fictional world they were trapped in, was perhaps the least interested in returning to reality out of all his friends. He found his thoughts turning homeward though, in a sort of morbid game of asking why.

Why would any of us want to go home? He asked, over and over. Dead end jobs. Dead end relationships. Terrible economic futures. Also, not heroes. We're heroes here.

Tobias had decided he liked being a hero, possibly almost as much as he enjoyed being a bard.

Cordelia, he noticed, was growing more comfortable in the skin she'd taken on in Revery as well. The first few months she, more than any of the others, felt the distress of being someone else. She was tall back in the real world, sure, but going by her ironically delicate new name Orchid here, with her muscular, half-orc barbarian frame, she uniquely took up space. She had presence. And everyone knew it, too, especially Cordelia, who did not like the attention it brought her.

But the town folk had become familiar with the adventuring party, even affectionate once they realized that having a group like theirs in town meant that their town, Garmond's Corner, was well-protected. Cordelia no longer hunched the way she had when they first arrived. She wore a sleeveless leather jerkin now too, showing off the striated muscles of her arms and revealing her gray-green skin. She might be an intimidating orcish barbarian, but the residents of Garmond's Corner knew she was *their* intimidating orcish barbarian.

But still, Tobias could tell she wasn't ready to stay here. He wasn't either, truthfully. Back in the first town they had encountered in Revery, Moderate Expectations, there was enough hustle and bustle for Tobias, in the guise of Oberon the Blue, to play for crowds at busy inns and taverns, making money as a performer, growing his renown.

I didn't have any renown in the real world, Tobias thought. *Failed actor, failed singer, failed everything, really. Here I'm a hero. Plus, I have a fan base.*

Tobias shook off the cloud of his thoughts and turned his attention to his companion. They were strolling aimlessly through the main thoroughfare, looking for something to distract or entertain them. Not that there was much to do here—the shops were functional, the residents friendly and rustic, the welcomes warm, but there was little trouble to get into in town. Meanwhile, the others all had their distractions, which, Tobias knew, was what Cordelia was referencing. He asked anyway.

"What do you mean, too comfortable?" Tobias asked.

"We're settling in," Cordelia said. "Don't you feel like we aren't meant to settle in? The heroes in fantasy novels don't pick a little town and set up shop and never leave."

The comment sparked a memory, a conversation Tobias had had with Jack one night when they were both a few too many drinks into the evening. Jack was talking about the mysterious strangers he'd encountered during his scouting missions; other players like themselves who had become trapped in Revery years before and had never escaped. The game, Jack said, did not like inaction. It wanted them to adventure. It was almost as if the game itself fed off adventure.

He'd thought Jack was just being his usual melodramatic self, but Tobias couldn't help admitting a certain nagging feeling himself the longer they stayed here. Something felt off.

"We're not going to get the others to move on very easily,"

Tobias said.

"Well, not Eriko, for sure," Cordelia said. "Seriously, how did the woman who could never make a relationship last more than fifteen minutes somehow become permanently smitten with a farmer's daughter in a fantasy game?"

Tobias stopped walking and looked up at Cordelia solemnly.

"You want to know my theory?"

"Sure," Cordelia said.

"The game gives us what we want," he said.

"Eriko was not a farmer's daughter type," Cordelia said.

"No, but she was goddamned lonely," Tobias said.

"She was?"

We all were, Tobias thought. But Cordelia was the one who hid everything best. Of course she'd not notice.

"I think so," Tobias said, going with tact over snark. "And then she saves the day and gets the girl."

"Well, that's just one thing," Cordelia said. "Right?"

"Have you seen Morgan with the guy who owns the stable?"

"Oh," Cordelia said. "I mean, it's hard not to notice, because Morgan's got zero subtlety with that stuff, but I hadn't thought…"

"Morgan has never come out to his family back home," Tobias said. "And here, he can be himself. And have you talked with Samlin, the stable owner? Dude is fucking delightful, Cordie."

Cordelia seemed to drift off into her own thoughts for a minute, then grimaced and turned back to him.

"But what about us, then?" she said.

"I wanted an audience," Tobias said. "My sister wanted magic. Jack just wants to be heroic. Honestly, darling, you're the only one I can't figure out."

"I was tired of being afraid," Cordelia said.

"Well, nobody's messing with you now, are they."

"I hate this theory, Tobias," Cordelia said. "Because if the game is giving us what we want…"

"What happens when it decides to take it all away," Tobias said.

"Shit," Cordelia said.

"I do not, do *not*, want to be here for this stupid game to fridge Samlin just to give Morgan's character pathos. But I'm afraid this game relies heavily on tropes, and that makes me think all of us are at risk just so whatever mysterious overlord running this thing can amp up the tension."

"You don't really think there's a… game master doing this, do you?" Cordelia said.

"Not literally," Tobias said. "But it feels… intelligently designed, doesn't it?"

"You think the game has AI."

"And I think it's a mean AI."

"We need to do something," Cordelia said.

"We do," Tobias said. "But you try telling the lovebirds we need to go off and slay a dragon or something."

"I don't like this."

"Neither do I," Tobias said. "Drink?"

"It's not even noon," Cordelia said.

"So, is that a no?"

Cordelia rubbed her forehead, the stress plain on her face.

"No, I'm just noting the time when we regret it later," she said.

Chapter 2: Ordinary life

Eriko finished buckling on her sword belt and looked down at the bed where Jin lay sleeping. Sunlight, soft and gold, filtered through her brown locks, splintering the color into a complex weave. Eriko found herself staring at the spray of freckles across Jin's face, the heaviness of her lashes.

I'm in trouble, Eriko thought to herself. I'm in so much trouble.

Jin stirred, eyes opening to catch Eriko's stare.

"Hi there," she said, breaking into a smile. "Heading out?"

"Yeah," Eriko said, her voice unexpectedly husky. "Jack's been gone a while, figured I'd go check on him."

"He seems to always come back alright," Jin said. "Why not stay a while instead?"

"Just need to stretch my legs," Eriko said, trying to ignore the urge to count the colors in Jin's hazel eyes. I'm not like this, Eriko thought. I don't act like this.

"You don't look right, Rouge," Jin said. She sat up and gathered a dressing gown around her shoulders. "What's wrong?"

"I..." Eriko chewed her lip. She hated when Jin called her Rouge, but that was her name here, the same way Jack was Raven or Tobias was Oberon. Their adopted names were who they were supposed to be in this world.

But I want her to know who I really am, Eriko thought. I don't want to play pretend.

"Can I tell you something?" Eriko said, sitting down on the bed, careful to not catch her dagger's scabbard on the sheets.

"Now you're making me nervous," Jin said.

"No, it's a good thing," Eriko said. "I—okay, Rouge is a nickname. It's my name, but it's not the name I was born with."

"You're saying Rouge is not your real name in a very roundabout way," Jin said.

"I just want you to understand I wasn't lying about my name. That's the name I go by here. But you're too important to me to keep letting you call me some ridiculous adventurer's name. It was a play on words anyway. It's not the name I want you to know me by."

"You have… another name," Jin said, her face stern.

"I would have told you my other name right away if I'd known I was going to fall in love with you," Eriko said. "How was I supposed to know that? I don't fall in love with anyone."

"You're in love with me?"

Eriko could suddenly feel her pulse in her eyeballs.

"I haven't said that out loud before, have I," she said.

"You certainly have not," Jin said.

The room felt incredibly hot for absolutely no reason. Eriko felt a line of sweat run down the hollow of her spine.

Okay. Okay, I can do this, Eriko thought. Just… do what normal people do and don't lie.

"My real name is Eriko, and I'm in love with you, Jin. And I don't know what that means, but I do know I need to tell you this."

Jin kissed her, then pressed her forehead against Eriko's, holding her head in her hands.

"I've heard the others call you Eriko at least forty times, you idiot," Jin said, bursting into laughter. "I knew you were lying about your name."

"My friends are idiots," Eriko said.

"And… Eriko?" Jin said, opening her eyes and tilting Eriko's chin up so they faced each other. "I love you too."

What did I do right to deserve this, Eriko thought, holding Jin's hands in hers. I'm supposed to be the lonely, angry girl. This makes no sense.

I am in so much trouble, she thought.

* * *

Morgan stood just outside the town's most prominent stable, where he could watch the stable master, Samlin, brush down one of the horses housed within. Samlin, a long-limbed man maybe eight or ten years older than Morgan, treated all the horses under his care with a warmth and respect that made Morgan smile every time. He'd known horse people back in the real world, but never really had an opportunity to be around the animals himself. If he were being honest, Morgan would admit he was a bit afraid of them, unable to get a read on their thoughts in those dark eyes, intimidated by the raw power in their hooves and teeth if moved to anger. The fact that he now, in this fantasy realm, found himself falling for not just a horse person but someone whose whole life revolved around the animals, was ever so slightly surreal.

I'm fooling myself, aren't I, he thought, not expecting an answer. He still sometimes forgot that the fictional goddess who gave him his powers here in Revery occasionally answered back, usually when he least expected it. Her voice, resonant and soothing, replied.

This world is more real than you know, Bastion, the goddess, Theana said, calling him by the name he went by here, where he played a battle priest, watching over his friends, and now this small town as well. *And the attachments you find here are as real as you let them become.*

That sounds dangerous, Morgan thought.

Love often is.

Did I somehow choose to follow a goddess of wisdom and perceptiveness when I rolled those dice? Morgan asked. Or did you choose me when I arrived here? I wonder what it would've been like if I were a priest of… I don't know. Fire. The hearth.

Revery ties together those who need to be, Theana said. *I needed you to be my warrior. You needed me to keep you safe.*

Before Morgan could answer, Samlin noticed him watching. The stable master's face split into a radiant smile. He often made fun of himself, saying he had teeth as big as the horses he cared for, but Morgan didn't agree. Samlin had that rarest of things: an honest smile.

"Inspecting my work, Brother Bastion?" Samlin said, patting the red-brown mare he'd been brushing on the rump.

"Just stopping by to say hello," Morgan said. He felt off-center, exposed, and knew he felt this way not just because Samlin seemed to be able to read him better than even some of his friends from the real world, but also because he was without his armor today. He worried the light tunic he wore might cling to his slight gut unflatteringly, or that he was less impressive without the cuirass he usually wore.

Samlin put a hand affectionately on Morgan's face.

"An afternoon visit by a dashing battle priest is always welcome," he said.

Morgan smiled self-consciously and laughed.

"I don't want to distract you from your work."

"This is stable hand work," Samlin said. "I'll have one of the boys finish up here. I do this because I enjoy checking on the animals. The hands need to keep busy."

Samlin's face darkened, looking past Morgan's shoulder out into the street.

"Speaking of work to do, my competition for your affections is approaching, and he looks distressed."

Morgan chuckled again. Samlin had teased from the first day they met that Morgan and Jack behaved like an old married couple, but it was always good-natured teasing. Jack, in his guise as Raven the ranger, leaned on Morgan more than the rest of their party because Jack knew they were the two… not the leaders, per se, but the group worrywarts. Jack would worry about something, need to tell someone about it, and go confess to Morgan, and vice versa. They'd been this way since childhood.

"He's probably just fretting over some goblins again," Morgan said. He turned and immediately knew he was wrong. Jack didn't look worried; he looked haunted. Even the wolf, Silence, seemed subdued, trotting obediently beside him.

"I'll leave you two to talk," Samlin said. "Looks like he has adventurer business to discuss with you."

"You don't have to," Morgan said.

"Trust me, I'm happy to not know what the Raven finds when he's out scouting," Samlin said. "I know enough about what's wrong with the world without hearing what he digs up every time he drags you and yours out into the field again."

That was the other process that they'd settled into, Morgan thought, sighing. Jack would find trouble—not melodrama, but an actual danger to the town or nearby travelers—and the party would gather, run off to be heroes, and come back to town to recuperate. Samlin had read the room correctly, as he often did, which Morgan very much enjoyed about him.

"Are you busy for dinner?" Morgan asked as he started toward Jack, not wanting to have whatever terrible conversation the ranger needed to have inside the stable.

"I'm not, but I have a bad feeling you might be," Samlin said, shooting Morgan another of his gleaming smiles. "Come find me if you aren't off slaying a manticore."

Morgan nodded, then trotted out to meet Jack in the street.

"When you named your character, you nailed it," Morgan said. "You are always a messenger of doom, Jack. What's wrong?"

Jack scanned the street, making sure no one was within earshot.

"Not sure yet," he said. "But I found an orc encampment."

"Simple enough to deal with," Morgan said.

"No," Jack said. "They were all dead. Heads on pikes. Something already killed our problem. And killed them ugly."

"And you're worried whatever did for the orcs…"

"Might come here next," Jack said. "I mean, I could be wrong. The enemy of my enemy, that sort of thing. But I don't think the good guys put heads on pikes. That's usually a bad guy thing."

"Yeah," Morgan said, a wave of disappointment and exhaustion washing over him. "Do we tell the others?"

"Better they're ready for trouble," Jack said.

"I was really hoping to have a date for dinner tonight, Jack," Morgan said.

"No reason you can't," Jack said, finally cracking into a grin. "Just bring your war hammer. Just in case."

"Nothing says romance like a maul," Morgan said.

Chapter 3: Dragged back to hell

Bennett awoke with a kick to the ribs, a heavy, hob-nailed boot thumping hard against his thin chest.

"Get up, Anders," the gruff, unfamiliar voice said, calling him by his character name. Anders the thief. Anders the scoundrel. Chaotic neutral Anders, all about himself in a group of companions who were all very much about themselves.

Fucking murder hobos, Bennett thought, blinking his one remaining eye furiously as he tried to come fully back to consciousness.

The camp was a slovenly mess, of course. A wild boar had been killed and messily butchered during the night, hanging like an accident victim from a spit over a sloppy fire. Men he didn't know—henchmen, Bennett suspected, non-player characters the group had coerced or charmed or hired along the way—sharpened weapons, adjusted mismatched armor, fought, argued, swore. One, a fighter of some sort with a red ponytail sprouting from the back of his balding head as if his long hair had started sliding off the rear of his skull en masse, was taking a loud piss uncomfortably close to where Bennet had been just sleeping. When he caught sight of Bennett staring at him, the red-haired henchman spit at him, only missing because somehow Bennett still retained some measure of the reflexes his roguish life had granted him.

"You're up," the soft voice of one of Bennett's childhood friends said. The voice emanated from within a deep black cowl, bony hands holding an ornate staff, resting it against one bony shoulder. Long fingers reached up to pull the cowl back, revealing a long, graying beard, the skin beneath it red and raw as if the wearer never learned to wash his facial hair properly. Above that scraggly beard the eyes were clear, sharp, smart. He tossed Bennett a rag. "For your head."

"Good morning, Craig," Bennett said, realizing his forehead was sticky with blood. He checked the rag to make sure it was moderately clean and then pressed it against a cut above his eyebrow, over his missing eye.

"Not Craig here, Bennett."

"I've known you since first grade, Craig. I'm not calling you Asptooth."

"You will if you know what's good for you," Craig said. "How's your head?"

"Ringing."

"You've got to stop trying to run off," Craig said, handing Bennett a wineskin. "Here, this'll take the edge off it. Every time you run off it gets worse. I don't know how long Blaggard is going to find it funny to have his men beat the shit out of you and just lets them kill you."

"Dom can go to hell," Bennett said.

"See, shit like calling him by his real-world name is just going to make it worse for you. He won't kill you. He'll just hurt you."

"The game turns Dom into the hulking warrior he always wanted to be, and he's still, decades later, just a little man trying to make up for his own perceived inadequacies," Bennett said.

"Goddammit, Anders, you know if he hears you playing junior psychologist he'll let the groupies kick you 'til you piss blood."

"Bennett. Come on, Craig, call me by my real name."

As he spoke, a small creature, monkeylike, red-skinned, with a pair of bat-like wings and tiny black horns, landed on Craig's shoulder. The imp whispered in Craig's ear. He pointed a bony finger at Bennett's face.

"Keep your mouth shut," he said, standing up and walking away. Bennett could hear strange sounds rattling from within Craig's robes, spell components in tiny jars and little leather sacks.

"Good morning, sunshine!" a booming voice said. Bennett sighed. Striding into the camp, adjusting his pants dramatically, was Dom. Dom was known in Revery as Blaggard the Black, a corrupted paladin. He wore only parts of his armor, blackened metal adorned with blood-stained spikes in places. He kept his long black hair, now shot through with gray in places, in a sloppy partial topknot. His beard was jet black, his pale, scarred face half-hidden by it. Dom had a massive two-handed axe slung across his back. He was flanked by a pair of hangers-on, sidekicks he'd picked up along the way, and one more familiar face further back, a long-haired man in pristine armor with a mace cradled in his arms. Brandon, the shadow priest, one of their original party. He went by Valamir here and shot Bennett a withering glare from just past Dom's shoulder.

"Anders! Glad you made it back in one piece. More or less," Dom said. He ripped a slab of meat off the boar with his bare hands and threw it to Bennett. "Eat up. We can't have our best rogue underfed. You look like you've been starving yourself."

"Why can't you just leave me be, Dom?" Bennett said.

Dom's face darkened. His lip curled for a moment, but then the storm of rage seemed to fade.

"We're a party, Anders. Remember? Warrior, wizard, thief, priest. We belong together. And we need you, my man," he said. "Even with nine fingers, there's no better at picking locks in this hellhole. We need your delicate talents, my friend."

"You can't tell me there isn't someone in this entire world who is more useful to you than a half-blind, nine-fingered thief, Dom."

Again, the bigger man's face twitched as he restrained his rage at the name. He exhaled heavily, nostrils flaring, and stood up.

"We did find a replacement in your first absence. Younger kid, lost his party from another campaign, you know how it goes. But he wasn't quite so... morally flexible as we needed. So, I terminated his contract with us."

"You killed him?"

"I bashed his brains in," Dom said. His sycophantic followers chuckled. "Last thing I need is a rogue telling me about ethics. This is our fucking playground. We make the rules in Revery."

Bennett just stared silently. He felt the cut on his forehead reopen, a thin line of blood running down his face.

"I never did understand what your problem was, Anders," Dom said. Now it was Bennett's turn to grimace at his name, a push-pull between their fictional identities and their real selves.

"It was the kids, Dom. I couldn't believe what you did to those kids."

There were no flaring nostrils or twitching lips this time. Dom crossed the camp in three steps and picked Bennett up by his shirt, lifting the rogue off the ground entirely. One large, gauntleted hand encircled Bennett's neck, the thumb pressing down roughly.

"Call me that name one more time, you little shit," he said.

"This game let us become heroes, and you just stuck to power gaming, Dom. It's pathetic."

Dom slammed Bennett to the ground, knocking the wind out of him. Bennett struggled to pull himself to his feet but couldn't.

"Show Anders over there what we do to deserters," Dom said with faux disinterest to the mouth-breathing onlookers. "But watch the hands. We can't have him losing any more fingers yet."

Fists and feet began to slam into Bennett's body. He felt consciousness slipping away. And just before blackness overtook him, he looked up to see Brandon, the cleric Valamir, shake his head disdainfully and walk away.

Chapter 4: No school of witchcraft and wizardry

Magic was not what Tamsin expected it to be.

No, she thought, studying the books laid out before her on the floor of her room at the inn the party had taken to staying at between adventures. No, that's not true. Magic is much like she expected, minus the fun. It was work. Not that she minded working hard. She'd always been studious by nature. But rooting through damaged spell books, torn scrolls, staring at arcane runes and languages long dead in this fictional world, all to parse out the words and gestures and strange materials she'd need to cast new spells… it was labor intensive.

In their travels, the group had been almost too successful at finding spells for Tamsin to unravel. They'd come across a spell book in an early battle that gave her access to several useful enchantments and invocations. Later on, Tamsin had found a burned but useable book in a treasure trove; a sheaf of scrolls which, though battered and incomplete in places, had several more useful spells for her. Another book also which had clearly been ransacked, pages torn out or ripped in half, but still had some secrets to share.

Many were beyond her comprehension, or at least her current abilities. She saved those, the ones whose spidery language danced on the edge of her vision but wouldn't quite take to memory. But others enabled her to scry over vast distances, or conjure elemental creatures—this process she researched but had not yet attempted, the idea of commanding a mystical being feeling too much like forced servitude for her liking. She unlocked a spell for teleporting across short but useful distances, another that would shatter locks on doors or safes, one that opened her mind to understand or read languages she didn't know on her own.

The one currently confounding her would, as she understood it, allow her to transform herself or one of her friends into an animal. This sounded cool, but the spell gave no indication, at least on the surface, whether that transformation would leave their mental facilities intact. It might be helpful in a fight to change her twin brother Tobias into a bear, but if that transformation meant he also thought like a bear, well…

Someone knocked politely at her door. She placed a strip of silk between the pages of the spell book she'd been reviewing and stood up to open the door. Jack, still in his studded leather armor, casually holding the ornate, enchanted bow he'd been given by an ally recently, stood there looking sheepish.

"You know you can just walk in," she said, gesturing for him to enter.

"Didn't want to interrupt your studying," Jack said.

"You too?" Tamsin said. "Everyone else hasn't let me forget the one time Tobias startled me and I almost set him on fire."

"I'm just saying, it's polite to knock first."

"But I didn't set him on fire," Tamsin said.

Jack shrugged. She studied his face. This world was hardening him, she observed. It was having a similar impact on all of them, but the more time Jack spent ranging alone, the sharper his features became, the grimmer his eyes. He was always a bit moody back in the real world— "Goth minus the black outfits" Tobias once said teasingly—but here it was less an affectation and more exhaustion. While Tamsin spent countless hours mentally wrestling with spells and Tobias earned the group coin through performing, Jack was out in the world looking for trouble, and usually finding it.

Even still, he seemed worse than usual. She put a hand softly on his arm, then slid down to hold his wrist.

"What did you find?" she said.

Jack told her about the orc massacre he'd encountered. He didn't hold back on the details, which Tamsin appreciated. Some of the others, Cordelia and sometimes Morgan, still handled her with kid gloves, because she and her brother were the least experienced with the sort of games that emulated Revery. Come on, she thought. I grew up in America. The real world is scary enough that they didn't have to hide the gory details about the monsters they faced.

"What are we going to do about it?" Tamsin said.

She followed Jack's eyes, where he stared at the books on the floor.

"You found some spells in those old books for detecting things, yeah?" Jack said.

"I have," Tamsin said. "There's some really useful stuff in the one we found in that abandoned tower. They're not flashy spells for blowing things up or setting them on fire, but they're like… perfect for searching for clues. For understanding things."

"Smart spells for smart people," Jack said, smiling.

"Just call me Detective Nimue," Tamsin said, invoking the name of her fictional character in Revery, Nimue the Silver. "We can start our own agency digging up clues."

"Well," Jack said, taking a deep breath. "I'm tapped out as far as simple tracking goes. Whoever killed those orcs made a mess and then stomped off into the wilderness. I could follow them well enough, but I was thinking, if we don't have to walk into a confrontation with them blind, we'd be better off."

"You want me to cast a few of these spells at the orc campsite and see if they tell us more about what we're facing," Tamsin said.

"Exactly," Jack said. "I don't know if that feels like a… I don't know. Beneath you? You're a wizard. This seems like it's below your pay grade."

"Jack, all I've ever wanted to do is look for clues," Tamsin said. "That's what magic is. It's learning things that do not want to be learned. I would love to give this a shot."

"Good," Jack said, relief spilling over his face.

"You know, you weren't so shy about asking me for things before we became… whatever we're calling this," Tamsin said.

"Yes, I was," Jack said. "But I found you intimidatingly attractive so I avoided asking you for anything, ever, at all cost, so you never noticed."

"I just thought you didn't like me much," Tamsin said.

"Funny how that works out, isn't it," Jack said.

"People are strange, aren't we," Tamsin said.

Jack nodded.

"So, when do we leave?" Tamsin asked.

"Camp's only a few hours away. Shorter if we borrow horses. We can head out whenever you're ready. Morgan's gone to find the others."

Tamsin stepped into a pair of boots by the door, threw a cloak around her shoulders, and tucked her wand into a holster she'd had made on her belt.

"Let's go be medieval detectives," she said.

Chapter 5: All I wanna do is scry, scry, scry

Cordelia didn't expect to feel this way.

Jack led the party several hours outside of town, up into the brush-laden hills that acted like a hint of things to come for the violet mountains beyond them. Cordelia could smell the death before she could see it. Jack's wolf, Silence, seemed to pick up on her distress immediately, nosing the palm of her hand like a family pet. She absently scratched behind Silence's ear and patted his neck firmly.

They broke through the tree line and were confronted by heads on spikes.

Orc heads.

Cordelia turned and emptied the contents of her stomach into the shrubbery they'd just emerged from.

"You okay, Cordelia?" Eriko asked, handing her a flask. Expecting water, Cordelia was surprised, not unpleasantly, to find it contained the powerful, clear alcohol the villagers were fond of brewing—bathtub hooch, as Tobias liked to call it. She swished the burning liquid around in her mouth, its antiseptic, stinging taste masking that of regurgitated breakfast, then spat it out ungracefully.

"You told me they were orcs," Cordelia said. "But I should have thought more about it. I forgot they look like…"

Well, not like me, Cordelia thought, not exactly. Her character, her avatar, was a human/orc hybrid, so she was smaller and not quite as heavily muscled than these powerful, green-skinned men and women. Her lower canines were prominent but not tusk-like the way theirs were. Her ears had a delicate point to them, whereas these people had oversized, almost knife-like ears. Her features, though green-tinged, were distinctly different from theirs, or at least that's how she felt.

But no, she thought. I look at them and I see myself. These might have been friends or allies or even family. And here they are, butchered and drying in the sun like hunting trophies.

"I'm not really orcish," Cordelia said. "Why is this hitting me in my guts like I knew these people?"

"Because Revery wants us to care," Tobias said, more softly than his usual delivery.

"What's that?" Morgan said. The cleric had already started tidying up the bodies, laying them respectfully side by side on the earth, though even he, not usually squeamish, seemed afraid to touch the spikes. Cordelia exhaled sharply through her nose and went to work removing the heads. There was no hope matching them up with the rest of their bodies, she thought.

"Working theory, I have," Tobias said, almost mumbling.

"Working theory? Care to share with the rest of us?" Morgan said. There was an edge to his voice Cordelia hadn't heard in a long time.

Tobias strummed his lute absently.

"A good roleplaying game makes you care about the story is all," the bard said. "And…"

"You think the world tells us what to care about," Eriko said, meandering in and out of torn tents looking for clues.

"My theory's just a work in progress," Tobias said. "Forget I said anything."

"I didn't bring you all up here so we could argue over meta-gaming theory," Jack said. "Tamsin, I hate to ask, but do you think you could try that new spell you learned?"

Tamsin looked worse than any of them, her face pinched, her eyes red-rimmed. The twins really were the soft-touch members of the party, Cordelia thought. She found herself momentarily annoyed at Tamsin before realizing she was more than a little protective of Tobias for being the same way. Gotta sort that bias out in my own head, Cordelia thought. Not sure where *that* came from.

"Help me find a clear space. I need three or four feet of sort of flat ground," Tamsin said.

It was easy enough to set her up once the butchered bodies were laid respectfully together, scattered, abandoned weapons tossed aside. Tamsin began drawing in the dirt, then pulled out a pouch from one of the endless pockets within her wizard's robes. She wiped sweat from her brow, then unclasped the blue cloak around her shoulders. The cloak, as if with a mind of its own, leapt from her back and coiled around Tobias, the bard patting the cape like one would a family pet. Cordelia regularly forgot the twins were sharing custody of an enchanted cloak, which all evidence indicated decided which sibling it preferred on any given morning and betrayed the other. It was like a long, flying, blue house cat and Cordelia had not once seen it do anything useful.

"I'm not exactly sure how this will go," Tamsin said, pulling her silvery hair into a messy ponytail, revealing pointed elven ears. Do Tamsin and Tobias feel more elf than human? Cordelia wondered. Or am I somehow more 'other' than they are? The stares they get in town are of a different variety than the ones I do, that's for certain.

Tamsin began muttering arcane words, her hands flitting like spiders as they created alien shapes in the air over the symbol she drew in the dirt. The lines she'd traced in the ground began to glow, and then her eyes lit up with the same hue.

"Humans did this," Tamsin said. "Or mostly human. Mercenaries or adventurers by the look of it. Mismatched armor. Good weapons. These weren't amateurs. Their leader is... no, they're all older than us. Forties or fifties at least."

Tamsin gritted her teeth and made a pained hissing noise.

"They were overpowered for this fight. The orcs never stood a chance. They have a mage, dark robes, maybe a cleric? Yes, a cleric, but not like you, Morgan, dark armor, his spells are a different color palette. Lots of others, but they're indistinct and follow the orders of the more unique men. I think... Tobias?"

"I'm right here, Tam," Tobias said, kneeling beside his sister and placing a hand gently on her shoulder. She seemed to acknowledge him without seeing him, a sightless nod in his direction.

"Your friend. From Moderate Expectations."

"The barkeep?"

"No."

"'I'm a bard. I had a lot of friends there."

'The player character, Tobias. The old man."

"Bennett? The rogue who was taken while we were away?"

"Yes! Eyepatch, missing finger, tired."

"That sounds like him."

"These people have him," Tamsin said. "He's not with them. He's bound. Not taking part in the slaughter. The others… they make fun of him. The big warrior in charge just flicked his sword at him so blood splashed on his face."

"Are they saying anything?" Morgan asked.

"This kind of scrying doesn't come with sound, sorry," Tamsin said. "Maybe that's a higher-level spell. Just video on this one."

"Are they doing anything that indicates why they did this?" Jack asked.

Tamsin shook her head.

"They're not even taking anything. They're just… killing. Like it's a game."

"I suppose depending on your style, killing is the game here," Eriko said softy.

"Guys, I think these are player characters, like us," Tamsin said.

"They can't be, can they?" Cordelia asked. "I thought we were the only ones."

"We're not," Jack said. "You know I met the druid outside of Moderate Expectations. There have always been other players here."

"But I thought they were all gone," Cordelia said.

"Or maybe the others went feral," Morgan said.

"Bennett told us his group became murder hobos," Tobias said. "Remember? Maybe I was the only one there for that conversation. But he said his friends leaned into the dark side of the game and that's why he bailed."

"And now they have him captive," Eriko said. "But why? What's the point?"

"Does your vision tell you which way they went?" Jack asked.

Tamsin nodded she extended her arm to her left, southward.

Toward the village.

"Shit," Morgan said, putting a razor's edge on the last consonant. "We have to get back. Right now."

Tamsin blinked her eyes as they returned to normal, squinting as if walking out into daylight from a dark theater. She squinted into the distance toward the village.

"Is that smoke?" she asked.

"I fucked up," Jack said, helping Tamsin to her feet. "We have to get back."

Chapter 6: Fate is a game mechanic

Samlin's stable was on fire.

Several buildings in the village were ablaze, but it was the stable that sent Morgan running ahead, the big man's armor clanking as he tried to sprint. Don't you dare do this to us, Tobias thought to himself. There are better ways to move us to action than cruelty, you terrible place.

The others began jogging after Morgan, but it was only Tobias who caught Eriko darting off in another direction. She saw him watching.

"I have to go," she said. "You all stay with Morgan. I just…"

"Splitting the party as usual," Tobias said. Eriko hesitated just the slightest bit before her expression went dark. "No, I'm not serious. Go see her, make sure she's okay."

Eriko's frown of worry broke just a bit before she turned and ran off on her own. Tobias broke into as much of a run as he could to catch up to the others. He still hadn't figured out how to run in these strange clothes, his lute clanging against his back.

He arrived outside the stable just in time to see Morgan throwing his arms around Samlin. The stable master looked smoky and weary but not harmed.

"I'm fine, I'm fine. I can't say that for everyone, but I'm okay," he said, patting Morgan on the back as if to make sure the cleric was really there.

"Who's hurt? I can…" Morgan started, but Samlin shook his head.

"Bandits, raiders of some kind," Samlin said. "Well-armed. Too well-armed to be raiding little villages like ours, if you ask me. They killed one of my stable boys who ignored my orders to just let them take what they wanted. We weren't ready to fight well-armed warriors. The boy… well, his death was quick, so at least there's that."

"Your stable," Morgan said.

"Took most of my animals," Samlin said. "Nothing compared to murder, but…"

"Who else was hurt?" Cordelia said. Behind her, Tamsin began making arcane shapes with her hand and drew a rune in the air. It sparked once, leaving a glowing imprint momentarily in Tobias' vision, and a small storm cloud formed over the stable and began to rain on the flames.

Samlin gestured down the street.

"They pillaged Jan, the blacksmith's shop. He tried to stand up to them and they took his arm off at the shoulder. We tried to help him, but it wasn't enough. A couple of the young folk from town decided to fight back when that happened and they were cut down, too."

"Horses, the blacksmith… what else did they take?" Jack asked.

"We don't have much here, you know that," Samlin said. "They just… took what little we had that was worth taking. Supplies. They were looking for mining equipment, I remember hearing them talk about that during the fight with Jan."

"We should have been here," Morgan said, his voice rippling with rage.

If we'd been here, they wouldn't have come, Tobias thought, but he kept the observation to himself. Cordelia knew it too, though—she stared at Tobias until he caught her eye. Revery doesn't want us settled. It wants us challenged.

Samlin looked back at his now rain-soaked and smoking stable, his shoulders slumped.

"I can raise more horses. I can build another stable. I can't bring Jan or young George back to life," he said. Then Samlin turned his attention to Tamsin. "Are you able to do that again? The rain?"

Tamsin nodded, a smile growing across her face with her realizing it. She always just wants to be useful, Tobias thought. We really are mirror images, not the same.

"Of course," Tamsin said.

"There's a few other shops they set on fire. Maybe I could show you to them," Samlin said. Tamsin nodded and the two started down the thoroughfare, Morgan walking beside them. Jack wandered into the burned out stable scanning for clues or tracks, Silence padding along beside him. Tobias backed slowly in the other direction so he could look just around the corner, where the nearest tavern was still standing, and not on fire.

"Where are you going?" Cordelia asked in a stage whisper.

"I can't sing a fire out. I can't strum my lute and bring someone back to life," Tobias said. "So I'm going to go get a drink and try to forget I predicted something like this was going to happen."

Cordelia looked openly torn between joining him or following Jack. She shook her head, but Tobias couldn't tell if it was in disgust or resignation.

"Just try not to make us look like assholes," she said, walking into the smoky shadows of the stable to find Jack.

Tobias took a deep breath, composed himself, then strutted into the bar with his usual swagger. Fake it til it's real, he thought, throwing his cloak onto a rack at the door. The barkeep, Miriam, watched him warily.

"Could've used your lot this morning," she said, placing a glass in front of her one other customer, a thin man in black robes, his back to the door.

"Miriam, if it makes you feel any better, I think they were waiting for us to leave," Tobias said. "And while we weren't here to defend you, I can assure you, we'll avenge you for what happened."

Miriam poured a generous amount of a local liquor into a stubby glass and placed it on the counter so it was waiting for him when he sat down.

"Is it true they killed the blacksmith?" she asked.

"I haven't seen it for myself, but so I've been told," Tobias said.

"Known Jan since he was born, you know," Miriam said, her voice almost wistful. "He came in here a few times a week. Always talking about the latest project. You'd think it wasn't possible for a man to be that enthusiastic about horseshoes."

Tobias raised his glass to Miriam, who hefted a glass of her own he hadn't noticed before.

"To Jan, then."

"To Jan. You'll get them for us, yeah?"

"We will, my dear. I promise," Tobias said. He tossed back the entire contents of his glass in one gulp and sighed as it burned all the way to his guts. *They could've killed Miriam*, he thought. *And where would I be then, huh? My favorite barkeep with her little gray head bashed in and nobody to ply me with free drinks.*

"Revery's a pretty little hellhole, isn't it," the stranger in black said. Tobias turned to get a better look at him. Fifties, maybe a bit older. Dark beard well-kept and flecked with silver. Sharp eyes. Smart. Very smart, taking in everything about Tobias with such casual observational skills it made him feel dirty. Male pattern baldness leading to a high forehead, but the man had the face to carry it off. Thin, hard, everything about him.

"Well, don't you just set off every Spidey-sense radar I have all at once," Tobias said. "Are we going to fight? I don't really want to fight."

"You're the bard," the man said. "What kind of a name is Oberon the Blue?"

"It's a name a bard would use," Tobias said.

The stranger laughed.

"This fucking world," the man said. "What's your real name, kid?"

Tobias raised an eyebrow as high as it would go.

"Oh, great."

"I'm not here to fight you. I just don't want to call you by some ridiculous name that isn't yours."

"Tell me yours and I'll tell you mine," Tobias said.

"Well, my stupid Revery name is Mordecai the Unholy," the stranger said. "But my friends called me Leo."

"Called. You said called. Past tense."

"Well, this world killed most of them… name?" Leo said.

"Tobias."

"Thank you. Revery killed most of my friends, Tobias," Leo said. "And the few it didn't I don't talk with too much anymore. Turns out when you pick the 'necromancer' character Revery wants you to be a solo player more than a group asset."

"There was a necromancer option?" Tobias said.

"We had the expansion set," Leo said.

"There's an expansion set?"

"Oh yeah," Leo said. "Revery is the biggest game world you've never heard of."

Tobias looked to Miriam anxiously, who refilled both of their glasses and walked away, humming to herself.

"I met another player before. Real name Bennett, went by Anders. Do you know him?"

"Oh, I know Anders and his crew," Leo said. "Revery is big, but it wants players to find each other. It finds ways to make that happen."

"But he wasn't a friend of yours."

"His group arrived after mine," Leo said. "And they're garbage people."

"Says the guy who raises the dead. I mean I might be jumping to conclusions but you said you're a necromancer. I assume there's dead-raising involved?"

"There is, you're not wrong," Leo said.

"Just checking," Tobias said. He threw back his second drink as quickly as the first. "This may seem awfully forward, but… why are you here?"

Leo laughed. For a necromancer, it was a shockingly pleasant sound.

"I'm here because I think my friend is wrong," Leo said.

"I thought you just told me your friends were all dead or didn't talk to you," Tobias said.

"This is true. But we do talk when we must. Especially when it comes to important things. And my friend Malcolm thinks one of you is destined for greatness."

"Clearly, you're looking for me, then," Tobias said.

"My friend doesn't think so," Leo said. "Revery is sick, Tobias. We always thought it fed off heroism, you see. That it needed heroes—players of the game, like us—to sustain itself."

"Okay, maybe I'm not the one you're looking for, then," Tobias said.

"My friend—his name is Malcolm—he thinks your friend Jack is the one we should keep an eye on."

"Well, the angsty ranger boy is a classic archetype," Tobias said. "That'd be my first pick. Or maybe Eriko, because why not go with the angsty rogue, right?"

"That was our original thought," Leo said. "But our dashing swashbuckler friend is long dead, and so is our glorious and selfless shining knight, but the shapeshifting overweight druid and the vile necromancer are the ones still here. And that fact that Anders' group is still alive tells you everything you need to know about whether Revery cares if you're the good guy or not."

"In my defense, I cut a very heroic figure," Tobias said.

It was Leo's turn to raise an eyebrow.

"You're seriously going to give me a hard time about that?" Tobias said.

"Your job isn't to be the classic hero, Tobias," Leo said. "You will be called to be brave. That happens to all of us. But you can do something I don't remember any other player in all these decades I've been here can do."

"A fantastic David Bowie impression?"

"You're a bard, you obstinate fool," Leo said. "You can tell stories. And it is my firm belief that more than adventurers and heroes, Revery needs stories."

"Oh," Tobias said, suddenly wishing Miriam would swing by one more time for a refill.

"I know what you did for the ghouls, learning their story. And I think you'll be called upon to do it again. I just want you to know it might be important."

"Might be," Tobias said. "So, you're not sure."

"Not at all," Leo said. "But there's nothing wrong with hedging our bets."

Tobias nodded, hoping to convey that everything he'd just been told made perfect sense, even though everything he'd just been told made absolutely no sense at all. *I really thought being trapped in a role-playing game would be less stressful,* he thought.

"So why tell me now?" Tobias said. "We met the ghouls a month ago."

"Because you're the one I'm betting on," Leo said, reaching for something Tobias hadn't noticed leaning against the counter beside the necromancer. "And the people Anders used to run with are notorious killers. They have no issues murdering other players here. Or anything else for that matter."

"PvP murder hobos?" Tobias said. "I'd rather face more undead."

"This might help," Leo said. He rested a sword encased in an aged leather scabbard on the bar. The scabbard was drab but the hilt and cross guard were elegantly crafted, the haft relatively long, as if it could be wielded with one hand or two.

"What's this?"

"It's a sword," Leo said.

"No shit," Tobias said.

"It's a sword that will only really work best in the hands of someone like you," Leo said. "I found it in a dungeon years ago and thought it was the stupidest thing I'd ever found, but for some reason I held onto it. And now here you are."

"Revery doing its thing," Tobias said.

"Revery is always doing its thing," Leo said. "It's very disconcerting when you realize fate might actually be a game mechanic, isn't it?"

Tobias picked up the sword and felt the entire weapon hum as his hand gripped the hilt.

"Don't unsheathe that unless you want attention," Leo said.

"I always want attention."

"I mean unless you really want attention," Leo said. "Like I said, I thought it was the stupidest thing I'd ever found."

"But it's perfect for me," Tobias said.

"Fate is a game mechanic," the necromancer said, smiling wickedly. He stood up, pulled his hood up over his head, and started for the door.

"Don't underestimate the other party," Leo said. "They don't care if you're from this world or back home. And players are always more dangerous than NPCs."

Chapter 7: I never liked PvP

Morgan grimaced as Eriko all but kicked in the swinging door to the tavern the rest of the party had gathered in, another damned near identical tavern below the rooms they rented here in town as the one they'd haunted in Moderate Expectations. He supposed most pubs in the real world became hard to tell apart if you spent enough time in them; maybe asking Revery to be more unique with its drinking establishments was more than they could ask.

The rogue was in a fury worthy of Cordelia's barbarian battle rage. Morgan couldn't say he blamed her. He felt a quieter, but equally powerful anger as he'd rushed to check on Samlin. The idea that Revery might allow them to find… love? Maybe not love, Morgan thought, not yet, but romance, someone to care about, and then immediately put them in harm's way, it was cruel and filled him with so much rage, but Morgan was well-practiced at hiding his feelings, and Eriko was an open book.

"Is Jin okay?" he asked quietly, hoping for the best, assuming Eriko wouldn't be in here pitching a fit if the young woman had come to harm.

"She's fine," Eriko said, her voice softening noticeably. Her body unclenched a bit, too, as she made eye contact with Morgan, as if realizing they had both faced similar demons today. "She hid. She's smart. She knew the only thing they'd do if they saw her would be to hurt her, so she hid. But what kind of hellhole of a world are we in? Her whole village is massacred by the undead and now this? Does this game just create NPCs to be victims?"

"But she's okay," Morgan said calmly.

"She is," Eriko said. "Is Samlin…?"

"One of his stable boys was murdered," Morgan said. "But Samlin is safe. They took half his horses."

Eriko sat down in a huff, turning her attention across the table to where the twins were sitting together. Morgan caught Eriko stealing a glance at the subtle way Tamsin had reached her hand over to place it on the back of Jack's, and Morgan instantly recognized a seething jealousy there. She opened her mouth to say something, then seemed to pivot to change to another conversation.

"Where the hell did you get that sword, Tobias?" she asked.

"It's a long story."

"You're a bard. Everything you do is a long story," Eriko said. "Where'd the sword come from?"

"I got it from a crazy old man in a bar," Tobias said.

"Y'know, fine, don't tell me. I don't care," Eriko said, ignoring a legitimately hurt expression on Tobias' face. If only she knew that everyone else had asked the same question and issued the same disbelief before she arrived, she might have found a brief glimmer of levity in the room.

But there was none to be found, really.

Cordelia sighed and stood up from her perch at the bar, stretching.

"We have to go after them, right?" she said. "I'm not misreading the situation?"

"They're murderers," Jack said. He was half hidden beneath his cowl, less for dramatic purpose but because Morgan could feel the shame emanating from him from across the room. As usual, their ranger was blaming himself for not being prescient enough to perfectly predict the future. "We have to stop them."

"But they're like us," Tamsin said. "We've killed a lot of monsters, sure, but these are… they're people back in the real world, too."

"The people here are as real as we are," Eriko said impatiently. "These bastards are running around killing whatever they want without a second thought. They deserve what's coming to them."

"I never liked PvP," Tobias said under his breath. Everyone looked at him. "What? Like any of you liked those games? We got ourselves stuck here because we liked to solve problems together, not kill other players."

"Are you saying we don't kill them?" Eriko said.

"I'm just saying I'm not looking forward to it," Tobias said. "But frankly, I think Revery wants heroes, not villains. It makes the villains for us. We'd be doing something the world wants us to by removing them."

"Removing is a very polite way of saying it," Morgan said.

Tobias smirked.

"I'm a bard. Tact is a class feature."

"Jack," Morgan said. "Will you be able to track them?"

The ranger nodded.

"They're not being subtle at all," Jack said. "Any one of us could follow their trail. It's like they don't care."

"From what I saw when I scryed on them, I don't think they do," Tamsin said. "Guys, I think they've been here a long time. What they're doing is… I mean maybe they're losing it? Trapped here, for decades. That's got to be hard."

"No," Jack and Tobias both said simultaneously. They both started and looked at each other.

"What was that about," Cordelia said.

"Long story," Tobias said.

"You and I might have to talk," Jack said.

"Maybe you two should talk right now, in front of us," Eriko said.

Jack turned to Morgan. Why me? Morgan thought. Why am I always the arbiter around here? Just because I pretend to be calm and level-headed doesn't mean I'm the leader of these fools.

"Fine," Morgan said. "Spill it."

"The druid I met, the old player," Jack said. "He seemed calm. The game might have changed him, but it didn't turn him evil, or mad. He felt at home here."

"Well, Bennett seemed to be in rough shape, but not evil," Tobias said. "And I might have met a wizard or something earlier today who was from the real world."

"You what?" Tamsin said. She punched her brother in the shoulder. "You're just telling us this now?"

"I told you I got this sword from a crazy old guy in a bar!" Tobias said. "You think I made that up?"

"You left out 'crazy old guy from the real world' in your

description," Cordelia said.

"Fine. That's on me," Tobias said. "But anyway. He didn't seem dangerous. Maybe a little weird, but not evil."

"Is he still here?" Jack said.

"He poofed," Tobias said.

"Poofed," Eriko said.

Tobias made an ornate hand gesture as if to indicate he was casting a spell.

"Poof. Gone. Couldn't find him."

"And he gave you a sword," Morgan said.

"The bard gets a sword. The ranger gets a bow from a ghoul. The barbarian receives an heirloom dwarven axe. I'm sensing a pattern," Eriko said. She pulled the ornate dagger they'd found in the ghoul hoard from her belt. "Reckon this means something?"

"It's magic," Tamsin said. "I checked. Not sure what it does. And I got a wand."

"I don't have anything yet," Morgan said.

"Clearly, it's your turn next when we roll for loot, big guy," Tobias said.

Morgan ignored the comment.

"Did your mysterious stranger tell you anything about these other players?" he asked instead.

"He thought we might decide to go fight the murder hobos," Tobias said. "But he didn't tell me we should or shouldn't."

"Why would he? That would've been helpful," Eriko said. She had finally found the barkeep and was begging for a drink.

"Well," Morgan said. "I guess we're fighting the murder hobos. If nothing else, Bennett seemed like a nice enough guy. He doesn't deserve to be left to whatever they're doing to him."

"Fair point," Cordelia said. "When do we leave?"

"Tomorrow," Eriko said.

"Not now?" Tamsin said.

"I want one more day here," Eriko said, a palpable edge of sadness to her voice. "We—we have this tendency to leave a place and never go back. I just want one more day, okay?"

She looked at Morgan, who found himself nodding to her, his eyes itching with hidden emotion. He wanted one more day as well, it seemed.

"Tomorrow," he said. "We'll leave in the morning."

Chapter 8: The big score

"That was for you, you know," Brandon said, the first time he'd spoken directly to Bennett in weeks. They'd all leaned into their characters during their time here, almost becoming one with them, but it was Brandon's transformation into Valamir that Bennett found most disconcerting. Dom had always been a bully in the real world, so of course living as a barbarian warlord would allow him to become more cruel and arrogant. Craig was Bennett's friend, or had been, but there had forever been an underlying hint of weird to him. Becoming a dark wizard suited him more than Bennett wanted to admit.

But Brandon's change into a cool, grim priest of evil. This was a more dramatic shift in personality. Then again, I hadn't expected to like thieving so much, Bennett thought. Revery changes us all.

"What was all for me," Bennett said, rocking idly on horseback. He didn't want the horse, not the way they'd acquired it, through blood and cruelty, but Dom had picked him up and slammed him into the saddle, ordering their NPC peons to tie his feet to the stirrups. "Go ahead," Dom said, grinning viciously behind his thick beard "Try to jump off. We'll just let the horse drag you for a while. See how long it'll take for you to beg to be put back on the horse."

"That was the mellowest village ransacking we've had in months," Brandon said from atop his own stolen mount. Bennett looked ahead toward Dom, his broad back swaying in the saddle of the biggest, darkest horse the stable had, his massive two-handed axe hanging from his shoulder.

Mellow. Bennett recalled the boy at the stable, the young man, really, big and strong but not a warrior. He naively thought his size meant something, but then Dom went full Blaggard on him, unsheathing that axe like it weighed nothing, bring it down in an overhead swing that nearly split the kid in half. Dom smiling at the stable master with blood on his face, blood staining his teeth, and politely demanding all the horses they needed, and feed and barding as well.

"Just a few fires and murders is mellow, then?" Bennett said.

Most of the time we don't leave anyone standing," Brandon said. "He'll let the henchmen loose on the town to take what they want, then we level the rest."

"And you're okay with this," Bennett said.

"It's not real," Brandon said. "It's never been real. Why should I care if we burn down a few villages?"

"You know that's not true," Bennett said. "We've been here long enough to know it's not true. These people are real, Brandon."

Brandon shrugged. The gesture was so nonchalant Bennett wanted to punch him.

"And what about you? Ever partake in mass murder?" he asked.

"Murder is boring," Brandon said. "I'm playing a different mini-game."

"Yeah?"

Brandon gestured at the henchmen all around them.

"Meet my flock," he said.

"Bullshit."

Brandon shook his head and smiled.

"True believers in the Lord of Blood, buddy," Brandon said. "I've been converting."

"You started a cult?"

"I started a cult," Brandon said proudly. "If things go my way, maybe I'll cap out at the Pope of Blood or something."

Bennett slumped deeper into his saddle. His friends weren't just psychopaths. They were the Revery version of televangelists.

"Brandon," Bennett said.

"Look," Brandon said. "I don't really care, but I swear Dom will start cutting your toes off if you keep using our real names. Just humor me, okay? I have enough trouble keeping him from torturing small animals without setting him off on purpose."

"Fine," Bennett said. "Valamir, what the hell do you need me for? You've been dragging me across the countryside for I don't even know how long and I still don't know why."

"We need a thief. Blaggard told you that already. The last time he let the boys beat the bag out of you."

"But why me, specifically," Bennett said. "I know for fact Cra— Asptooth has spells that can knock down a door with a word."

Brandon leaned in conspiratorially.

"We found the big one, Anders," he said, smirking when Bennett flinched at the use of his game name. "The ultimate dungeon. The big score. It's called the Tomb of the Maker."

"This still doesn't answer my question."

"According to the lore, the Tomb of the Maker is sealed with a lock impervious to spells," Brandon said. "Another one of those Revery things. This tomb wants you to have a rogue with you to pick the lock and disarm its traps. It's designed for a co-op game setting."

"And I'm the only rogue you know? You couldn't hire a thief from the Guild or something?"

"That's the other thing, if we're reading the lore right," Brandon said. "The lock can only be broken by 'a rapscallion not born of this world.'"

"It really says 'rapscallion.'"

"Look, I didn't do the translating, that was Asptooth," Brandon said. "But it makes sense, right? This is a game. It wants you to play a certain way, as sandbox as it makes itself out to be."

"And the name. The Tomb of the Maker. It's not… you don't really think it's the game designer's own tomb, do you?"

Brandon raised his hands.

"I don't know. Could be a great smith, could be some sage or scientist. Or maybe it's the game designer. But it's supposed to be one of the great lost sites of Revery. And we found a map."

Bennett shot Brandon a doubtful look with his one good eye.

"And all this time, it's been here, at the edge of the continent. Not off in some remote locale, not hidden on an island or on a glacial mountain top or at the bottom of the sea. Just here."

"Hey, I was the one who always complained that Revery is annoyingly Euro-centric in style," Brandon said. "And the research we found said the Maker wanted to be buried near his home.

Bennett sighed heavily, swatting a fly away from his face.

"What are you hoping will be in this tomb, Valamir?" Bennett said, trying to keep the edge of sarcasm out of his voice as he used Brandon's game name.

"I don't know. What would you want buried with you if you built an entire world?" the cleric said.

"Maybe the way to leave it?" Bennett said, not sure he'd want to find that at this point. *Would I even know how to exist in the real world anymore?* Brandon interrupted him before he could wallow any deeper into that line of thought.

"Or maybe the way to control it," Brandon said, a broad grin spreading across his face.

Chapter 9: We can't learn this all on our own

Jack wandered out of the forest and into the warm light of the party's camp fire, his anxiety-riddled perimeter check finished. Silence strolled beside him jauntily, bumping into Jack's hip with the top of his furry head. Jack leaned down a bit to scratch the wolf behind the ears, smiling at how much the creature could seem like any other dog when things were peaceful.

The camp was quiet but humming at the same time. Morgan slept in full armor, his massive hammer within arm's reach. Cordelia was asleep as well, but with her back against a tree, sitting up, her axe across her lap in an almost meditative pose. Despite Jack's deft step he made enough noise to cause the barbarian to open one eye cautiously, see him, and go back to sleep.

The others were faring even worse. He saw Eriko blatantly pretending to sleep, her back to the fire but her fingers drumming nervously on her own shoulder where she held her blanket in place. Tobias lay on his back staring up at the stars, that mysterious sword by his side.

And sitting by the fire, wide awake, was Tamsin, spell books open as she took notes and practiced arcane hand gestures absently.

Jack took a moment to watch her. It still took him by surprise when he saw the pointed ears sneaking out from beneath her hair. All of them still looked very much like themselves here, even Cordelia with her green skin and pointed canines, so when one of the changes Revery made to their physical forms stood out, it was more a reminder how far from home they were than any monster or magical spell. The other changes felt more powerful, in personality, in actions, but those little details were often the hardest to get used to.

The scar on his face itched, reminding him of his own physical transformations. He wondered, should they ever find their way back to the real world, if the scar from the bogeyman's blade he received on their first adventure would come with him, or disappear.

Tamsin looked up from her books and caught him staring.

"What are you staring at?" she asked, a hint of a smile crossing her face.

The way the fire casts shadows on your face, he thought, but instead he just sat down next to her, setting his bow and short swords aside. Silence curled up on the opposite side of the fire to watch them, head on his front paws.

"What are you working on?" Jack asked.

"The books we've found along the way have spells that are beyond my abilities," she said. "But the longer we're here, more of them make sense—like we're leveling up."

"That would make sense," Jack said. "Learn anything new?"

Tamsin spun one of the books around to show him. The spidery letters creeping across the page were beautiful, but meant nothing to him.

"This is the one I can't quite commit to memory. It's just outside my reach. But the sigils here on the page tell me it's a transformation spell. I think it would let me transform one of us into another creature."

"Forever?"

"Temporarily."

"Polymorph," Jack said. "A staple of every fantasy setting."

"From games to Harry Potter," Tamsin said. "I think it'd be a lot of fun to mess around with."

She flipped backwards a few pages.

"This one I can cast," Tamsin said. "I can create illusory copies of myself. Not sure how much help it'd be in a fight, but if something tries to kill me, I could use it to hide, I suppose."

"Just you?"

"For now," she said. "Who knows what else is in this book though."

She flipped another few pages back.

"This one I need some components for, but it'll let me summon a familiar. I've always wanted a familiar."

"Like a little imp or something?"

"More like a daemon from Pullman's books," Tamsin said. "An animal companion."

Jack nodded to Silence.

"How would you feel about another furball around, buddy?" Jack asked.

The wolf huffed and closed his eyes, luxuriating in the warmth of the fire.

"What's in the other book?" Jack said, pointing to another leather-bound tome Tamsin found during one of their excursions.

She winced and shook her head as if encountering a bad smell.

"I don't like that book," Tamsin said. "Awful stuff in there. Animating corpses. Instilling fear in people. Mind control. I mean, a lot of it would be useful, right? I'd almost rather control someone's mind if it means you or Cordelia won't have to kill them. But that book feels strange. Wrong. Like whoever wrote down those spells had ill intent."

"We could destroy it, if you want," Jack said. "Seems like the other books we've found have been serving you well."

Tamsin exhaled sharply.

"No," she said. "I won't use it, but these books have power, y'know? They have value. I keep wondering if we meet the right person, another magician, I could trade it for something I *can* use myself. Y'know? Or…"

She trailed off, hesitant.

"Or what?" Jack asked.

"Or maybe I can trade it for lessons," she said. "Jack, all these things we're learning, all the things we're capable of. We can't learn this all on our own. Or maybe you all can. But I can't."

"The druid I met gave me some suggestions," Jack said. "And your brother seems to meet random people offering him words of wisdom everywhere."

"And Morgan has his goddess," Tamsin said. "I think I need a wizarding school. Or at least a mentor. Someone I can bounce ideas off. Because a lot of these spells are just, just beyond my grasp. I keep thinking if I could ask the right question I could do so much more."

"Then we'll find you a wizarding school," Jack said.

"The others won't want to go," Tamsin said.

"Then we'll go for a while without them," Jack said.

"You tell Eriko literally every day that splitting the party is bad," Tamsin said.

"It's not splitting the party. It's a side quest," Jack said, smirking. Tamsin didn't smile back. "Honestly, I think maybe we could all use a breather after we stop these guys we're chasing. Nothing says we have to split up permanently."

"I can't leave my brother."

"Your brother is slacking off on learning to cast spells," Jack said, fully aware Tobias was listening. "Maybe he'll come with us and learn a few tricks to add to that song-magic he uses. We can all learn a thing or two. And then we'll reconvene and go dragon slaying or something."

"Is it weird we haven't fought a dragon yet, by the way?" Tamsin said. "I'm new at this sort of game."

"I think they're more like endgame bosses," Jack said. "We're still fighting low-level monsters."

"Good to know massive ogres and tribes of murderous troglodytes and hordes of ghouls are just low-level monsters."

"Hey, I don't make the rules."

They sat in silence for a few moments, the fire crackling, Tamsin absently skimming through the open book.

"I suppose we should start making plans. If we're never going to go home, I mean," she said.

"We don't have to give up on going home," Jack said. And then: "Do you want to go home?"

Tamsin looked into the fire, not making eye contact.

"Does it make me a terrible person if I said most days, I'm not sure?"

Jack listened to the forest sounds, ran a hand along the magic bow at his side. He watched his wolf companion sleeping by the fire and felt the warmth coming off Tamsin sitting close beside him. He thought about the life he'd left back home, and realized how rarely he did that anymore, how he barely gave it a moment's thought.

"No," he said, his own gaze falling onto the flames. "No, I don't think it does."

Chapter 10: Interlude – Old men making plans

"You gave the comic relief an ancient relic," Malcolm said. The old druid sat on a downed tree, his hands folded across his belly as he looked up at Leo in his usual dark necromancer's robes.

"I gave the bard a classic weapon for bardic heroes," Leo said, reining in his tone. "And he's not the comic relief."

"We've been watching. He's the comic relief."

"He is a performer, and that is the role he has, until recently, believed was his to fill," Leo said. "And I think he was allowing the narrative to undercut his potential. I have decided to give him a boost."

"You think he's the one, then."

"I have no idea which is 'the one,'" Leo said. "And frankly, you and I both know there is no 'one.' Revery wants heroism, not one single hero. I think they all have roles to play, and call me crazy, but keeping the natural storyteller in the party alive when Revery all but lives off story and legend seems like a good idea."

Malcolm put his hands up in a conciliatory gesture.

"I'm not really disagreeing with you," the druid said. "You just know I hate that fucking sword."

"Everyone hates that fucking sword," Leo said. "But in the hands of a bard with enough guts and a bit of skill, it's an incredible weapon."

Malcolm scratched absently at his gray beard. A small bird landed on his shoulder and fluttered its tiny wings. Leo resisted the urge to club the bird with his staff.

"The orc barbarian hasn't figured out that axe yet, has she," Malcolm said.

"No, but either she will, or she'll find an artifact more suited to her. This world is lousy with magical weapons for warriors."

"She's the one I worry about," Malcolm said.

"She's the one I worry the least about," Leo said. "She's pretty straightforward, Malcolm."

"She doesn't strike you as being detached?" the druid said.

Leo paused, pursed his lips, raised his eyebrows.

"You're not wrong," he said. "Ever since the dwarf died in front of her, she's been coasting."

"There's got to be something we can do to help her," Malcolm said. "The others have all found roots here. And we need them to care about Revery, Leo. That's the one thing that matters. They need to give a shit or they're no use."

"No use?" Leo said. "This world will kill them if they don't care."

"This world will kill them if they do," Malcolm said, his tone growing soft and tinged with remorse.

Leo felt a stab in his heart he hadn't felt in a long time.

"I miss them, Malcolm," he said softly.

"I do too," the druid said. "More, lately, if that's possible. I suppose not all heroes make it to the end of the story. That's what makes it a good story. Sacrifice and loss. I just didn't figure it'd be you and me here at the end of ours."

Leo shook off the sense of nostalgia and cleared his throat.

"The party is going to confront those idiot grognards we've always taken issue with," the necromancer said.

"Maybe they'll finally be the ones to put an end to those Chaotic Asshole alignment nitwits," Malcolm said. "I'm surprised Revery hasn't course corrected those monsters yet."

"Everything here serves a purpose," Leo said. "Even old necromancers and druids past their expiration date."

"Maybe Revery's been saving them for this fight."

Leo sighed and sat down on the fallen tree next to Malcolm.

"Honestly, that'd make more sense than them somehow gaming the system. They've been a cancer on this world since they showed up."

"Heroes need foils."

"We should've killed them ourselves," Leo said.
"Could we have, though?"
Leo rubbed his eyes tiredly.
"I don't know," he said. "But it would've been fun to try."

Chapter 11: Blood rage

Cordelia stretched her neck and shoulders, waiting for the others to finish preparing for the day's travel. They'd all become efficient at it—only Morgan with his heavier armor took much time, really—but Cordelia, unarmored, unencumbered, started the morning by buckling on the belt her axe was looped through, so she had time to sit and watch the others.

I think I made a mistake, Cordelia thought to herself, observing as Jack checked his bowstring, Tamsin packed her books, and Eriko made sure all her thieves' tools were where they should be. I thought the simplicity of a barbarian would be a pleasant change from the real world, she thought. I worried about everything in the real world. Work, budget, clothes, the car, too much time fretting about aesthetics or social graces.

The first few months here in Revery truly had been revelatory, though, as she found herself able to stop caring about almost anything other than the safety of her friends. The greatest responsibility she had was keeping her axe honed sharp. The others did all the worrying. She was just here to hit things.

But lately she'd started to feel if not bored, at least unfulfilled. She needed more. Battle-raging had been a wonderful escape for a while, but it wasn't her, not deep down. She hated to admit it, but she needed more purpose in her life.

Maybe I can reroll into a paladin, she thought, laughing quietly to herself.

And then she broke into a run.

Cordelia had no idea what part of her brain told her to move; she'd heard something, or just sensed it, and suddenly she pounced on Tamsin, covering the mage with her body.

"Cordelia, what—" Tamsin started to say, shock and confusion on her face, but her voice faded as the crossbow bolt lanced into the thick muscles of Cordelia's shoulder, right where Tamsin's head had been just a second before.

Before Tamsin could say anything else, Cordelia turned in the direction the quarrel had been fired from and started sprinting. She felt her heart swell, her vision growing red around the edges. Time slowed around her.

The campsite flickered with a golden light as Morgan, his armor not fully buckled, called out to his goddess for protective magic. Pale celestial runes glittered across the party's armor and flesh as the spell took hold.

Eriko launched a dagger into the forest with an underhand flick of her wrist. Cordelia, her battle fury heightening every sense, could see the edge glint as the blade spun, saw a spray of crimson from the brush as the dagger struck home.

Jack broke into a run as well, nocking an arrow and letting fly. Cordelia could see the shaft wobble in slow motion; could see the fletching shiver as it cut through the air.

And then Cordelia was on the first attacker, her axe buried in his shoulder so deep it split his collarbone. She could hear Tobias yelling to leave one alive, but those words were meaningless right now. In this moment, there was only battle and blood, enemies to put into the dirt.

Another ambusher had the misfortune of falling under her gaze. The crossbowman, struggling to reload his weapon. He dropped the quarrel he had been trying to lock into place, and Cordelia brought her axe down on the weapon, smashing it into splinters. She could see the shards of wood embedded in the man's hand clear as day, and then a second swing from her axe nearly took his head completely off his shoulders.

A grimy man with red hair and beard drew a worn sword from his hip and prepared to face her, but Silence stole the kill, pouncing from the shadows and clamping down on the bandit's wrist, crushing it until he dropped the blade. The wolf carried the red-haired man to the ground with the force of his weight, and Cordelia heard screams of pain and fear.

She came face to face with another attacker, too close to get her axe up in time to swing as he raised a spiked club. Cordelia brought her head down against his nose in a smashing head butt. Bone crumpled under her forehead, and she smelled blood, hers or his she did not know. The half-hearted swing of his club connected, slamming into her shoulder, but Cordelia batted the hand away and grabbed him by the throat, head butting him again, and again, until he dropped limp to the ground.

Growling, she spun around looking for someone else to fight, but the battle was over. The blood still pumped in her ears, but as it slowed, she could hear Tobias singing. Cordelia took a deep breath, exhaled, felt her limbs grow heavy and liquid. Pain burned from the shoulder where the crossbow bolt remained embedded.

"You in there, Cordelia?" Morgan asked, approaching her slowly. He seemed to identify the fury fading from her eyes.

"Yeah," Cordelia said. She recognized the song Tobias sang as one of his spells. It sounded hypnotic, and probably was.

"Let's get that bolt out of your back, huh?" Morgan said.

She nodded, wincing as the pain began to radiate out from her shoulder all the way down to her fingertips. She let Morgan lead her to a fallen log and watched Jack and Eriko drag the still-living red-haired man to the camp as well, Tobias trailing behind them, singing.

"This is bad," Morgan said. "I'll throw some healing magic on you but it's going to hurt coming out."

"It'll hurt more if we leave it in," Cordelia said, watching as the red-haired man's face went from aggressive to blank to almost warm, his eyes glassy as he looked up at Tobias like a long-lost friend.

Cordelia felt the soothing tingle of Morgan's healing magic and almost broke into a string of curses as he pulled the bolt from her shoulder. Even unable to see, she could sense the flesh knitting back together. She may not even get a scar from this, she thought, mildly disappointed.

"Hello, friend," Tobias said in a sing-song tone. Using his music magic, Cordelia realized. The bandit seemed to ignore the injuries he'd sustained and looked up at the bard with a smile.

"Hi there," he said. "I'm Garm."

"Nice to meet you, Garm," Tobias said. "People call me Oberon the Blue. We're friends, yeah?"

"Of course we're friends," Garm said.

"I have never liked this spell," Eriko said, walking away as she wiped blood off one of her daggers.

Tobias held up a hand.

"Mind telling us why you attacked us, Garm?" he said.

The bandit nodded.

"The boss said to slow you down. Knew you'd follow," Garm said.

"The boss?"

"Blaggard the Black," Garm said. "Deadliest mercenary this side of the Silver Spine Mountains. We're his crew."

Tobias nodded and exchanged a glance with Jack, who was hovering behind Garm, ready to strike if needed. Jack turned to Cordelia and Morgan as if to read their reactions.

"Where's Blaggard going now?" Tobias said.

"He found a barrow," Garm said. "A tomb. It's gonna be our big score!"

"Is Bennett with him?" Tobias said.

"Who?"

"Anders, the thief," Tobias said. "Sorry, you know those rogues with their fake names, right friend?"

"Oh, the coward? Yeah, he's with them," Garm said. "He's good for target practice, but the boss said he needs him."

Again, the party exchanged glances, reading thoughts.

"How far a head start does he have, Garm?" Tobias asked.

"Not sure. They're marching into the night," Garm said. "Maybe a day ahead. Maybe more. You're slow. We waited for you for a while."

"Sorry to disappoint you, Garm," Tobias said.

"That's okay. You're here now."

"How many men does Blaggard have?" Jack asked. Garm looked over his shoulder at him, then turned back to Tobias.

"I know. He's speaking out of turn," Tobias said, then repeated Jack's question word for word.

"Fifteen plus his core crew. A priest and a dark spell caster," Garm said.

"That's a big crew," Morgan said.

"We can take them," Cordelia said. "We've fought worse."

"Better if there were fewer, though," Jack said.

Tamsin had been listening quietly, but chimed in.

"What are we going to do with him?" she asked.

Cordelia gripped her axe and started to stand up.

"Whoa," Tamsin said.

"Can't leave a threat alive," Cordelia said.

"Whoa, whoa," Morgan said.

"I don't think she's wrong," Eriko said.

"Better idea," Tobias said. "Hey Garm?"

"Yes, friend?"

"I want you to do me a favor."

"Of course," Garm said.

"I want you to run ahead of us. Day and night if you must, to get to Blaggard as soon as you can. And tell him we're all dead."

"But you're not dead."

"It's more like a practical joke," Tobias said. "Just tell him there was a fight, and you won, and we won't be following anymore."

Garm started at Tobias for a full minute, then nodded, as if his brain had hiccupped briefly before responding.

"I can do that."

"Good job, Garm. Run along now, okay?"

"Okay, friend. It was very nice meeting you," the red-haired bandit said.

Jack helped the grimy bandit to his feet and stepped back. Garm made a sort of sloppy salute and took off running.

"Right back at ya, kid," Tobias said, making finger guns at the fleeing captive.

"Tell me you've never used that magic on us," Eriko said.

"Only when I'm desperate," Tobias said. Eriko gave him a withering look. "Kidding. I'm kidding."

"Will it hold?" Jack asked.

"As long as no one questions him too hard," Tobias said. "Or dispels the charm. Either of which is possible, but hey, at least it might help."

"Also," Morgan said. "Were you seriously going to murder him on the spot, Cordelia?"

Cordelia looked at the axe in her hand, still dripping with blood. She rotated her shoulder, testing to see if it had healed properly.

"Nah," she said, not really convincing herself. "It was just the blood rage coming down. Adrenaline, y'know? Barbarian stuff."

"Okay," Morgan said, making eye contact just a little longer than Cordelia liked. "That's fine. It happens."

"So, what do we think of this Blaggard guy?" Eriko said.

"Kills villagers, burns down towns, puts heads on spikes, and tried to get us killed," Jack said. "Sounds like someone we absolutely need to meet."

Chapter 12: Grognards

Standing before the Tomb of the Maker, its doorway barely hidden behind a striking waterfall, Blaggard looked out over his gathered henchmen and companions with contempt.

Blaggard—who still thought of himself as Dom, though he maintained a strict illusion that he was fully invested in his Revery persona—wasn't sure when contempt became his default emotion. He knew he wasn't a good man before they came here. He could fake it well enough. He was kind to his mother, tolerable to his siblings. Hated his dad, but the old man earned that. He was unpleasant to his coworkers, but only within the limits of social interaction. He just had no need for friends at work.

He had his own friends. Though he wasn't always great to them, either.

Maybe when they first met they were social outcasts. Dom, a thick-faced, angry young man who would have been a bully if he'd had more social standing. Craig, now the magician Asptooth, had been the weird one, always awkward around people, even their crew, though he was *their* weirdo and they guarded him as one of their own. Brandon, the cleric Valamir here, bookish, almost brilliant, but impatient. And Bennett of course, a little shy, more than a little awkward, happy to have friends even if they weren't anyone's first choice of companions.

Still, they outgrew the true awkwardness of youth, and stuck it out together. They weren't bad guys when they got here. Hell, Blaggard thought, we were even heroes for a long time.

But then they realized they couldn't go home. And that was when they got angry. And they started breaking things.

It started small, of course. Refusing to accept surrender when offered. Blaggard would always remember the first time that happened, the cathartic thrill of it as an orc chieftain offered peace and he answered it with a blade through the orc's head. They played by the rules for a long time, taking their treasure and buying what they needed in town, paying for rooms at inns, buying rounds of drinks for the simple-minded locals. But at some point Blaggard joked to Asptooth that they were more powerful than anyone in any town they visited. Why were they paying for anything when they could just take it?

So, they took what they wanted and left. Asptooth laughed. Valamir shook his head, weighing not the morality of it but the consequences they might have to deal with later. Anders showed his first signs of weakness. Blaggard knew he should've seen the signs their rogue would betray them then, but they were all still friends then.

It got worse from there, of course. Villages resisted, and they'd slaughter whole militias. Blaggard couldn't even remember how many towns they'd watch burn to the ground. Eventually they became hunted, by king's men, by soldiers, by mercenaries. Once even by other players. But winning is easy when you no longer care about ethics or rules. Blaggard's crew left a trail of blood wherever they went. And it turned out Revery had no end to where they could go seeking fortune. It was years before they decided to head back from where they came.

Unexpectedly, others pursued them as well, not to fight them, but to join them. Warriors who wanted to follow them for fame and fortune. It wasn't an army, exactly, but it was a war band, a force to be reckoned with, and Blaggard was at the front of it, his friends by his side.

If we can't go home, he thought, then we'll make this place ours.

Anders disappeared one night. At the time, Blaggard didn't think much of it. He was tired of him by then. Tired of all his friends, frankly, but Anders was the only one who made his problems known. The others just followed his lead.

They killed dragons, good and evil. They found a castle in the sky and slaughtered the giants who lived there, stealing all the treasures they'd hidden among the clouds. They delved deep into the earth, to the forgotten places. It was there in the darkness he found the axe he carried now, the Hunger, thrumming with malevolent power, with a patina of rust that never came clean. Demons came to fear them.

But they grew bored. Each new challenge was just another box to check off. Another head to mount on the wall of their fortress in the Blackspire Mountains. It was then they began to ask questions about those who came before them. Other adventurers. Other stories. The things those players left behind. Artifacts of legend. Maybe even a way home.

And then they found the map to the Tomb of the Maker.

Valamir of course tried to temper their expectations; that was his job. Asptooth was convinced it was the tomb of whoever wrote this game. The creator of Revery. The man who, whether by accident or design, trapped them here.

They were going to find that tomb, Blaggard said, accepting no argument. And they were going to take whatever was left behind.

And now the tomb's entrance stood before them, a simple archway of stone barred by doors slick with spray from the waterfall, carved in bas-relief to depict all manner of mythological creatures, as though the artist tried to capture all the greatest beasts this world had to offer.

They'd traveled Revery north to south, east to west. They'd seen rivers of lava and castles in the clouds, towers carved of ice, forests of glowing fungus far beneath the earth. Blaggard was almost disappointed to find the Tomb of the Maker here, so close to where all their adventures began, the least exotic, least impressive place any adventurer might go. It's in the goddamn starter zone, he thought. The waterfall it hid behind was decorative at best, a thin veil over what he hoped was a treasure trove.

Blaggard waved Asptooth forward. The wizard shuffled ahead of their armed men and examined the door, his nasty little imp hovering on his shoulder like a bad thought. Both wizard and imp batted at the spray from the waterfall like they were shooing away mosquitos. He hunched over in an uncomfortable, affective manner.

Asptooth nodded to himself, stood back to his full height, and scurried back to Blaggard.

"It's as we suspected, based on the notations on the map,"

Asptooth said in that raspy affectation he'd picked up so long ago Blaggard could barely remember what he sounded like in the real world. "The door is enchanted in such a way that spells won't open it. It's quite clever. The lock requires a master thief to pick it, relying solely on his own skill. No cheating."

Blaggard reached down to put a gauntleted hand on Anders' shoulder. The rogue looked up at him with his one good eye with a combination of loathing and fear.

"You dragged me back into your shit just to unlock a door for you, Dom?" Anders said. "I thought you were kidding."

"Get to work, old buddy," Blaggard said, offering his most malicious smile. The rogue didn't move, so Blaggard grabbed him by the back of the neck and dragged him bodily to the door, throwing him on the ground in front of it, splashing water across his trousers and tunic.

"I'm not opening this goddamned door for you, Dom," Anders said, wiping mud from his cheek.

"Really," Blaggard said, his voice echoing in the confines of the stone behind the running water, drawing himself to his full height. The metal and leather of his blackened armor creaked dramatically. "This is the hill you're going to die on? Opening a door?"

"It's not about the door and you know it. It's about who we've become."

"That's cute," Blaggard said, spitting on the ground between them. "There were plenty of years you were right there beside us, smiling as we watched churches burn and counted our money."

"I never wanted to be a villain, Dom. And as big an asshole as you are, I don't think you did either."

"Open the door, Bennett," Blaggard said, almost flinching as he himself broke character, using Anders' real world name.

"You can't make me."

"Maybe not," Blaggard said, still rattled by his slip in names. "But I can start cutting more parts off you and try to change your mind. You still have all ten toes, or did you lose a few of those along the way?"

Anders stared up at him, both defiance and fear growing in equal parts.

"You wouldn't."

"You've seen what I've done in the past, little buddy," Blaggard said. "You've seen me enjoy it. You think I won't do to you what

I've done to our enemies?"

"We were friends, Dom. Since we were kids. You wouldn't… you'd torture me? Me?"

"We haven't been friends in a long time. And the part of me that was Dom died even further back than that. Now open the door, Anders. I have a headache, and I don't want to have to listen to you scream."

Blaggard had to give him credit—the rogue held out a few seconds longer. He almost thought he'd have to start cutting pieces off. But finally, Anders relented.

"My tools are in my pack," he said, resigned.

Blaggard made a motion over his shoulder for the bag to be brought to them.

"Good lad," he said. "I knew you had it in you."

Chapter 13: The Tomb of the Maker

"That's a waterfall," Morgan said, as if he were asking for verification.

"It's a waterfall," Jack responded without irony.

"Our cleric and our ranger, just pointing out the obvious," Eriko said. She pulled her hood back and ran her fingers through her hair, partly to fix her faux-hawk and partially because she was running entirely short on patience.

"We tracked them to a waterfall, and they… disappeared?" Morgan said. They'd taken up position from the woods, on a ridge to the north of the waterfall. The tracks led directly to the water and then just ended. Jack and Silence had scouted ahead to see if the war band had crossed the river the waterfall fed into, but came back with nothing.

"Hang on," Eriko said, hopping to her feet and dusting off her pants.

"No," Jack said, standing up to join her.

"Uh-uh. You: outdoor scout. Me: sneaky scout. This is my job, Aragorn. Now sit down and let me do it."

Not waiting for a response, Eriko darted down the ridge, not pausing until she reached the stone outcropping adjacent to the waterfall. She edged her way behind the water, doing her best to avoid getting wet and mostly failing. But it was worth it, she thought. Footprints. Soggy, starting to fade, but footprints, leading directly into a carved wall beneath an archway. If that's not a door, I'm not a rogue, she thought.

She turned around to run back to her companions and nearly crashed directly into Jack and Cordelia.

"Shit!" Eriko said.

"Sorry," Jack said.

"How did you not hear us?" Cordelia said.

"Waterfall. The waterfall is really loud, darling," Eriko said. "Sidebar, there's a door here. They went into the door."

Jack stepped past her to examine the relief.

"Gryphon, manticore, dragon, eagleboar," he said. "Goblins and demons and ghouls and wights. It's like a fantasy literature greatest hits montage."

"It's also a door," Eriko said.

"Can you open it?" Jack asked.

Eriko held her hands out at her side and did her best Han Solo impression.

"I don't know what that's meant to convey," Jack said.

Eriko struck the Han Solo pose again.

"So, you can unlock the door," Jack said.

Eriko patted him on the cheek.

"You got it, babe. Get the others."

"I'll watch her back," Cordelia said, sliding her axe from the loop on her belt as Jack disappeared.

Eriko took out her lock picks and found an almost imperceptible gap in the stone where dull metal showed through. She looked inside, seeing nothing but darkness, and began to tinker, testing the mechanisms, listening with her ear pressed against the stone. Gears whirred and clicked. She exhaled sharply, removed her picks and began again.

The others shuffled in behind her. Cordelia shushed them. Tobias ignored her.

"Need help?"

"Shut up, bard," Eriko said. Again, the mechanism slipped and went back to its default, locked position. "Just everyone be quiet. I can get this."

Again, Tobias ignored her, but this time, he started singing.

"I swear to god Toby if you don't shut it I'm going to stab you in the…" Eriko drifted off, leaving the threat unfinished. She felt her mind grow calm, her hands steadier, all distraction fading away.

She closed her eyes and truly went to work on the lock, moving minute pieces, creating a tiny symphony of clicks and whirs.

She heard the tiniest of scrapes of metal on metal, and the door began to slide open.

"Got it," she said, turning back to her friends. Tobias stopped singing. "What was that? The song you were singing?"

"It's bard magic," Tobias said. "I think my job is more to make all of you better than to be the best myself. That's the song of clarity, or something. It's supposed to help whoever hears it. Steadies their hand, focuses their concentration."

"I would've had it without you," Eriko said.

"I'm sure you would have," Tobias said. "But we're all getting wet."

"Can we just go inside?" Morgan said, hefting his hammer. "You can tell us about your wonderful bard spells later, Tobias."

Eriko held up a hand.

"Not we," she said. "Let me check ahead."

"I'm getting wet. Wet armor chafes," Morgan said.

"Just give me a minute. Rogue stuff. Remember the last time I didn't check for traps before we went into a cavern?"

"Go on," Tamsin said.

Eriko slid inside the cavern, and for a moment, her resentment and anger about this quest faded. This is what she was made for, sneaking through shadows, scouting for dangers, exploring forgotten places. This is why she played these games, why she chose to be Rouge the Rogue. For a moment, she set aside her worries and felt the thrill of the hunt.

She found no traps, but she did find footprints. The war band had certainly come this way, trampling the dusty floor of the tomb. Someone had lit a torch and abandoned it in a sconce. It burned low, but provided enough light for Eriko to see the general dimensions of the first chamber. It was large, and mostly vacant, like an antechamber. One wall was covered in writing she couldn't recognize. To her left, a set of stairs led down into pitch darkness below. She listened for a moment but heard nothing. Well, either they're deeper into the tomb, or they're waiting to ambush us, but either way, here we are, she thought, jogging back out of the tomb.

"Hey, twins," she said. "One of you has got to have a spell that lets you read languages, yeah?"

"I do," Tamsin said. She had the flying cape she and her brother shared custody of wrapped around her like a tarp, cowled around her head to keep her hair dry from the waterfall.

"Come on, then," Eriko said, leading the party inside. She pointed to the word-covered wall. "Can you read that?"

Tamsin reached into a pouch and withdrew a slip of paper. She whispered to the paper, which spontaneously caught fire. Tamsin dropped the burning page, which was all but disintegrated before it touched the tomb floor. Her eyes glowed with a fire instead, though, and she gazed upon the wall with understanding.

"This is old draconic," Tamsin said. "One of the first languages of Revery."

"Does it say anything interesting?" Morgan asked.

"Crossword puzzle, clearly," Tobias said.

"Shh," Tamsin said. "It's a greeting. A greeting and a warning."

"What does it say, Tam? Can you read it to us?" Jack asked. Silence padded around the edges of the room, sniffing at shadows.

"Before you lies the Tomb of the Maker. Last resting place of the Dreamer who Dreamed, whose Reveries made Revery," Tamsin read.

"Humble," Eriko said. She drew one of her daggers and took up position near the stairs leading down. Cordelia saw her and joined her, weapon ready just in case.

"The dead join the Maker in his slumber. They will not wake unless you wake them; they will not stir unless stirred," Tamsin said. "I feel like something might be lost in translation there."

"The dead," Morgan said. "I know we've dealt with undead before, but I really don't look forward to doing it again."

"Life blooms below as well. Be wary traveler, for breathing deeply of life can hasten you toward your end," Tamsin said.

"Booby trapped. Of course the tomb is booby trapped," Tobias said. "Maybe we should just let them get themselves killed and pick off any stragglers who stumble back out?"

"The Maker's allies await beyond. Their judgement is their own, their loss endless, their longing, eternal," Tamsin said.

"Allies. Did the Maker inter their party here as well?" Jack asked.

"I want to know what they want from this place," Morgan said. "I know we're here to avenge the town, but this feels bigger than that. The Maker? The person who made Revery? Is that what we're hearing?"

"I think I know what they're looking for," Tamsin said, her eyes still pools of fire as she looked back at her friends. "This last line: The Maker's heart made Revery. Whoever holds his heart reveals all. Revery's future beats within."

"There is… absolutely no way to interpret that in a manner I'm comfortable with," Tobias said.

"The future of Revery? What does that even mean?" Eriko said. "Like, did he bury the game master's rules in here?"

No one spoke for a few seconds as Eriko's voice echoed in the darkness. Morgan finally broke the silence.

"I have a terrible feeling you're a lot closer to the truth than you meant to be, saying that," he said. "Guys, I think we have to stop them. We can't let people like this run the game, can we?"

Chapter 14: The Interred

The first thing Morgan noticed as they descended from the antechamber was that the stairs were wet. He closed his eyes and took what he hoped was a calming breath. Crouching down, he touched the fluid with his fingertips and sniffed it, expecting the coppery tang of blood.

"Water," he said, noticing the growing sound of dripping in the darkness.

"It's raining in here," Tobias said.

"We're under whatever body of water is feeding the waterfall out front," Jack said, not sounding thrilled about it.

"What do you think the chances are this place floods on us?" Eriko asked. Morgan couldn't find her in the dark where she'd dropped into the shadows.

"Tomb's been here a long time," Morgan said. "I'd hope we didn't show up the day it finally decided to cave in."

"You say that like you don't know how bad our luck is, traditionally," Eriko said. "You okay, Tamsin?"

The mage made a small, gurgling grunt in the back of her throat. Morgan half expected to see her fighting off some monster, but the only monster she was facing just then was claustrophobia.

"I don't like the idea of being underwater like this," she said. "You know that stretch of highway back home that's under the harbor?"

"You're really going to bring that up right now?" Tobias said. "You've been actively afraid of that tunnel since we were toddlers."

Morgan wanted to tell the twins to knock it off, but if he was being honest with himself, the idea of being under a river or lake right now was more than a little unsettling for him as well. It didn't help that he could barely see down here.

"Could one of the wonder-elves cast a light spell so the lowly human over here doesn't trip over his own two feet?" he said, trying to cover his anxiousness with annoyance.

Tamsin softly spoke the single arcane word of her spell, conjuring a pleasant glow in the palm of her hand.

Morgan found himself looking down at a corpse, its head bifurcated by a vicious blow between the eyes.

"Shit!" Morgan said, stepping back involuntarily, his heel landing on the dead man's shin. The room spun and he found himself falling, armor and weapons clanking as he rolled down the entire flight of stairs.

"Morgan!" Jack called from the top of the stairs.

"I'm fine, I'm fine," the cleric said, flexing his fingers and toes to make sure he was telling the truth. He could still see Tamsin's light spell from above, but he himself was surrounded by shadow. He almost jumped out of his skin when he saw two glowing eyes appear in the darkness, only to exhale in relief as Silence padded toward him, nudging his face with a cold, wet nose.

"Morgan, have you ever not failed a stealth check?" Tobias yelled.

"Do not push me, bard," Morgan said, a slow bruising ache creeping across his shoulders from the fall.

"Oh. Hey. It's Tobias' buddy," Cordelia said.

"Garm?" Tobias said. "Oh, shit. It's Garm. They killed Garm?"

"Probably because they knew you cast a spell on him," Jack said, barely restraining the annoyance in his voice. The ranger appeared from the shadows as well and offered Morgan a hand. He took it and together they got him back on his feet.

"You'd think we'd get better at this by now," Jack said, resting his hand on the short sword at his waist.

"Guys, Garm is super dead," Tobias said. "I'm thinking that spell was a mistake."

Eriko emerged from the shadows at the foot of the stairs as well, running a hand along the dusty stone walls of the chamber.

"Where are we now?" she asked. "I'll see if I can find a torch or something."

Before Eriko could step away, Silence began to growl at the darkness. Jack drew his sword. Morgan hefted his hammer.

"He doesn't usually growl at good things," Morgan said.

"No, he certainly does not," Jack said.

Then they heard scraping.

"The poem on the wall," Jack said. "The dead won't stir unless they are stirred."

"Hey, find anything interesting?" Tamsin said, appearing with her light at the foot of the stairs. The glow filled the entire chamber, and it revealed exactly what Morgan had hoped it would not.

The walls were lined with interment niches for bodies, in stacked rows of three niches each. And the bodies within those niches were moving.

Boney feet dragged across the dusty floor. Empty eye sockets stared blankly in the party's direction. Dried tendons creaked as vacant jaws opened wide, hissing as their teeth snapped open and shut. Some held rusted weapons; others reached out with bare hands, the ancient bones of their fingers worn into points.

"I think we stirred the dead," Tobias said.

Cordelia grumpily pushed her way past the bard and shattered the skull of the closest walking corpse with a swing of her axe, then splintered its ribcage on the backswing when the creature didn't fall. Jack unleashed a series of quick slashes on another skeleton, much to the same effect.

"Anyone got something that'll make these guys fall down and stay down?" Cordelia asked, brutalizing another skeleton as the now bodiless arm of the first grabbed onto her booted ankle. She shook it until it fell off and then began stomping on it until the bones splintered. "This isn't going well."

Morgan closed his eyes and, with profound discomfort, prayed to the goddess he didn't believe in.

I still don't quite understand our relationship, he thought. I don't know what we are to each other. But if you have any advice on how to help these poor dead bastards find their final peace, I'd be most appreciative.

Theana, the goddess, said nothing. Instead, the head of his battle hammer began to glow, flickering with a gold-white flame.

"Huh," Morgan said. "That'll do."

The flame danced in the dark, then leapt from his weapon to the blades of both Jack's and Cordelia's, so all three of them held implements wreathed in holy light.

Cordelia shot Morgan a curious look, then backhanded the nearest skeleton with her axe. The undead creature let out a soft, mournful cry, but then crumbled, bones falling apart as if time itself had caught up to it.

"Ha!" Cordelia said, before diving into the oncoming horde of walking dead, smashing and slashing away. Jack joined in beside her, less brutal but equally effective. Morgan stepped up as well, swinging his heavy hammer with practiced ease. There was little violence to it, he found; instead, it felt with each strike that he was doing something right, that these beings wanted to be released from this undeath. The grotesque sound of cracking bones was softened by the relief he could hear in the creatures as they fell to pieces.

He had no idea how long the battle went on, but as he caught his breath, he realized he no longer heard bones clattering to the floor. Jack was scolding Silence to drop a tibia. Cordelia prodded a pile of rags near her feet, and a skull rolled out, grinning up at them with broken teeth.

"Who do you think they all were?" Tamsin asked, delicately avoiding stepping on any of the long-dried corpses with a grace Morgan found himself almost jealous of. "They couldn't all be players like us, right?"

"We could ask," Tobias said, picking a skull up off the ground.

Morgan's stomach twisted unexpectedly.

"You don't really know how to do that, do you?" he asked.

Tobias gave him an uncomfortable smile.

"You're kidding," Morgan said, a growing unease settling across his limbs like a chill.

"You better be kidding," Cordelia said.

"I think we should do it," Eriko said.

"Toby," Tamsin said sharply.

"I'm a bard in a world where bards use talking magic, guys," Tobias said. "I literally have a magic song that can make the dead speak. I'm not joking."

"I don't even want to know how you learned you can do this," Jack said.

"Good, because I don't particularly want to tell any of you how I learned it," Tobias said. He put his hand under the jaw of the skull and used it to speak like a puppet in a dopey, exaggerated voice. "Do you want to know who I am, Jack?"

"Put that down," Morgan said.

"Put me down," the skull said. It did not speak in Tobias' voice. The bard dropped the skull with a start and took a long step back.

"I didn't do that," Tobias said.

Tamsin knelt in front of the skull and looked it in the eyes, or at least where the eyes should have been.

"Hello," she said. "We're sorry about your body."

"Hello," the skull said back. "No need to apologize, little wizard. My body was destroyed long ago. I am not like the others. I was… special."

"Special how?" Tamsin said.

Jack took a step forward as if to intercede, but Morgan put an arm on his shoulder and shook his head.

"Let her talk," he whispered to Jack.

"We were all servants of the Maker," the skull said. "Servants. That's a nice word. We served. He took us with him, so no one else could have us. He took everything with him. Locked us away here in the dark. The cold, cold, endless dark. Does the sun still shine? Does the world still go on without us?"

"It does," Tamsin said. "How long have you been here?"

The skull made a strange sound by chittering his teeth, somewhere between laughter and derision.

"What is time to the dead," the skull said. "We've been here as long as we've been here. But you've sent my brothers to their rest. You've done a good deed. Cleric, what god do you serve? I saw your light. I saw you glow."

Morgan did not join Tamsin with the skull, but spoke up.

"Theana, the Wise, the Lady of Light," Morgan said. "In a way."

The skull made the tittering noise again with its teeth.

"No gods are wise, but there are worse than her," the skulls said. "If the gods were wise they would have stopped him."

"Him?" Tamsin asked. "The Maker?"

Again, the skull clicked his teeth, but it was more aggressive this time, more unpleasant, if that were possible.

"Can you tell us about him?" Tamsin said.

"A wizard. Like you. Cold. Without conscience. A builder. Everything was part of the plan. Everything was for a purpose. Like us. Like his friends. They're here too, you know. In the dark. I saw them go in. They never came out."

"This is horrifying," Eriko muttered.

"Others came through before us, right?" Tamsin said.

"The brute. Yes. I saw him. He knew not to wake us, though. I watched him pass, but he let my brothers sleep. They were very quiet."

"We need to find them," Tamsin said.

"Then you go deeper," the skull said. Go deeper, but know that no one has ever come back the way they entered. I have watched. I have seen."

"Thank you for the warning," Tamsin said. "Do you have a name?"

The skull was silent for a moment. Then he exhaled, a ghostly, rasping sound.

"I… do not remember. I had a name, once. I remember having a name."

"How do you like Yorick?" Tobias said.

Tamsin gave her brother a ferocious glare, but the skull clacked his teeth in approval.

"That is a fine name," the skull said. "I will be Yorick, until I can remember my true name."

"See, he likes it," Tobias said.

"Do you, um, want us to leave you here?" Tamsin asked.

"Whoa, whoa, whoa," Eriko said. "That implies there's another option."

"Would you take me with you?" the skull, now Yorick, asked, his voice plaintive.

"Tamsin, please don't," Morgan said.

"Of course, we can take you with us," Tamsin said. "You'll be here all alone if we don't!"

"I love this so much," Tobias said.

"I absolutely hate this," Morgan said, more repulsed than he'd been for as long as he could remember.

Silence shuffled over to Yorick, sniffed him, then licked the curved dome of the skull.

"It's settled, then," Tamsin said, scooping Yorick up off the ground. "We need to get you a Baby Bjorn or something."

"The twins are officially slowly descending into full-on goth-lite status," Eriko said. "Not how I thought this would go."

"Fine, we bring the skull," Morgan said. "But one Shakespeare joke and I'm turning this party around and going home."

Chapter 15: The Grove

The only exit out of the catacombs was a stairway of rough-hewn stone leading up. Eriko again took the lead, with Jack and Silence close on her heels. Tamsin sighed as she hung back. She knew once she really got a hang of the magic at her disposal she'd be unstoppable, but for now, she felt like the rest of the group treated her like glass, and she couldn't argue with their logic—the others were all better in a toe-to-toe fight, even Tobias. I'm less of a fighter than the guy with the lute, she thought tiredly.

Then she noticed the faint blue-green glow at the top of the stairwell, and Eriko, face half-bathed in that glow, looking down at the rest of them.

"You're not going to believe this," she said, stepping aside to allow the others to look into the chamber ahead.

"Life blooms ahead," Tamsin said, quoting the poem from the antechamber. "This is not what I was expecting from the poem."

It was a grove of sorts, but not like a garden. The room, more cave than chamber, was covered in alien fungus, every inch coated with life. Much of the fungus gave off a faint light, the glow they'd seen from the stairs.

"We've already dealt with killer fungus before," Tobias said. "Can we just assume the mushrooms want to eat us?"

"Wouldn't be surprised," Jack said, a hand on Silence's shoulder as if to keep the wolf from running ahead.

"Why does it have to be killer mushrooms?" Morgan muttered.

"We don't know they're killers," Tamsin said. "It said not to breathe deeply of life. That was the warning."

"I think they'd beg to differ with that assessment," Eriko said, pointing into the weird darkness ahead. Tamsin hadn't noticed them before, but following Eriko's gesture, she saw them: corpses, sprawled out on the floor. No blood, no signs of combat; just men on their backs, motionless, lifeless.

"I can see an exit," Cordelia said. On the far side of the cavern, the floor sloped up into a stone pathway. Tamsin thought she could hear running water.

"The warning was to not breathe too deeply. Maybe we need to just get across as quickly as we can," she said.

"Could be a warning to move quickly, could be a warning not to stop and smell the flowers," Jack said. "Either way, our only option is through. Move quietly and be ready to run."

Tobias started humming the Super Mario Brothers theme song. Jack gave the bard a long, unhappy stare.

"What," Tobias said.

"Why are you like this?" Jack said.

"Mario, Luigi, knock it off," Eriko said. He stretched her legs as if getting ready to sprint. "On three?"

Cordelia ignored everyone and just walked ahead, pushing past the entire group to enter the grove.

"Or we could just follow the barbarian," Eriko said, shrugging and joining her.

Halfway across, Cordelia nudged one of the corpses with the toe of her boot.

"Who do you think they were?" she asked.

"They're dressed like Garm," Tobias said.

Tamsin stared at the closest corpse's face. It showed almost no signs of decay—instead, bits of fungal growth appeared around the eyes and lips, a dusting of lichen or some other substance, but otherwise, the bodies looked fresh. She said so to the party.

"These haven't been here long," she said. She pulled the skull of Yorick out of her satchel and showed him the body. "Do you know these guys?"

"The living all look vaguely the same to me," Yorick said.

"Keep moving, everyone," Morgan said, irritation peppering his tone. "This isn't the best place to…"

The eyes of the nearest corpse popped open, filmed over and milky. Tamsin let out a small gasp of surprise and put her hand on Morgan's arm.

"What? Oh. Uh-oh," Morgan said.

"Guys," Tamsin said.

"Go," Jack said, drawing his short swords. "Go, go, go."

"Um," Tobias said, pointing toward the ceiling.

"Um?" Tamsin repeated, and then spotted what he was looking at—a massive toadstool, maybe five or six feet in diameter, swelling and shifting, as if it were about to burst.

Another corpse had risen to its feet shambled toward the group. Cordelia put out a foot and shoved him back with a stiff kick. The dead man opened his lichen-lined mouth and looked as though he were about to roar at her.

Instead, spores started to pour out from his open jaw.

Don't breathe deeply, Tamsin thought.

"Everyone get down!" she yelled. Instinctively, the party all dropped to the ground, some flopping onto their bellies, others crouching low. She drew her wand from her belt, dropping Yorick to the ground to leave her other hand free to make a series of arcane sigils in the air. And then, as if lighting a match, a burst of flames erupted around her in all directions. The two corpses both caught fire immediately; the spores pouring from their mouths burst into flames in the air like cinder. She aimed the wand up into the air toward the toadstool just as it exploded, pouring greenish-gray spores down onto the group, Flames erupted from the tip of the wand, consuming the falling material and turning it to ash. It drifted down onto them like snow.

She felt a rough arm around her waist and suddenly Morgan had her over his shoulder like a sack.

"Keep burning it!" he yelled, and she did, almost torching her brother in the process as he tried to follow. Tobias, holding Yorick like a bowling ball, fingers in the skull's eye sockets, ducked to avoid her spell, looking at her as if offended.

"Sorry!" she gasped as Morgan's metal armor dug into her solar plexus.

The party sprinted over a stone bridge, water running below them nearly black in the darkness of the cave, no way to tell how deep it ran. Tamsin banged the heel of her fist against Morgan's back as they reached the other side.

"Put me down, put me down," she said, and the cleric roughly set her on her feet. "Everyone across?"

The others nodded, faces streaked with soot and grime.

On the far side of the bridge, Tamsin could see one of the walking corpses, still on fire, shuffling toward them. A low-hanging cloud of spores trailed behind him like Pigpen from Peanuts.

Weakest party member, sure, she thought, tracing new arcane symbols in the air.

"What are you doing?" Eriko asked. Tobias waved the rogue off, hushing her. If Tamsin weren't concentrating so hard on the spell, she might have laughed at the filthy look Eriko gave Tobias at the thought of being shushed, particularly by him.

She completed her spell, and the air in front of her gleamed with faint magical light. She watched as the spore cloud drifted closer and then stopped as if striking an invisible barrier.

"It won't be able to follow us," Tamsin said. "We're safe for now."

"I hate to be the party pooper, but…" Cordelia started.

"You're sort of becoming our resident party pooper, Cordelia," Tobias said.

"First, don't make me throw you back across the water," Cordelia said to the bard. "Second… if it can't follow us here, doesn't that mean we can't go back there? So we're stuck here?"

"Do you want the optimistic answer to that question, or the pessimistic answer to that question," Tamsin asked.

Cordelia just stared at her.

"Look, we can cross that bridge when we get to it," Morgan said, who caught Tobias about to make a bridge joke. "You really can't help yourself, can you."

"For the record, we just walked through a room full of fungus and I made no dirty jokes," Tobias said. "I, frankly, think that I deserve some credit for that."

"I admire your restraint," Eriko said.

"Thank you," Tobias said.

"How long will that hold?" Jack asked. "The shield, Tamsin. Is it permanent?"

"I can maintain it for about eight hours," Tamsin said. "If I remember the spell book's instructions correctly."

"So, we have eight hours before this place fills with deadly spores," Jack said.

"Better than no hours," Eriko said.

"Not disagreeing," Jack said. "Any idea what's next?"

Tobias lifted Yorick's skull and struck a very Shakespearean pose. "Yorick, old friend, what delights await us?"

"It's been so long," the skull said, his raspy voice forlorn.

"Do your best, little buddy," Tobias said.

"I think, perhaps, you must enter the Last Chapel," Yorick said. "Yes, yes, I believe the Last Chapel will be waiting for you soon."

"Nothing quite like ominously named religious locations to brighten your day, huh?" Eriko said.

"Not like we've got much choice in the matter," Morgan said, resting his hammer on his shoulder. "A chapel's a chapel, right?"

"This is a fantasy setting, dude," Eriko said. "A chapel is never just a chapel."

Chapter 16: The Last Chapel

"Y'know," Tobias said, brushing his cloak back from his hip to free up his weapons. "I honestly didn't think it would literally be a chapel."

The chamber had been hidden behind a pair of ornate, closed doors, but the doors hadn't been locked. He and Cordelia pushed them open easily enough, though they made an alarming racket as they scraped against the stone floor. What lay beyond made no sense, not after the overgrown fungus garden and the room filled with the walking dead. It was wide, built in stone bricks, with a high ceiling, torches flickering with warm light. Pews created a sort of semi-circle, their backs to the door as they aimed toward a short dais upon which an engraved altar stood. Unidentifiable religious instruments sat upon the altar, a bowl of some kind, folded cloth, other items of indeterminate purpose. Behind it, a gorgeously painted mural decorated the wall. It depicted what Tobias assumed were the gods and goddesses of Revery: a nature goddess, nude, surrounded by deer and other harmless beasts; a storm god, eyes gleaming with lightning; an armored woman with a spear in one hand and a book in the other; a trio of goddesses, one young and dressed in white, one older, eyes wrapped in a gray cloth, hair hidden by a hood of the same color, and a third, whose face seemed both elegant and skull-like depending on how long you looked at her. Others were less prominent, an old man covered in arcane tattoos, a god pulling deeply from a wineskin. To the far left, a slender god with the face of a fox seemed to look Tobias directly in the eyes.

"We're not alone," Jack said quietly, and Tobias tore his eyes from the mural to see an armored man sitting in the front row of the pews, his back to them.

"Hello?" Eriko said, drawing her daggers and walking forward. Morgan tried to put a cautionary hand on her shoulder but the rogue seemed to almost evaporate as she deftly dodged his grip. "Mind if we pass through? We're looking for a bunch of assholes."

The figure said nothing at first, remaining perfectly still. But then he stood up and turned to them, removing a finely crafted helmet and setting it down on the bench. The tabard covering his breastplate was deep blue, emblazoned with a black tree as lightning struck its branches. He had a ceremonial weapon, a mace, swinging at his side, almost too ornate to be useful. His face was ashen, his hair colorless. Only his eyes showed signs of life.

"I take it you have not come to pray to the god of sea and storms," the armored man said.

"If it would help, we can make the time," Tobias said.

The apparition glanced at the bard for just a second, then turned his attention back to the rest of the group.

"It's fine. My god hasn't answered me in so long I can't remember what his voice sounded like. He's abandoned me here," the man said.

"We're, ah, hi. Hi, there," Eriko said. "We're sorry to bother you, but... who are you?"

"I'm a member of the First Campaign," the man said. 'I was the cleric. My name was…"

His eyes unfocused and he looked at the ground nervously.

"I was the cleric. My name isn't important. I had a name, but I think it was taken from me. Either by him, or by time. Or both."

"Him?" Morgan said. "Your god?"

The cleric looked Morgan up and down and nodded.

"You serve the lady of light. That's good. You'll need light here. It's been so very long since I've seen the sun."

"Are you trapped here?" Tamsin asked.

The ghostly cleric nodded slowly.

"He trapped us all here, you see. The First Party. The Maker was finished with our story, and he wanted it to end, and we could not be allowed to go on without him. So, he bewitched us, and brought us into the darkness, and now here we stay for all eternity."

"The Maker," Jack said. "This is his tomb."

"The Maker. Our wizard. He wasn't just a wizard," the cleric said. "Or rather, he was the first of all wizards. He made this place, with his magic, with his mind. This world. He was the Maker."

"And now he's dead," Cordelia said.

"So it would seem," the cleric said. "But I'm not, am I? Or I'm dead, but I'm not gone. Perhaps he's not gone either. Perhaps we're all trapped down here waiting for the end of all things."

"What do you mean by the end of all things?" Jack asked, but Cordelia spoke over him at the same time.

"Who's we?" she asked loudly.

"My friends. We were the First Party. The cleric, the wizard, the warrior, the rogue. I will tell you the others are not what they once were."

"I'm guessing you aren't what you once were either, sparky," Eriko said.

The cleric did not seem angered by her sarcasm. Rather, he just took her in as if fully seeing her for the first time.

"That's true," he said mechanically. "I am not what I once was. I am less. An echo. That's what time does to you, I think. You become an echo waiting for someone to hear you. Do you hear me now?"

"We hear you," Morgan said. "Were there others? People like us who came through before?"

"There were," the cleric said. "They were like you. Like me. Not from this world. Not from Revery."

"You're not from Revery?" Tamsin said, her tone sharp.

"No," the cleric said. "We were the First Party. Perhaps you are to be the Last Party. That would be a relief. Revery has outlived its purpose, I think."

"That would be unfortunate for all of us," Jack said.

"Can you tell us about the others?" Morgan asked.

The cleric nodded.

"They were not as respectful as you. I smote some of their number, but their priest made the dead walk again. I let them pass. The others will deal with them."

"The rogue and the warrior," Morgan said.

"Or the Maker's toys," the cleric said. "Before this was a tomb, this was his workshop, and his creations still walk. Everything in this tomb is eternal."

Tobias watched Jack and Morgan exchange matching grimaces.

"Which way did they go?" Cordelia asked. "I see two doors ahead."

And she was right, Tobias realized—he'd been so distracted by the mural that he didn't see a door in each of the far corners. Neither was closed.

"I don't remember," the cleric said.

"Do you have a recommendation?" Eriko said, her voice slick with sarcasm.

The cleric looked to one door, then the other, then shrugged.

"Both ways lead to doom," he said.

"Do we flip a coin?" Tobias said.

Morgan let out a heavy sigh, and then beckoned the party to huddle up.

"I have a feeling we're screwed either way," he said.

"I vote left," Jack said.

"You always vote left," Eriko said. "I say we split up and scout ahead."

"What is it with you and splitting the goddamned party?" Morgan said.

"I agree with Eriko," Cordelia said. Morgan started to protest but she held up a hand. "We won't engage. I think we split up three and three and each take a corridor. Then we come back here and reconnect when we know which way we need to go to catch them."

"As long as you don't engage alone, I'm okay with this," Jack said. "Between Eriko and I, we've got the ability to scout. And we're a big party. Three and three should be safe enough."

"Fine," Morgan said. "How do you want to do this?"

"Boys and girls?" Tobias said. Everyone simultaneously gave him some variation of a dirty look. "What? I'm not kidding. Jack, Eriko, sneaky. Cordelia, Morgan, muscle. Me and my sister, your magical utility player. Am I wrong?"

"Tamsin and Jack go together," Eriko said. Instantly, Tamsin and Jack looked at her as if offended. "Seriously. If the love birds split up, you'll be worrying about each other. At least this way you know where the other one is."

"That makes perfect sense, and I'm trying to figure out why you sound mad at me about it," Tamsin said.

"Because I've got this shitty feeling I'm never seeing my girlfriend again and I'm jealous, okay?" Eriko said. "It's fine. Can we go?"

"Yeah," Jack said. "We'll go—"

"Left," Eriko said, giving the ranger a warm smirk. "I'm mad at me, Jack, not you. It's okay. Love you, dummy."

"Love you too, you maniac," Jack said. "Be careful."

"You too."

"One moment," Morgan said, walking up to the cleric once more. "Is there anything we can do for you?"

The cleric regarded him with tired eyes, more emotion in his face than they'd seen before.

"There are gems, in the Maker's final resting place. We cannot destroy them ourselves, but they are what bind me and my friends here. If you break them, we may finally rest."

"May?" Morgan said.

"I don't know for sure what will happen," the cleric said. "Perhaps we'll finally go home. Perhaps we'll just cease to exist. But I hope, if nothing else, I can finally leave this room."

"We'll do what we can," Morgan said.

The cleric dipped his chin, acknowledging the promise. He reached for the mace looped to his belt.

"Here," he said, handing the weapon to Morgan. "This is a weapon sacred to the god of sea and storms, but he has always looked at the lady of light as an ally in the darkest of days. He would want it wielded for a good cause. You seem strong enough to carry that burden."

Morgan hesitated, then accepted the weapon. Blueish lightning crackled from the head down the haft and across Morgan's hand and wrist.

"I can't take your only protection," Morgan said.

And for the first time, the cleric smiled.

"You know as much as I do that people like us are never truly unarmed," he said. "And with any luck, I won't be here much longer. I hope we never meet again, cleric of the light."

"I'll do my best to make sure we don't, cleric of the storm," Morgan said. "I promise."

Chapter 17: Elemental

Jack knew they were in trouble when the door slammed shut behind them as soon as they entered the tunnel. He closed his eyes and leaned his head back, simultaneously hiding and telegraphing his annoyance.

Morgan tried the door. It wouldn't budge.

"I don't think we're going back that way," he said.

"We didn't just split the party. We bifurcated it," Jack said. "Goddammit."

Tamsin examined the door as if looking for locks—searching for arcane sigils, Jack knew, something to dispel to release the door from its hold. She shook her head.

"We're in it, boys," she said. Then she wrinkled her nose. "Do you smell bacon?"

Jack sniffed and then looked down the hall before them. It ended in a right-hand turn, and then into darkness.

"That definitely smells like bacon," Jack said.

"I know it's bacon," Tamsin said. "Bacon's the only thing I miss from deciding to become vegetarian."

"Guys, I know I might sound irrational, but bacon in a long-forgotten tomb makes me uneasy," Morgan said.

"Do you not want to investigate the bacon?" Jack said.

"Do we have a choice?" Morgan said.

"Then we investigate the bacon," Jack said. "You two hang back.

I'll scout ahead. You as well, Silence."

The wolf bowed his head as if in understanding and took up a protective position at Tamsin's side.

Jack reached the bend in the corridor and turned to see a dimly lit room ahead, the smell of cooked meat—which, the closer he got to the source, smelled less and less like bacon—growing stronger the further he traveled. He looked back to Morgan and Tamsin and beckoned them to join him. The cleric drew his new mace and held it at the ready. Jack could see faint blue sparks of electricity bounding around the weapon's head.

"Nice new thumper you've got there, kid," Jack said.

"Not bad, is it," Morgan said, smiling back at him. He almost looks like he's enjoying this, Jack thought, and realized how much he missed his oldest friend's enthusiasm. Worry had worn Morgan down more than any of them, and Jack wished he could find some of the joy he once found in their pretend adventures back in the real world.

Tamsin coughed and cleared her throat. She winced at Jack.

"Not bacon," she said.

Jack pointed toward the light at the end of the tunnel where something dark and long lay sprawled on the ground.

"I'm thinking it's people," Jack said.

"Please don't make a Soylent Green joke right now, Jack," Morgan said. "I'm a half-step away from puking on my tabard."

"You're saying I should keep my long pig jokes to myself?" Jack said.

Morgan's skin turned almost ashy around his cheeks and neck.

"You know cannibalism is one of my phobias, dude," Morgan said.

Jack bit his tongue between his teeth playfully and trotted ahead, his soft-booted feet not making a sound. He peered into the room ahead and found it empty of anything alive, but certainly containing a few occupants no longer qualifying for that description.

Silence trotted past him quietly and marched right up to the nearest burned corpse. Jack almost gagged.

"Don't eat that, buddy," he said, his voice raspy as he choked back the bile.

"Oh, shit," Morgan said as he emerged from the tunnel behind him. Tamsin made a choking noise and covered her mouth.

"Those are what I think they are, aren't they," she said.

Jack scanned the room. The walls were the same rust-colored stone making up the chapel, but the chamber comprised of an open floor made of flat gray tiles was otherwise empty. It was rectangular, and in each of the four corners a brazier stood glowing with a different colored light. Jack noted only one with flames, and the others emitting an arcane light, one blue, one white, one green-gray. The varying light gave the room a sickly, uneven gleam.

Jack counted the bodies. Three in total, all intact but burned into unrecognizable, blackened husks. He could make out melted bits of armor, weapons warped by heat. He turned away when he recognized bone.

"They must've activated a trap or something," Jack said. "What do you reckon those braziers do?"

"It's probably oversimplifying, but my inner fantasy-novel reading dork is telling me the colors correspond with fire, water, air, and earth," Tamsin said. "Do you think Revery has that sort of thing? I mean it's super trope-y. Everything in Revery is trope-y. They'd have elementals, right?"

"They've had everything else we'd expect them to have," Morgan said. "Found the exit, by the way."

He pointed with his new mace toward a gap in the stonework on the right-hand wall furthest from where they'd entered. Also, Jack noted, closest to the corner with the flame-filled brazier.

Tamsin made a quick gesture with her hands in the air and her eyes unfocused. She then scanned the room.

"Magic there, magic there, magic there… this place is booby-trapped like the house in *Home Alone*, guys," she said.

"Well, maybe our villains here set off the fire trap and we don't have to worry about that now," Morgan said. "Does this room smell like propane?"

"Does propane have a smell?" Jack said.

Morgan ignored him and walked with more confidence than Jack was comfortable with toward the next door. The whole way, Jack cringed, waiting for his friend to hit a pressure plate or a trapped rune and set the whole room on fire.

Nothing happened. Instead, Morgan called back over his shoulder to them.

"It needs a key!" he said. "There's four keyholes. The one carved with flames is filled in, like someone snapped the key off in the lock."

Tamsin and Jack shared an uncomfortable glance, then each, in turn, looked at the three remaining corners.

"How do we want to do this?" Tamsin said.

"You pick," Jack said.

"Oh no, I'm not picking the form of the destructor, Venkman," she said.

"God, I love that you just picked the Bill Murray Ghostbuster for me," Jack said.

"Well, he was the hot one," Tamsin said. Jack raised an eyebrow at her. "I was a weird kid, of course I had a crush on Bill Murray. Like you didn't."

"You two are so well-suited for each other, it actively annoys me," Morgan said. "Tamsin, what spells do you have ready? I've got absolutely nothing that will help with a rock creature, so my vote is air or water."

"Water," Tamsin said. "I have a bad feeling whatever air creature we wake up will be invisible and I'm not prepared for that."

Morgan trotted over to the blue brazier and searched it. He reached down below the light and lifted a simple key at the end of a thin chain.

"That was too easy. My money's on the fight being the hard part here," he said. "You two ready?"

"No, but that's okay," Jack said. He watched as Morgan touched the holy symbol of Theana around his neck, then his throat, and then pointed at Jack, Tamsin, and finally the wolf. "What was that?"

"A spell of water breathing," Morgan said. "Just in case this thing tries to suffocate one of us."

'Aren't you clever," Jack said.

"I've been playing these games my whole life," Morgan said. "Give me a little credit."

The group gathered around the door and Morgan handed Jack the key. Jack looked at him quizzically.

"Working on the assumption this is some magical water creature," Morgan said. "You figure your bow is going to be the most effective weapon this time?"

Jack nodded.

"I bow to your superior logic," he said. He located the lock carved to look like a wave. "You ready?"

"The answer to that question is never going to be yes," Tamsin said.

"Okay then," Jack said. He slid the key in and turned the lock.

Nothing happened.

"Awesome," Morgan said.

"Wait," Tamsin said. She pointed at the floor. Between the cracks in the tiles, water began to bubble up into the chamber.

"Drowning. We're going to drown. That's how this room works. This is so disappointing," Morgan said, but then the water began to pull together, no longer just puddling but taking on a form, first a pair of watery legs, then a thick, translucent torso. "I take it back. I wish it were just flooding. I seriously take it all back."

The transformation neared completion as an enormous, squat-bodied water monster, shaped like an unearthly mishmash of ape and frog, roared a challenge at them.

Jack reached for an arrow from his quiver and nocked it in the ornate bow he'd been given by the ghoul hunter. He pulled back the bow string and let fly, the arrow bursting into mystical flames as it lanced toward the creature's face.

It struck true, landing with a splash and a hiss. The water elemental roared again, this time as if in pain.

And then its long, fluid arm shot forward, grabbed Jack by the neck, and yanked him forward, plunging his entire body into its own torso.

The world went very quiet as Jack found himself floating within the creature. The world outside was distorted, the sound muffled. He panicked for a moment as he tried to inhale, but then remembered the spell and hoped it would hold. He could see Silence growling and snapping at the watery monster, watched as Morgan charged forward, electricity dancing as he swung his mace at the creature's legs. That sound he did hear, an echoing, rich thump as the magical weapon struck home, and then his whole body seized up as electrical energy coursed through the water, amplified by the moisture. He screamed, and bubbles came out of his mouth, blinding him momentarily.

When his vision cleared, he could see Tamsin yelling at Morgan and gesturing, waving her hand violently. The cleric stepped in front of her as Tamsin knelt down, hands outstretched. Violet arcane energy gathered between her fingers, creating symbols in the air around her, and then she slapped both palms against the ground.

A terrible rushing sound filled his ears, and without warning he found himself freefalling, plummeting to the floor below. Unable to right himself, he landed hard, barely able to prevent himself from colliding face-first with the tiles. He coughed and water spurted out, undignified and alarming as air flooded back into his lungs.

He looked back to where the creature had stood, but now nothing remained. Just puddles, the blackened human corpses now soggy and flopped over. He felt a strong hand grip his arm and help him to his feet, and then Morgan's arm slipped under his own to make sure he wouldn't fall over.

Tamsin stood up, the purple symbols she'd summoned still drifting around her, spinning like mathematical poetry.

"What did she do?" Jack asked Morgan. Silence sidled up to him and licked his hand. He ruffled the wolf's furry head.

"Banishment spell," Morgan said.

"I didn't know you could do that one," Jack said.

"I haven't had need of it yet," Tamsin said. Her eyes, he noticed, glowed with that same violet light. "I'm going to hold the spell a little longer, until we're out of the room, just in case."

"Lucky she decided to figure that one out in that spell book," Morgan said. "Our other options were turning the creature to steam or electrocuting it, and I had a feeling either of those would've cooked you inside."

"Yeah, your magic mace gave me some electro-shock therapy, by the way," Jack said. He looked down at his hand and saw it was still trembling a little.

"You going to be okay?" Morgan asked.

"It'll pass," Jack said. "I hope."

He saw the chamber door had opened, and so, soaked and exhausted, the trio and wolf stepped through. It immediately swung closed behind them. The first thing Jack noticed was the sound of running water.

"It's gonna take a while before I'm comfortable with that sound," Jack said. In front of them, an underground giver—possibly even the same river that fed the waterfall by the entrance, he realized—flowed with deceptive strength in front of them. A path continued to their left, a blank stone wall on their right, where the river appeared to flow underground.

Silence stepped in front of them and stared, deathly still, across the rapidly moving water. A similar entrance mirrored theirs on the other side.

And they heard screaming.

"Tobias," Tamsin said. "They're all on the other side."

Chapter 18: The Workshop

The look of disgust on Eriko's face would have been hilarious in a different context Instead, it was directed at the dungeon door that had slammed shut behind them, cutting them off from the rest of their party.

"This is why we check for traps, isn't it," Tobias said. Cordelia's stomach twisted as she saw the glare Eriko leveled on the bard, and, for a brief moment, feared for his life.

"Whatever," Eriko said. "Done is done. Let's see what's up ahead."

"Do you want to stealth up, or should we stay right with you?" Cordelia asked, not really having a preference. She thumped the heel of her fist against the door to see how solid it was and knew with some certainty there'd be no breaking it down with her axe.

"Normally I'd scout, but now I have a bad feeling we'll run into some other trap door and then you two will be stuck for eternity in a lightless corridor," Eriko said. "Stick with me."

Eriko didn't wait for the others, padding ahead silently and swiftly as she always did, hunched over as she ran, like a ninja. The corridor turned sharply to the left revealing a dimly lit room ahead.

Cordelia struggled to keep up without making noise and failed, her muscular frame averse to soft footfalls. But her concerns for her own stealth went away when she heard Tobias catch his lute on the corner of the stone wall with a hollow, melodic thump.

"Are you even serious," Cordelia said.

"You try hauling around multiple instruments and being sneaky at the same time!" Tobias said. "This thing is designed to break stealth. Look at it!"

"Hush," Eriko said, edging her way to the door. "Oh look. More dead things."

Cordelia joined her and was greeted with the distinctive sight of a horrific wizard's workshop. Vials, bottles with mystery liquids, a strange titration unit long unused and covered in dust, body parts in glass jars, including a large glass container with just eyeballs, and more unidentifiable parts from creatures clearly not humanoid.

"That hand is definitely waving at me," Tobias said.

Cordelia ignored him, focusing instead on the massive, dried out corpse sitting in casual repose at the far end of the room. Whatever it had been in life, it looked human enough, with a powerful physique, long limbs, a symmetrical face. Stitching ran across its entire body—his body, really, Cordelia said, the creature looked like an eight-foot-tall, powerfully built human male. The corpse wasn't rotting, but some entropy had set in, skin dried out and wrinkled, turning leathery, like a mummy, rather than moldering putrescence.

"This is a workshop," Eriko said. "Who builds a workshop in a tomb?"

"Someone who didn't consider it a tomb when they started," Cordelia said.

"Or, alternately, someone who didn't plan on staying dead forever,' Tobias said. Cordelia grimaced at him. "What? Did I say something wrong?"

"No, just thinking about the consequences of if you're right," Cordelia said. "Not wild about some sort of immortal undead mage who used to be like us."

"Well, if he's coming back from the dead, he hasn't been here," Eriko said, running a finger across the surface of a glass beaker. "This place is covered in dust. Even the big guy over there has a layer on him."

"What do you suppose he was?" Cordelia said.

"Experiment seems to be the obvious option," Eriko said.

"Um," Tobias said. He had wandered over to one of the desks and started thumbing through the books there.

"Um what," Eriko said.

Tobias held up one of the books from the desk.

"The Art of Golems, Volume 3," Tobias said, holding up the tome.

"Golems," Cordelia repeated.

"Volume 3," Tobias said. "I assume this means the wizard successful completed Volume 1 and Volume 2."

"We should move on," Cordelia said, but Tobias, tucking several of the books from the desk into his satchel, started walking toward the body.

"I mean what if this is like Frankenstein's monster," Tobias said. "Frankenstein basically made a meat golem."

"Do me a favor and never, ever say the phrase meat golem again as long as I live," Eriko said.

Tobias turned back to her and smirked.

"Meat golem," he said. And then the meat golem grabbed Tobias by the head like a man palming a basketball and threw him into the nearest wall with a grotesque thump.

"Toby!" Cordelia yelled, instinctually drawing her axe and charging. The creature stood up to his full height, lumbering toward her awkwardly, its eyes burning with a faint red glow. She could hear tendons and muscles creaking like old rope as he reached for her as well. She swung upward, lodging the axe in the palm of his hand, nearly bifurcating it, but the golem did not react to the wound. Instead, it swung its other hand, balled into a fist larger than her head, and punched her so hard the whole world flashed white and then went dark. She felt herself flop and skid across the laboratory floor.

When she opened her eyes, she saw two Erikos dashing across the lab, nimbly dodging a backhand blow and planting two daggers deep into the creature's chest. She swung downward, daggers in reverse grips, and embedded her weapons just above the collarbone. The golem emotionlessly reared its head back and then slammed its forehead into Eriko, sending the rogue to the ground in a pile of long limbs.

The creature strode toward Eriko's prone form, hand outstretched as if picking up refuse from the ground. Tobias stirred, climbing to his feet, and Cordelia watched as the bard almost fell over, pin-wheeling around. But then he started doing something with his hands and she knew he at least had enough wits about himself to try one of his tricks.

The barbarian climbed to her feed and charged the monster,

throwing all her weight and strength into his midsection. It felt like she'd crashed into a wooden cabinet, not a living thing, but she was strong enough to knock him back, getting his feet out from under him and slamming him into one of the laboratory tables. She tried to stand up and take a step back, but the golem grabbed hold of her, his hands so large he was able to almost encircle her waist. He punched her, and Cordelia was surprised to feel a sharp pain along with the dull blow. My axe, she realized, seeing blood pouring from a puncture wound in her chest. It's still stuck in his hand.

Tobias uttered an incantation and Cordelia saw the red glow of the monster's eyes wink out. The creature made a strange sound, almost bewildered, and reached up to his own face to examine its eye sockets. As his hands were placed over his face, Cordelia summoned as much power as she could and slammed her fists down onto the golem's left hand where her axe was still stuck in the gristle and sinew.

The thunderous blow of her fists was accompanied by a gut-churning cracking sound. For the first time, the monster used its voice, a mournful, twisted howl. He pulled his right hand from his face and tried to do the same with his left, but horrifically, it was as though that hand was stapled to the golem's head, one side of the axe still trapped in his hand, the other deeply embedded in the monster's face.

As if blind, the creature flailed around with its good hand. Cordelia tried to dodge out of the way, but she underestimated the golem's reach. He clubbed her clumsily with a forearm, then grabbed her by her leather armor on the backswing. She grabbed at his fingers, trying to free herself, each digit thick as a tree branch, but she couldn't break the grip. She felt her feet leave the ground as he lifted her and then charged at the nearest wall, massive feet slapping with an almost comical, arrhythmic sound across the floor.

When her back hit the stone wall it felt like being in a car accident. Everything hurt at once, the back of her head most of all as she heard the muffled sound of bone on rock. The creature finally freed its left hand, yanking it free, and Cordelia was almost thankful to see the axe clatter to the ground. At least he won't punch me to death with my own weapon, she thought. Small favor in that. He reared back with his left hand, preparing a blow that Cordelia was convinced would flatten her skull, and she felt this strange, alien voice inside her. This would be a good death it said, this is how orcs die, a good death against a worth enemy—but her own voice, her real voice, cried out as well—no, no, this is not where I want to die, not like this, I don't want to die in some stinking cave and never see my mother again, no…

The tip of a gleaming blade slide silently through the monster's eye socket. A familiar gloved hand wrapped itself around the golem's neck, and Eriko—road rash across one cheek, a deep purple bruise growing around her eye, blood trickling from her nostril—appeared, clinging to the creature's throat. The rogue's whole body shuddered; Cordelia could tell that Eriko was pushing with all her might on the dagger she'd embedded in the golem's head, twisting it, searching for a brain that might not be there.

The golem's grip on Cordelia loosened. She slid with merciful slowness to the ground as the creature fell to his knees, shoulders slumping, and then lowering his head to his chest. If not for the ornate hilt sticking out of the back of his skull, the golem would almost seem as though he'd fallen asleep while meditating.

"Hey, gorgeous," Eriko said, offering Cordelia a lopsided smirk. She retrieved the two daggers she'd stabbed into the monster first, and then struggled to pull the third, which Cordelia now realized was the fancier one Tamsin had found in the ghouls' lair, from the golem's skull.

Cordelia tried to thank her, but when she spoke, nothing but coughing came out. She wrestled with her own guts to avoid puking and bent over to pick up her axe, which she promptly dropped. It was then that she noticed the blood running all the way down her right arm, pouring from the wound in her chest.

"We gotta get you patched up," Eriko said.

Cordelia shook her head.

"Tobias," she croaked.

When she spotted the bard, she almost laughed. In another situation, it might have been a comedy routine—Tobias, blood running from his nose and one ear, clothes torn, his lute absolutely destroyed but still hanging from his shoulder like detritus, hair sticking straight out to one side, and the flying cloak he and Tamsin shared holding him up like a sober friend trying to keep an intoxicated companion from wandering into traffic.

"I'm sorry," he muttered. "I think he knocked me the hell out."

"He did," Eriko said. "How are you feeling?"

"Like I broke a wall with my face," Tobias said. Then he focused his eyes on Cordelia. "You!"

He tried to run to her side and would have fallen back down again if not for the cloak. He knelt beside Cordelia and delicately checked on her wound.

"What was that thing you did before?" Eriko said. "That was new."

"I'm picking up little bits of magic," Tobias said. "Nothing like Tamsin or Morgan can do. Like little knockoff, cover band versions of their spells. That was a blinding spell."

"It was good work," Eriko said.

"I wasn't even sure the thing had eyes, to be honest," the bard said. "It was the only thing I could do without passing out. Here."

He started humming a song. Between the pain throughout her entire body and the ringing in her ears, it took a few seconds before she realized which song it was.

"Are you… singing Marvin Gaye?" Cordelia asked, slurring her words.

"Listen, my magic is music-based, okay?" Tobias said. "If I weren't concussed I'm sure I could have come up with a better song with the word healing in it, but this is all I got right now, so you'll just have to deal with it."

'That's fine," Cordelia said. She watched as the blood slowed from the savage wound on her chest. The pain remained.

"I don't have much," Tobias said. "You're going to need Morgan to really put you back together. I'm sorry. I'm basically a spell thief. I wish I could do more."

"Better than bleeding to death," Eriko said. "Can you walk, Cordie?"

Cordelia struggled to her feet. Her whole body was shaking. She wondered if this was what shock felt like.

"I'm fine," she lied, looping her axe into its usual spot on her belt.

"That's got to be the worst of it, right?" Tobias said.

Cordelia aimed a withering look at him, and caught Eriko doing the same.

"Okay then," Tobias said. "Onward to the next terrifying experience.'

Chapter 19: The Sharpest Blade

Morgan hung back as Jack took the lead, running past the rapidly moving underground river and up into the next series of tunnels, trying to find a way around or across to get to their friends. Even above the rush of the water, the sounds of combat they'd heard were horrifying, though the silence that soon followed was worse still.

A sharp left turn led them into another open chamber, this one looking truly like a tomb. A raised bier at the far end; low tables covered in dust and offerings, torches burning with a flickering, illusory light.

But what Morgan found Jack staring at were the walls.

"What happened in here," Jack said. Morgan followed his line of sight and saw lined grooves carved into the wall, countless vertical lines, every brick carefully, meticulously notched.

Tamsin entered the room last, and she walked directly up to the nearest wall, touching the grooves with the tip of her finger.

"Any idea what those are, Tam?" Jack asked. "Runes? Art?"

Tamsin peered at the pattern and shook her head. She cast a quick spell and a spark of light passed from her palm to the wall, but nothing happened after.

"They're not enchanted," she said. "I'm no expert, but they almost look like they were just, like, scratched into the wall. The eerie thing is they're all so uniform. Each one is the same length and I kind of think they're all the same depth, too."

"What can I say," a new voice said from the shadows. Morgan's hand went immediately to his mace. "I've had time to perfect my art."

"And what art is that?" Morgan said. He stepped closer to Tamsin, shielding her, knowing he could take a hit better than the wizard could if it came to that. Jack drew his short swords and entered a predatory stance. Silence emitted a low growl.

"Why, those lines mark the passage of time," the voice said, closer now. The speaker revealed himself, stepping into the light from a hiding place Morgan knew no one could naturally disappear into. It was as though he'd been embedded the shadows themselves.

The newcomer was whip-thin, dressed head to toe in black leather armor. His long, almost colorless blonde hair was pulled back in a tidy ponytail with a dramatic, almost anime-like lock falling across one eye. A joyless, cruel smile dominated his face.

"How long have you been here?" Tamsin said, trying to keep her tone casual, as if she were asking him about the weather.

"That many," the man in black said, gesturing to the walls.

"Years? Days?" Morgan said.

The man in black cocked his head, a puzzled look taking the place of his smile.

"You know, I'm honestly not sure," he said. "I suppose that's a mercy, isn't it? Not knowing. Nobody tells you that about undeath. You want time to matter, but eventually… is it even possible to keep track? Day and night, year after year, nothing changes down here in the dark."

"Are you like the cleric?" Tamsin asked. "Trapped here by the Maker?"

"Oh, you met the cleric," the man in black said. "Is he still staring at that altar, hoping his god will save him? Nobody's coming to save us. We were used and betrayed and now we'll stay here beneath the earth until Revery itself finally comes to its much-deserved end."

"Not a fan of Revery, then," Morgan asked.

"Oh, I was very much a fan of Revery," the man said, closer now, uncomfortably close. "We were the first real heroes, you know. And I can tell from your armor and weapons you're like us. You want to love this place. You want to be its saviors."

"Maybe not saviors," Jack said. "But if we're stuck here, we might as well do right by it."

"Well I have terrible news for you, little heroes," the man said.

"Revery is cruel. It either makes you cruel or punishes you for not becoming so. When I started, I wanted to be a simple thief. But by the end I was an assassin of kings, the greatest murderer the world had ever seen. And still, as dangerous as I was, somehow my friend bound me here. So, tell me, little heroes. Why do you come to our final place of unrest?"

"We came here looking to stop a bunch of murdering bastards," Morgan said. "But the longer we're here, the more I think we're supposed to do something else."

"That's too bad," the man in black said. "I was hoping you were here to feed me."

Before Morgan could respond, the man disappeared, melting into the floor like a puddle of shadow. Morgan put a protective hand toward Tamsin, and as he raised his weapon, he felt a searing pain across his neck. The man in black stood before him, one wickedly curved dagger dripping bright red blood from the tip of the blade. Morgan had the presence of mind to keep his grip on the mace, but slapped his free hand over his neck to check the wound. It came away soaked with blood.

Morgan took a wild swing at the shadowy man and missed. He felt as though the movement of his arm forced blood to spurt out of his neck wound and almost went down to one knee.

But then Jack was on the assassin, slashing blindingly with both swords. The shadowy man hissed, darting away, bits of his cloak separating as Jack's blades picked away at the man's garments but never seemed to draw blood. The assassin retaliated with a swing of his hooked dagger, but Jack darted back, narrowly avoiding having his own throat cut.

The chamber brightened as a blast of arcane fire erupted within the assassin's cloak. Tamsin held her wand outstretched, unleashing her spell. The shadowy figure disappeared again, turning to smoke and oil in the darkness.

Morgan lost his footing and fell to one knee. He tried to speak, but instead of words, blood came coughing up from his mouth instead. Tamsin tried to help him, her face drained of color and her hands outstretched as if she realized she simply did not have the magic to fix him. He waved her off and clutched at the holy symbol he wore around his neck.

Okay, Theana, he thought, feeling his life slipping away, the world growing colder by the second. I don't know how this works, but your-not-quite-faithful but doing-his-best servant is dying and could really use a hand here…

Morgan didn't even have time to wait for the goddess to respond when the assassin materialized out of thin air behind Tamsin and raised his blade. Startlingly, Silence launched into Morgan's vision, the wolf clamping down on the man in black's forearm, not knocking the dagger from his grip but changing the trajectory enough for Tamsin to stumble back and out of the way. The assassin swung his arm with shocking strength the and dislodged Silence, sending the wolf spiraling through the air.

Morgan's vision went hazy. He looked down at his hands to see warm, golden light gathering in his palms. Inside his mind, he heard Theana's calm voice.

Your work is not yet complete, priest. Heal yourself.

Morgan desperately pressed both hands into his own neck as if choking himself. He instantly felt an incredible burning; his eyes watered and his mouth went dry with pain. But soon that pain faded into something else, an almost antiseptic sharpness that faded into numbness. He coughed again, and another glob of blood flew from between his teeth, but he gasped in deeply and felt the tomb's cold, musty air flood his lungs. He'd never been so happy to smell stale air.

When he looked back up, he saw Jack in a losing battle with the assassin. The ranger was almost holding his own, admirably blocking blows that should have gutted him or slashed his eyes out, but it was purely defensive. Jack couldn't turn the wicked tide of slashes away to give anything back.

"Morgan!" Tamsin said. "I need a distraction!"

Morgan staggered to his feet. His limbs felt watery, his guts twisted, but he hefted his mace and let out what he thought was a war cry; instead all he could muster was a raspy, growly snarl, but it was enough. He charged at the assassin, foregoing any grace or tactics, and instead spear-tackled him, throwing all his weight and might into driving his shoulder into the undead rogue's midsection.

It worked, too, for just a second. Morgan had him trapped, pinned against the nearest wall, the slimy feel of the assassin's leather armor squirming against his face and arms as he held him tight. He felt a sharp pain in his side and found his arms were empty, the man in black disappearing once again into the floor like shadow made real. Morgan fell to the ground, unbalanced, gritting his teeth as he felt blood running down inside his armor and pooling at his belt. He rolled over to see Tamsin preparing a spell, arms waving in that alien, elegant way her magic had, but then the assassin reappeared blade aimed at her throat.

Silence reappeared, not attacking the assassin but rather, in a maneuver that would have been funny if Morgan were watching it online and not fighting for his life, swept Tamsin's legs out from under her. The wizard fell into an unceremonious heap, her arms pin-wheeling to try to regain her balance. The assassin's blade passed over her head where her neck had been just an instant before, chopping off several inches of her silvery hair. A much better result than a beheading, Morgan thought.

As Tamsin crashed to the ground, Jack jumped over Silence, blocking a swing by the man in black that would have raked down the wolf's back, saving the beast but putting Jack right back into death's sights.

And then Tamsin yelled a single arcane word and slapped her hand down on Jack's booted foot.

The ranger seemed to shimmer right then; his form became blurry. Morgan wondered at first if it were his eyes, if the blood loss had gotten to him, but Jack truly seemed to be moving at a different speed than the rest of the world. He was suddenly as fast—maybe faster—than the assassin, making up for what he lacked in skill with unnatural speed.

The assassin was still incredibly swift, though. He soon caught on to Jack's sloppier tactics and regained his footing. And the two exchanged blows for what felt simultaneously like an eternity and just a split second, blades ringing out like silver bells. Then the assassin kicked Jack square in the chest and sent the ranger skidding back, both swords falling from his hands and clattering to the ground, the mystical energy imbued in him leaving a trail like a photo taken with the shutter left open too long.

Jack made no move to regain his swords. Instead, in one smooth motion—something impossible without the spell Tamsin had channeled into him—he unslung his enchanted bow, nocked a single arrow, and let it fly. The arrow burst into flames as it was released, flying at an impossible speed. The assassin, charging in with supernatural swiftness to finish Jack off, ran directly into the blazing arrow, his own speed making it impossible to dodge out of the way.

The arrow pierced the man in black's forehead and exploded out the back of his head. Instead of blood and bone, shadow poured forth, a mixture of liquid and vapor, darkness where viscera should have been. And as that oily shadow gushed out like a geyser, the assassin began to disintegrate, his body turning to ash and darkness.

Morgan heard a single word from the darkness, and it filled him with equal parts dread and relief.

"Finally," the man in black said. And then he was gone.

Morgan crawled back to his feet, hand at his side, once again coming away red with blood. He unbuckled his armor to examine the wound.

"Morgan!" Tamsin yelled, rushing over to him. "I almost got you killed!"

"Nah," Morgan said, feeling the raspy-ness from his neck wound already starting to fade. Thank you, he muttered silently to Theana. I think you saved my life.

The goddess said nothing in return, but Morgan could have sworn he felt a warm hand on his shoulder as he bent down to retrieve his mace.

As he looped the weapon onto his belt, he turned to Jack, who was sitting down looking at his hands.

"What the hell was that spell," Jack asked. "I can't stop shaking."

"It was a spell of speed," Tamsin said. "I—I guess the spell book didn't say anything about side effects. How do you feel?"

"Alive," Jack said. Silence sidled over to him and bumped Jack's shoulder with his muzzle. The ranger put a shaky arm around the wolf's neck. "Which is better than the alternative. I just… I think I just need a minute so I don't throw up."

"Nobody's going to judge you if you throw up," Morgan said. "I can try a healing spell if you want."

Jack shook his head.

"You look like you need it more I do," Jack said.

"Nah," Morgan said. "I just got stabbed in the love handle. Didn't hit anything vital."

Jack clumsily crawled over to pick up the first of his short swords. Tamsin, the only member of the party still in reasonably healthy shape, retrieved the other for him from across the room. She stopped and stared at another passageway, previously shrouded in shadows, leading deeper into the tomb.

"Do we keep going, or do we backtrack?" she said.

"I think we need to press on," Morgan said. "The current looked too strong to swim it and I don't want to know where that current takes us."

"I think you're right," Jack said. "We just need to hope the others are doing okay and that these passages all lead to the same place."

They sat together in silence for a moment, partly to let Jack stop shaking and for Morgan to bandage his side, but also to listen for their friends. They hadn't heard a sound since the initial yelling on the other side of the river.

"What do you think he meant by 'finally?'" Tamsin said.

"Lot of scratches on the wall," Jack said.

"What if he's been waiting all these years for someone to come along who was strong enough to kill him," Morgan said. "And hell, we almost weren't. He could have killed all three of us if things hadn't gone just right."

"Do you think he's right about Revery?" Tamsin said. "That Revery makes you cruel?"

Morgan shrugged.

"How are we to know for sure," Morgan said. "But I think, from what we've seen, Revery makes you what you truly are. Maybe he and his party were cruel all along and didn't know it. Maybe they blamed their own darkness on the world itself."

"Or maybe it corrupted them," Tamsin said.

"Tell you what," Jack said. "You start showing the first signs of Slytherin behavior, we'll call you on it, okay?"

"You go full Boromir on us and I'll let you know," Tamsin said.

"Sounds like a plan," Morgan said. He grunted as he got to his feet, the gash in his side throbbing. "Now let's go find our friends."

Chapter 20: The Wall of War

Tobias did his best not to let Cordelia notice him staring. The barbarian did anyway. Tobias was never made for subtlety.

"I'm fine," she said, but he knew she was lying. Her breathing was ragged, and her gait uneven. Each step brought a grimace of pain to her eyes as she gritted her teeth and tried to ignore it.

Tobias couldn't ignore it, but he decided for her sake—and possibly for his own safety, so as not to annoy her—to pretend to ignore it.

Eriko dashed ahead, then came back almost immediately.

"Around the corner," she said. "Another chamber. There's a weapon rack, some other stuff. And a suit of armor."

"A whole suit of armor?" Tobias asked.

"Just standing there, like it's on display," Eriko said. "Dead center of the room."

"Are you sure it's empty?" Tobias asked.

"Of course," Eriko said. "Or, well, no, not at all. I have no idea. I didn't get that close."

"We should assume the suit of armor can kill us," Cordelia said, pressing past both of her companions. They scurried to catch up with her just as she walked into the new chamber.

"Interesting that the suit of armor is in the middle of the room, as if to prevent us from passing," Tobias said.

The armor was dull gray metal, almost black, and held a battle axe at the end of a long handle in one hand as if at attention. It wore an ornate helmet, reminiscent of a Roman gladiator's. And as they entered the room, it picked the axe up and held it across its body.

"Welcome to my chamber," the suit said in a deep, male voice. As it spoke, red pinpricks of light appeared where its eyes should be.

"Oh, come on," Eriko said. "I don't want to fight talking armor."

"I'm not talking armor," the suit of armor said. "And I recognize that tone. You're not from Revery, are you."

"No," Tobias said. Uncomfortably, this was the moment his lute, or what was left of it, decided to finish falling apart and collapse to the floor with a resonant bong sound. Tobias sighed, wondering if he would live long enough to need to find a new lute or if this was just the inevitable end of most bards. "We're from the other side."

"As am I," the suit said. "We were the first. The fighter, the mage, the assassin, and the priest. The first to arrive, and the first to never go home. We died here."

"So, you're currently dead," Eriko said.

"You know how this world works," the armored figure said. "Death isn't a single definitive state. I'm not alive. Nor are my friends. Our own wizard buried us here, to guard his tomb, as if he were somehow the most important among us."

"I don't suppose you're really mad at him and just going to let us pass," Tobias said.

"I'm afraid not, elf," the armored man said. "Part of the curse, you see, is that we are compelled to destroy anyone who enters these halls. I'll be honest with you. I don't want to kill you, but I have to."

"I am starting to hate magic," Cordelia said.

"I wish you'd live long enough to realize how wise that opinion is," the armored man said. "I was, in life, a warrior of honor. I will grant you one opportunity to turn back. Leave now and I will not shed your blood. Move forward and your deaths await."

"See, the thing is, the door locked behind us," Tobias said. "And we're trying to find our friends, so, I guess we're kind of at an impasse. Maybe I can play you a song for your troubles instead?"

"I will make your deaths as painless as you let me," the warrior said, raising his axe with both hands.

Cordelia charged forward, jostling Tobias as she charged.

The warrior brought his massive weapon down on the barbarian, who side-stepped it, swinging her own axe one-handed at his torso. Her blade skidded off his chest plate, sparks flying. The warrior shouldered her in the chest, catching her in the solar plexus, knocking her back. Pushing in, he brought his axe up again. Cordelia tried to step out of the way, but only partially dodged, taking the gripping gauntleted fists holding the weapon to her face rather than the blade itself to her skull. She careened backward, smashing into the weapon rack behind her, and Tobias could see in every striation of muscle, every twitch of her arms, that the fight with the golem had taken everything out of her. She was running on fumes.

Eriko ran in, daggers drawn. She leapt into the air, trying to repeat her success against the golem, but the armored man, without turning to look at her, reached out with his left hand and caught her by the throat in mid-air. Eriko hung there, feet dangling, her daggers clattering to the ground as she clutched at the gauntleted hand holding her aloft.

Cordelia started to stagger back to her feet, but a metal-plated boot slammed into her sternum, pinning her to the wall. The barbarian slammed the heel of her hand into the warrior's knee, trying to bend the joint and free herself, but the armored figure was unflinching, unwavering, as if he felt no pain at all.

Tobias looked at the broken lute on the ground, thought about the mind-manipulating magic he had at his disposal, and then saw his friends, outmatched by a deathless juggernaut. He placed a hand on the hilt of the sword the necromancer had given him in the tavern.

"You better not have been lying to me, you old bastard," Tobias said. And he drew the sword.

Instantly, Tobias heard the opening guitar riffs to Queen's "Princes of the Universe."

"Oh, shit," Tobias said.

And then, the sword began to sing.

The sword's voice wasn't a pitch perfect match for Freddie Mercury, but, Tobias noted, it was damned close, like an excellent cover band or a world-class karaoke singer. He was just marveling at the high notes when the sword yanked him forward, forcing his body into a dance of violence.

The armored apparition dropped Eriko to the floor, the rogue dragging herself away on her hands and knees, fingers scrabbling across the stone floor for her daggers. The warrior removed his boot from Cordelia's throat as well and focused all his attention on Tobias.

"Where did you get the fucking song-sword," the armored figure said, his tone somewhere between awe and absolute, uncut disgust.

Before Tobias could respond, the sword dragged him across the floor, his feet flailing beneath him like terrible ballroom dancing partner. The warrior brought his axe down in a killing blow, but the song-sword forced Tobias to dart out of the way, and with a flick of his wrist—a movement, Tobias noted with horror, had nothing to do with any will or volition on his part—the tip of the blade pierced the slimmest gap between the undead warrior's armor at the elbow, stabbing all the way through and then pulling back out again.

The armored figure's battle axe dipped as if the strength in that arm suddenly dissipated. The warrior swung again, one-handed, and somehow the massive axe seemed to move even faster now, but the song-sword pulled Tobias out of the way, back and around, jabbing forward with almost sadistic precision as it pierced the warrior's hand between finger and thumb. Tobias felt the point of his sword scrape against the leather-wrapped handle of the axe and then pull back again, darting away like a dancer.

"I hate that fucking sword," the warrior said, squaring up again, preparing to charge.

"I'm thus far undecided," Tobias said, feeling his body coaxed into what he had to think of as an "*en garde*" position, or possibly a very elegant reimagining of "come at me, bro."

The warrior let out a gut-churning battle cry and thundered forward, kicking up ancient dust from the stone floor, moving with deceptive speed.

I guess I need to trust you, Tobias thought, and he felt a warmth, welcoming, almost loving, creep up his sword arm. Steadier than he had any right to be, he waited until the warrior drew dangerously close, then ducked down, dropping to one knee, the song-sword wailing a high note as it passed through the undead adventurer's armored knee. The warrior toppled forward with the sound of dishpans dropped on a restaurant floor.

"Not like this," the warrior said, struggling to his feet. He swung his axe in two massive, perfect arcs, so fast the blade blurred in the air, but Tobias let the sword guide him and he danced out of each attempted killing blow. With a deft spin, he twisted to the warrior's side and drove his sword up under an armored armpit, sinking the blade to the hilt and then withdrawing as if he'd never been there. For the first time, the warrior cried out in pain.

"I just wanted to die with dignity," the warrior said, hefting his axe once more. There wasn't nearly as much strength in it, Tobias could tell. Though the adventurer did not bleed, ghostly wisps of gray-black smoke drifted from the wounds, as though his essence were leaking from each slash and stab.

"I've wanted to rest for so long I can't remember the years," the warrior said, stomping clumsily toward Tobias. "I wanted a good death. I will not be killed by the goddamned song-sword like a Highlander knockoff."

"Honestly, dude, I wish I could give you a better death," Tobias said. "This is as undignified for me as it is for you, I mean it."

The warrior didn't respond with words, but with action. He hurled his axe at Tobias, and the song-sword twisted just so, severing the axe-head from the haft, sending both parts flying. And then it felt as though Tobias was flying as well, guided forward by the sword, tossing it in the air as a wailing scream of guitar filled the air. He caught the sword in a reverse grip and followed through, the blade's edge passing through the thinnest gap between the warrior's helm and breastplate. More smoky material poured out, and the warrior, now weaponless, reached out to him, red eyes gleaming from within the helm.

"Gods, I hate bards," the warrior said, and then collapsed to the floor. As he fell, his armor came apart, falling onto the stone as if it had been previously held together by nothing more than force of will. His helmet spun on the floor dramatically before coming to rest.

Tobias sheathed the sword, and the music, thankfully, silenced immediately. He turned to Cordelia and Eriko and smiled.

"What the fuck was that?" Cordelia said.

"Bard stuff," Tobias said.

"Bards are so weird," Eriko said, helping Cordelia to her feet.

"You don't even know the half of it," Tobias said.

Chapter 21: It requires a sacrifice

Valamir couldn't get the smell of burning human flesh out of his nose. It was in his clothes he knew, and in his hair, and it would be a good long time before he could eat pork of any kind again. He seemed to be the only one in their cadre fazed by it. Blaggard ignored it easily, and the surviving henchmen brushed it aside. Asptooth looked alarmingly hungry. And Anders just looked like he had bigger worries on his mind, which, Valamir knew, was more than a little accurate.

He wondered briefly what they would have encountered had they chosen to go right instead of left through the chapel. The fire elemental caught them off-guard and deep-fried several of their peons before Asptooth locked the creature down. The undead rogue was stealthy but not terribly observant as they passed through his chamber unseen under the shadow of masking spell Valamir himself had cast.

And now they found themselves in what had to be the end of the tomb.

The large stone chamber was lit with recessed globes glowing with mystical energy. A simple spell, Valamir knew, but it was often the simplest spells, not the most powerful, that would last forever. The room was wide and open, runes carved into every brick and stone. A waterfall cascaded down the back wall, and a statue of a demonic figure—a strangely obscene figure, Valamir noted, though if someone asked he could not tell them exactly why his mind found it obscene. Somewhere in his subconscious, it struck a nerve and made him uncomfortable, and yet couldn't take his eyes off it. The statue stood on a raised platform, behind which the waterfall disappeared into a tunnel under the floor, though it was easy enough to hear the water rushing beneath their feet. Curved steps led up to the dais, and a coffin, elegant, ornate, even ostentatious, rested there, sealed and gleaming with a wealth of gems embedded in its surface.

"It's about fucking time we found this place," Blaggard said, wiping a dark substance from his face. Valamir was almost certain the substance was soot from one of the burning henchmen, but Blaggard took no notice of it, as was his usual style. The big warrior slapped Anders on the back in a congratulatory manner, though the one-eyed rogue, wrists bound in front of him, looked as far from celebratory as he could be.

The Tomb of the Maker, Valamir thought. He wasn't sure what they'd find here, exactly. When they started searching years ago they thought it might be a way home. But back then they wanted to go home, and Valamir was fairly certain everyone except maybe Anders had no intention of that anymore. They'd been here too long, "gone native" as that old offensive saying went. They'd stayed long enough to realize that being the villain was more fun.

But even being a villain got boring after a while.

Had they thought the tomb would hold a portal home, they may have stopped searching for it long ago, truthfully, Valamir thought. But Asptooth had uncovered in his research vague notes, stories and hearsay that the Maker had somehow wrested control over parts of Revery—had, in terms their party understood best, become a game master himself, usurping a god and taking his place. Other stories hinted that the Maker was the original game master, the one who built Revery to escape the real world. Whatever the truth was, the group all concluded that these were secrets far more interesting than just returning to some nine-to-five job. They'd grown powerful enough to no longer fear dying at the end of a goblin's spear. Valamir's divine magic was powerful enough that he could cure a rotten tooth or heal a burst appendix—an event Valamir would never forget, holding a screaming Blaggard down, the big man dying and begging for his life in ways he never had in all the bloody battles they'd fought before then. And once they'd reached that level of power, the idea of returning to modern medicine seemed pointless.

Anyone they'd known in the real world had long forgotten them, they thought, and here they could be kings.

Better still—with the secrets of the Maker, here they could be gods.

But now, with the coffin of the Maker in front of them, Valamir felt a sense of vague disappointment. Not fear. It had been a long time since they'd been afraid of anything in Revery. But somehow the lack of majesty, the absence of greatness… he began to wonder if perhaps the Tomb of the Maker was just a tomb. All the trickery, the undead guardians, the hidden dungeon left in plain sight, it all felt like an elaborate ruse.

Don't tell me I came all this way for a practical joke, Valamir thought.

Blaggard was louder about it.

"Look at this shit hole," Blaggard said. "A statue and a fancy coffin? You told me this place was full of secrets. I expected something more. I wanted to see behind the game master's screen."

"Let's look around," Valamir said softly. Decades of dealing with Blaggard's outbursts had perfected his ability to find the right tone to keep the dark knight from going too far off the rails.

Blaggard gestured violently at Asptooth.

"Get to work, then," he said. "Do your magic shit. Figure out what we're missing."

The dark wizard nodded gleefully, his filthy teeth gleaming in the arcane light. His imp, the little ruddy-skinned bastard none of them had ever felt particularly comfortable around, danced a little jig on Asptooth's shoulder then darted up to fly a circuit of the room. Asptooth himself wandered around, seemingly without reason, but Valamir had watched his ally work often enough to know the chaos of the path he took was just part of his affect. He always found what he was looking for, and he liked making those discoveries look like an accident.

If Valamir was to be honest with himself, that was the extent to which he truly understood Asptooth. He'd been a strange man in the real world, and Revery had only made him stranger. Valamir might have spent decades learning exactly how to read Blaggard and how to manipulate him; in that time, he still barely knew what went on in Asptooth's head. And, frankly, he was glad for that. He suspected the wizard's mind was a cesspool.

"Nothing about this place feels right,' Anders said, his voice ragged and dry. "What do you want here, anyway?"

"To rule the world, right?" Blaggard said, ruffling the rogue's gray hair.

Anders gave Blaggard a morose, almost contemptuous look.

"You never wanted that kind of responsibility. Come on."

Blaggard's eyes darkened for a brief second, but then his black beard split into a grotesque smile.

"You're not wrong there, little buddy," he said. "I think we're just so goddamned bored. Y'know? Maybe remaking this place in our own image will break up the monotony."

Valamir turned his back on Anders, unwilling to watch Blaggard torment their former ally for sport any longer. He motioned to the remaining henchmen to take up guard duty at the door they'd come through, as well as a second doorway on the opposite side of the chamber. There were only seven left now, less than half what they'd set out with. Several were killed by the elemental; a few others were taken by the undead earlier in the tomb; one was eaten by a reptilian creature that darted out of the river running through the tomb, silently dragged into the depths. He long ago gave up worrying about the NPCs here, sure that their suffering was all a figment of the players' imagination, but the logistics of needing to refill their war band when they got back out of the tomb was exhausting.

"How's it going over there, you mystical freak?" Blaggard yelled. Valamir closed his eyes, inhaled, then turned to see where Asptooth was meandering now. The wizard had stopped near one of the sets of stairs leading up to the dais, his imp back on his shoulder, and together they both appeared to be reading something on the stonework.

"Got something," Asptooth hissed. "One minute. I need time to translate."

The others had all taken time to learn to talk in character here in Revery, Valamir remembered. Some still slipped back and forth easily enough. Blaggard could let his Dominic voice out at any time, the two being so similar in their bullying tones. Valamir himself had no trouble distinguishing his dark cleric persona from himself. And Anders had gone into full regression—his thief character was all but gone, his real-world voice and mannerisms having long taken over again when he got tired of their dangerous games. Asptooth though; he seemed to delve deeper and deeper into his character the longer they remained here. Valamir could still get Craig to emerge when he needed to talk to the real person inside the wizard's cloak, but there were days he wondered if Asptooth had been inside Craig all along and Revery just let him out.

"Sacrifice," Asptooth said, grinning at his companions grotesquely again. "It requires a sacrifice to awaken the tomb."

Blaggard raised a thick eyebrow at Valamir, and they both looked awkwardly at the henchmen. Neither had an issue sacrificing one of their servants, but even knowing they weren't truly real, Valamir knew there was only so far you could push the NPCs before they would fight back, and that wouldn't help matters here.

"Important," Asptooth said. "This says the sacrifice must be something intrinsic to yourself. It must be part of who you are. A blood sacrifice."

"Like a limb?" Blaggard asked, incredulous. "I'm not cutting off a hand for this."

"No," Asptooth said. "No, this word here—why is this all written in arcane runes? The Maker spoke the low language like the rest of us. This is just showing off."

"Why don't you read us the text as best you can, Asptooth. We can try to fill in the blanks."

The wizard sighed in annoyance. His imp whispered something in his ear, and the mage waved his hand at the creature muttering "I know, I know" quietly. He cleared his throat.

"Here Lies the Maker of Worlds, sealed beneath that which he wrote. That which he wrought, it's wrought," Asptooth said, his tone almost theatrical. "None of us enter Revery alone, but that is how we all leave it. Someone's story ends tonight. You must choose the ending, and their tale will feed the great river. Huh. And I thought I was melodramatic."

"It's asking for a fucking human sacrifice," Valamir said, louder than he intended. The henchmen behind him stirred. Blaggard noticed this as well and, in his ever-horrifying, ever-decisive way, grabbed Anders by the scruff of the neck.

"Well, Anders, it's been a good run," Blaggard said, his tone dripping with feigned regret.

"You're shitting me," Anders said, voice cracking. "Come on, Dom. I've known you my whole life. You're kidding, right? You're just trying to scare me. Trust me, I'm scared. You got me."

"Eh, scaring you is easy," Blaggard said. He hauled Anders to his feet and dragged him over to the lower ground below the dais.

Valamir followed, staying a few steps behind. He hadn't noticed before from the entranceway, but a short stone table stood there at the base of the rise. It was covered with red-black blood stains, so old they almost looked like faded paint.

"No!" Anders shouted, struggling against his bonds and the superior strength of Blaggard's grip. "Not like this, man, not like this. What is wrong with you?"

Blaggard slammed Anders down on the table and the rogue went silent, his eyes turning pleadingly to Valamir. The cleric felt only the slightest pang of regret, but then he thought: *you never wanted to be here anyway, Bennett. This is a mercy. You've been ready to leave Revery for far too long.*

Seeing no help would come, Anders started swearing and violently shaking his body in an attempt to escape. Blaggard held him down easily with one hand and drew his massive blade with the other.

"Boss!" one of the henchmen yelled, interrupting the drama. Asptooth groaned and Valamir was uncertain if the sound indicated relief or annoyance.

"What?" Blaggard barked, eyes wild with frustration. *His blood's up,* Valamir knew. *He'd lose control soon if he didn't get what he wanted.*

"There's a lot of noise coming from the tunnel!" the henchman shouted. He was guarding the door they hadn't used to get to the tomb. Valamir reached for the morning star on his belt, the chain rattling as the spiked metal ball jangled loose.

"Either we were followed, or Anders' shouting woke up whatever was in the path not taken," the cleric said.

"Boss!" this time one of the guards at the door they *had* used started shouting. "I think I hear something too!"

"What does it sound like?" Valamir asked, trying to keep a level tone. "Do you hear footstep, or—"

Before the guard could answer, an arrow burst from his shoulder, its point ripping through the man's leather armor in a spray of blood.

Valamir turned to Blaggard, waiting to see what the warrior would do.

"Well, keep them busy," he said, choking up on his two-handed axe as though it were a kitchen tool. "I have work to do."

Chapter 22: The hero route

Jack strode into the chamber arrow nocked and bow drawn, ready to fire. Morgan flanked him on the left, his mace in both hands like a baseball bat. Tamsin stood on his right, the heat of a fiery spell already building in her hands. Silence hung back in the shadows, ready to launch like a homing missile at anyone who moved.

The raider guards backed off slightly from them, weapons drawn, one of their number dragging the wounded man away. Past them, the room was wide and strangely well lit. A massive man with heavy armor and a black beard stood beside old Bennett, the rogue situated on his knees. Behind them a raised platform held a large, gemmed coffin, and beyond that a tall statue, then a waterfall. The waterfall made a distracting amount of noise.

"Hi there," Jack said. He counted the combatants: Six unwounded grunts; a long-haired fella in armor who looked like a cleric; a magic-user with an imp on his shoulder; and the big warrior. "We were trying to find the subway, have you seen it?"

"Hey look, guys. Tourists," the big man said, smiling broadly. It was exactly the kind of wide, faux-friendly grin Jack had always distrusted in the real world, and it was no different here. He instantly hated this man. "What can we do for you, fellow travelers from faraway lands?"

"You killed some folks we were watching out for," Jack said.

"Well you did a shit job of that," the big man said. "But it's cute you're still in hero mode. You must be new here. Do you still call each other by your other names when nobody's listening?"

"These guys seem like real treats," Morgan muttered over Jack's shoulder.

"I'm Blaggard, by the way. Leader of this merry band of ne'er do wells. That there's Valamir and that's Asptooth," the man said. He grabbed Bennett by the hair and shook his head like a puppet. "Do you know Anders? He always had a soft spot for newbies."

"We're familiar, yeah," Jack said. "You okay up there, Bennett?"

"Hey, kid," Bennett said, not answering Jack's question, which, Jack knew, was answering it in another way.

"Look at you guys, all brave and daring," Blaggard said. "I remember those days. We were heroes once, right, Asptooth?"

"It was so boring," the wizard said in a strange tone Jack couldn't parse out as an affectation or his real voice.

"So, you don't recommend the hero route?" Morgan said, too loudly. He's trying to warn our friends, Jack realized. Hoping his voice carries down the other cavern entrance.

"Everything is more fun when you're the villain," Blaggard said.

"Well you're all charming," Tamsin said.

"Hey look, a girl," Blaggard said. "Man, I wish girls played our games back in the old days. It was always just us guys. Right, Valamir?"

"Not that we never asked," Valamir said. His voice was softer, calmer. Jack knew instinctively that the cleric was the one to watch in the fight. Blaggard seemed dangerous and impulsive, but there was a quiet calm to Valamir's vibe that made him particularly nervous.

"I can't imagine why you couldn't get anyone to join in on your game," Tamsin said. "Was it the BO, or the thinly veiled misogyny?"

"Kid, we've been here decades. Insulting me like that doesn't work," Blaggard said. "We've had a great run in Revery. We did just fine."

"What are you doing here, then," Jack said. "Run out of dungeons to delve? Decide to go through the low-level stuff again to see what you missed?"

"You have no idea," Blaggard said. "This tomb is the cheat code. We're here to collect it."

"Cheat code," Morgan said.

"Yeah, see, this place is called the Tomb of the Maker. Which has a nice ring to it in any fantasy world, right? But here, in Revery?

Think about it. Who is the maker of a game world?"

"The designer," Jack said.

"Or the game master," Morgan said.

"Now you're getting it," Blaggard said.

Jack sensed the expendable henchmen tensing as if they were waiting for a signal to attack. He regretted the choice to walk in with his bow. If they charged him in melee he could fight them off with the Dragon's Breath bow; it was designed for that. But an up close and personal fight was not what he'd been hoping for.

"So what, you're here to open the Tomb of the Maker and become the game master?" Jack said.

"That depends on what happens when we open that coffin," Blaggard said. "Want to find out with us?"

"I'm thinking no," Jack said.

"That's too bad. If you turned out to be even moderately villainous, I might've invited you to join our little party," Blaggard said. "Instead, well, I guess you're going to be making some death saves."

"Don't make us kill you," Jack said. "I don't like the idea of killing someone from back home."

"Funny," Blaggard said. "I really don't mind doing it."

And then he swung his sword down at Bennett's neck.

* * *

Tamsin didn't know where to look.

Jack was doing most of the talking, which was fine—she wasn't sure what to say just now anyway, and Morgan seemed to be plotting something, so letting Jack take the lead and fake some bravado seemed to work.

But with so many targets ready to lash out at them, she had no idea where to focus her fire if it came to a fight. There was the big jock one, Blaggard, of course; but she was picking up on quiet menace from their cleric. And the wizard at the far wall with the imp on his shoulder gave her the creeps immediately upon making eye contact.

All the monsters we've faced in this world, she thought, all the creatures and things that go bump in the night, and the first time she felt truly uncomfortable, the first time she felt like a creature was looking right through her, and of course it was a man from the real world. This was a familiar threat. Give me ghouls and ogres any day over a man who thinks he can take whatever he wants.

Morgan joined in on the conversation, yelling awkwardly. It shook Tamsin out of her own thoughts, and then she sensed it—not in some supernatural way, but she just knew that her brother was nearby. Was that why Morgan was acting strangely? To get the attention of their friends? She could see another entrance into the tomb, almost a mirror image of the one they'd just exited themselves. It would make sense, she thought, to have two pathways through the tomb, even if the wizard who built this had no intention of ever leaving. A secondary route would be a logical precaution during the building process.

She tried to follow everything Jack and this Blaggard guy were saying, but she couldn't take her eyes off the wizard—what did Blaggard call him? Asptooth. Of course they were villains. They entered a game with villainous names. They never wanted to be the good guys. Just like people in the real world, they lied about their intent and telegraphed their plans.

Then Jack said something about killing, and Blaggard tossed out a retort, and then blood arced through the air like a monochromatic rainbow.

Tamsin didn't look. She didn't want to know. Instead she unleashed a ball of flame at Asptooth, trying to get the jump on him. Go for the spell caster, that was what Morgan and the others had told her—the enemy will always go after you, so hit them first.

But the imp launched off Asptooth's shoulder and muttered an incantation in a guttural, incoherent language that made Tamsin's mind cringe and her guts squirm. A semi-transparent curve, almost like glass, bubbled up to surround the imp and the caster, and Tamsin's fireball exploded against it harmlessly. The room grew warm with the flames, but Asptooth stood without a scratch on him.

She expected him to laugh, but instead Asptooth's face went stoic. His eyes turned oily black and he pointed at her. She tried to counteract his spell but her aim was unsure—she had no idea what his gesture meant, not until black, leathery tendrils burst from the stones beneath her feet and battered her way like ropey clubs.

I'm outmatched by a veteran wizard, she thought, trying to call to mind any spell that would help, but every time she started an incantation one of the tendrils would knock her off her feet. Her wand clattered across the floor and soon it was out of reach as she scrambled to regain it.

A tendril caught her with a backward blow across the face, sending her sprawling. Furious, hurt, she turned around from the assault, and yelled out the one thing that came to mind, the one name she could always count on.

"Toby! Help! We need you!" she yelled, just as a sickening green hue took over the chamber's light.

* * *

Morgan picked up nothing but malevolence from the chamber the moment they walked in.

Not just the chamber itself, though the tomb thrummed with dark, miserable energy. The men they found there were hardened killers, and he knew it instantly. He'd spent most of his life with people looking at him with hate; he knew it when he saw it. But these men were somehow worse. Travelers, like Morgan and his friends, but bloodthirsty, violent—somehow, even compared to the monsters they'd fought, the sensation of encountering someone from their world, from back home, capable of that level of dark violence was more off-putting, more sickening than any undead creature or cannibalistic troll.

And when he saw Blaggard holding Bennett by the hair, he immediately knew: he's going to kill that man.

Yes, he is, Theana said in Morgan's head, her voice soft, mellifluous. *This place demands a sacrifice.*

We need to do something, Morgan thought. He was suddenly very aware of the wound in his side where the undead rogue had stabbed him. The bleeding had lessened, but his whole side had begun to stiffen.

Whatever action you take, beware the priest, Theana said. *He serves my rival.*

Y'know, we really haven't talked enough about the other gods, Morgan thought. Jack was still talking with the death knight-looking dude, getting him rambling, trying to find out what they were doing here.

Morgan noticed the other door to the right, with more of the unfortunately red-shirted henchmen guarding it. He could hear noise from within, noise those guards were clearly also hearing and trying to pretend to ignore.

Jack and the Blaggard jackass were talking about good and evil now. Naturally these guys were murder hobos, Morgan thought. Leave the wrong players in any game setting long enough, they'll start abusing the system just to see how far they could go.

"So you don't recommend the hero route?" Morgan said theatrically. Come on, Eriko, you know you heard that. You had to. Don't walk into a trap. Better yet, come bail us out.

Morgan caught the cleric, the one Blaggard called Valamir, staring at him with if not contempt, something akin to it.

What can you tell me about his god? Morgan thought.

I am the goddess of light and knowledge. I seek to burn away the darkness. He serves my opposite. The one who creates a fog of war to obscure the light.

But I'm a war priest, too, Morgan thought. So I should be able to match him, yeah?

The problem with my eternal enemy's children, my Bastion, is that they are unrepentant cheaters.

Awesome, Morgan thought. I'm the world's worst poker player and I'm going up against a professional liar.

Jack had turned the conversation with Blaggard onto the tomb, about its use, about why Blaggard and his party had come here. The words were getting more unpleasant by the syllable.

"Don't make us kill you," Jack said. "I don't like the idea of killing someone from back home."

Morgan's heart sank. He knew the minute they walked in here that they'd have to fight these people, but nothing about this felt right.

"Funny," Blaggard said. "I really don't mind it."

Morgan expected Blaggard to launch an attack at Jack. Instead, he turned his blade on bound, helpless Bennett.

And the blood began to flow.

Chapter 23: Straight-up murder

Eriko held up a hand as they worked their way along the tunnel toward. She could see shapes silhouetted there, armed men clearly taking up a defensive position, waiting for them. She glanced back at Tobias and Cordelia and held up three fingers.

Hypothetically, she thought, they should be able to take out three guards. But Cordelia looked as though someone had hit her with a bus, her entire body a mass of bruises and cuts, armor stained red with blood from the chest wound Tobias had partially healed. Tobias was, without a shadow of a doubt, severely concussed, Eriko knew. She'd seen enough concussions to identify the signs. He joked about the golem breaking the wall with his face, but it felt more than a little literal now.

The gamer in Eriko almost laughed. Always the rogues who get through a fight without a scratch on 'em, she thought. Not that this would do them much good. She could probably stealth up and slit the throats of two of those guards before they even noticed her, but who knew how many men were waiting beyond them? Those three were just the ones assigned to watch this door.

Tobias caught her eye and made a "wait" gesture. He waggled his fingers in that spidery way both he and Tamsin cast spells, and then he flung his hand out back toward where they came from, like a dog owner pretending to throw a ball.

Sounds of battle began to ring out from the room they'd just left.

Creepily, it sounded like their own voices fighting.

"What was that?" she asked in a harsh whisper.

"Illusion. Audible trick," Tobias said. "They'll think we're still back there fighting for our lives. Let's us sneak up on them easier."

"Or now they'll be waiting for us for sure," Cordelia said.

It looks like it hurts her just to talk, Eriko thought, reassessing their chances in a fight with their barbarian severely hobbled and their bard solidly concussed.

Then she heard Jack start talking.

It wasn't combative, she could tell, though she couldn't make out the words. It almost sounded like negotiation. She started tiptoeing further up the hallway toward the sound, hoping the shadows in the dimly lit corridor provided enough cover for her to approach unnoticed. As she got closer, she realized that the guards were no longer looking down the hall toward them—they were, it seemed, keeping an eye on Jack and whomever he was talking with. Eriko curled a finger at Cordelia and Tobias, urging them to follow.

The closer they got to the doorway, the more of the room Eriko could make out: The waterfall at the back, which helped mask their footfalls; the massive statue; the fancy coffin; and then the armored man with his captive.

"Bennett," Tobias said softly.

The big warrior, whom they heard introduce himself as Blaggard to Jack, was gesturing melodramatically with a cartoonishly large battle axe. Tamsin chimed in, too far away to hear her, but Morgan said something loudly about heroes. They're all alive, Eriko thought. That's a start. We can work with that.

Without warning, Blaggard choked up on his axe so he held the handle just beneath the double-bladed head. And then he dragged the edge swiftly across Bennett's throat.

"Holy shit!" Eriko said, unable to hold in her thoughts.

"No!" Tobias said, as Cordelia said nothing but made a horrified choking sound in the back of her throat.

The men at the tunnel entrance started to turn around to look at them. Eriko didn't hesitate. She drew a dagger in each hand and darted forward, doing her silly anime run, and ducked under one guard's swinging sword, then jabbed the point of a blade into another guard's throat. Then, with her off-hand, she repeated the attack, perforating the other guard. As both men began gurgling, clutching their necks, she threw a dagger underhand at the third guard, missing her intended target of his throat, instead embedding the dagger in the man's eye. He fell over, screaming.

The entire room in view now, she saw a wizard or something preparing to cast a spell, his attention on Jack, who let loose an arrow and cursed as Blaggard deflected it easily with his axe. A third man, clearly not a flunky like the guards, held a morning star in one hand with his other outstretched. A sickly, poisonous green stream of light flew from his palm, engulfing Morgan, who was covered in blood, Eriko realized in horror.

More blood flowed across the stone floor, a dark, growing puddle beneath the fallen form of Bennett. Eriko took aim with her other dagger, hoping to hit the armored warrior with a head shot, but then the room shook.

And the coffin began to glow.

* * *

"He straight-up murdered my friend," Tobias said, running past Cordelia to follow Eriko into the fray. Cordelia tried to run with him, but she found herself almost unable to sprint at all; her limbs were sore, muscle and bone, and felt like they were responding long after she demanded they move.

Still, she drew her dwarven axe and stormed out of the corridor as best she could, past the corpses of the men Eriko had so efficiently dispatched.

That was something she was still having trouble accepting, Cordelia had to admit—she found her own rage and aggression uncomfortable, but knowing that one of her best friends had somehow become a talented assassin here in Revery was hard to believe. *She's a goddamned vegan back home,* Cordelia thought. *Someone who won't eat turkey shouldn't also be capable of slitting two men's throats in a quarter of a second.*

The room had erupted into pure chaos: two spell casters were hurling arcane energy down on Tamsin and Morgan; Jack was interrupted in his attempt to charge the massive warrior who killed Bennett as three more henchmen surrounded him, the ranger holding them off with the bladed edge of his magic bow, spinning it like a staff. Cordelia hobbled past Eriko, deciding the dark-armored cleric would be a good target, but as she did, one of the dead men grabbed her ankle.

She almost screamed. Instead, though, she kicked at the hand, shaking her leg free. Surveying the room, she saw that the creepy, bearded wizard was looking right at her. He held up a hand and made gestures that would have been at home if made by a marionette's puppeteer.

The other guard Eriko killed climbed to his feet, eyes blank and lifeless. And then the third—she killed three in one swoop, Cordelia realized, a pit growing in her stomach—pulled Eriko's dagger from his own eye and started stumbling toward her, slack-jawed and mute.

He's making zombies, Cordelia thought. Okay, let's kill them all over again.

She spun her axe in her right hand, a bit of flair before the fight, but the wound in her chest, where the golem had stabbed her with her own weapon, suddenly shot through with burning, brutal pain, and her weapon clattered to the ground. She clutched her shoulder and found the wound had ripped open again. He did warn me it wasn't much of a healing spell, Cordelia thought, but this is ridiculous.

The first undead guard grabbed at Cordelia, going for the throat. She grabbed him by the hair and slammed him bodily to the ground with her one good arm. The one-eyed, dagger-wielding corpse came at her next, and she grabbed him by the wrist and shoved the dagger back at him, piercing his other eye. This seemed to leave the creature hobbled and confused, but still walking, so Cordelia knocked his feet out from under him. He landed hard, flat on his belly, and Eriko's dagger burst out the back of his head, shoved the rest of the way through his skull by the fall. The body stopped moving forever, then.

Cordelia felt a weight hit her in the back, and the congealing blood of the third and final newly-minted zombie began pouring down the back of her armor. She reached back with her uninjured arm and, roaring in rage and disgust, hurled him like shot-put over her head. He landed in a tangle against the nearest wall.

"Okay, then. Three down," she said.

And then her leg went out from under her as her own axe, swung by the first of the undead guards, bit into her quad.

Roaring in frustration and pain, she grabbed the handle and yanked the axe out of her leg, kneeing the zombie in the face. She brought the axe down directly between his eyes, and he went still. She went to one knee, trying to catch her breath, watching as the dark knight who killed Bennett began running for the now glowing coffin.

Axe in her off hand, one leg barely able to support her own weight, she started limping toward the dais to stop him.

Chapter 24: Sound and fury

He killed my friend, Tobias thought, dashing in the room and almost slipping on the pooling blood on the ground from the men Eriko had killed. Well, maybe friend is overstating it. But still. Bennett was a nice guy. I liked that one-eyed weirdo.

Tobias tried to scan the room, but his eyes kept being drawn back to Bennett's body, the way his blood was pouring out like water from a fountain, gathering in a shallow basin near where the armored psychopath who killed him had dropped the body. He had that little healing magic, but he knew a slit throat on a dead man was more than he could repair.

Next, he located his sister. Tamsin was hanging back behind Jack and Morgan, exactly where the wizard should be in this situation, but Morgan looked beat to hell and not exactly a bastion of protection for Tam.

The room's lighting began to change, not just with the flashes of arcane energy all the casters were tossing about, but also a bright, almost antiseptic glow. It came from the gemmed coffin, which now lay partially open, the light spilling out from under the lid.

The evil, knight-looking guy—Blaggard, he'd called himself—stepped over Bennett's body and ran for the stairs leading up to the coffin, all mirth gone from his face. Replacing it was determination, and something else—greed, Tobias thought. Whatever was in that coffin was valuable to him, somehow. And he was ignoring everyone else to get at it.

One of Eriko's daggers whirled over Tobias' shoulder with a skin-crawling hiss, its trajectory heading right for the evil warrior. But Blaggard, without missing a step, swung his battle axe timed to perfectly deflect the dagger with the flat of the blade. Eriko's weapon went spinning off in another direction—that direction ending at Jack's body. The blade tore through the ranger's shoulder, more a glancing wound than grievous, but still enough to cause him to cry out in surprise and pain as he ran after the knight.

The handful of remaining guards were closing in on Tamsin, who made a series of alien gestures with both hands, summoning a protective barrier around her that knocked the fighters back. Tobias ran in her direction and reflexively flinched and ducked as a sickly greenish light flew overhead. He stopped dead in his tracks as that light splashed against Morgan, who let out a shocking grunt of pain. Tobias almost gasped as he watched Morgan's skin take on a grayish, deathly pallor. The ray of light did not stop after it struck, but rather remained tethered between Morgan and the dark priest's outstretched hand.

"Tam?" Tobias yelled. His sister looked right at him, then to Morgan, then back to Tobias.

"Help Morgan! I got this!" she said. Dropping her shielding spell, she slapped her hands together, stretching her fingers, then slammed both palms on the ground. Gas-blue flames erupted around her in a blast, engulfing the guards and knocking them off their feet, causing them to cry out in pain.

"Okay. She's got that," Tobias said. He turned his attention instead on the cleric, who seemed to be sucking the very life out of Morgan's body.

He reached for the song-sword and started to draw it from the scabbard. As soon as he did, the first riffs of David Bowie's "Heroes" began to echo through the burial chamber.

"Oh, absolutely not, you musical theater garbage fire," the dark cleric said, dropping his attack on Morgan and casting another spell at Tobias. Tobias flinched again, preparing to take the brunt of another spell attack, but instead, everything went deathly silent. The song-sword stopped singing. He couldn't hear the sounds of battle.

He started swearing. His voice made no sound.

Shit, he said. Out loud. But nothing came out of his mouth.

"I hate that fucking sword," the dark priest said, raising his maul to take a swing at Tobias, who scrambled out of the way as best he could, hoping the priest would telegraph his attacks enough to enable Tobias to dodge. The maul connected with the ground, kicking up dust, shattering stone, but all without a sound. A spell of silence, Tobias thought miserably. He knows my kryptonite. All my magic is song-based.

Even the song-sword was obviously effected. He still drew the blade, and here in Revery as Oberon the Blue, Tobias was moderately skilled with a sword. But without the song seemingly guiding his strikes and parries, he was quickly back on his heels, fighting for his life. Sparks flew up as the maul hit stone once again. Tobias struggled to not imagine what the weapon would do to his bones if it hit him.

Tobias slashed at the cleric and marveled, despite being half-convinced this was how he was going to die, at how strange it felt to sense the reverberations along his blade as his attack was parried but heard no clang of metal on metal. Apparently, sword fighting benefits from sound and I never noticed, he thought. Funny how the scuffle of feet or the exhalation of breath all helped him in battle and he never picked up on that. The maul came rushing past his head, but somehow the bard ducked out of the way once more. More reflexes than brains, he thought, imagining his brains splattered on the stone floor.

The cleric lifted his maul above his head for a killing blow. Tobias found himself frozen like a rabbit, unsure if he should jump left, right, or try to stab the priest and just hope he could pierce his armor. But then a gauntleted hand grabbed hold of the haft of the maul and yanked backward, catching the priest off-balance and sending the weapon crashing to the floor. Again, the eerie silence of it made Tobias' head spin, an ugly lump of metal landing without a sound on the ground.

The dark cleric spun around to face his new attacker and got a blow to the head for his efforts as Morgan clobbered him with his electricity-sheathed mace. The cleric fell to the ground in a heap, and sound returned to Tobias' world, blades crashing, flames roaring, someone screaming.

Morgan fell forward, and Tobias caught him one-armed, careful to not hurt him with the song-sword. He helped Morgan take a knee, leaning heavily on his mace. His skin was still drawn and gray but the effect of the spell seemed to be waning.

"Whatever that was took a lot out of me," Morgan said, his voice raspy. "Sorry I didn't step in sooner."

They were interrupted, though, with Tamsin yelling from across the chamber.

"Jack!" his twin yelled out, and Tobias watched as she crushed a small vial in her hand and pointed at the ranger, whose entire form flickered for a split second as he ran up the steps to the dais, gaining on the big, bearded fighter who had murdered Bennett.

And then the wall beside Tamsin exploded.

* * *

Tamsin found herself in the strange position of seeing the entire battle unfurl unobstructed.

It started of course with the murder, her stomach churning at knowing there was nothing she could do to save the old rogue bleeding out on the floor. She wasn't surprised when Eriko came charging out of a doorway on the far side of the chamber—she knew, just knew, that Tobias was nearby, and Eriko whirling like a dashing blender meant her brother would soon follow.

Then things started to overlap—another man, the quiet one with the lanky hair, hit Morgan with a spell so clearly dangerous it even looked evil in the light it gave off. The creeper of a wizard against the far wall cast a necromantic spell, animating the dead bodies of the men Eriko struck down, trapping Cordelia in a desperate fight. The coffin opened, and Blaggard sprinted toward it; Jack bolted to intercept. And then Tamsin remembered that she was surrounded by flunkies and no longer had a ranger or cleric watching her back, so she instinctually threw up a protective spell to give herself a minute to think.

Her brother, in typical Tobias style, distracted the cleric from his attack on Morgan, but got tied up in a fight himself. Looks like I'm on my own, Tamsin thought, running through the process of her arsenal of spells and realizing her only option here was overkill.

Her spell barrier held, but she knew she only had seconds before the guards would break through, but rather than worrying for herself, she saw the glow pulsating from within the coffin, watched Blaggard running for it, and knew, whatever power that light would grant him, the dark warrior was absolutely the wrong person to have it.

And only Jack was close enough to stop him.

"Jack!" Tamsin cried out, dropping her protective spell and hitting him with another boost of speed and agility with the same spell she'd cast in the previous chamber. She worried, briefly, what using it twice on him would mean, if it would hurt him in some way, knowing what it cost him on the come-down last time, but she had to trust him to finish the fight before that happened. She watched her partner's shape blur and then speed up, almost cartoonish in how quickly he crossed the distance to the dais.

The guards were on her now, weapons raised, ready to strike down an unarmored magician. This was not in Tamsin's plan. She folded her hands together, structuring the spell, drawing power from the well of the beyond, and summoned an expanding wall of mystical flames that burst out from her. The men screamed. She tried not to hear it, to remember that it was kill or be killed, that this was something she had to do.

Then she caught the bearded, grimy wizard and his imp staring at her. He held out one boney hand and the air filled with the smell of ozone. Lightning arced out from his fingertips. Without thinking, Tamsin threw herself to the side, yelping as stone and dust crashed against her back and legs. She belly-flopped on the ground and looked up, squinting against the dust.

She had to trust the others, she thought, struggling to get to her feet, ears ringing, barely able to string together the concentration she'd need to cast another spell. She felt drained, tapped out.

She turned to look at the dais in horror as Blaggard and Jack stood toe to toe before the statue and waterfall, bathed in the light of the coffin.

Chapter 25: Knives out

Eriko wrinkled her nose at the metallic smell that filled the room right before an explosive blast of lightning nearly took Tamsin's head off. Blinking away the afterimage of the spell, she turned her sights on the source: the grimy, bearded wizard who had thus far stayed as far out of the fray as possible.

Well, my greasy friend, that's about to change, she thought, picking up the short sword one of the guards had dropped and pulling her last remaining dagger from the sheath on her hip. The fancy one, she noted, feeling the ergonomic, soft-leathered grip. That'll do.

She broke into a run, leaping over an ornate, fallen vase nearly as tall as she was, shattered and spilling dust on the floor. The magician only noticed her at the last minute, slapping his hands together and throwing a spell at her like a softball.

She dodged out of the way gracefully, pirouetting around a ball of flame, hoping it didn't hit her friends behind her. She caught herself laughing, entertained by the idea of dodging a spell like an action hero dodging a bullet.

As she finished spinning, though, she bit back a scream as the small, spikey body of the imp—the little, red-skinned creature on the wizard's shoulder this whole time—flew into her face, claws slashing, his alarmingly wide mouth filled with rows of needle teeth.

"Holy shit!" she said as she felt the little creature's claws rake across her cheek. Instinctually she dropped the short sword and reached up, snagging the imp around the neck without looking. She threw the beast at the ground as though she were spiking a football. It made a grotesque, wet thumping sound, but instead of killing the imp, she seemed to have only enraged it. It skittered to its feet, red wings flapping furiously, and it launched itself back up at her.

"Back off, you little creep!" she said swinging at it with her dagger and missing. She felt those tiny claws scratch her forearm and, furious, she swung with her unarmed fist with a sloppy haymaker.

Instead of whiffing entirely, which she expected to do, or connecting with its nasty little face, which she hoped to do, Eriko instead punched the imp in what could only be called the groin area. It let out a half-shriek, half-grunt and flittered away from her, it's little hands held up in a defensive posture as if asking her to stop.

She didn't.

She reversed her grip on her dagger and punched again, this time a solid left cross that landed dead center on the imp's nose. It squawked out a choking sound and dropped to the ground like a dead bird.

Not bothering to check if she'd killed the demonic creature, she kicked it away and sent the red, spiny body skidding across the floor like a doll. Then she turned her attention back on the wizard, who seemed absolutely appalled she'd dared to punch his diminutive friend.

"Did you punch Cheremy in the crotch?" the wizard said, incredulous.

"Your imp's name is Cheremy?" Eriko said.

"I heard you go by Rouge the Rogue," the wizard said. "You have no business making fun of my familiar."

"That's fair," Eriko said, flipping the dagger to her other hand and lunging at him.

The mage lashed out with another spell, and this time Eriko couldn't get out of the way fast enough. She felt something icy and sharp dig into her shoulder, and she willed herself to ignore it. Instead, she dropped into a roll, under yet another spell attack, and then flipped back to her feet, this time close enough to draw blood.

The magician raised his hand violently, palm out to her, and she saw a faint shimmer surround him. She recognized it immediately— a protective spell Tamsin used all the time when she needed to block an attack aimed her way. Dammit, Eriko thought, already committed to stabbing him, knowing it would fail. I wasn't ready to break through magical defenses. I really thought I could get to him in time…

The ornate dagger, with its excessively glamorous handle, its elegant blade far more for show than function, passed right through the shielding spell, shattering it like thin glass. The point of the blade continued forward, stabbing into the palm of the wizard's hand and then through it, sending blood spraying in both directions.

The wizard screamed in pain as Eriko herself screamed in surprise.

"Where did you get a spell-breaker?" he said, sounding as though he might vomit at any second. Eriko yanked the blade back out of the palm of his hand mercilessly, and the wizard's knees buckled. "How did you…"

"Asptooth!" someone yelled from across the chamber.

The cleric, clutching his head, scalp bleeding as he dragged himself to his knees. Morgan stood near him, electric sparks glittering around the head of his mace, the light turning Morgan's drained face into a ghastly mask. Tobias had a shoulder under him, looking as though he were the only thing keeping Morgan on his feet.

"Asptooth? Craig! We gotta go! Where are you!" the cleric yelled.

"Don't you dare," Eriko said, pointing her dagger at Asptooth's face. "Also, Craig? Seriously?"

The wizard smirked at her and flipped her the middle finger. He disappeared in a puff of blackish-purple smoke.

"Shit," Eriko said. She spun around back to Morgan and the others and saw Asptooth appear next to his dark cleric companion. She felt a puff of air on the back of her neck and then the imp used her head as a launching pad to shove himself into the air, gliding swiftly back to his master.

"I hate that thing," Eriko said as she felt a trickle of blood run down her forehead from her scalp.

She risked a glance over her shoulder to Cordelia, who was a mass of bruises and blood. Even from here she could see the barbarian's eyes were glazed over with exhaustion and pain. Morgan was on the verge of collapse. Tamsin looked mostly uninjured from the explosive spell that knocked her off her feet, but at the same time tapped out—her face was drawn and her skin pale, as though all the spell casting had taken too much out of her.

And there was Jack up on the dais.

The ranger was moving at an impossible speed, boosted, Eriko assumed, by a spell from either Tamsin or Morgan, something they hadn't tried before. But he'd needed it. She hadn't noticed until now just how big the armored man was. Morgan was a big dude, football player big, and this guy made him look average. Jack, meanwhile, was never particularly intimidating, and now, seeing him square off with this brute of a man in full black plate, Eriko began to worry.

Jack nocked and fired an arrow with blinding speed, but the arrow—even glowing with fiery, mystical energy from his enchanted bow—careened off the dark warrior's breastplate with a spark of red-gold light. The knight ignored him, reaching instead for the coffin, where light gleamed from beneath its jeweled lid. Jack crossed the distance between them as if he were moving in fast-forward, jumping up onto the coffin lid and swinging down at the other man with the bladed edge of his bow. The dark knight seemed almost annoyed as he was forced to bring his two-handed battle-axe up to block the blow.

Jack whirled, bringing the magic bow down like a staff, but the warrior shoved him back, giving up his grip on the coffin lid, and then climbed on top of him, towering over the ranger and upsetting his footing.

And then he started to swing that axe as though it weighed nothing at all, and Eriko started to run.

Chapter 26: All I ever wanted, really

The spell Tamsin cast on Jack was having a strange effect.

Maybe it was because she reapplied it so soon after the first time; maybe it was simply that he was more aware of it now. But as his body raced faster than it should ever have been capable across the chamber, moving to intercept Blaggard and keep whatever was in that coffin out of his hands, his thoughts seemed to move with equal speed. His eyes took in with high-definition quality everything happening in the tomb: Cordelia bleeding to death; Morgan wasting away; Eriko facing off with Asptooth; Tobias battered and lost; and Tamsin surrounded by the burning bodies of men she'd set ablaze with her magic. But not only that: he felt almost as though his mind could be in two places at once.

His friends laughing around a table. Sharing secret adventures with the same joy as they shared secrets of themselves. The bliss of telling stories together. The safety of knowing who you could trust, who you could love, who would trust you and love you back.

His friends. He didn't have many of those. All the friends he had were in this room, and they were suffering.

I brought us here, he thought, the gleaming beneath the coffin boring into his brain like a knife. I wanted my friends to have an adventure together, at home, on a rainy night, with too much pizza and all the laughter we could ever want. In a place where nothing could hurt us.

All I ever wanted was for them to be happy.

Well, no, he thought, feet barely touching the ground as he sprinted up the short staircase, preparing to fire an arrow at Blaggard. He took aim at the big man's heart and let fly, the arrow bursting into brilliant golden flames as he released it, ridiculously overdramatic, like something he'd seen in a sci-fi cartoon as a kid. The arrow splashed against Blaggard's armor and disintegrated. The dark warrior's eyes rose from the coffin to watch him, and Blaggard smiled. There was no joy in it.

There was one other thing Jack always wanted. A shadowy shape entered his field of vision, darting up the stairs behind Blaggard. Silence, his wolf, eyes almost glowing in this slow-motion reality Jack found himself living in. Silence's teeth were glittering, pristine white, perfect arrowheads glistening with saliva as the wolf tore toward them both.

This game gives us what we want, Jack knew. He wondered about this, as he swapped his grip on the bow to swing it like a bladed weapon. Jack felt as though he were in someone else's body as he moved with surreal, unearthly grace, like some alien combination of stuntman and martial artist.

Morgan wanted something to have faith in when his own faith had crumbled, and he wanted to find someone to care about without fear. Eriko wanted adventure, she wanted risk without risk, to be the dashing scoundrel. Cordelia, poor Cordelia, all she ever wanted was to be strong enough that the world would leave her alone, to be powerful enough the no one would ever truly threaten her.

And the twins. I dragged them into this. But Tobias found his voice when the real world told him he was worthless every moment of every day of his life. In Revery, Tobias could be himself when reality refused to let him exist at all. And Tamsin just wanted magic. Sadder than anyone would ever know, and lonelier than she'd ever admit, Tamsin wanted to disappear into stories of magic because the real world didn't offer her enough magic of her own. She could be something here, something great, if she wanted.

This game knows what we want, Jack knew, and his heart went very cold in his chest, as if it refused to beat.

Blaggard was insanely strong, Jack realized, as the bigger man easily shrugged off every one of his attacks. He wielded an axe that must've weight as much as Eriko as though it were a conductor's wand. Parry, swing, block, swipe, they sparred back and forth, Jack only surviving because the spell gave him the supernatural speed he needed to avoid having his head taken off by a swing of the battle axe.

He ducked under a wide slashing blow and brought the bladed edge of Dragon's Breath up along the side of Blaggard's armor. It drew no blood, but it did exactly what Jack wanted; in his heightened vision, he saw the leather straps holding the black, iron-like breastplate in place tear and split, opening a gap in Blaggard's armor. The dark knight's next blow might have taken Jack's arm off, but Silence reached them just in time, clamping his slavering jaws down on Blaggard's knee, finding a weak point in the joint of his armor. Blaggard let out a roar more in anger than pain, but his body buckled, his right knee no longer seemingly able to support his weight. He turned his axe on Silence then, but Jack was faster, hooking the haft of the weapon with Dragon's Breath so it altered the course of the blade. Still, Jack's heart skipped as he heard Silence emit a high-pitched whine when Blaggard's gauntleted arm connected with the wolf's ribs and sent him sprawling to the floor below.

Holding the axe with one hand, Blaggard grabbed hold of Dragon's Breath. His armored glove protected him somewhat from the blade, but still, Jack could see blood pouring between Blaggard's fingers as he tightened his grip. Then, with monstrous force, he yanked the bow out of Jack's hands and threw it away. Jack heard it splash into the waterfall to his right and disappear.

Revery knows what we want, Jack thought as he drew the two curved short swords from his hips. He stepped back as Blaggard swung wildly, sparks flying as the axe clashed against the coffin's lid.

"I didn't survive this long to be the villain in someone else's story, you little shit," Blaggard said, slashing without a care about what he hit. The axe smashed into the tall, demonic statue in front of the waterfall. For a moment, Jack thought Blaggard might lose his grip on his own weapon, but he held on, grimacing in pain as the vibrations shook his arm. Jack slipped in an upward, hacking attack of his own, once again not penetrating the warrior's metal armor, but splitting another leather strap holding his pauldron in place.

He felt the spell beginning to fade. His arms still jangled with nervous energy and adrenaline, but the world began to move closer to its natural speed, the eerie accuracy of his vision lessoned. The memories of his past playing in his mind turned gray and faded.

Blaggard reached for him with his bloody, ruined hand and Jack tried to slip out of reach, but without the spell's help, he wasn't fast enough. The dark knight's fingers closed around the neck of Jack's armor, and he dragged him in close, so close Jack could see the flecks of gray in Blaggard's beard, and smell the rancid fury on his breath.

"I never get tired of killing real people," Blaggard said. "It's so much more fun than killing the pretend ones here."

Jack felt a sharp pain in his chest as Blaggard's other hand jabbed upward. The decorative point of his battle axe, something barely worth noticing before, pierced through his armor easily, just below the sternum, splitting his leather armor as if it were paper. Strange, Jack thought, it doesn't hurt like I thought it would. It almost feels like a stomach ache.

The game knows what we want, Jack thought. He smiled at Blaggard as the massive warrior held him aloft, impaled on his battle axe, framed by a waterfall to nowhere. He could hear his own blood splattering on the coffin lid, could taste it in his mouth.

"I always wanted to die saving the day," Jack said, and he jammed the short sword in his left hand up through the gap he'd made in Blaggard's armor. With nothing to stop it, the blade passed through his flesh up under Blaggard's arm until Jack could feel the blade's crosspiece scraping against the plate armor.

"No," Blaggard said. A thin trickle of blood began to run from the corner of his mouth.

"Yeah," Jack said, and he brought the sword in his right hand down through the space where Blaggard's pauldron had come loose. The sword slid easily inside, scraping grotesquely against Blaggard's collarbone until it pierced the soft flesh of his lung. Now *that* hurt, Jack thought, the violent motion of lifting his arm causing him to shift on the point of the axe.

"I hate this fucking game," Blaggard said, a bubble of blood bursting from his lips. He collapsed to one knee, digging the axe deeper into Jack's chest as he maintained his death grip on the ranger's neck.

"I'm sorry," Jack said, but he wasn't sure exactly who he was talking to then. He looked down from the dais one more time, unsure who he was searching for. He heard Morgan yelling his name, and Tamsin, further away, but it was Eriko, his oldest friend, whom he locked eyes with, her face bloody as she ran toward him, arms outstretched, his name on her lips.

He felt Blaggard's arm flex and tighten.

"You killed me," Blaggard said. "Rot in hell."

And then Blaggard threw him toward the waterfall. There was nothing to stop him from going over the edge. All the strength had gone out from his legs. His arms felt loose and useless. There was an awful pulling sensation as the axe ripped from his chest, and he felt his shoulder bump into the knee of the demon statue as he passed by, but by then, nothing hurt anymore. The sound of the waterfall engulfed him, and then darkness.

This game knows what we want. And this this is all I ever wanted, really.

I just wanted to…

Chapter 27: Those who remain

Morgan watched his best friend's body plummet into the waterfall and felt more helpless than he'd ever felt in his entire life.

He pushed himself away from Tobias and started running slowly and sloppy toward the dais. Blaggard's corpse was sprawled out on the coffin, blood running down the surface in a grim parody of the waterfall behind him. He limped past Valamir and Asptooth and stared them down furiously, only to see Asptooth cast a spell that sent both men blinking out of existence. The dark priest shrugged nonchalantly at Morgan as he passed, as though everything they'd all just been through was nothing more than a way to pass an afternoon, and then they were gone.

Silence the wolf let out a long, devastating howl, and Morgan knew Jack was gone, really gone. He didn't need to see the body to know, not when Silence howled like that. But still, he wasn't ready to give up. Not yet. We are in a land of gods and magic, Morgan thought. Death a mutable thing here.

Theana, I struggle with believing in you, Morgan thought. But if there were ever a time I needed you to be real, this is it.

He slapped his hand down on the symbol of Theana on his tabard and felt a warm, soothing energy pour through his veins. The agony of Valamir's spell faded. His limbs no longer felt withered and exhausted. But still, no matter how strong he became, he wasn't fast enough. By the time he reached the top of the dais, he found Eriko staring down into the pit where the waterfall poured into impenetrable darkness.

"I don't see a bottom," Eriko said. "Morgan, I don't see a bottom."

"It's a waterfall," he said. "It's got to empty out somewhere, right?"

"Can you see him?" Tobias yelled. He had joined his sister, who stood in shocked silence, looking at the empty space where Jack had been just seconds before.

"Where does this waterfall go?" Eriko said, loudly. "Can one of you goddamned magic users figure out where it leads to? We need to find him!"

"The river," Cordelia said. She'd lost a lot of blood, Morgan realized, seeing her take a knee, unable to stand any longer. "The river runs all the way through the temple, remember? It's got to be the same stream we crossed under to walk in. Right?"

Eriko locked eyes with Morgan, then leapt off the dais to the floor below and began to run.

"Wait!" Morgan said. "There's elementals on the way back. Traps and monsters."

"Not the way we came," Eriko said sharply. "We took care of our monsters."

Eriko darted back down the corridor she'd emerged from originally with Cordelia and Tobias, and Silence ran after her like a shadow. Tobias watched her go, clearly torn between staying with his sister and helping Eriko. He looked to Morgan pleadingly.

"Go," Morgan said. "I've got things here."

Tobias nodded, kissed his sister on the side of her head, and bolted after Eriko as well. He flung off his magic blue cloak as he ran and it flew through the air behind him to coil around Tamsin like a hug. She drew the cloak closer around her shoulders and started toward Cordelia, but the barbarian waved her off, standing up on her own. Instead, Tamsin walked slowly, deliberately up the stairs to join Morgan by the coffin.

"We're not going to be able to save him," Tamsin said softly. Her eyes were wide, her voice giving off the illusion of calm, but Morgan could feel the emotion roiling off her.

"We'll find him," Morgan said. "Let's catch up with the others. Come on."

"Not yet," Tamsin said, turning to the coffin and the dead man who lay atop it. "Jack died to stop Blaggard from getting whatever is in that coffin. We need to make sure no one ever does."

Cordelia hobbled up the opposite set of stairs, clutching her bleeding thigh.

"Could use a little help, doctor," she said.

Wordlessly, Morgan strode to her, once again calling on Theana for her grace. His hand became engulfed in a gentle golden light, and he pressed his palm against the brutal wound on Cordelia's leg. The light mercifully prevented him from watching the knitting and reforming of her torn flesh, but when he drew his hand away, only a faint scar remained. Her other wounds had also faded as well, though it was hard to tell, as covered in blood as she was.

Cordelia placed a strong, gray-green hand on Morgan's shoulder.

"Thank you," she said. "Now let's see what's in that box."

The barbarian brushed past him and grabbed hold of Blaggard's armor, hauling his limp corpse away and throwing it on the ground. She spat on his face, which Morgan hadn't expected. Cordelia shook her head.

"You see people do that in the movies," she said. "It doesn't feel as good as I thought."

She picked up Blaggard's battle axe and instantly Morgan's stomach twisted. He hadn't noticed it before, but something emanated from the weapon, a malice that was almost sentient.

"Get rid of that," he said. "It's... unclean, somehow. There's something wrong with it."

Cordelia examined it for a few seconds, then tossed it away.

"I can feel it," she said. "God, I can feel it. That thing is... wrong. It's wrong."

"Don't touch it again," Morgan said. He watched the door where Eriko the others had run through, listening for combat or worse, but nothing came. He put his hands on the coffin's lid. "Here, help me with this."

Together, he and Cordelia pushed the lid off and let it clatter to the floor. He expected to see the Maker within, either a desiccated corpse or some strangely preserved body, waiting to be discovered. Instead, as the coffin was laid open completely, the light from within began to fade, and all they found was an empty box.

"He's not in here," Morgan said.

Tamsin joined them by the coffin, tracing runes in the air with her index finger. Her eyes began to glow a faint violet.

"Blaggard never said how he knew this tomb was a way to control Revery, did he," she said.

"Not that I know of," Morgan said. "We barely know anything about this place at all."

"There's magic throughout everything here. The stonework, the gems on the coffin, the statue. The whole place is built with magic," Tamsin said. "But I think this place wasn't made to control Revery. I think this place was made to think the Maker no longer controlled it. Morgan, I don't think he's dead."

"What do you mean, not dead," Cordelia said.

"I don't know," Tamsin said. "No body, no mechanism. The magic in his place is dangerous, but ordinary. It's a game element, not a control panel."

Tamsin squinted at the coffin, examining it closer, then reached inside. She withdrew a single, simple gold ring.

"Do you think that's what Blaggard was looking for?" Morgan asked.

Tamsin shrugged, then studied the waterfall. It was hard to tell, Morgan thought, if the moisture gathering on her face was from the water, or if those were tears.

"We should find the others," Tamsin said, pocketing the ring.

"And Jack," Cordelia said.

Tamsin took Cordelia's hand gently, her long elven fingers entwining with Cordelia's rough orcish digits.

"I got him killed with that spell," she said. "I got him killed for a useless plot twist. I should have seen this right away. I should've known."

Cordelia pressed her forehead against Tamsin's.

"Come on," she said. "Let's get out of here. Don't give up yet."

"One last thing," Morgan said. He lifted the hammer he'd received from the ghostly cleric and brought down on one of the gems adorning the Maker's coffin, blue, like the cleric's tabard. The gem cracked and crumbled. He did this twice more, smashing an obsidian gem, and then a deep red one. Each became powder under his swings.

"What are you doing?" Cordelia asked.

"The cleric who gave me this weapon asked one favor," Morgan said. "I don't know if those were the right crystals, but I said I'd try to set him free if I could."

He looked at strangely artful, ostentatious tomb and shook his head.

"I don't know," he said. "I hope this is enough."

* * *

Because you're the one I'm betting on. And the people Anders used to run with are notorious killers. They have no issues murdering other players here. Or anything else for that matter.

That was what the necromancer had said to him back in the tavern, Tobias thought. He warned us. Warned me. And he put his chips on me instead of Jack. And now I'm here with a stupid magic sword and my friend is dead.

This game is bullshit.

He and Eriko had passed through the tomb without incident, back through the rooms they'd fought their way through, and found the previously locked door back to the chapel unlocked as well. The spirit cleric was gone when they arrived, though whether destroyed or simply hiding he didn't know. They avoided the attention of dangerous fungus in the Grove and did not wake the dead again on their way out.

It was dark when they exited the tomb, but that didn't stop Eriko, with Silence at her side, from first attempting to climb down the waterfall to look for Jack's body, and then, seeing where the water ran from the tomb, following its path down to a river further down the hill. Tobias positioned himself so he could still see the tomb entrance while watching the rogue and wolf, silhouetted in the moonlight, walk along the edge of the water looking for the body.

How far does this river flow? Tobias wondered. Was this the only path the river took? Or did it split somewhere within the tomb and empty out elsewhere, somewhere we'll never find?

The necromancer thinks it's my job to tell stories, Tobias thought. He thinks I'm here to bring Revery new life by being its voice. But this world took my friend away, and now I'm watching the people I love suffer. Well, Revery, I'm not going to doctor this story to make you look good. The world will get the harsh truth about how you treat your heroes.

The wolf howled again into the night. He was always so deathly quiet—the reason Jack named him Silence, naturally—that hearing the beast's long, piercing cry was heartbreaking. He saw Eriko sink to her knees in the sand beside the river, punching the ground. He forgot sometimes how much longer the others had known each other. He and Tamsin were latecomers to this circle. Eriko had known Jack since before they could spell their own names, Morgan and Cordelia nearly as long. Morgan might be—might have been, Tobias corrected himself—Jack's best friend, but Eriko had never really remembered a world without him. Almost the way Tamsin and Tobias himself were.

The others emerged from the tomb not long after. Cordelia, at least, was looking better. Morgan clearly hit her with some of his healing magic, fortunately. She had looked like half a corpse herself for a while there. And Tamsin, still stoic, her mouth a grim line.

This game gives us what we want, and it can take it all away from us any time it wants to, Tobias thought. The theory he'd put forward to Cordelia days ago. I was worried about Eriko and Jin, or Morgan and Samlin, because I assumed Jack was the hero of this story. Tragic backstories were for the supporting cast. You don't kill the lead.

I should have been worried about my sister, he thought. And it turns out I was looking in the wrong place anyway.

He approached his twin awkwardly, unsure of her reaction. She could be emotional or she could be the very opposite depending on whether she felt threatened by showing her true emotions, he knew. That had been Tamsin her whole life, all or nothing, the opposite of himself, who had no filter, no control over his emotions. She seemed to be holding everything in, but when she saw her brother, her face broke. He threw his arms around her and felt her face press into his neck. The magic cloak wrapped around them like an embrace.

The world became quiet, except the mournful howl of a wolf, his cry honoring the fallen.

Chapter 28: Interlude – Tools of gods

The tomb became peaceful when the survivors left, only the sound of the waterfall breaking the silence. It had been an empty burial place for a long time, but now the room was true to its name, with dead warriors slowly rotting on the floor. Most were nameless soldiers in a war they never knew they were fighting. Blaggard, the man once known as Dom, held a place of mock honor, left to molder beside an empty coffin.

Even Blaggard would have said that this was a fitting end, dying alone and friendless in the dark. He had never been a good man, and his friends were allies of convenience at best, even in the real world. This was the end he deserved. Glorious deaths were for men who inspire people to care about them. He had only really inspired himself, and even then, only to violence and greed.

Hours passed, then days. Blaggard's friends never came for him, either to inter the body or to try to restore him to life. Again, Blaggard would admit this was a fate he had asked for. He'd never been kind to his friends. And for decades, they'd been stuck together here in Revery, led by his force of personality and threats both real and veiled. Letting him rot was something he wouldn't blame them for. He'd do the same for them as well, just as he was willing to let Anders, the man he'd once called Bennett, to decompose in the same way.

Sorrow is for those who deserve it, after all.

But eventually, the tomb did show signs of life. The eyes of the demonic statue began to glow a deep orange shade, like a fading fire. Its great stone head looked down at Blaggard's body, and then one massive hand reached down and picked him up like a doll.

With its other hand, the statue began to trace symbols onto Blaggard's breastplate. With each swish of its talon, the dark paladin's body transformed, reformed, became something more than what it was, and at the same time, became something less human. Surgical slices with that massive claw turned a powerfully built human man into something alien, simultaneously recognizable and unmistakably different.

The statue broke free of its moorings, its stony skin taking on a dark red hue as life breathed into it that was not there before. It set down the mutated body of Blaggard onto the dais and waited. Eventually, the paladin gasped for air, scrambling as though electrocuted as life poured back into the mangled body. He didn't seem to mind, though.

Rise, the statue said, in a voice both audible and not, a sound Blaggard felt reverberating in his chest. He was momentarily confused, unsure why he was alive, where he'd been, what had been done to him. Instead, he complied with the order, sitting up in someone else's coffin.

Rise, agent of death, the statue muttered. The pain of death seemed to drain away from him like dirt in a bath.

Blaggard looked up at the statue, who regarded him with passive curiosity. The demonic thing seemed almost amused that the dark knight seemed to want to challenge him. No, no, the statue said, into his ears, into his mind, voice both real and ethereal at the same time. Your time is not done yet, Blaggard. My master has further work for you to do in his name. That is your reward for overstepping your place in the natural hierarchy of things. You thought you had earned a higher place in the chain, but in the end, men like you are always first to the pits.

The statue once again scooped up Blaggard, but this time, the creature placed the knight on his shoulder.

You have a role yet to play, little Blackheart, the demon whispered. You were never a hero. You were a one-note villain. But a different story has yet to unfold for you.

You belong to us now. And you will do nicely. Yes, Blackheart, you failed Revery in life, but in death, you will do quite nicely. We've

waited for you a long time.
    Welcome home.

Chapter 29: Answers and questions

Time passed.

Eriko spent her days ranging, traveling up and down the river, hunting for clues to Jack's whereabouts, or if that failed, a body to give them all some closure. Over and over again, she returned emptyhanded.

Often Cordelia went with her, because together, they had the least to do. Morgan could tend to the town, and Tamsin had her own research. Tobias performed to keep their coffers filled. But a small town in the middle of nowhere had no use for a thief and little use for a barbarian. Cordelia could still find some purpose guarding the town, but Eriko felt as though she were simply… nothing.

She had Jin, but she could feel the fear Jack's death instilled in her creeping in. Jin would find Eriko in the dead of night standing in the bedroom, dagger in hand, listening, half-expecting some ambush to come crashing through the door. She told Jin that her fear was that there would be revenge for their stopping whatever power move Blaggard and his men had tried to commit, but what Eriko did not say, what she would not say, was that the fear keeping her awake at night was that someone would come and take Jin away from her.

She couldn't get Tamsin off her mind. The magician had not been the same since that night. All joy was gone from her eyes. She hadn't been involved with Jack long, but in this world, this group was all they had, and it didn't take long to find out you needed someone here. Tamsin had taken on a haunted look, softer and harder than she'd been before at the same time.

I don't want to be like that, Eriko said. And so, she slept softly and woke with a blade at the ready several times a night. She checked the windows and the doors, and she made sure Morgan or Tobias or Cordelia would check on Jin when she was off hunting for Jack's body.

Once, she found some tracks by the edge of the river. They were probably just a hunter's or a fisherman's, she knew, but she took a chance and followed them as best she could. Unfortunately, of all the skills Revery gave her as a rogue, tracking was not one of them. That was Jack's purview, after all. She wished Silence was with her. The wolf sometimes traveled with her on her excursions, but he had wandered off on his own this day. She traced the footprints perhaps a mile into the forest before becoming lost in the brush.

And so, she went home again.

Jin was already asleep when she returned, and so Eriko kicked off her boots, set aside her weapons, and crawled into bed, still smelling of forest and sweat. She lay in the dark for a while, waiting, thinking, listening. After a few hours, she got out of bed, wrapped herself in a spare blanket, and sat on a chair by the windows, looking out into the moonlit street. She stole glances at Jin sleeping peacefully.

I'll miss this when I'm gone, she thought. But she could think of no other way to stop being afraid.

* * *

Morgan prayed for answers he knew he'd never receive.

He quizzed the goddess about resurrection and restoration, about ways to bring his best friend back to life. The goddess was vague in her responses, and Morgan quickly realized that such magic had both rules and flexibility, and those added up to no clear answer at all.

Except, of course, they needed his body.

He watched Eriko leave one morning on her daily excursion. Alone on this particular day, except for Silence. Those were the treks on which Morgan feared they'd lose Eriko, too. He couldn't go every time, and there were days when Eriko wanted no company, but he always worried something would catch her unaware in the wild. Or worse, that she'd finally give up and leave. They'd none of them been right since Jack's death. It had put the fear of mortality into all of them, had turned this grand adventure into something deadly and true.

Samlin sat across from Morgan, his breakfast finished as Morgan's lay half-eaten.

"You worry enough for all of them, you know," Samlin said.

"That's my job," Morgan said.

"No," Samlin said. "You're a battle priest. We don't get many of you here, but we know what you stand for. You keep your friends safe, not through worry. You're a warrior, Bastion."

Morgan smiled sadly. He hated that Samlin only knew his fictional name. His game name. He wanted to be honest with him in all things, but they had long ago found that Revery's magic protected its denizens from the corrupting forces of anachronisms and meta-knowledge. Morgan wasn't sure if Samlin would even hear his voice if he told him his real name.

"And now you're worrying again," Samlin said.

"I'm sorry," Morgan said.

"I'm amazed you don't make yourself sick every day," Samlin said.

"How do you know I don't?"

Both men laughed. It was a comfortable laugh. One he could get used to living with every day. Except, of course, the world pulled at them. He knew they all felt it. They'd overstayed their welcome. That was what brought death to this town in the first place, and it would so again. He'd seen Eriko prowling her windows late at night watching the sky for trouble.

If we stay, we live in fear. We live in fear if we leave, too, but at least we know that trouble follows us. The old man and the scorpion, we lead the danger away so that others might live.

"Ever thought about being something other than a battle priest?" Samlin asked.

"Like what?"

"I don't know. A stable owner," Samlin said, laughing again. "Or maybe a priest of the not-so-battle kind. We don't have one of those here, you know. You'd have customers."

"You know, when I was younger, I considered that," Morgan said, and meant it. As a boy, he thought about joining the clergy when he grew up, but he'd been born into a church and a time in history when his own religion rejected his truest self, and that daydream felt too much like lying and even more so like self-flagellation.

"Well, it's something to consider again, maybe," Samlin said. "Look, I know you have other things to do. I know you have to go, but if you ever get tired of this life you live…"

"If it's ever safe for me to stay in one place, Sam," Morgan said. "This is the place I'd choose."

"But you can't."

"I can't," Morgan said. "I need to find a way to save my friend."

* * *

Unless Eriko needed her company, Cordelia no longer slept at night. She'd find a dark room during the day and hide, sleeping restlessly, and rise as the sun set. She'd patrol the town, mostly the perimeter, out of sight from the view of the town folk.

She knew they weren't afraid of her, this powerful orcish woman with an axe and spiked leather armor. She kept her hair shaved into a reddish crest and had taken up a habit, for reasons even she wasn't quite sure of, of applying war paint to her face and upper arms.

I think I'm trying to scare ghosts away, she thought.

She found weak points in the town walls and fixed them where she could, or dropped hints to the town leadership when she couldn't. She ran into a small cadre of orcs passing through and, rather than seeking blood, talked with them and advised them to avoid the town. They saw reason, and she was relieved. The longer she wore this body, the less comfortable she was with fighting creatures who were just slightly different from run of the mill humans, and the orcs of Revery, though universally hulky and gray-green, were more human than not.

She killed a rabid bear. Mercy killings broke her heart. But if not her, who? Someone had to walk these woods and keep the town safe.

But the longer this went on, the more she thought back to Tobias and his theory. That trouble followed them, that danger was forever in their wake, that wherever they went, they'd get people killed, and she grew anxious. If not for her friends she would have moved on right after the battle in the Tomb of the Maker. She could feel the world calling to them. It smelled like a storm on the horizon.

But the others needed time. She understood that.

Sometimes, on patrol, Silence emerged from the forest. The poor creature, she thought. If the rest of them were broken by the loss of their friend, Silence seemed utterly lost. He sometimes would accompany them on their searches, but then disappear for days at a stretch. Tamsin worried there would be a time he simply wouldn't come back, and Cordelia suspected that would ultimately prove true. He was a wild beast tied to them only by his bond with Jack, and now he seemed to just cling to the last vestiges of that brotherhood.

Maybe he'd be better off without us, Cordelia thought. Honestly, I suspect everyone would be.

She watched the town from the darkened woods, the rare lit window, the hushed quiet of a peaceful town.

Cordelia hoped her friends were ready to move on soon. She did not like the scent of danger in the air, and it grew stronger every day.

* * *

He didn't tell anyone about it, but Tobias had begun composing his own music.

He continued to stick to the classics while performing at the local tavern after an obnoxious side quest to find a new lute to replace the one he'd smashed in the dungeon. That, he thought, was a story in and of itself, but perhaps of more interest to bards than ordinary folk.

His work at the tavern kept his group fed, and paid for their rooms upstairs, and all of that was well and good, though he'd started singing different songs since the Tomb of the Maker. Less glam pop and more melancholy tunes. He'd dipped into 1980s New Wave stuff a lot. Til Tuesday seemed to be quite popular among the villagers, and he converted quite a few folks into Cure fandom, which was a bright spot in his life, to be honest. Depeche Mode seemed to frighten them a bit, but they adored Blondie, and he had nightly requests for the Eurythmics "Sweet Dreams."

It was almost enough to make him forget how much guilt he felt about Jack's death.

The more days passed since the battle the more he could not remember why he never drew the song-sword. He professed profound guilt about this to Cordelia one night when they were in their cups and the barbarian almost took his head off.

"You had a catastrophic concussion and were trying to save Morgan's life," she said. "And you've never been our fighter. Your job was not to be the warrior. That was my job, and that was Jack's. And we failed that night. Not you."

Well, it's my job now, Tobias thought, but did not say. He just ordered another round and thought about lyrics.

The lyrics, you see, were their story.

He pictured it in a bit of a prog rock style, a bit of Rush, a bit of Coheed and Cambria. He wouldn't be able to perform the songs alone, of course. He'd need percussion and backup vocals, maybe a bass guitar if he could find the medieval equivalent of one. He was writing a concept album, not a ditty. Eat your heart out, Led Zeppelin, he thought. We've put real blood into our fairy tales.

He shared the lyrics with no one. They weren't ready yet. They had more adventures to experience first, more adventures to weave into the tapestry of these epic ballads.

If he survived this, Tobias thought, he'd have a job to do, and he planned on getting it right.

But until then, Tobias thought, entering the tavern as the evening crowd gathered, it's pop songs 'til I have a room full of smiles.

He strummed the first chords of "Come on Eileen" by Dexy's Midnight Runners, a popular number with the weekend crowd, and as always, he had the room in the palm of his hand.

* * *

Tamsin had all her arcane research materials spread out across the desk in her room and was ready to set it all on fire.

Not literally, she knew. But she was reaching the end of the line. She'd ransacked every scrap of material they'd found, the good spell books, the scrolls, something written on what was clearly the tanned hide of a pig that made her skin crawl. Even the one she knew contained dark magic. That one she did not commit to memory, because the words tickled the inside of her brain like spiders. She'd never wanted to even open it before, but now, she could bring herself to, if not learn the spells, at least take stock of the book's contents.

None of it told her how to bring Jack back.

Bring him back. That very thought turned her stomach. Not because she didn't want to restore him. Yes, they'd been romantically involved, but it all felt so new, she knew, and she felt shame at how much she missed his presence. We weren't there yet, she thought. I think I miss the potential though. We had potential, and that was snuffed out, and now I'll never know if this was meant to be or just two homesick people who fell into each other at the right time.

He was just a good man, and she had never, in her life, known many of those. He deserved better than what Revery gave him. She wanted to be able to give him a second chance.

But nothing she had in her collection could tell her how. She threw one of the less powerful, but heavier, books across the room with a thud.

"I need a magic school, that's what I need," Tamsin said, rubbing her eyes with the heels of her thumbs.

"I know where a magic school is," a voice said from the other side of the room. Tamsin felt her hair stand on end.

"Who… is there?" Tamsin said.

"It's me," the voice said. It's coming from my satchel, Tamsin thought. The leather one she'd carried into the Tomb of the Maker. Holy shit, I never unpacked it. I threw it in the corner and just left it there for days and days.

"Oh my god. Yorick?" she said. The talking skull. I put a talking skull in my satchel and I've completely forgotten about him.

"That is what your brother called me, yes," the voice said. Tamsin raced across the room and flung open the satchel. The skull wasn't even facing up at her—the poor creature was face down, eyes pointed at the bottom of the bag.

"Yorick, I am so sorry," Tamsin said, drawing him out and setting him down gently on the desk. "Things got really crazy in there and I forgot we found you."

"You were the first people to speak with me in a civilized manner in hundreds of years," Yorick said, his tone remarkably pleasant for someone who had spent a few weeks at the bottom of a bag. "Honestly, the bag was a change of scenery."

"Well, in any event, it was rude of me," Tamsin said.

"All is forgiven," Yorick said. Tamsin could have sworn he was smiling.

"So, you said something about a magic school?" Tamsin said.

"Yes, yes," Yorick said. "The Hawksmith Academy. They've always trained great minds there."

"It's a wizard school?" Tamsin said, feeling incredible guilt at how excited she was by this news.

"Not just wizards," Yorick said. "In my day, they trained priestly spell casters like your big friend there as well, and other kinds of magic. It was a repository of knowledge and a treasure trove of talent."

"In your day," Tamsin said. "No offense, but how do we know it's still there?"

"Magic schools don't just close their doors," Yorick said, his tone almost snarky. "Of course it's still there. It's situated fifteen miles outside the capital, to the northwest. Or it was back then."

"Might it have moved?"

"Magic users have done stranger things," Yorick said. "But if you're looking for a school of magicians, I'd recommend starting there."

Tamsin scooped Yorick up in both hands and kissed his boney forehead.

"You are marvelous," she said. "Do you think they might know how to bring someone back to life?"

"Are you planning on restoring me?" Yorick said. "Oh, you are the most wonderful of saviors!"

"Oh," Tamsin said, trying to hide her confusion. "I mean, of course, if we can restore you, why would we not bring you back! Especially letting us know about the school. I owe you that much, Yorick."

"Well then," Yorick said. "Bring me a map, and I'll show you exactly where it is."

Chapter 30: Splitting the party

"So, you're saying the talking skull told you how to find Hogwarts," Cordelia said, with only the faintest hint of incredulity.

The party sat around a large table in the tavern. It was late morning and the bar was mostly empty, except of course, for the usual day drinkers. They had food and drink but none of them did much more than fiddle with their meals. Tobias ignored his meal entirely and busied himself by restringing his lute.

"I know it sounds ridiculous, but I don't think he's lying," Tamsin said. "And if we're going to bring Jack back…"

"Do we even know resurrection magic exists in this game?" Cordelia said. Both Eriko and Tamsin visibly flinched. No one had ever cast any doubt, after years of playing games just like Revery, that such a thing would be outside the mechanics of the game. But the truth was, they'd seen a lot of permanent death here and no evidence it was reversible.

"My, um, patron says it's possible," Morgan said.

"Great, so your fake goddess has told you we can resurrect people," Cordelia said.

"What's the matter with you, Cordelia?" Tamsin said. "Why are you bringing all this up now?"

"Because she feels helpless. I do too," Eriko said. "The two of you—three, I guess, if we count your spell thievery, Tobias—all of you might be able to do something. We're just good for killing stuff and getting through locked doors."

"You're not useless. We need you," Morgan said.

"No, you need this Hawksmith Academy," Eriko said. "And I'm not doubting it exists. I actually think you should go."

"We should go? Not all of us?" Tamsin said.

"Yeah," Eriko said. "I can't sit around while you talk to scholars and read old books. I need to do something useful."

"You sound like you have a plan," Morgan said.

Tobias said nothing. The truth was he already knew everyone's proposed plans and he wasn't wild about any of them, but none of this was his decision. He just kept his mouth shut and kept stringing his lute.

"I do," Eriko said. "Two of those old grognards got away. I want to backtrack to where this Blaggard guy and his crew came from. Maybe find what clues they've left behind. Piece together their motivations."

"And maybe find and kill a high-level magician and cleric, on your own," Morgan said.

"Not on her own. I'm going with her," Cordelia said.

Morgan's face twisted into a look so baffled Tobias almost laughed. His expression read as if he'd just walked through a particularly offensive fart.

"We can't... split the party!" Morgan said. "You know that's the first rule! Oh, who am I talking to. You love splitting the party."

"I don't love splitting the party," Eriko said. "But think about it. This is more efficient. We can do our investigation, you can do yours."

"If it makes you feel any better, we won't go after these Valamir or Asptooth guys without you," Cordelia said. "If we find them."

"How are you going to get in touch with us if you do find them?" Tamsin said. "We don't exactly have iPhones here."

"One of you has to have a spell that can send a message," Cordelia said.

Tamsin glared at Tobias. Tobias grinned back at his sister.

"We both have one," Tobias said.

"What?" Morgan said.

"I thought it only worked on us because we're twins," Tamsin said. "I thought it was an elf thing or something."

"Until I tried it on the pig guy the other day," Tobias said.

"What do you mean, tried it on the pig guy," Morgan said.

"I used it to make the pig farmer think one of his pigs was talking to him telepathically," Tobias said.

He felt four different judgmental looks landing on him at the same time and strummed his lute.

"Like you wouldn't have done it if you could," he said.

"Did he answer the pig back?" Cordelia said, at first dead serious, but then breaking into a whispery laugh on the last word.

"He looked at that pig like he'd never eat bacon again," Tobias said. "Anyway. It's not like these spells come with instruction manuals."

"Technically, mine do," Tamsin said. "I just didn't know how we obtained that spell until later."

"Anyway," Morgan said. "Okay, fine, we have whatever that's called, magical voicemail. But what if we run into trouble? We're already missing someone. We can't afford to split up."

"I think we can't afford not to," Cordelia said. "This world gets more dangerous all the time. If we stay together, we're wasting so much time."

Tamsin sighed.

"I hate that you're right," she said, resting her head in her hands. "And if we do this right, Morgan and I can catch a ride on a trade caravan to the capital. We don't have to travel alone."

"And with our skill sets, Cordelia and I can travel overland without much notice," Eriko said. "We're less conspicuous than when we've got a wizard and cleric in tow."

Tamsin eyeballed Tobias suspiciously.

"What about you, sunshine?" she asked. "Are you coming with us or going with them?"

"I don't know," he said, and meant it. "On the one hand, if I go with you maybe I can pick up a few more spells. Maybe learn a bit about my own abilities. But someone needs to keep the disaster darlings over there out of trouble."

"I resent that," Cordelia said.

"I don't," Eriko said. "I think that's our new title."

"If we're going to move quiet and fly under the radar, I think we leave the bard at home," Cordelia said.

"And here I thought we were BFFs," Tobias said.

"We are. But you are a circus sideshow, Toby," Cordelia said. "And you know it. Your sword literally sings power ballads."

"Also, Morgan and Tamsin need you there to make sure they

have someone with a good bullshit meter when they meet all the magical academics," Eriko said.

"I love that somehow the *bard* is the one who is expected to keep both groups out of trouble," Tobias said. "Take that and stuff it in your D&D joke."

"Also, I kind of feel like it's bad luck to break up the twins," Cordelia said.

Tobias and Tamsin turned to each other with an almost eerily timed, identical expression.

"Fair point," Tobias said. "Bard loose at Hogwarts. What could possibly go wrong?"

"Everything," Tamsin said. "But I'll be there to rein you in."

"So, we're really splitting the party," Morgan said.

"Don't call it that," Cordelia said. "Consider it the Breaking of the Fellowship."

The party was quiet for a moment.

"Pretty sure whenever a group splits up in a fantasy story, some of the members never see each other again," Tamsin said.

"Don't," Morgan said.

"*Lord of the Rings*?" Tamsin said.

"The *Dragonlance* Saga," Tobias said.

"*Game of Thrones*," Eriko said.

"You people are so morbid," Cordelia said. "If anyone can break the trope, it's us."

"Well then," Tobias said, raising his glass. "To Breaking the Fellowship. Nobody else gets to die. If you do, I will haunt you with 80s synth pop for the rest of eternity."

Epilogue: Revenant

Two skeletons stood hip deep in a rapidly flowing river, arms held aloft as if they were trying not to slip. They both wore armor.

One wore a hat.

Sitting on a fallen tree beside the river was a thin man in a black robe. Mordecai the Unholy to many, though he honestly preferred if people just called him Leo. The Unholy thing had lost its luster over the years.

This is more Malcolm's thing, he thought, somewhat put off by the way the sun glistened through the leaves, the soft gurgle of the water. This is druid stuff. It's a bad place for a necromancer. But he was here for a purpose, and would not leave until he fulfilled that purpose.

One of the skeletons waved an arm his way, catching his attention. Leo looked out to see what had the undead husk all worked up. It held in its bony hand a beautiful longbow, adorned with draconic imagery. A magic weapon, of course, and one Leo had seen before.

"Yes, yes, keep that," he yelled out to the skeleton. The creature looked at the bow for a moment, almost as if it had never seen such an object before, and then slung it across its desiccated back for safe keeping. It started to return to shore, but Leo waved it back.

"No, keep looking," he said. "You hold onto that for now. I'll get it from you later."

Leo knew the skeletons were not capable of real communication, but he could have sworn the skull nodded at him before returning to work.

Leo wondered what someone might make of this. Undead were not unheard of anywhere in Revery, of course, but usually if you saw the walking deceased, they were up to something truly diabolical. Murder, or cannibalism, or something equally ugly. Not engaging in what appeared to be fishing without a pole or net, which was exactly what these two skeletons were doing.

Something took the legs out from under one skeleton, sending the other scrambling, marionette-esque, after its companion to the rescue. Another thirty or forty feet downstream the first skeleton popped back up to the surface, and its companion reached beneath the water to grab whatever had wiped the first out. Together, they began to drag the heavy object to shore.

The object, of course, was a body.

The skeletons dropped the corpse on the reddish clay of the riverbank. Leo walked slowly over to the body, careful to not drag his cloak through the mud, and threw back the hood.

Beneath it he found the drained, deathly face of the ranger Malcolm thought would save Revery.

"I knew the world was messing with our expectations," Leo said. He commanded the skeletons to pull the corpse further inland, away from the water, and as they did, Leo rummaged through his pouches and pockets until he found a small glass sphere filled with fine ruby dust. He traced an emblem with his finger on the surface of the glass, which left a trail of light that melted into an etched rune. He hunched down over the body.

"Gentlemen," he said to the skeletons. "If you would, please hold his arms. This spell can sometimes result in a violent reaction."

The skeletons silently complied, but exchanged what Leo had to actively convince himself wasn't a questioning glance to each other. I spend too much time around the dead, he thought. They're starting to develop personalities.

He placed the sphere over the ranger's heart—just above the grievous wound in his chest, which was convenient, Leo mused—and uttered a few words in the language of demons. A shadowy thrill passed through him, as it always did when manipulating the darkest of magic. And then he slapped his palm down on the sphere, shattering it.

The glass exploded, and the red crystals poured out like a fine mist. The chest wound began to knit itself closed, the crystals sinking into the ranger's skin and becoming one with it. Color began to return to his sunken face.

Then his eyes opened, and he inhaled violently.

His eyes were no longer what they were before he died, of course. That was part of the price. They reflected light like an animal's a reddish glow when viewed from just the correct angle. The ranger tried to sit up, but the skeletons held him in place. He started shaking, and Leo gave it a few seconds to make sure he wasn't having a seizure. No, Leo saw—he's just struggling to move his arms, making sure they're still attached to his body.

"Let him go," he commanded, and the skeletons complied.

The ranger sat up, touched his chest, then his face. He coughed several times, hard, and then twisted to vomit up muddy river water. There was blood mixed in as well.

Leo handed him a rag. The ranger took it, wiped his mouth, then stared at the blood on the fabric.

"I died," the ranger said.

"Very definitively," Leo said. He stood up and wandered in a small semi-circle until he found a stump that looked relatively comfortable to sit on.

"What did you do to me?" the ranger asked.

"Well, I brought you back, of course," Leo said. "You're welcome."

The ranger staggered to his feet but immediately went back down to one knee. One of the skeletons offered him a hand, and the ranger looked up at the creature incredulously, but then accepted the help. The undead thing delicately helped the ranger to a nearby rock wide enough to act as a seat.

"Undead," the ranger said. "You're what, a necromancer?"

"I am. You know my friend. The druid, Malcolm."

The ranger nodded. He looked sick, but that was all part of the spell's toll.

"Okay, necromancer."

"Leo. Or Mordecai if you insist on in-game names."

"Leo, then," the ranger said. "Am I undead too? Did you bring me back to be one of your minions?"

"Oh no," Leo said. "I never make minions of people I know. And I've been watching your group for a while now. You go by

Raven, yes? Raven the ranger?"

"Yeah. But my real name is…" the ranger moved his mouth and looked as though he'd lost all control of his words. He swallowed several times, then looked at Leo as though he'd kill him with his bare hands.

"Why can't I say my real name?"

"Ah, that's part of the cost of the spell," Leo said. "I'm no priest. I can't bring you back out of the goodness of my heart. But as one who trucks with death, I can retrieve a person from beyond at a cost."

"And that cost is my name," the ranger said.

"The cost is a task," Leo said. "After which you earn your name back, and true life. For now, you are a revenant, trapped in between. Fulfill your geas and you will be free. I don't make the rules, sorry."

"Geas. Like Cuchulainn. The magical command he couldn't break in the myth."

"You know your mythology," Leo said. "That helps."

"You think someone who plays a game like this doesn't like myths?" the ranger said. "So, I'm not dead, but not alive. I've lost my name but I can get it back. Can I see my friends?"

"No," Leo said. "That is part of the geas. You must remain a secret to them until you have finished the task set before you."

"Why do this?" the ranger asked. "Why bring me back at all?"

"Because I need something done, and you're the one who got yourself killed," Leo said. "And that means you're about to play a different game."

Book 5:

Splitting the Party

Prologue: The Revenant

The ranger stared into the fire, trying to remember his name.

He chased the thought around his mind, like a shark after a smaller fish always just a little behind. I had a name, and now it's gone, he thought. He said as much to the skeleton sitting casually next to him. The skeleton nodded and shrugged.

"It's driving me insane," the ranger said. "My name is on the tip of my tongue, and then it's gone."

"That's part of the spell," the necromancer said. The necromancer had two names. Mordecai the Unholy, or simply Leo. He preferred the latter, though the ranger could tell he had some pride in the former. "You still have your second name, though."

"Raven," the ranger said. "The one I picked. I could've been so much more creative if I'd tried."

"I think it suits you," Leo said. The skeleton nodded, as did his counterpart, a skeleton in a kilt who had been stoking the fire politely.

"I suppose," the ranger said. Raven. A bird associated with the dead. That hadn't been his intent when he picked it. He was just being melodramatic at the game table. And now that silly, melodramatic name was the only one his brain could hold onto. "Am I dead?"

"Not really," Leo said. "You're somewhere in between. Fulfill this task for me, though, and the resurrection will be complete.

You'll be restored to life once more, name and all."

Raven the ranger chewed his lip, unsure if he should keep his next thought to himself. The necromancer looked at him as though he were already reading Raven's mind anyway, so he just said it.

"What if I don't want to come back?" he said.

Leo looked mildly surprised.

"You'd rather not be resurrected?" Leo raised an eyebrow.

"I think… I think I was ready," Raven said. "I was okay with where I was. And then a few moments later I was here, and everything hurt again. I'm so very tired."

Leo seemed to ponder the comment for a moment, then shrugged.

"I suppose you can be released back to where I found you," he said. "That's not the request I was expecting of you."

"I get it."

"Can I ask," Leo said, taking a swig from a flask within his robe. "What did you see on the other side?"

Raven exhaled, chasing thoughts around his mind again.

"Do you dream when you sleep?" he asked.

"Sometimes," Leo said.

"Always?" Raven said.

"No," Leo said. "Sometimes. But not always."

"So you know what it feels like when you sleep without dreaming," the ranger said.

"I suppose."

"Not fear, not emptiness… you're just not there anymore, y'know? That's how it felt." Raven took a sip from a waterskin, then set it aside. "And now I'm here again. How long was I gone?"

"A few hours at most," Leo said. "We fished you out of the river pretty quickly."

"Felt longer than that."

"Maybe time moves differently on the other side," Leo said.

"You're the necromancer. Aren't you supposed to know these things?"

"I only deal with this world. Not the next."

"If there is one," Raven said. "Part of me wondered if I'd end up back in the real world when I died. I'm relieved I didn't. Bad enough to come back here. It's worse there."

"I could've told you death here was real," Leo said, taking a sip from his own skin, filled with wine rather than water. "I've lost most of my friends here."

Raven nodded and sat in silence for a bit. One of the skeletons handed him some fish it had been cooking over the fire. The ranger nibbled at it without any hunger or interest.

"Why bring me back, though? What's the point?" he asked.

"Because I need something found, and I've learned that the only people who can find it are those whose stories have ended," Leo said. "Revery wants us to stay and keep making stories. We're the world's lifeblood. At least that's my theory. But there's a seam tearing this world, and I want to find it and fix it. And I needed someone who had taken their story to the very end to search for it."

"And my story is over."

"It was," Leo said. "You met your tragic end. Sacrificed yourself for your friends."

"I don't know that I did it for them," the ranger said. "I think I'd been looking for a way out my whole life."

Leo took another drink and then leaned forward on his knees, his gaunt face eerie in the firelight.

"And I took that away from you," he said.

Raven nodded. Leo shook his head ruefully.

"It won't mean much, I suppose, but I am sorry," Leo said. "I thought you'd want to see your friends again, and I could get the piece I need to fix this broken world, and we'd both be happy. If I'd known…"

"You still would've brought me back," Raven said. "You needed a finished story. You needed me."

"I suppose I would have," Leo said. "But I mean it, kid. I'm sorry to ask you to do this."

"I find this… seam, this tear, whatever it is you're looking for. And it'll save the people who live in this world?"

"I think it will," Leo said.

"Not just my friends. Or yours. The people who live here."

"That's my hope," Leo said.

"These people are real," Raven said. "They're not game pieces. They're not NPCs in a videogame. They're as real as we are. Aren't they."

"In so many ways, kid, I wish that weren't true. But they are real. They love and suffer as much as we do."

Raven nodded, drawing his hood down over his face to hide his eyes.

"Okay," Raven said. "One more quest, then. One more job. I'll do this thing for you. And then…"

"Then, whatever you need to happen, I'll make sure it happens," Leo said.

Something moved in the brush behind Leo, who turned to look, curious. The skeleton next to Raven pointed, while his companion stood up and hefted a spear to protect the necromancer. Leo waved them off, though.

"It's fine, boys. We know this one."

A familiar canine shape emerged from the underbrush. Silver and black, eyes gleaming in the firelight, Silence, Raven's wolf companion, slinked into view. He trotted across the small camp and sat down in front of the ranger, watching him.

Raven reached out a hand and placed it on the wolf's long snout. A rasping pink tongue looped out to lick his palm.

"You made it," Raven said.

The wolf huffed, then turned three circles before plopping down on the ground at Raven's boots contentedly.

"At least you won't have to make the journey alone," Leo said. And for the first time, the necromancer betrayed just the barest hint of a smile.

"Yeah," Raven said, running a hand absently down Silence's back as his mind drifted to the friends he hoped he would not have to explain this to. "I guess not."

Chapter 1: Not a real orc

The wolf wandered away their first day on the road and never came back, leaving Cordelia and Eriko alone.

Cordelia had seen it coming, the way Silence had been exploring without them, ranging further and further away. She knew he was fixing to leave, and, if she were being honest with herself, she didn't feel much about it one way or another. He'd been a fixture since they arrived in Revery, sure, but he had been so eternally at Jack's side, so singularly attached and protective, that it felt strange to have him along in the first place. She pitied the creature, who had been so obviously looking for his dead friend for days now, and she thought she'd feel something in his absence. But the gnawing emptiness in her own belly overwhelmed any concerns she had for Silence now.

Eriko, however, was uncharacteristically despondent. And Eriko, also uncharacteristically, traded sadness for anger.

"Stupid fucking dog," she said, as evening drew close and Silence didn't return. They were working their way up an old hunting trail north of where their last battle took place, backtracking where Blaggard's group had made their way from before the encounter at the Tomb of the Maker. It was slow going, but if they stayed to the path they felt reasonably sure of themselves.

"We knew he was going to leave and not come back some day, Eriko," Cordelia said.

"Stupid fucking dog abandoned us," Eriko said, sneering. "He's probably not even a real wolf. What kind of wolf acts like that?"

"A wolf in a fairy tale," Cordelia said softly. "Maybe he found a pack to join."

"Or maybe he hurt himself and he's dying in a ditch somewhere and we can't help him," Eriko said. "Stupid fucking dog."

"You okay?"

Eriko glared at Cordelia, then shrugged.

"Stupid dog was all we had left of him, is all. Are we making a mistake?"

"Everything we do is a mistake," Cordelia said. She saw the loneliness in Eriko's eyes with sudden clarity. "Did you want to go back?"

"We can't go back," Eriko said. "Everyone we care about dies. I can't go back."

Cordelia took a deep breath and tried to center her patience. She hadn't made attachments in the town they'd been protecting, and she was strangely numb to the death of their friend. Eriko had given up love to seek out their vengeance, and she'd always been just that much closer with Jack than the others. She's just feeling all the feelings, Cordelia said. Why can't I feel any of them?

Eriko began tromping off, walking fast enough to annoy Cordelia, but Cordelia reached one long, gray-green arm forward to grab the rogue by her shoulder.

"You smell that?" she asked.

"There is no right answer to that question."

"Stop it. Do you smell… food?"

As they'd bickered, the sun had fallen further in the sky, and now Cordelia could make out the light of a small fire ahead, just off the path.

"We should go around whoever it is," Eriko said. Cordelia couldn't tell if her friend wanted to avoid the camp ahead as a precaution or if she simply didn't want to talk to any strangers tonight. Either way, Cordelia agreed.

"Okay. We'll head into the woods a bit, wend our way around, and…"

"Or you could join me for dinner," a gravelly voice said from their left, the speaker invisible. "I've got stew on. You're welcome to some, if you'd like."

"Not crazy about dinner invitations from invisible people," Cordelia said. "No offense."

"Can't say I blame you," the voice said again. "I'm coming out. Can't be too cautious these days, you know. Had to make sure of you."

"How can you be sure of us?" Eriko said. "We could be bandits. Very dangerous bandits."

"Arguing over a dog loud enough to scare the game away?" the voice said again. Cordelia heard movement in the brush to her left, too loud, too obvious to not be on purpose, as though he were signaling to them the direction he was moving from. She gripped her axe tightly but kept it hooked on her belt.

Finally, the speaker emerged. Pale green skin, the color of lichen, yellow-gold eyes, visible tusks poking up from his lower jaw. An orc. His head was shaved bare, visible as he pulled a furred hood back from his face. The orc was thick-framed, built like a brick standing up on its narrow end. He had a pair of axes hanging from his belt, nowhere near as artistically crafted as Cordelia's but fine weapons nonetheless, weapons made for killing.

"Come on, then," he said. "Stew's gonna burn if I don't get back to camp."

He led them a few hundred feet up the path until they came upon his fire. True to his word, a pot hung over the flame, bubbling and smelling of freshly picked herbs and some sort of game animal Cordelia preferred not ask about. A few packs had been set aside there, a spear leaning against a tree, but no tent or other camping gear.

"I'm Hark," he said, dragging a heavy log closer to the fire and sitting down with a grunt.

"Rouge," Eriko said, giving him her character name. Cordelia did the same.

"Orchid," she said.

The orc studied her for a moment, then nodded at some unspoken conclusion. He stirred the pot a bit with a ladle and then handed Eriko a small wooden cup.

"Help yourself," he said.

Cordelia half-expected Eriko to play the vegetarian card, but she didn't, taking a respectful scoop of the stew and sipping at it from the cup. Cordelia did the same, and then Hark, seeing his guests fed, took a heaping amount for himself.

"If you—okay, this is going to be a rude question," Eriko said. "But why are you out here alone?"

Hark nodded and chewed at a bit of meat from his stew.

"Well. Not a rude question. Traveling alone in these parts isn't common. Or smart, to be fair," he said. "But I wasn't alone. Not until recently. I was a scout for a local band of orcs."

"Was," Cordelia said.

"Oh no," Eriko said.

Hark shook his head.

"You heard about the massacre, then," he said.

"Our friend… found the camp," Eriko said. Jack's discovery of the slaughtered orcs had been what led the party to Blaggard's warband. They thought there hadn't been any survivors. Cordelia felt her stomach turn to acid remembering the mutilated bodies. How she'd felt seeing faces like her own torn from their bodies.

"Yeah," Hark said, exhaling loudly. "I was off scouting for a path around that human settlement when it happened. Came back and…"

"Our friend had been hoping to parlay with you," Eriko said. "To ask you to leave the town alone."

"We meant no harm," Hark said. "Were driven off our land by human cattle farmers a while back, trying to find a place to settle away from…"

He waved his hand around.

"I don't know. I'd like to think I wish I'd been there, to die by their sides. But I wasn't, and I'm still here, and life goes on, I guess."

"We killed the leader of he men who did that to your friends," Eriko said. "Or our friend did. He didn't survive, but he got the bastard, in the end."

"That's good. Not that your friend died. But that someone got the butcher. I wouldn't have done been able to do it on my own."

"We're looking for his allies," Cordelia said softly. Hark looked up.

"Allies."

"His men scattered, but his priest and his wizard escaped. We're tracking them," Cordelia said.

"And what do you plan on doing when you catch them," Hark said.

"Haven't got that far yet," Cordelia said.

Hark nodded.

"Well, then," he said. "Vengeance. It has its place."

***

Eriko eventually nodded off, curled in a ball near the fire. Cordelia wrapped a blanket around her and ran a hand through her hair, then settled down near the fire herself.

Hark was watching her, passively, as he prepared to bed down himself.

"You're staring," Cordelia said.

"Nah. Observing," Hark said.

"See anything interesting?"

"You're not a real orc, are you," he said.

Cordelia wrapped a pulled a blanket around her shoulders and shot him a dark look.

"What's that supposed to mean?" she asked. "Am I not orc enough for you?"

Hark shook his head, lips curling as if fighting off a smile.

"Nah," he said. "I'm nor orc enough for some, myself. I mean, though—you weren't born an orc."

Cordelia touched the tip of one of her small fangs.

"You're the first person to notice," she said.

"It's the little things," he said. "And it's not… it's not that you're not orc enough. It's that you don't feel like you belong. Neither of you do. You feel like you're both very far from home."

Cordelia looked over to the sleeping bundle that was Eriko.

"We are," she said.

"And the men who killed my people?"

"They were very far from home as well," she said. "But not with us. Not like us."

Hark grunted. He looked terrifying in the darkness, the fire playing across his features, turning his kind eyes almost demonic.

"I've met people like you before," he said. "Travelers. Most treat orcs like toys to be broken."

"The men who killed your people treated everything like toys meant to be broken," Cordelia said.

"But not you."

"Not us," she said.

"And your friend died for that."

"He did."

"This world has a strange way of treating heroes," Hark said. "It's like the gods are addicted to tragedy."

"I think all gods are addicted to tragedy, in this world and any other," Cordelia said. She imagined her grandmother's rage at hearing her say that and almost smiled. Almost.

Hark said nothing for a few moments, long enough for Cordelia to wonder if he'd fallen asleep. Finally, he spoke.

"I'd like to help you, with your revenge," he said. "It seemed stupid, to seek it out on my own. But now…"

"Revery places the things we need in front of us and sees if we'll reach for them," Cordelia said.

"It does," Hark said. "Good night, Orchid."

"Good night, Hark," Cordelia said.

She sat awake by the fire a while longer, listening to the sounds of a living forest at night. In the distance, she heard a howl. She thought of her friends, and wondered if they'd ever find their way home.

Chapter 2: Birdcage

"I think we found the middle part of *The Hobbit*," Tobias said, stopping on the side of the road to shake a rock out of his boot.

"I don't follow," Morgan said. He looked at Tobias with a hint of annoyance, but then sat down on a nearby rock, his exhaustion visibly catching up to him.

"It's all the walking," Tamsin explained. "We're just walking. Pointlessly. Forever."

Not technically forever, Tobias thought, but they'd been on this major trade road west for days, often going hours without even seeing a passing dog let alone a caravan or other travelers. He'd been worried when they split up from Cordelia and Eriko that they'd run into trouble they couldn't handle without them, but their journey so far had been catastrophically boring. Even more so since Morgan forbade Tobias from singing yesterday. My own fault, Tobias thought. I was the one choosing songs with travel puns in them. It was The Proclaimers song that set Morgan off and inspired the moratorium on singing.

They'd been told this Hawksmith Academy lay several weeks' travel to the west of the Tomb of the Maker. They traveled ready for danger, be it bandits, monsters, or both. And instead, their greatest enemy had been the quiet. Tamsin and Tobias bickered a bit, and so had Morgan and Tobias. The bard had come to realize that, as Tamsin and Morgan did not bicker, he himself was probably the source of the problem.

"Am I annoying?" Tobias blurted out, as if his companions could hear his inner dialogue leading up to it.

"Yes," Morgan said.

"Just checking," Tobias said.

He turned his attention to his sister. She'd been more withdrawn the past few days, coming up for air from whatever dark thoughts she'd been having to seem almost herself, but inevitably, she'd spiral back into a dark mood again. Tobias had no frame of reference for what she'd been going through, losing a relatively new, still genuinely happy relationship to a tragic end with Jack's death. Before this, Tamsin had always been the sort of person who stayed with someone to make them happy, rather than herself. Jack, for all his faults, had made Tamsin happy instead, and even Tobias, as deeply cynical as he was, had harbored some hope for them, that they'd get out of this insane game world they were trapped in and find something neighboring ordinary happiness together.

He was almost jealous, if he were being honest with himself. No one had ever taken Tobias as seriously in any way as Jack and Tamsin had treated each other. This world seemed to want happy endings, in a roundabout way. Morgan's relationship with Samlin, Eriko with Jin, it seemed like everyone here was capable of having a healthier relationship than they'd ever hope for back in the real world.

Except, of course, Revery would then yank that love away from you for maximum agony. It was as if the world thrived on melodrama and pain as much as it did on heroics. Tobias didn't have much trust for whoever built this place.

"What's that?" Tamsin said, knocking Tobias out of his thoughts. His sister was pointing into the distance at what looked like a barren tree.

"It looks manmade," Morgan said. "Signage? A crossroads?"

There was something hanging from the horizontal branch of the structure. It took a moment for Tobias to realize what it reminded him of.

"It's like a birdcage," he said.

"Not a birdcage," Morgan said. "It's a cell."

"There's a body in it," Tamsin said, starting to walk faster.

Tobias and Morgan trotted to catch up, Morgan cursing under the weight of his heavy armor. The closer they got, the more clearly Tobias could see that his friends were correct. A bell-shaped cage, a humanoid figure lounging in it, unmoving, one foot hanging out from between the bars.

"Are they dead?" Tamsin said.

Morgan brushed past her, hefting his war maul.

"I don't think a corpse in a cage is going to hurt you, He-Man," Tobias said.

"In this world? I don't trust anything," Morgan said.

"That's a good policy to have," the body within the cage said. "You folks have anything to drink?"

Morgan cursed, taking an involuntary step back. Tamsin and Tobias exchanged a worried look.

The figure in the cage, lean and dressed in battered rags, sat up a bit straighter and draped their arms through the bars.

"Come on," they said. "You've got to have some water. Wine. Beer. Gatorade, I don't care."

"Gatorade?" Tobias said.

He approached the cage, studying the face within. Lean, with cheekbones sharp with hunger; dark hair shorn close to the scalp; a sardonic mouth, quirking up in one corner.

"You gotta be shitting me," they said. "Of call the people who could have walked by. You're players, aren't you."

"Toby," Tamsin said, but Tobias waved her off.

"You're like us," he said. The prisoner nodded.

"Yeah," they said. Their face was hard and sharp, but Tobias saw the water welling up in their eyes and it surprised him. They wiped their eyes with the heel of their hand. "Shit. Why am I…"

"Where are your friends?" Tobias asked. "The other players?"

"Gone, man," they said. "Shit, they're gone, and I thought I'd die in this fucking cage—are you going to let me out? Please don't leave me here."

"What are you doing in that cage?" Morgan asked, a looming presence just past Tobias' shoulder.

"Pissed of the wrong noble, I guess," they said. "It's easier to be the big tough hero when you have your friends with you."

"Someone locked you up on the side of the road," Tamsin said.

"Yeah," the prisoner said. "There's… you're coming from the east, yeah? Things get harder the further you get from where you started."

"We've noticed," Morgan said.

Tobias pulled on Morgan's arm. The cleric yanked his arm away from him.

"What are you doing?"

"I need you to come with me so I can try to pick the lock on this cage," Tobias said. "Let me get on your shoulders."

"Are you serious?"

"What's the problem?" Tobias asked.

"We don't know if they're telling us the truth," Morgan said. "Everything here is dangerous. What if this is a trap?"

"I don't think Revery sets traps using people who know what Gatorade is," Tobias said.

While the men argued, Tamsin stepped past them and handed a waterskin up to the prisoner, who took it gratefully.

"Thanks," they said.

"I'm Tamsin," she said. "I guess my name here is Nimue, but my real name is Tamsin."

"Kit," the prisoner said. "My ridiculous game name was Sabre. We all have ridiculous game names, don't we?"

"Tobias is my brother, also goes by Oberon. And the big guy is Morgan, aka Bastion."

Tobias had crawled onto Morgan's back, and the cleric was begrudgingly allowing him to clamor up to reach the lock. Tobias struggled with the lock for a moment, then got irritated and whispered a magic word into the keyhole. The lock became red with inner heat, and Tobias used the butt of his dagger to smash it open.

Gingerly, Kit pushed the cage open and climbed down. Morgan offered a hand, and they took it, landing clumsily on their feet.

Kit immediately went down to one knee. Tobias helped them sit down properly, catching their long-fingered hand in his own. They smiled at each other awkwardly.

"Always had a soft spot for bards," Kit said. "I don't think I can walk yet. You don't have to stay, I'll be fine. Just getting me out of there was more than I hoped anyone would do for me."

"We're not just leaving you here," Tobias said, faster than he expected to. Morgan shot him a questioning look. Tamsin ignored it all, instead handing Kit a hunk of hard bread from her pack.

"Bread and water? I'm a warm blanket away from feeling like I'm actually a human being," Kit said. Tobias immediately dropped his own blanket over their shoulders without warning. Kit chuckled a bit.

"We'll stop for the day," Tamsin said. "Get you fed and warmed up. You can come with us, if you'd like."

Kit studied each of their faces on at a time. Tobias smiled awkwardly, annoyed at himself for breaking character. Tamsin looked infinitely more alive than she had in days with someone to care for, rummaging through her pack for the skin that contained wine instead of water. Morgan, taking it all in, softened, sitting down to start pulling together what they'd need for a fire.

"You're really from our world," Tobias said.

"Unless there's more than one," Kit said. "Honestly, the shit I've seen, I can't be sure of that. But yeah, I'm from a place with Gatorade, and cars, and boardgames, and pizza, and… shit, I liked it here for so long, y'know? And then everything went wrong. Every single thing went wrong."

"I think I know what you mean," Tamsin said.

"You lost some of yours too, huh," Kit said.

"Just one, but…" Tamsin said.

"Everything fell apart after that," Morgan said.

Kit nodded, silent and understanding.

"Where are you headed?" they said, breaking the melancholy silence.

"Hawksmith Academy," Tamsin said. "We were hoping to…"

"We're looking for answers," Morgan said.

Kit took a long swig of wine, then looked first to Tobias, and then to Tamsin. They winced and gritted their teeth.

"I have some bad news for you," Kit said. "Last I heard, Hawksmith Academy was empty."

Chapter 3: A new kind of villainy

He'd thought of himself as Valamir for so long it felt strange to even say his real name. Brandon? I haven't been Brandon for a decade. More than a decade, maybe, he thought. He hadn't lost himself in the Valamir persona, not like some of the others. Valamir was more of an amplified version of himself, and he eventually became that amplified version, and it worked. It helped him survive in Revery. And as far as he was concerned, he'd stay Valamir until he had to go home.

Now Asptooth, on the other hand, he'd never be Craig again. Valamir watched as his companion, the one surviving member of their party, rummaged through his belongings he'd left at the safehouse they now stood in. This was always their plan, if things with Dom went wrong. They always had a feeling at some point Dom would blur the line too far between his murderous Blaggard persona and the man they used to call their friend. Dom was always a bully, but the longer he stayed in Revery, the more he got used to lording power over people, and the more Valamir assumed that this was who Dom had always wanted to be. Vicious, creatively cruel, blind to consequence.

Asptooth left that line behind long ago, but there was something endearing about the creepy wizard he'd become. Disconcerting, yes, unpleasant, often, but Asptooth could always be counted on. He was a survivor. He might have been the most suited to surviving here in

Revery, if Valamir was being honest. The man embraced the madness rather than fought it, and he played this world's game smarter than any of them.

It was that mad persona that allowed Valamir and Asptooth to set this place up, actually. Dom, or Blaggard, never quite knew what to make of Asptooth's weirdness, and so when the wizard wandered off for a few days, the warrior just assumed he was doing more of his usual inscrutable magic nonsense. In fact, Asptooth had taken some coin he and Valamir set aside, bought a small house in a lakeside town they were passing by, and carved into the floor all the necessary arcane sigils to let him use the place as a safe haven they could retreat to using one of his spells. This was always meant to be their backup plan. Valamir had hoped to never have to use it, but with Dom and Beckett, or Blaggard and Anders, both dead, he was glad they'd had the forethought to set it up.

Asptooth plopped down on a chair in the main chamber of the safehouse, dust poofing out as his arse hit a cushion long-unused.

"So Blaggard's dead, then," Asptooth said.

"Looks to be," Valamir said.

"Huh," Asptooth said. He scratched at his scraggly beard absently. "I don't think I want to go back to being Craig now that he's gone."

"You don't have to."

"I mean, I don't feel like a Craig anymore."

"That's understandable."

"Not for a long time, either."

"I'd be lying if I said I wanted to go back to my old name, too," Valamir said. "We can keep being who we are. Just because Dom's not around to threaten anyone who uses their 'real world' names doesn't mean we have to stop using our Revery names."

"Asptooth just feels more natural."

"Sure," Valamir said.

Asptooth traced a sigil on the floor, which light up with sickly green light. A line formed on the floor and Asptooth whacked it with the heel of his hand. A small hidden hatch opened a crack, which Asptooth then pulled open fully. Sacks of gold and gems, sellable goods, and other items they'd squirreled away during their journeys lay hidden within.

"Say this much for Dom, the man couldn't do math to save his life," Valamir said. He picked up a sack of coins and jangled it casually.

"Not like he had any plans for us to have a retirement fund," Asptooth said.

"Everyone needs a backup plan," Valamir said.

Asptooth reviewed what remained in the cache, nodding to himself.

"It's enough to live off of for as long as we want," he said. "But not…"

"Not our usual level of luxury," Valamir said.

"Solidly middle class."

"I'm not keen on spending the rest of my life solidly middle class in a knockoff Middle Earth," Valamir said.

"I was kind of hoping for something more luxury living style," Asptooth said, grinning wickedly. "Not sure there's much money in continuing to follow Blaggard's obsession over that dead god wizard guy."

"No, most of the money there was from the pillaging," Valamir said. "I'm going to be honest, I'm not ethically against pillaging, but I always found it boring."

"The screaming was fun," Asptooth said.

Valamir shook his head, hiding a smirk.

"You sick bastard," he said. "Something is wrong with you."

Asptooth showed his crooked teeth between his beard, making a goofy grin.

"You have something else in mind other than pillaging?"

"To tell you the truth, old friend, I've had my eye on white collar crime for quite some time now," Valamir said. "Isn't that what a proper adventurer does? You outlive your friends, and then you go back to your home village and, I don't know, start a bank or something."

"So you want to switch from D&D to Monopoly?" Asptooth said. "I thought you were less boring than that."

"I'm serious," Valamir said. "Why run across the countryside, killing and breaking into tombs… when we can make other people do it for us?"

"Like nobles?" Asptooth said.

"Better," Valamir said. "Like CEOs."

"Do we have enough cash saved to do something like that?"

"Not yet, my friend, but I know exactly how we can start building up that capital," Valamir said.

"Yeah?"

Valamir tapped the holy symbol of the deity he proclaimed to worship here in Revery emblazoned on his breastplate.

"Asptooth, my man… we're going to start a church."

Chapter 4: A person with theories

Eriko had no idea where they were.

Thinking back, it had always been Jack, as the ranger, who led them in their off-road searches. None of the rest of the party was equipped in any way for hiking into the unknown. Hark seemed to know where he was going, but the problem there was that neither Eriko nor Cordelia was able to really express where they wanted to go.

And Eriko was strangely calm about this.

Cordelia was not, and she'd finally started making her concerns known.

"I don't know where we are," she said out loud, as if echoing Eriko's thoughts. "Do you know where we are?"

"North," Eriko said.

Cordelia stopped in her tracks and looked around at the green nothingness that surrounded them. Hark had disappeared into the woods an hour before, offering to try to scrounge up some food so they didn't have to dip into their supplies, leaving Eriko and Cordelia to follow a vague hunting path that may or may not have just been dirt.

"North," Cordelia said. "We're not only never getting home, we're never going to find our friends again. We're going to die out here. And not because a monster got us. Nope. Because we got lost."

"We'll be fine," Eriko said.

Cordelia raised both eyebrows so high onto her forehead Eriko thought they were going to appear on the back of her head.

"Fine? Really?"

"I have a theory about all this," Eriko said. She stopped and pulled off one of her boots, shaking it until a loose stone fell out.

"Oh, you're a person with theories now," Cordelia said. "This is a thing you do. Theories."

"I'm serious. I have a theory."

"Let's hear it."

Eriko sat down on a nearby fallen tree to fix her boot.

"Revery gives us what we want," Eriko said. "And it seems to want us to adventure."

"Okay," Cordelia said, the skepticism rich in her voice.

"Jack didn't want to survive the Tomb of the Maker," Eriko said. "That was the story he's always wanted. Revery gave it to him, because it wants drama."

"Jack died because we couldn't save him."

"We couldn't save him because this world, the story, wanted a certain ending," Eriko said. "Morgan's greatest wish was a normal, happy, out relationship. Tamsin's is to go to magic school. Where are they going? Magic school."

"Morgan lost his happy relationship," Cordelia said.

"Because Revery wants us to face hardships," Eriko said. "It gives and it takes away."

"Like you and Jin."

"We're not brought into this world we know nothing about to have healthy relationships," Eriko said. "Revery manipulates our relationships with the people here to push us to action. Look what happened with Ingo."

"We didn't have a relationship with Ingo," Cordelia said.

"We did. He was the bigoted old dwarf who redeemed himself a bit at the end. And now you're carrying his axe around like it means something to you."

"It doesn't mean anything to me."

"Doesn't it, thought?" Eriko said. "Everything here means something."

"What does this have to do with us being lost?" Cordelia said.

Eriko stood up and dusted off the seat of her pants.

"We want to find the things Blaggard and his crew uncovered. We don't have to know how to find it. If we're meant to find it,

Revery will put what we're looking for in our path just to see what we do with it."

"This sounds way too much like we've lost all free will," Cordelia said.

"In a way we did. We're all under the gaze of some grand designer," Eriko said. "A game master deliberately fucking with us."

Both women turned around, reaching for weapons, when they heard a barking laugh from the woods. Hark stepped out with a couple of rabbits slung over his shoulder.

"Haven't heard talk of the Grand Designer in a long time," Hark said.

"Listening in on private conversations, Hark?" Eriko said.

"The way you two talk, I could hear you from a quarter mile away," Hark said. Don't have to listen in order to hear you."

"Fair point," Cordelia said. "You said Grand Designer like it was a proper name."

"Because it is a proper name," Hark said. ""They don't teach you about the pantheon where you're from?"

"Secular society," Eriko said. "What's the Grand Designer?"

"And why doesn't anyone talk about him?" Cordelia asked.

"Oh, people talk about him," Hark said. "But not the way they used to. The Grand Designer is a god. Of industry and invention. A thinking man's god."

"Doesn't sound too bad," Eriko said.

"He wasn't," Hark said. "Until about forty years ago, when he stopped answering prayers."

"What do you mean, stopped answering prayers?" Cordelia said. Hark shrugged.

"Not a religious man myself, but I guess them that revered him say he went completely silent," Hark said. "Their spells stopped working. They didn't hear his call anymore. It was as though he ceased to exist."

"That happen often?" Eriko said. This line of conversation had caught her interest. Real world religion didn't intrigue her, but mythic pantheons made up of fictional gods were definitely her thing.

"Not in my lifetime," Hark said. "Not in most lifetimes. But I guess gods can come and go. And the Grand Designer, he went away and never came back. I guess there's a whole group of folks who went on to study where he went, but nobody ever figured it out. Or at least that's what I heard. But what do I know."

Cordelia and Eriko exchanged a long, baffled look.

"What's the point of gods if they just piss off?" Eriko said.

"Maybe people just need to have faith in something," Cordelia said.

Hark shrugged.

"In fairness, if your god isn't purifying your village's well or curing the sick, I don't see much point in them either," he said. "But I'm a simple man. Easily entertained, easily disappointed."

"Huh," Cordelia said, and then wandered ahead, outpacing Eriko and Hark, who watched her leave without a word.

"Something I said?" Hark asked.

"She used to believe in something, a long time ago," Eriko said, realizing she'd never sat down to talk with her friend about her beliefs since finding themselves in a world where divine intervention was a casual affair. "Might be she still does. I don't know."

"Whatever helps you get through the day," Hark said. "I said a few prayers for my people, when I buried them. Don't reckon it did a bit of good, but they would've done the same for me, so I figured, what harm."

"It was probably the right thing to do," Eriko said.

"Mm," Hark said, as noncommittal in his response as Cordelia had been in hers.

He gestured to the departing Cordelia with his chin.

"What was it she wanted?" the orc asked.

"Wanted?" Eriko said.

"I heard the two of you talking about the world giving you what you want. Your friend with the death wish and such."

Eriko exhaled deeply. She'd never known what Cordelia wanted, in this world or the last. Cordelia had always been the most closed book in their group, the hardest to read, the least likely to ask for anything.

"I don't know," Eriko said.

"That's too bad," Hark said. "Everyone must want something, yeah? Even if it's a simple thing. Or grand. Doesn't matter. Just something."

Eriko grimaced, suddenly uncomfortable with knowing what she didn't know about her friend.

"You figure the world will give you what you want from this hunt you're on?" Hark asked.

"Honestly, I think so," Eriko said. "But that's not what worries me."

"What worries you, then?"

"If the world gives us what we want, but does so at a cost, I think there's going to be a fight when we get there," Eriko said. "And I'm afraid that she and I aren't enough to handle what we might find."

Chapter 5: Real life was hard enough

Tamsin had trouble containing her wretched level of disappointment at Kit's words.

Hawksmith Academy is empty.

Maybe they were wrong, Tamsin thought. Maybe they'd just heard a rumor. But the idea that this school of magic, where she or Morgan might learn a way to bring Jack back, where they might learn the sort of magic that might keep them all alive here, was abandoned had her teetering somewhere between despair and tears of rage.

She bit both back, chewing on her lip as Morgan and Tobias calmly asked Kit questions about what they'd seen so far.

"I haven't been to the academy," Kit said, graciously accepting a bowl of vegetable stew Morgan has put together when they camped. The newcomer clearly fought the urge to wolf the entire bowl down in one go.

"How long were you in that cage?" Tobias asked.

Kit shrugged.

"I got a little delirious after the first few days, to be honest," they said.

"You end up in there for any particular reason?" Morgan asked.

"I backed the wrong side in a rebellion against a corrupt noble," Kit said. "I… after I lost my party, I just started taking up lost causes. What else could I do, y'know? I was on my own. No idea where to go. I figured maybe if I gave the game what it wanted, a heroic story, it might point me in the right direction, but instead, I ended up in a birdcage."

"This is going to come across as either weird or rude or both," Tobias said. "But what… do you do?"

"What do I do?"

"What's your thing. What, I guess what class are you? I can't tell."

"On account of I'm wearing sexy rags and completely unarmed," Kit said.

"Yeah, that," Tobias said.

Kit laughed.

"I'm just a warrior," Kit said. "I mean, I know a couple of little spells I learned along the way, but when we were picking our characters back home, I just… my life was complicated enough already. I just wanted to be a hero and hit things with a sword. So that's what I picked."

"Just a fighter, making their way through the world," Tobias said.

"You gonna write a song about me?" Kit asked.

Tobias smirked and shrugged.

"Don't put the thought out there if you don't want it to come true."

Tobias unbuckled his pack and pulled out the curved sword he'd started out with, the one he'd set aside in favor of the stupid musical sword he'd picked up among the ghouls.

"It's not much, but I figured you might want something," he said, offering the sword and belt to Kit. They nodded appreciatively and started buckling the belt around their waist.

"I see you've got an upgrade over there," Kit said. "What's the deal with that?"

"Don't get him started," Morgan said.

"I don't want to get me started either," Tobias said, patting the blade on his hip. "It's the Singing Sword. It kills people while performing power ballads."

"Of course it does," Kit said. "Why wouldn't the bard have a singing sword. This world makes an uncomfortable amount of sense."

Kit pointed to Morgan and Tamsin.

"Cleric and mage, yeah?" they said.

"Yep," Morgan said.

"Odd party makeup," they said.

"Our ranger… didn't make it," Tamsin said, trying to remain

stoic. "And our rogue and barbarian went off without us."

"Split the party?"

"Different responses to tragedy," Morgan said gruffly. "We thought we might find some answers at the academy. They wanted to go looking for clues about this group of murder hobos we stopped."

"Murder… you mean Blaggard's group?" Kit said.

"You know him?" Tamsin asked, trying and failing to not sound over-eager.

"By reputation. Just a destructive piece of shit who destroys everything he touches."

"He killed my—our friend," Tamsin said. "But he's gone. We killed him."

"Huh," Kit said. "I never met him, but I had a feeling he was another player, like us. This world is cruel but nothing here even remotely matches the cruelty back home. I knew it had to be someone from our world."

"Well, he's gone now," Tamsin said. "And we were hoping Hawksmith could—"

"We want to bring our friend back. There's got to be a way," Morgan said.

"There is. I've seen it," Kit said between mouthfuls of stew. "I can't do it. You might."

"Where would we learn that, though?" Morgan asked.

Kit shrugged.

"Can't say for sure," Kit said "I mean, even if Hawksmith is abandoned, the rumors say the place is full of libraries. Maybe something was left behind."

"So it's worth the trip no matter what," Morgan said.

"I'm not an expert, but it seems like a reasonable guess to me," Kit said. "Who knows what they left lying around."

"So I guess we keep going, then," Tamsin said. "To Hawksmith, empty or not."

"Well, I'll go with you, if you don't mind the company," Kit said. "I've been on my own for a while. It's weirdly, ah, comforting to run into folks from home."

"Absolutely. Please stay," Tobias said, then looked vaguely shocked at himself for blurting it out.

"Happy to have the company," Morgan said, settling in to sleep near the fire. "We'll see about getting you some armor soon."

"I appreciate it," Kit said. "I know the area pretty well. Can steer you away from the shadier folks."

Tamsin wrapped a blanket around herself and settled in as well.

"Usually we rely on Tobias to be the shady one," she said. "Don't let him play you any songs tonight though. He'll wake the dead."

"The dead, as it happens, like my music," Tobias said. "Everyone does."

Tamsin closed her eyes, trying to tune out the quiet conversation Tobias struck up with Kit. For half a second, she could pretend things were back to normal, that they hadn't broken the party up, that Jack wasn't dead, that this was still a game. But her mind kept latching on to the image of an empty academy, bereft of answers. She wondered if Eriko and Cordelia were okay, or if she'd ever see them again.

Sleep was a long time coming, and when she drifted off, she dreamed of fairy tales, and how rarely they had happy endings.

Chapter 6: Her story

They were days into the journey when they came upon the first statue.

It was entirely out of place, a once-perfect representation of a man, some kind of hunter, poised to take a shot with his bow. The bow had had been broken over time and lay at the man's feet, and his expression, Eriko noted, was not one of ferocity or courage but of... not fear, she thought. Surprise? He looked surprised, like someone caught him with his pants down.

"Odd spot for a statue," she said. Both Cordelia and Hark grunted noncommittally and moved on.

They found another statue a quarter mile later, made of the same pristine stone, a warrior raising his sword arm in battle. The arm had broken off and lay on the ground, crumbling at the break. Another statue had tumbled and shattered nearby. Beyond that, they could see a half-dozen others, all in different poses—combat, shock, begging for mercy, one even smiling. They were all supremely detailed, but in different stages of disrepair. Chipped here and there, stained by the elements, crusted with pale green lichen.

"Strange place for a statue garden," Cordelia said.

"These aren't statues," Hark said. The orc was examining one figure up close, running a hand over the statue's armor.

"You might be right," Eriko said, leaning in to look at one statue's face. "There's no artistry to these. They're like facsimiles.

And the expressions—too ordinary to be intentional, too mundane for it to be by accident."

"You're saying they're what… people turned to stone?" Cordelia said.

"Gotta assume there's at least a few creatures who can turn things to stone," Eriko said. "Classic trope. Unavoidable."

"I hate this trope," Cordelia said, her face close to one of the statue's, staring it in the eyes. "I can never stop wondering if they're alive in there. Awake. Staring at the same spot in their vision for all eternity."

"Well that's morbid," Eriko said, feeling very claustrophobic.

"Or what if it hurts when parts chip off," Cordelia said. She looked over to Eriko and cocked her head. "Imagine your arm falling off and you can still feel it. Just an eternity of silent screaming."

"Can you stop?" Eriko said. The nudged on of the broken limbs with the toe of her boot. "Any idea what did this, Hark?"

"A few things could have," he said. "Basilisks. Cockatrices."

Eriko followed the gaze of the statue in front of her, then turned to the one beside him, and the one after that.

"Cordelia," she said. "They're all looking in the same direction."

"So we should look the opposite direction, then," Cordelia said.

Eriko ignored her and walked cautiously forward. Ten of fifteen paces along, she saw a cave, half-hidden by vines draped across the entrance like lace curtains.

"Cordie," Eriko said.

"If you turn to stone I'm not carrying you home," Cordelia said.

Eriko said nothing, padding silently toward the cave entrance. With her outstretched hand she gently brushed the vines aside. The cavern was larger inside than she expected, and cool. She could hear running water. She crept soundlessly down a formation of stones that acted as a short, natural staircase and tilted her head to listen.

"I know you're there, little one," a woman's voice said from the dark. Something moved in the periphery of Eriko's vision and she flinched. Great, I'm going to turn to stone and spend the next thousand years in some stupid, panicked pose, she thought. But she flexed her fingers and they moved just fine. Nope, not stone yet, she thought. Eriko searched the darkness for the source of the voice and saw, half-silhouetted by the light of the cave entrance, a woman's shape, tall, shoulders thrown back, head held high and proud. On top of that head, Eriko saw a writhing mass.

Medusa, Eriko thought. She winced, trying to avoid looking, but she couldn't help herself from staring The woman's skin in the light of the cave seemed almost stonelike, and Eriko could make out the faintest dusting of emerald scales where the light touched her neck and arm. Something was wrong about the writing atop her head, Eriko noticed—one half moved with fluid, snakelike undulations, but the other half seemed... wrong. Less lithe, less formless.

"Have you come to steal from me, little one? Come to kill me to make a name for yourself?"

"No," Eriko said. "I'm looking for answers, and my search led me here."

The medusa stepped into the light more fully, so Eriko could see her face. Sharp lines, large, alien eyes gold and split with jet-black vertical pupils. She smiled at Eriko, revealing distinct, pointed canines. Eriko could now identify the snakes where her hair should be, the left half of her head covered in a roiling mass of snake heads, writhing with almost sensuous, unending movement. On the right half, though, the snakes were headless, a collection of mutilated stumps, twitching with grotesque, silent pain.

"What happened to you?" Eriko said, taking an involuntary step forward. The medusa held out a hand to stop her.

"Come no closer," the woman said, circling Eriko like a predator, her long, diaphanous gown drifting around her legs like mist. "You said you seek answers. What answers do you seek?"

A clatter arose behind Eriko, and she realized her companions had found the cave entrance and had begun to clumsily make their way inside.

"Cordelia, wait. It's okay," Eriko said.

The medusa stepped back into the shadows again, speaking softly.

"You've seen my work. You know what I can do," the medusa said. "Enter only if you have no malice in your heart. I will know. And I will do to you as I have done to all the others."

Cordelia reached the bottom of the stone stairs and stopped next to Eriko.

"What's going on," Cordelia whispered.

Somewhere on the steps, Eriko could hear Hark waiting, his breathing faintly audible in the dark.

"Hark blindfolded himself," Cordelia said. "I couldn't, I would've fallen down the entire flight of stairs, but..."

Eriko hushed her with a gesture of her hand.

"We have no malice," Eriko said. "We seek… some terrible men killed one of my best friends. They came this way, looking for something. I want to know what drove them."

"So that you can attain it for yourself?" the medusa asked.

"I don't think so," Eriko said, perhaps more honestly than she intended. "I want to understand them. Why they've done what they've done."

"All men are monsters," the medusa said. "All humans are, in truth, but men more readily accept the monster in each of their hearts. Perhaps these men you seek to understand had simply given over to their darkness."

"We stopped them at the Tomb of the Maker," Eriko said. "They wanted something there, but failed to find it."

There was a long pause, a terrifying silence as she said this. Finally, the medusa spoke again.

"You can come out, orc," she said. "I have no quarrel with your kind. It's humanity who leaves nothing but death in their wake."

Hark stumbled down the stairs, bumping into Cordelia, who righted him and reached for the blindfold around his eyes.

"It's okay," she said. "We're not hiding our eyes."

The medusa stepped forward into the light once more. Eriko could make out the details of her ravaged head more clearly now, could see the scarred over stumps of her dead snake-hair. Cordelia hissed.

"Who would do this kind of thing," she said, her teeth bared.

The medusa held out a hand, and a long, milky yellow snake slithered across the floor, coiling around her legs and hips and coming to rest across her shoulders. The serpent flicked his tongue toward the adventurers casually.

"Men. Men seeking the Tomb of the Maker," the medusa said.

"But how?" Eriko asked. "All those warriors up above, you stopped all of them. How did this happen?"

"These tomb raiders knew of my kind," the medusa said. "We are powerful, but not without our weaknesses. They'd clearly fought one like me before. Likely one of my sisters."

"And killed her," Eriko said.

The medusa nodded gently.

"Killing women who scare them is a rite of passage for men," she said.

"These men cut your hair," Cordelia said.

"And demanded I answer their questions," the medusa said.

"Did you escape?" Eriko asked.

The medusa shook her head.

"I think it entertained them that I should live," she said, gesturing to her butchered hair. "Live like this. Men love the power that cruelty gives them."

Cordelia exhaled loudly through her nose. Eriko, surprising herself, took the medusa's hand. The being locked eyes with her, an angry glare softening into something else.

"We killed their leader," she said. "I know it's not enough, but…"

"What's done is done, and only what will be is up to us," the medusa said. "I told them they were wasting their time. That the Maker is not who he is said to be. But they wanted to see their greed through to the end. And cared nothing for what they destroyed to find it."

"What led them to you?" Eriko asked. The medusa's hand was cool in hers, long fingers, a soft gleam of pearlescence beneath her skin.

"There's a myth that medusa steal all the memories of those we turn to stone. They thought someone out there knew what they wanted to know, and thus, so would I."

"But you don't," Eriko said.

The medusa nodded, punctuating the gesture with a slow, thoughtful blink.

"What did you tell them?" Cordelia said.

"What they wanted to hear. I knew where the Tomb of the Maker is. And if I told them the truth, that all gods and magicians are liars, they wouldn't have believed me anyway. So I simply said the things I knew would make them leave."

Eriko squeezed her hand and rose to her full height.

"Where I came from, you're the monster of the story," Eriko said. "But you're not, are you."

"The monster in almost every story is not the villain, little one," the medusa said. "But stories need villains, and monsters are there, strange and unknowable. It's an easy tale to craft."

They stood together, unspeaking for a few moments, the water running softly deeper in the cavern.

"I'd tell you that we will kill these men for what they've done, but I don't think that would help, would it," Eriko said, finally.

The medusa shook her head.

"Fate will drop the blade where and when it belongs. Maybe you will wield it. Maybe someone else. I have time. I am patient."

The medusa touched Eriko's face, a soft finger caressing her jawline.

"But if you could make it hurt when you do, I would not be upset."

Chapter 7: Alignment shift

When they first saw the riders heading toward them on the road, Morgan was, at least momentarily, excited to have someone new to talk to. The road itself made for easy traveling, but they'd gone literally two entire days without seeing a soul and the solitude was beginning to make him anxious. Other humans, or at least something akin to human, felt like a welcome distraction.

Then Kit cursed under their breath and Morgan's anxiety came walloping back into his chest.

"We should avoid these guys if we can," Kit said. "They're flying the colors of the local lord."

"The one who put you in that cage," Tamsin said. For some reason, Morgan noted, Tamsin drew her cloak up over her head as the riders approached, shadowing her eyes.

"The lord who abuses his subjects," Tobias said.

"Look, I'm okay with a fight," Kit said. "But if you're hoping to keep a low profile, getting into a brawl with the lord's enforcers is kind of the opposite of that."

Morgan looked north and south from the road. They were in the lowlands now, with nothing but flat ground and scattered brush for maybe a half mile in either direction before they could find a tree line to hide in.

"What do you think our chances are of talking our way out of this?" Morgan said. "We're not going to be able to hide before they get here and I have to assume running to hide from them is only going to draw their attention more."

"I can talk us out of anything," Tobias said.

"I'm not doubting your gift of persuasion, but his enforcers are always looking for a shakedown," Kit said. "And if they recognize me…"

"In the very least, we can fix that," Tobias said, and made a series of small gestures with his hand.

"Oh," Kit said, and when Morgan looked over, he saw the fighter now had a mop of long, red hair spilling down over their eyes, and looked a bit taller, broader of shoulder, with a slight paunch. "Thanks. I hate it."

"I can drop the spell if you want," Tobias said.

"Maybe skip the pot belly next time," Kit said.

Morgan almost laughed, but the sound of hoofbeats drawing closer spiked his nervousness all over again. The horses slowed and one rider pulled ahead, a man who might have been handsome if there weren't a glint of overt cruelty in his eye. All of the riders wore reddish-brown armor and were geared with solid, if not glamorous, weapons.

"We don't see many travelers heading this way," the man said. "What's your business?"

The man locked eyes specifically with Morgan. For a moment, Morgan wondered if he should have hidden his cleric's vestments. I really need to learn more about the religions of Revery, he thought absently. One of these days I'm going to walk into the wrong town worshiping the wrong god and…

"A pleasure to meet you," Tobias interrupted, stepping forward and offering a bow. "We are indeed travelers. We were making a pilgrimage to the libraries of the Hawksmith Academy, though we recently learned…"

"The Academy's gone, elf," the lead rider said.

"I was going to say, we recently learned that the school has been abandoned. We were planning on traveling as far as the next town to restock our supplies and then head back home."

"And where's home, then?" the rider asked. "And if you came this far, how'd you hear about Hawksmith's condition? We haven't seen any riders on this road for miles."

"Moderate Expectations," Tobias said.

The rider's mouth tightened.

"Roundabout way to get here from Moderate Expectations," he said, his hand visibly resting on his sword. "Would've thought you'd take the Granite Pass and make your way through Dark Pines instead."

"That would be my fault, my lord," Morgan said, immediately feeling slimy for using the honorarium. "I asked my companions to travel with me to check in on a few local parishes before heading to the Academy. It was an inefficient route."

The lead rider turned his full attention to Morgan now, taking in his armor, noting the war hammer he carried.

"Expecting trouble, priest?" he asked.

Morgan attempted his best casual shrug.

"Shouldn't anyone, traveling these days?"

"Not on Lord Zayne's roads," the rider said. "Nothing happens out here we don't know about. And you still haven't answered my question. How'd you learn the academy is empty?"

"We..." Morgan began.

"The prisoner," Tobias said. For a flash, Morgan panicked that Tobias has given them away, but he realized—the riders would know they passed the cage. Tobias knew they'd be aware they passed the cage, and Kit. Use the truth against them. Not for the first time Morgan was involuntarily impressed by Tobias' ability to work in half-truths.

"That piece of shit is still alive enough to talk?" the leader said, and his men chuckled behind him. Morgan sensed Kit tense beside him but remained silent.

"They were looking for anyone to talk with," Tobias said. "Couldn't shut 'em up."

"Guess we'll need to poke a few more holes in the prisoner, keep 'em from disturbing travelers, then." Again, a rough peal of laughter. It made Morgan's skin crawl. "Well, you're a day out from the nearest town. We'll let you pass once you've paid the Lord's Tax for use of the road."

"The Lord's Tax?" Tobias said.

This elicited a different kind of laughter from the riders.

"How do you think we maintain such pristine passage through the territory?" the lead rider said. "If we let everyone use it for free, we'd have nothing but trouble. It keeps order, you know. Makes sure nobody uses it who can't help with its upkeep."

"Sure, right," Tobias said, shooting a quick glance at Morgan, and then at his sister. "That's not unreasonable, I suppose. How much do we owe you?"

"How much do you have?" the rider said.

Morgan could hear loosening of swords in scabbards. One rider slid from his horse and dropped to the ground, walking toward them casually. Another absent-mindedly checked on his crossbow.

"Ah, I see, it's, um, income-based," Tobias said. "It's a tax, of course it's income-based."

"If you want to put it that way to make yourselves feel better, sure," the lead rider said. "You can just leave most of it with us. Keep, oh, the copper pieces you have so you can take part in the local economy. We'll take that fancy sword, though. And I like your cloak. We'll take that, too."

The cloak around Tobias' shoulders shifted of its own accord, and Morgan realized the flying cloak had chosen Tobias today instead of Tamsin. They were about to rip a sentient cape from Toby's shoulders and Morgan had no idea how that would go over. He thought about reaching for his hammer, but the lead rider's eyes were already on him.

"And you won't need that fancy armor in Lord Zayne's territory. We're here to protect you."

"Uh," was all Morgan could stutter out before the smell of ozone split the air and a blinding blue-white flash went off in front of him.

The screams of pain were loud, but they were mercifully short. Morgan watched as a bolt of lightning struck the lead rider first, then proceeded to bounce between his men, lighting up the crossbowman with such force Morgan could hear his skull rattling around inside his domed metal helmet. Another guard fell with a thump and clatter from the back of his horse, steam emitting from within his armor. The lightning danced among the men, returning to electrocute a few riders more than once.

In a split second, the riders went from a band of dangerous-looking warriors to smoking, half-cooked corpses.

The leader, barely alive, crawled toward them, grabbing hold of the toe of Morgan's boot with a hand weeping blistered fluid from splitting burns. Kit's own boot swung into Morgan's vision as he watched the blackened, splintered fingernail's on the rider's left hand touch the toe of his boot. The leader went sprawling away from Morgan, and as he clawed at the ground, trying to pull himself back to his feet, Kit drove the point of their borrowed short sword into the back of the leader's skull.

"That's for Nathan," Kit said as their blade point emerged from the lead rider's mouth.

"Holy shit!" Morgan said. He looked at Tobias in shock, who was looking at Tamsin.

"Holy shit!" Tobias said. "Tam! You just electrocuted the whole fucking gang!"

"I didn't electrocute their horses," Tamsin said, her face still vaguely shrouded by her cloak. She reached up to the leader's horse and put a calming hand on the beast's neck.

"We were going for low-profile!" Tobias said. "I was low-profiling! What the hell!"

"This was Sir Darius," Kit said. "Scumbag who locked me up. All of Zayne's men are garbage, but he was the worst. Small and petty and cruel. The world won't miss him."

Kit looked at Tamsin for a hard few seconds.

"But when they don't report in, others will come to investigate," Kit said. "We should move."

"Tamsin," Tobias said.

"I made an executive decision," Tamsin said. "They were just about to either rob us or figure out we were lying. We don't have time to deal with little garbage dictators. We need to find whatever is left of Hawksmith and bring our friend back. I'm not wasting time on talking our way out of situations with people who don't deserve it. They tortured Kit and were going to go back for more."

"And when they found I was gone, They would have come looking for us again," Kit added. They looked at Morgan imploringly. "I don't want to kill people in cold blood any more than you do, I promise. But the wizard made the right decision."

Morgan shook his head, then sighed.

"Nothing we can do to fix this now anyway," he said. "Let's get the bodies off the road. Tamsin, Tobias, do either of you have a spell that will help us hide them?"

"I've got something," Tamsin said.

"Great. Okay. Hide the bodies. We'll take the horses to get some distance between us and… this mess, and then we'll set them free so if anyone finds them they'll be far enough away from the corpses it'll just add to the confusion. Good enough?"

Tamsin nodded. Tobias gave a thumbs up and then started rifling one of the riders' pockets.

"What are you doing?" Morgan said.

"Looking for the Lord's Tax," Tobias said. Morgan shot him a disapproving look. "Hey, if they were running a shakedown operation, no reason we can't benefit from it. We'll give it to charity, right? Most of it. Some of it. A fair percentage. We'll give a fair percentage to charity."

Morgan shrugged and began his consistently awkward process of climbing onto one of the bigger horses.

"Fine. Just be quick about it. We can't stay long."

Chapter 8: What he is believed to be

Conversation was muted for several hours after the conversation with the medusa. Eriko was visibly turning thoughts over and over in her head. Hark seemed noticeably shaken by a close encounter with such a powerful being. Cordelia suggested they stop once they'd traveled far enough to feel like a respectful distance from the medusa's lair, and Eriko dropped her pack without hesitation.

"They cut her hair," she blurted out. "I'm going to kill every last one of them."

Cordelia shrugged.

"Won't get an argument from me."

"They killed my friends," Hark said before kneeling down to rummage through his own backpack, his assent more than implied.

"So—not to change the subject from justified homicide," Cordelia said. "But something the medusa said has been stuck in my head ever since we left."

"Yeah?" Eriko said, kicking away some brush to find a comfortable place to sit.

"She said the Maker is not what he is believed to be. What do you think that means?"

"That gods are full of shit?" Eriko said.

Cordelia turned to Hark, who appeared to only be half-listening.

"Hark, how much do you know about the Maker?" Cordelia asked.

The orc shrugged.

"As much as anyone not raised to worship him, I guess," he said. "You really don't know anything about him?"

"Imagine the two of us grew up in a place where we hadn't heard of the gods of Revery," Cordelia said. "We're kind of learning on the fly."

Hark settled down and pulled out a bundle of dried jerky. He picked out a piece for himself and then passed the open bundle around.

"I only know what everyone knows," he said.

"Pretend you're talking to a little kid, teaching her the basics," Cordelia said. She sensed Eriko's rage subsiding as she leaned in, her curiosity piqued.

"Well," Hark said. "He's the Maker. The Grand Designer. He's the god of crafting, of science. He's the god of creating things. That he was both a mortal man, and the builder of the world."

"Why would the medusa say that he wasn't what he's believed to be? Maybe he's a fraud?" Eriko said.

Hark pondered the question a moment, chewing slowly.

"The Maker does have two very different origin stories," he said. "But most of the gods do, depending on who tells it. Some say he was the first of the gods. That he made Revery and everything sprung from his designs. He set down the rules and structure the world was built on, and then the other gods began to appear to fill out the places he didn't want to oversee."

"Would that make him, like, *the* god? The god over all other gods?" Cordelia asked.

Hark shrugged again.

"There really isn't a hierarchy. I guess if there's gods who are… worshipped? Revered? More than others, the three sisters would be it. But the gods traditionally all have equal footing. They oversee unique parts of life and death."

"The three sisters?" Eriko asked. Cordelia shot her a glance as if to say not to interrupt. Eriko smirked. "Just a small detour. Who are the three sisters?"

"The goddesses of life and death itself," Hark said. For the first time, he seemed to be engaged with the theology lesson. Cordelia wondered if perhaps these goddesses were who he himself worshipped. "The Lady of Hope, She Who Waits, and the Mother of Graves."

"That last one sounds terrifying," Eriko said.

"No," Hark said, and the grim-faced orc actually smiled. "The Lady of Graves stands between her sisters. The Lady of Hope believes that all life is sacred, and we should treat it so. She Who Waits is her opposite, a death goddess, who believes that life itself is meaningless, and only the void awaits."

"And the Mother of Graves is the go between?" Cordelia said.

"The Mother of Graves says that life and death are not our toys to be trifled with. She balances her sisters. Life is precious, but impermanent. Death is sacred and necessary. Both balance the universe."

"Seems to me like Revery only really needs one sister," Eriko said.

Hark barked out a brief laugh.

"Perhaps you are right," he said. "But three sisters we have, and all three sisters have their followers."

"And all of these gods, the Maker, the sisters, they do things for their followers," Cordelia asked. "We have a friend whose magic comes from Theana."

"The Lady of Light and Words," Hark said. "All the gods do have their chosen few they grant magic to, yes. Though as you know, the Maker has grown quiet of late."

"Yeah," Cordelia said. "What was his other origin story? If he wasn't the first god, who is he?"

"There's a myth that the Maker, or the Grand Designer, was first a mortal man," Hark said. "A scientist and wizard who, through his own machinations, ascended to godhood. They say that's why the Maker could be absent-minded, almost neglectful of his worshippers, because he is forever tinkering, changing and altering reality to make the experiment more perfect. In this story the other gods don't trust him, because his power isn't granted by some cosmic right, but learned, and taken."

"So he's a dungeon master in that story," Eriko muttered.

Hark's brow furrowed.

"In both stories, the Grand Designer is a builder of structures, hidden barrows and subterranean lairs," he said. "Filled with unnatural corridors, traps, monsters of his own design. Would that make him a master of dungeons?"

Eriko's eyes went wide and stared at Cordelia, mouth open.

"What if the god Blaggard and his crew were looking for is

Revery's game master," she said.

"Or worse, what if he's the game designer," Cordelia said.

"I don't understand anything you're saying," Hark said.

Cordelia shrugged apologetically to the orc.

"I guess it's our shorthand," she said. The orc continued to look at her as though she were speaking a foreign language. "Code. A code we speak with each other."

"Finally, something that makes sense," Hark said.

"Hey, Hark," Eriko said. "I know you're not a religious man, but if we were looking for a temple of the Maker, would you know the closest one?"

Hark looked up at the sky as if to assess his place in the world, then looked east, and then to the west.

"There's one in a town about a day's travel that way," Hark said. "But…"

"But?" Eriko said.

"But there's a… what do you call it. A place where a bunch of priests all live together and study."

"A monastery?" Cordelia said.

"Sure," Hark said. "If you say so. If we go east, we're a bit further away, but if you're looking for answers, that might be an option."

"To the monastery of the Maker, then," Cordelia said.

"Sounds thrilling," Eriko said, hefting her pack and following Hark eastward.

Chapter 9: The reality of the situation

Morgan and the others made camp as far from the road as they reasonably could. They hadn't seen any signs of other patrols, but none of them wanted to take the risk. They made a small fire, kept it lit long enough to make dinner, and then doused it, sitting quietly in the dark, one eye always to the road in the distance.

Morgan watched the others silently, trying to read the room. Tobias seemed to be hitting it off with Kit in a pleasant way, the bard and the newcomer chatting quietly about their lives before Revery. But Tobias looked to his sister every few seconds, observing her in ways only twins know how to, a glimmer of concern etched across his face.

Tamsin said nothing, huddled in the sentient cloak, which had taken to shrouding her eyes dramatically. If she weren't sitting up, Morgan might have assumed Tamsin was asleep. He slid over to her so they were side by side. He noticed, uncomfortably, that she had Yorick, her talking skull, sitting on the ground beside her, probably to give him a break from being inside her backpack. The skull seemed to smile up at him, and Morgan resisted the urge to ask Tamsin to turn the skull to face away. Instead, he dove right in.

"You want to talk about earlier?" he asked. It was strange, Morgan thought, to speak this way now. He'd been a counselor back in the real world, working toward a degree, hoping he might help people one day, though the work paid so badly he knew he should find something else. He was good at it, though, and he desperately wanted to be someone who helped.

And here I am in this fantasy world, a healer, he mused. Maybe Eriko is right. Revery gives us what we want. It just doesn't give it easily.

"What's there to talk about," Tamsin said.

Morgan heard the tenor of Kit and Tobias' conversation change. They still made small talk, but he could tell they were both listening, gauging Tamsin's mood the same way Morgan was.

"You killed a lot of people back there," Morgan said.

"We've all killed people here," Tamsin said sharply.

"I'm not judging," Morgan said. "It's just not like you. So wanted to make sure you were okay."

Tamsin twisted her hands in her lap with idle energy.

"I'm fine," Tamsin said. "This is just the reality of the situation."

"The reality of the situation," Morgan repeated.

"We thought this was a game. We thought having magic was fun. But it's not a game, or at least not the kind of game we wanted it to be. We thought this was a roleplaying game. But it's crueler than that. So if we're going to make it, we need to be cruel, too."

Tobias had stopped talking entirely, now. Morgan glanced over at him and saw Tobias staring at his sister. Kit placed a hand gently on Tobias' shoulder.

"I don't think we… is that what you think this place is?" Morgan said.

Tamsin drew back her hood so she could look him in the eyes.

"It taunts us with what we want, Morgan. And if that's the game it wants us to play, then fine. I'll fight fire with fire."

Morgan took a deep breath, rubbed his eyes, rested his elbows on his knees. He exhaled deeply and then locked eyes with Tamsin.

"Maybe the game is offering us a temptation to be cruel because it wants us to be heroes," he said. "It's giving us the chance to be better than who we are."

"This place killed your best friend, Morgan," Tamsin said. "Why aren't you angrier?"

Morgan thought about it for a moment. Her words felt like a icy stab in his guts. Revery had killed his best friend, his oldest friend. Someone who had been kind to him when being kind to someone like Morgan wasn't easy. How have I made peace with it so quickly? He thought.

"I don't know," Morgan said, finally. "I think I… I think I still have hope we'll see him again."

Tamsin let her cowl droop back down over her eyes. She made a sound in her throat such that Morgan couldn't tell if she were scoffing or sobbing.

"We saw what that other party was like, Tobias said, joining them. "They took the cruel path. Turning on each other. Abusing the world. And they lost."

"Did they though, Toby?" Tamsin said. "We both lost someone. That was it. One and one. The others got away. Nothing changed."

"My party split," Kit said. They sat down next to Morgan, limbs untangling as though they were still adjusting to life outside the birdcage. "And it wasn't because of the reasons you'd think. Half of us wanted to be heroes, and half of us thought it was just a game."

"What happened to them?" Morgan asked.

Kit shrugged.

"I know some are dead," they said. "The others might as well be. Look, I don't know much more about this place than when I arrived. But I know this much. You need each other, or it starts to tear at you. I don't think it wants to separate us to hurt us. I think it wants to teach us that we need each other, somehow."

"And it teaches us this by killing our friends." Tamsin said.

"I don't know," Kit said, running a hand through their dark, spiky hair. "Sometimes it feels like there's nobody at the wheel and we're all on our own."

"Like the real world," Tobias said.

"Like the real world," Morgan said.

Tamsin scooted off away from the group by herself, the magic cloak tightening around her protectively. Tobias dragged his blankets to curl up near his sister. Morgan made a few small gestures with his hand and a glimmering circle appeared for a split second around the camp, a trick he'd learned recently that would warn them if approached. He laid down on his back, keeping most of his armor on, war hammer by his side.

"It's harder when you know they're real, isn't it," Kit said softly in the dark.

"The people?" Morgan whispered back.

"Everything," Kit said. "They're not pixels on a screen. They're not miniatures on a board. I've been here long enough to know it's true. They're real."

"I know," Morgan said. "And it doesn't make things easier, that's for certain."

"I used to think Revery was meant to teach us empathy," Kit said. "To think about our actions more."

"Used to?" Morgan asked.

"Like I said. Sometimes it feels like there's nobody at the wheel."

"I don't know what's scarier. If it's all by design, or if it's all meaningless," Morgan said.

"Why not assume both," Kit said. "The existential crisis will be that much more intense."

Morgan laughed in the darkness, looking up at the stars. He gestured vaguely at the lumpy shape of Tamsin in the dark.

"I can't wait to see a more intense version of this," Morgan said.

"Give it time," Kit said, rolling over to sleep. "Just give it time."

Chapter 10: The Boneyard

The ranger turned the memory of his real name over and over in his mouth, fiddling with it like a loose tooth. The name was always somewhere on the tip of his tongue, a ghost barely concealed by a mind unwilling to see it. It's absence was infuriating. I should know who I am, he thought. I can remember so many other details. Where is my name?

He was going to ask the necromancer this very question just as they crested a hill, but what he saw below them stole the words from his mouth. The sky above was dark and sunless, and the ground turned rapidly from faded green grass to gray, dead ground. Scattered across the lifeless soil were bones, endless bones, as if a great massacre had occurred here and been forgotten by time.

Some of the bones moved.

Skeletons, mostly human, some certainly not, shuffled aimlessly in a mockery of life. Raven stole a glance at the necromancer's two skeleton companions. Over the weeks of travel, he'd come to have a sort of odd affection for the undead creatures, whom he'd started thinking of as Bert and Ernie, because Leo refused to tell him their real names. They were expressionless skulls, but compared to the shambling horrors below, they seemed full of life, almost smiling. The undead in the valley moved as though pulled by invisible marionette strings.

Silence padded up beside Raven and let loose a low growl that slowly turned into a whine. Raven reached down to scratch the wolf behind his ears.

"These friends of yours?" the ranger asked as Leo joined them on the top of the crest and leaned heavily on his staff.

"Shit," Leo said. "Either the swarm migrated, or we're a few miles off course. I planned on avoiding this place."

"Great directions," Raven said.

"You're the ranger. Aren't you supposed to detect these things?" Raven shrugged.

"I assume we have to go around," he said.

"Not necessarily," Leo said. "They'll leave me alone because, well, I'm me. You're mostly dead at the moment so they won't pay you much mind. That leaves only…"

Leo looked at Silence and sighed.

"The dog."

"Wolf. And I'm not leaving my friend behind," Raven said.

"We could kill him and reanimated him like these two here," Leo said, gesturing at his skeletal companions.

Raven raised a finger aggressively at him.

"Not even remotely funny," he said.

"I thought I was funny," Leo said. "I really was a dog person in the real world, you know. I wouldn't actually hurt him."

He stared at the wolf again, this time Silence returning the stare with a judgmental glare.

"This is a tremendous waste of resources, but if you insist," he said, reaching into a pouch and pulling out a pinch of bone powder. He threw it in the air and said a few words in a language that made Raven's skin crawl. When he finished, Silence sat in the same spot he'd been seconds before, but now, his skin was sloughing off, revealing sharp bone and rotting meat

"What did you do to him?" Raven hissed, barely containing his anger.

"Nothing," Leo said. "It's an illusion. But it's good enough to fool the undead. Provided we move quickly. They'll just think he's another reanimated corpse."

Raven moved to pet Silence, but found himself too repulsed by the rotting flesh to follow through.

"It's temporary. Temporary enough we should start moving now," Leo said. "Don't worry, your corpse dog will be back to normal in a few minutes."

"C'mon, buddy," Raven said, gesturing for Silence to join him. Together they walked downhill, slowly but with purpose, trying to avoid tripping over old bones or getting too close to the shuffling dead.

"What is this place," Raven asked once he heard Leo catch up. The necromancer pointed at a skeleton, not one of his own, who got just a little too close, and said "don't" in a soft, firm voice. The skeleton meandered off in another direction as if chastised.

"It's called the Boneyard," Leo said.

"Creative," Raven said. He felt a bit of bone splinter and crunch beneath his boot. "I came back to life for this. So worth it."

"It's the southern edge of the Badlands," Leo said. A marker of sorts. The bones are from a cataclysmic event they call the Blightstorm. Nothing good lives out past this marker, but most of it stays on the other side."

"And why are we headed into a place that sounds as welcoming as the Badlands, which has been poisoned by something even more charming, like the Blightstorm?"

"Is now really the time for this conversation?" Leo said, pointing at another skeleton who wandered close enough to get a stern finger wag.

"Look, you brought me back from the dead for something. The least you can do is educate me about why."

Leo looked up at the sky and muttered something about gods and patience. His two skeleton companions seemed to look at each other sympathetically, shrug awkwardly, then resume their vigilant stance.

"We're going into the Badlands for two reasons," Leo said. "One, there's something there I need you to look at. Something that will only make sense to someone whose story has ended."

"See, that makes no sense and yet also makes me feel useful. I'm not asking for much here," Raven said. Silence trotted past him, deftly avoiding any of the walking dead, looking back with a half-skull face, eyes burning with irritation as if to tell him to hurry up.

"And second, there's a seer out here I'd like you to meet," Leo said. "Like you, he exists outside the story. I think he'll open up to you. He speaks to me in riddles, but you might intrigue him enough to get him to speak plainly."

Raven could see the end of the Boneyard now, where the broken detritus began to give way to a blackened, angry plane. The horizon seemed to glow reddish gold, as though with heat.

"Look," Raven said, counting off the distance between himself and the edge of the Boneyard. A hundred feet, ninety, eighty. "You said I could find this seam, this rip in the world. Do you think the Badlands had something to do with it?"

"I don't know," Leo said. One of his skeleton companions tripped over a femur and almost fell on his face, but the other skeleton caught him and helped right him. "I've found tears. Ulcers in reality. But that's all they were. We need to find the source before it truly tears."

"What do you mean, ulcers?"

"Holes in reality. Places where I could look through."

"And what did you see on the other side?" Raven asked. "Did you see… did you see home?"

Leo shook his head. Together, they shuffled across the edge of the Boneyard, gritty, shattered remains giving way to silky black powder beneath their feet.

"I saw this world but better. I saw this world but worse."

"Alternate realities?" Raven asked.

Leo threw his hands up noncommittally.

"Maybe they were just mirrors to another time. I don't know. That's what I need you to find out for me."

As they crossed out of the Boneyard, Raven turned back, watching the sleepy movements of the skeletons as they drifted aimlessly in the lifeless ground behind them. He felt a sudden pang of empathy for them, forever haunting a place no one cared about, in a world that seemed half-made and half-forgotten.

"Do you ever think about setting them free?" Raven asked, gesturing at the undead. "That maybe there's someone in each of those bodies, trapped and suffering?"

Leo leaned on his staff once again, staring out across the Boneyard as if seeing it with fresh eyes.

"I've never considered it," he said. "I don't know what's inside them. Even these two."

He gestured at Bert and Ernie with a false dismissiveness that gave the barest hint of affection.

"I don't know what they remember, or who's in there. It could be it's just bones, reanimated by magic, following the ghosts of instinct long buried. Or maybe these are the last vestiges of a soul. Maybe undeath has kept them from whatever amounts to heaven or

Valhalla or whatever here. Or maybe undeath keeps them from oblivion. Frankly, my alarmingly nihilistic friend, you know better than I do what awaits them. Is it better than this?'

Raven thought about the quiet emptiness he'd seen on the other side. The silence. The utter isolation. He felt, in that moment, every inch of this almost-living body. Its limits, but also its presence, the weight and realness of it. And in his heart, he did not know which was worse.

"Leave them, I guess," he said, and he began walking into the blackened desert of the Badlands, thinking about eternity, and emptiness, and impossible answers.

Chapter 11: Hate and fear

Cordelia awoke to the sound of birds in the trees and a soft hissing noise she knew was Hark sharpening his axes. She rolled over to see Eriko out cold, drooling slightly in her sleep, and sat up gingerly. Her legs were tired from their journey, of course, but it occurred to her that this was also the best she'd felt in some time. She hadn't taken a beating in a battle since the Tomb of the Maker, and it almost felt as though her body had forgiven her for the punishing damage she'd put it through in recent months.

Probably means a dragon will come tromping over the next hill, she mused. But it was nice to not feel like she'd been pushed down a cliff for once.

She found Hark a respectful distance away, trying to work on his weapons without disturbing his companions. He barely looked up at her but nodded in welcome as he sensed her approach.

"I'm jealous of you," he said. "That axe you carry is enchanted, isn't it. Doesn't dull."

"I suppose it is," she said. She drew Ingo the dwarf's axe from the loop on her belt and looked at it, really looked at it, for the first time in a while. Hark's weapons were all function, built to last, but not with an artist's flair, not like the one she carried.

"Where'd you get it?" Hark asked. He checked the edge of one axe, then started sharpening the other.

"A dying dwarf gave it to me. Asked me to take his to his

daughter." She slid the axe back into its loop. "I guess I failed on that promise."

"You'll find your way there eventually," Hark said. "And by then the weapon will have a story. A blade like that, it deserves a story behind it."

"I guess," she said, thinking back to the hate in Ingo's voice when they first met, the glimmer of reconciliation at the end, the way she didn't want to forgive him but rather forget him. She'd dealt with bigoted old men her whole life. His attitude wasn't new. She didn't care enough to want to redeem him, either. But then there was the stupid axe, and what to do with it. She returned her attention to Hark. "Can I ask you a question?"

"Of course."

"Why does this world hate orcs?"

Hark stopped the rhythmic motion of sharpening his axe and set it aside, looking her in the eyes now.

"I said you were different when I meet you," Hark said. "I knew it. What are you, really? Did you grow up among humans? Have friends in the right places? I'm not judging you, mind. I'm just curious. You're different."

"I'm not…" Cordelia trailed off. "I'm not from here."

"This region?"

"Sort of," Cordelia said. "I don't have any point of reference for this world. But I know what it's like to be hated, and I know people hate people like, well, us. And I just want to know why. I understand hate in general, I mean. I'm talking about orcs specifically."

Hark stretched out his legs, rolled his neck until something popped back into place.

"I figure people just need someone to blame their troubles on," Hark said. "We're different, so we scare them, and we don't have much, so we're easy to strike down upon. We believe different things, and that makes us dangerous, in their eyes. And in the end, it's easier to hate someone else than blame yourself for all your problems."

"Yeah," Cordelia said.

"I've been among humans. They bring their own pestilence, they inflict violence on each other, they hate other humans who are more similar to them than different, but just different enough. And not just humans. Elves, dwarves, even orcs, we're all capable of hating ourselves as much as we hate others. But it's easier to lash out at someone different. To assert power. To create a villain."

"People need villains, don't they," Cordelia said. "They make society afraid to change."

"And the more different that villain is, the shorter the leap to making them a monster."

"I was hoping, when we came here, that it'd be different. That it'd be better," Cordelia said. "Hate like this is just so… mundane, y'know? It's just such a cheap, sloppy way to make you feel better about your own misery. God, I thought I'd want to stay here to escape everything that was wrong with where we came from and it's just a different flavor of terrible."

"Do you want to go back?" Hark said. "To wherever you came from?"

Cordelia found herself off her footing. I haven't thought enough about this, she realized. It's been one crisis to another, one terrible experience to another, and there was no way home anyway, so why waste time daydreaming about it.

"I don't know," she said. "What would you do?"

"I don't know anything about where you came from," Hark said. "I can't answer that. But before I ran into the two of you, I was going to go north into the wildlands and disappear. I thought I'd had enough of other people. The ones you love get taken away, and everyone else isn't worth knowing."

"But you're still here. With us."

"I know a good person when I meet one," Hark said. He gestured at the still sleeping Eriko with his chin. "Maybe even two. You seem the types to leave the world better than you found it. Thought maybe I could help a little."

Cordelia hesitated, then placed a hand on the back of Hark's. She'd never been good at casual affection. Touching his hand felt awkward and strange. But he smiled at her, his craggy face close enough she could see the creases in the laugh lines.

"Thanks for staying. We couldn't do this without you."

"I reckon you could," Hark said. "But a little help never hurt."

Chapter 12: Hawksmith Academy

They could see the Hawksmith Academy long before they arrived Tobias thought this was really more of a tease than anything else.

It looked like an oil painting; a tall, classic fortress atop a craggy hill, with a long, winding, elevated road leading up to a massive portcullis. The academy had multiple spires, at least a half-dozen Tobias could spot at this distance, and conical roofs of red, with green ivy crawling up the stone walls. The front faced a wide-open field, long blades of golden grass swaying in the breeze of an oncoming storm. Gray and purple mountains stood in the distance behind the academy like a canvas backdrop.

"I'm sort of disappointed it looks exactly as I pictured it," Tobias said, swaying easily on the back of his stolen horse.

"I don't see a soul up there," Morgan said. "No one manning the walls. No guards."

"I told you it was abandoned," Kit said.

"Empty of people doesn't mean empty of answers," Tamsin said. She spurred her horse on, and the others followed. Not as though we have anywhere else we can go, Tobias thought.

The road to the academy looked more harrowing from a distance, but the closer they got, the less alarming it appeared. There were no guardrails, leaving the path open on either side as it rose steadily higher into the air, but the path was wide enough for two wagons to pass side by side. Still, Tobias dismounted and walked his horse up the road rather than ride, as vertigo kicked in from the raised view he had on horseback. Tamsin and Kit dismounted as well, though Morgan stayed on a bit longer, saying he could get a better view from the back of his horse.

"Also," he said, "I'm wearing heavy armor, and this is a long walk."

They reached the portcullis, a waffled pattern of black iron, etched with runes. It was closed.

"It's enchanted," Tamsin said, waving an irritated hand at the gate.

"And too heavy for us to lift, even if we wanted to," Tobias said after a few half-hearted attempts. He had a spell that could open a locked door, but after looking at the arcane sigils Tamsin had pointed out, Tobias began to have visions of casting his spell and being knocked back by protective enchantments so violently he would fall over the edge of the road.

"We should figure something out soon," Morgan said. He pointed out southwest from where they'd come. A dusty cloud was moving toward them. Riders of some kind.

"Think it's Zayne's men?" Tobias asked.

"Can't tell from here," Kit said. "But I'd rather not find out."

Tamsin began softly chanting the words of a spell. Her eyes glowed briefly and she scanned the entire portcullis quickly.

"I don't see a way to break the enchantment," she said. "Who would've thought an academy of magicians would be good at their security?"

"They're definitely headed this way, whoever they are," Morgan said. Tobias saw him place a hand absently on the hilt of his war hammer and realized he'd already half-drawn his sword from the scabbard.

"Maybe we try knocking?" Tobias suggested.

Morgan gave him a long, irritated stare. Tamsin just shook her head. Kit shrugged.

"Why not?" they said.

"Sure," Tobias said. "Why not."

So he walked up to the portcullis and politely rapped his knuckles against the frame.

"Bonjour!" Tobias said. "It's just a few traveling salespeople! Are you interested in buying cosmetics?"

"Look it'll be fine," Kit said. "It's not like they know we killed the other soldiers."

"Aside from the fact that we have their horses," Tobias said. "Also we're traveling with a former inmate of a roadside jail cell."

"Shit," Kit said. "Y'know what? I actually missed being in trouble like this."

"Hey, big guy," Tobias said to Morgan. "Any chance you've got some sort of divine intervention up your sleeve?"

"The lady upstairs doesn't seem to be answering," Morgan said. He slid his hammer from its loop and prepared to fight, a look of resignation on his face.

Tobias drew the Singing Sword and began to hum a tune from *Les Misérables* under his breath. The moment he turned from the portcullis, he heard a clunk behind him, and the sound of chains moving. He whipped around to look at his sister.

"What did you do?" he said.

"I didn't do anything," Tamsin said, wide-eyed, holding her empty hands out at her sides. "This wasn't me."

The gate began to rise, revealing the interior of the academy, a wide quad that might have been serene once, now overgrown and sloppy. Kit grabbed the reins of their horses and began leading them inside even before the portcullis was fully opened. Morgan and Tobias hung back as Tamsin ran inside, watching the oncoming horses, the livery of the guards they'd encountered the day before.

"I know they were bad guys, but maybe let's make sure your sister doesn't rage murder a bunch of guys who work for a local evil lord until we have a game plan next time," Morgan said.

"Y'know, they always said I was the impulsive twin," Tobias said. Together, they stepped inside the gate, which immediately began to lower back into place. He raised an eyebrow at Morgan. "Good sign?"

"Or we're trapped in here," Morgan said.

"I am so happy to have you along on this journey," Tobias said "Every party needs a pooper."

"Guys?" Tamsin said, and the men spun around, weapons drawn.

"What now," Morgan said. And then: "Oh."

In the center of the quad was an enormous tree, a weeping willow that seemed to Tobias to have a semblance of a face naturally formed in the trunk. Sitting beneath the tree was a tiny creature, not but three feet tall, green-skinned with ears like chef's knives, dressed in shabby wizard robes.

"If this guy speaks in a weird syntax, I'm going to be thrilled," Tobias said.

The little goblin clambered stiffly to his feet and waddled over with the help of a staff that would have just been a cane for any of them. He stared at them with enormous yellow eyes for a long moment, saying nothing. Tobias thought about making a joke but thought better of it. Look at that, he said. I'm gaining emotional maturity.

"You were very loud out there," the goblin said, finally.

"Yeah, well, we were in a rush," Tobias said. "Bad guys chasing us."

The goblin looked at their horses, then back at them.

"Worse than horse thieves?" he said.

"Possession is nine-tenths of the law," Tobias said.

"Ah!" the goblin said, pulling a thin chain around his neck from within his robes. A set of monocles, with glass of different colors, hung there. He held one up in front of yes eye, squeezing the other closed tightly, then switched between several monocles until he nodded in satisfaction.

"Yes," he said. "You're from the Third Plane," he said. "I knew it the minute you showed up on our doorstep."

"The Third Plane?" Tamsin said.

"Our?" Morgan said.

"Typical Third Planers, all sarcasm and questions," the goblin said. "Come along. I'll put some tea on. I haven't had company in a while."

A banging came from the portcullis, accompanied by men shouting to open the gate.

"So about those guys," Tobias said.

"Ah. Yes," the goblin said. He made a gesture in the air, said something in an arcane language, and then the voices at the door started to cry out in fear, or pain, or both.

"Hang on, what just—" Morgan said, but the goblin continued to walk away, toward a cozy little building to the left the quad.

"So many questions," the goblin said. "Do you take milk in your tea?"

Chapter 13: Not exactly Hogwarts

Tamsin had always imagined herself at a school for magic. Long after she had been expected to grow out of it, she'd still daydream about being whisked away to some school of wonder and whimsy, where she could learn to summon mysterious creatures or control flames or wind.

In exactly none of those fantasies did the school look like the Hawksmith Academy. When she'd first heard the name, she envisioned a sort of Hogwarts, but college. Or maybe Brakebills. She would have settled for Xavier's School for Gifted Youngsters. But Hawksmith, in its current state, was nothing like any of those places. It reminded Tamsin, strangely, of the castle of Tir Asleen in the movie *Willow*, a once-beautiful, but eerily abandoned, structure of stone and shadow. Following the diminutive goblin inside for tea, she found herself scanning darker places for wandering trolls.

The goblin handed Morgan a steaming cup of tea in a surprisingly delicate teacup, already prepared as though the group had been expected. Morgan looked at the tea with confusion.

"What about the men outside?" Morgan asked.

"Oh, those ruffians? They can't get in," the goblin said. "Nobody can get in."

"Without your permission," Morgan said.

"No, without…" the goblin gestured all around. "Without the academy's permission. Lord Zayne's been trying to get people inside for years now. It's fun to watch them try."

"I'm sorry. We weren't properly introduced," Tobias said as the goblin handed him a cup next. "I'm Oberon the Blue."

"No you're not," the goblin said. He made a dismissive tsking noise with his tongue. "I know people from the Third Plane when I see them. You're not fooling anyone."

Tamsin had been inspecting a bookshelf that had seen better days when the goblin corrected her brother, and she turned her attention fully on the small creature.

"I'm sorry, the Third Plane?" she asked. The goblin was holding a cup of tea to her expectantly. Somewhere in few seconds she'd been turned away, Kit had also been furnished with a cup.

"The Third Plane. You're from the place above, yes?"

Tamsin shook her head.

"You're going to have to forgive our ignorance," she said. "We haven't heard the term before, um…"

"Gristle. I'm Gristle the Destroyer, the Second," the goblin said.

"Gristle the Destroyer," Tobias repeated.

"The Second," the goblin said. "It's a family name."

"I inferred," Tobias said. "If we're from the Third Plane, where are we now?"

"Revery. The one in-between. The Second Plane," Gristle said.

"Hey, Gristle," Kit interrupted, sitting languidly in a chair that cracked underneath them loud enough they stood back up again immediately. "Where is everyone?"

"Define 'everyone,'" Gristle said.

"I'd heard Hawksmith was a bustling place, not too long ago. Where did the students go? Where are the teachers?"

"Oh!" Gristle said, slurping his tea loudly. "They evacuated."

Tamsin looked over to Morgan who was staring back her with the same worried look she'd given him.

"Uh, why'd they evacuate?" Tobias said.

"And where?" Morgan said.

Gristle pulled down a jar from a nearby shelf and unscrewed the top, placing it down on the table between all of them.

"Biscuits," he said. "Try dunking them."

"Where did everybody go, Gristle?" Morgan repeated.

"Oh," Gristle said. "Most went to the First Plane."

"Is the First Plane like the Third Plane?" Tamsin asked.

Gristle shook his head.

"It's more like Revery, of course," he said. "Because Revery is a dream of the First Plane."

"This makes perfect sense to me," Tobias said. "How about you all?"

"Gristle," Tamsin said, softly. "Why did they evacuate?"

"Because Revery is dying," Gristle said. "And they thought it would be better to not lose so much knowledge when it is no more."

"I thought that was a myth," Kit said. Tamsin raised an eyebrow at them quizzically. "It's an old faerie tale they tell to scare kids, that you can find the edge of the world, where Revery is dying. But I've never seen it, and I've been all over."

"So they just… abandoned Revery, and the Hawksmith Academy," Tamsin said.

"Well, no," Gristle said. "There is a Hawksmith Academy in every plane."

Tamsin felt a spike of excitement in belly. Every plane?

"Even the Third Plane?" she asked.

"Yes," Gristle said. "But nobody likes it there."

"But they still left this world to die," Morgan said. "That doesn't sit right."

"They seek knowledge elsewhere," Gristle said. "Ways to save this world. Revery is a young place. The thinkers here thought they might find answers elsewhere."

"And if not, at least they wouldn't be on a sinking ship," Morgan said derisively.

"Hey Gristle," Tobias said. The goblin looked up at him expectantly. "Why are you still here if they're gone?"

The goblin smiled proudly.

"I volunteered to stay and mind the place," he said. "Answer the door, take any messages that might come our way."

"But the world is dying," Tobias said, his tone uncharacteristically serious. "Doesn't that mean you'll die too?"

Gristle shrugged his bony little shoulders.

"This is my home. I didn't want to leave it. So I stayed," he said. "It was the choice I made."

Tamsin's breath caught in her throat. Determining your own fate. Being willing to die for it. She felt a pang in her chest.

"Gristle, if we're from another plane of existence, are we really here?" she asked. "I mean, physically. Is this my body, or is it some shell, or projection, or something like that?"

"Of course you're you," Gristle said. "You're always you. Unless you're someone else. But no, you're not an avatar. This is the you of the Third Plane."

"Out of curiosity, do you know if time works the same way on all the planes?" Tamsin pressed. "Like, for example, ten days pass in Revery, does, say, only one does in the Third Plane?"

"No, that's not correct," the goblin said.

"So every day we're here, we lose a day back home," Morgan said.

The goblin nodded. Morgan put a hand over his own mouth as if biting back a scream.

"We've been gone for months," Morgan said. "Our lives, Tamsin. Everything we had back home must be."

"Holy shit," Kit said. "I've been here four *years*."

"I am so glad I decided to put off getting a dog," Tobias said. "Are we all going to be fired from our jobs when we go back?"

"Are we going to be legally dead when we get back?" Morgan said, his voice cracking. "Toby, this is even worse than I expected."

"Your expectations for a right and just universe needs to be adjusted before you explode, Morgan," Tobias said. "Of course we're screwed. Why wouldn't we be screwed?"

Morgan sat down and put his face in his hands.

"We are all screwed," he said .

There was a pause, as though nobody knew what ask next. But the answer to that was simple.

"Gristle, if we die here, we die for real, right?" Tamsin said, her stomach churning.

Gristle nodded affirmative.

"Oh, Jack," Tamsin said, exhaling sharply.

"Wait," Morgan said, standing up. "Just hang on one second. These aren't the questions we came here to ask."

"No," Tamsin said, rubbing her eyes tiredly. "They're not."

"Gristle, we were told the Hawksmith Academy might know something about bringing someone back from the dead," Morgan said. "One of our friends fell in combat, and we want to bring him back."

Gristle nodded sagely, and rubbed his chin with a small, clawed hand.

"Resurrection? Yes, we knew how to do that," he said. "There were many ways."

Tamsin exhaled sharply. Morgan waited for her to speak, but she gestured for him to continue leading the conversation.

"And can you teach us how to do that?" Morgan said.

"I can't, not me, not me, I'm sorry," Gristle said. "But the things you need are in the vault."

"Great!" Tobias said. "So you can just let us into the vault and we'll be on our way."

"Small problem," Gristle said. "But it's nothing you can't handle I'm sure."

"Don't think so highly of us," Tobias said. "What's this small problem? I'm sure it's not small at all, I can tell by the tone of your voice."

"The academy brought as much of their knowledge and magical items as they could when they evacuated, but what they couldn't carry, they put in the vault for safe keeping. But to keep evil-doers away from their stores of knowledge, they put protections in place."

"Traps?" Kit asked.

"Locks?" Tobias asked.

"Guard monsters," Tamsin said rather than asked. She already knew the answer before she said it.

"All of the above," Gristle said. "Also some varmints that got in there after everyone left."

"Varmints," Morgan said, the exhaustion in his voice palpable.

"But if you can get past them, you can certainly find teachings on resurrection," Gristle said.

"I don't suppose they left you with the password to bypass all these protections, did they, my new friend?" Tobias asked.

"I'm afraid I'm just the gatekeeper, not the true guardian," Gristle said. "But I can show you to the vault! And also give you snacks if you'd like."

"Great!" Tobias said, springing to his feet. "Look on the bright side, gang. If one of us gets killed breaking into the vault, the survivors, hypothetically, should be able to bring them back to life. It'll be fine. Lead on, my good man, kindly show us snacks and vaults."

Chapter 14: Why is it always crawling

Gristle lead them down a disconcertingly long spiral staircase in one of the central buildings on the Hawksmith Academy quad, the way lit by candles that clearly no one had been around to light. Morgan looked at how far off the ground the candles were compared to Gristle's three-foot-tall frame and assumed they were either magic, or there were ghosts who just wandered the halls on candle maintenance duty, and neither option appealed to him very much.

They reached a landing at the bottom of the stairs, a relatively square room ending in a massive, barred door. Morgan reached out to run his hand along the frame, looking for flaws.

"That's a good door," Morgan said.

"It is of very high quality, yes," Gristle said.

"Any chance you've got the key?"

The goblin held out his hands apologetically.

"No key," Kit said, running a hand impatiently through their hair.

Tobias walked up to the door, rapped it a few times with his knuckles, and shrugged.

"Another dungeon, another crawl," he said. "Why is it always crawling? Why can't it be dancing? Strutting?"

"Dungeon crawl and we're down one rogue and one barbarian," Morgan said. "I knew splitting the party was stupid."

"We're down one ranger, too," Tamsin said. "That's why we're here."

She pushed her brother gently aside, placed her hand on the lock, and uttered a single arcane phrase. Morgan heard gears click into place, and the door creaked open.

"New trick?" Tobias asked.

"New trick," Tamsin said.

Morgan started to push past the twins to take the lead, but Kit put a hand on his shoulder.

"This was my job," they said. "I was a professional door kicker. Let me go first."

"This isn't your fight," Morgan said. "You don't have to come with us. No reason to risk your life for someone you never met."

Kit shot him a crooked smile and then slid the sword they'd borrowed from Tobias from its sheath.

"I haven't had a good group to go delving with in a long time," they said. "This'll be fun. Besides, if they locked up spell books and other secrets in here, maybe I can replace this toothpick your bard gave me."

"Okay, new friend," Tobias said to Gristle. "Provided nothing in there kills us, what are we looking for?"

The goblin considered the question for a minute, scratching his chin with sharp little nails.

"Tomes of white magic, to start," Gristle said. "They left many spell books and scrolls behind, which you might use to learn the spellcraft you need."

"Spell books, naturally," Tamsin said. "Anything else?"

"Resurrection spells require powerful ingredients," he said. "They did not bring all of those valuable items with them when they left, just in case there was ever a need in the future. There should be stockpiles of those components in storage within."

"Awesome. Do you know what sort of items a resurrection spell would need, though?" Morgan said.

Gristle shrugged.

"Expensive ones? The spell books will tell you, I'm sure."

"Right. Why make it easy," Tobias said. "Y'know, I genuinely enjoyed Revery for a little while. Clearly I was bamboozled."

"Hey Gristle," Kit said. "Any magic weapons in there?"

"Probably," the little creature said.

"Mind if I take one if I find one I like?"

Again, Gristle shrugged.

"No one else is using them," he said.

"Great," Kit said, rubbing their hands together and slapping Morgan on the shoulder. "See? No reason to feel bad about me coming along. I get to pick out a prize."

Kit led the way through the door, with Tobias close behind. Morgan and Tamsin brought up the rear. As they walked inside the doorway, Morgan looked back at Gristle.

"You're not screwing with us, right?" he asked.

Gristle shrugged.

"I'm just the gatekeeper," he said. "I'm sure there is plenty down there to screw with you so I don't have to."

And the door slammed shut of its own accord.

"Guys, I don't think Gristle was being entirely honest with us," Tobias said.

But before Morgan could answer, the floor dropped out from beneath the entire group.

They found themselves sliding down a wildly steep ramp where the floor once was. Morgan immediately felt like a trash can thrown down a flight of stairs, his armor clanking and scraping the entire way down the chute. Tobias became a stream of obscenities as he rolled ass over teakettle past him. He saw Kit struggling to use their sword to slow their descent unsuccessfully, and then Tamsin, almost trance-like, just riding the fall calmly, waiting for the inevitable end.

That inevitable end came abruptly as the ramp dumped the party out onto a flat stone floor. Morgan remained laying on his back for a moment, trying to assess the damage and entirely unwilling to stand back up in his heavy armor yet.

"Everyone okay?" he said, a little louder than he'd intended.

"I think I broke my coccyx," Tobias said.

"I changed my mind," Kit said. "I want to go back. Can I go back?"

Tamsin was on her feet, a light spell drifting above her palm to brighten the room. She wobbled a bit as she got her bearings.

"Another empty room," she said. "Two doors."

"I love when a dungeon gives us options," Tobias said, irritably getting back to his feet. "Multiple choice torture."

"Maybe take the volume down a notch, Toby," Tamsin said. "Gristle said something about guard monsters."

"He also said nothing about trap doors, so who knows what the little jackass knows," Tobias said. "Hey, the Hawksmith people… they're supposed to be the good guys, yeah?"

"It's what I'd been told," Kit said. "Never met anyone. Never really believed when anyone said they were the good guys, though. Why?"

"Just thinking," Tobias said.

"We've talked about this. Don't do that," Tamsin said.

"No, seriously. If they're the good guys, why would they put guard monsters in their basement?"

"To keep idiots like us from stealing their stuff?" Morgan said.

"No, I mean, wouldn't that be cruel? Trapping something in a dark dungeon for all eternity?" Tobias said. "That seems kind of awful."

"Depends on what they've trapped down here," Tamsin said. "Maybe they only used monsters that were safer kept underground."

"This new version of you where you're an eternal ray of fucking sunshine is a great improvement, Tam," Tobias said. "I feel reassured by literally everything you say now."

"Shush," Morgan said. "Does anyone else smell sulfur?"

"You need me to be quiet so you can smell more clearly?" Tobias said.

"I will slap you upside your damned head, Tobias," Morgan said.

"I smell sulfur," Kit said.

"Is that what that is? I thought it was just the general funk of an abandoned dungeon," Tobias said. "Yes, I smell sulf—"

Tobias was cut off mid-sass as an inky black tentacle dropped down from the ceiling and wrapped around his neck, lifting him off his feet. His eyes bulged and his hands wrapped around the coil trying to free himself.

"Toby!" Tamsin yelled, and she sent her arcane light source spiraling up higher in the room to illuminate what had her brother in its grasp. Clinging to the ceiling was a roiling mass of oily, thick fluid that seemed to move with if not an intelligence of its own, certainly a sort of hungry malevolence.

Tamsin reached her hand back as if to throw a spell, then turned quickly to Morgan.

"Is sulfur flammable?" she asked.

"I don't know!" Morgan said.

"Usually!" Kit yelled, and then they kicked off the wall, sword in hand, and leapt toward Tobias and the black tentacle holding him aloft. His blade bit into the tendril, tearing it, but not enough to cut Tobias loose as he continued to rise closer and closer to the shapeless monster above. The bard was scrambling to draw his magic sword from its scabbard, but every time he released one hand from the tendril he'd start kicking desperately as it choked him more.

Tamsin cursed under her breath and made a series of mystic gestures with both hands. A sliver of ice formed in the air above her, like a rough sketch of a sword, and she pointed aggressively at the mass of ink-colored movement on the ceiling. The icy blade darted forth like a missile, exploding on impact and sending a cloud of ice and half-frozen bits of black gelatin down onto the party below. Morgan turned to cover his eyes just in time to see another tendril, which had coiled down the wall behind him, lash out to grab at him. He swung his hammer with adrenaline-fueled speed, knocking it aside with an amount of force that surprised even himself, but the tentacle seemed to just brush off the blow and continue toward him.

A blade flashed and the tendril fell to the floor, still wriggling and squirming to rejoin the greater mass of the creature. Kit saluted him with their sword and adopted a fighting stance.

"It's the whole ceiling," Tamsin said, putting her back against Morgan's. Tobias had his sword out, casually hanging at his side. "Any bright ideas?"

"I could sing to it," Tobias said, sounding vaguely nauseous.

"Bright," Morgan said, laughing to himself. "Hang on."

He reached his free hand beneath his tabard and drew out the holy symbol of Theana. It still felt strange, asking favors of a fictional goddess, but he couldn't deny that it worked here in Revery. He didn't like the idea of praying, but he asked her for her help. If you wouldn't mind, he thought, we could use a bit of your light right now.

The holy symbol began to glow with an intense golden light. It drove all shadow from the room, and caused the twins and Kit to all shield their eyes. From above them, there came an alien squealing noise, though fear or pain Morgan couldn't tell. The oozing creature, whatever it was, peeled back, recoiling from the light, until it was completely hidden under the ramp the party had slide down to get here.

The group backed away together into the right-hand doorway leading out. Morgan wondered if they were choosing the wrong path, but at this point, either seemed better than staying here.

"Quick thinking there, priest," Kit said, lowering their sword halfway, not taking their eyes off the room they'd just left.

"Only problem I can see is it'll be there if we have to go back out the way we came in," Tamsin said.

"That's a problem for later-us to deal with," Tobias said. "Now-us have other issues to worry about."

They continued down the corridor, Morgan remaining at the back with his holy symbol held up in case the shapeless monster pursued them. He heard Tobias swearing and turned his attention his companions.

"Oh, that's not ominous at all," Morgan said.

The corridor ended in a doorway. A doorway with eyes. A doorway, with eyes, designed so that the frame of the door itself was surrounded by pointed, serrated teeth.

"Do we just… open it?" Tobias said.

"No," Tamsin, Morgan, and Kit all said simultaneously.

"Fine then," Tobias said. "Hello, door!"

The eyes opened.

"Shit!" Tobias and Tamsin said in the exact same tenor and tone.

The door blinked at them, and then it began to laugh. It was a melodic laugh, rich and musical. It reminded Morgan instantly of Audrey II from *Little Shop of Horrors*.

"I swear to God if this thing says 'feed me' I'm gonna—" Morgan started to say.

And then the door said:

"Feed me."

"I hate this place so much," Morgan said, and lifted his hammer again.

Chapter 15: Old Bobby

The ranger awoke at dawn, the sun in these badlands was never much more than a red sliver on the horizon, casting angry shadows across a blackened, dusty landscape. The necromancer was already awake, puttering with a modest breakfast, some sort of gruel he'd made in a pot over their small fire. He handed Raven a bowl, which he accepted, though he found he never really grew hungry anymore. He ate the food offered because it made him feel warm inside, some small semblance of normalcy in this cold body.

Leo stared off into the distance as if looking for something. Raven placed his bowl on the ground so Silence could finish off his meal, the wolf happily making short work of whatever breakfast it had contained.

"What are we doing out here, anyway," Raven said, hand-feeding strips of jerky to the wolf. Normally Silence was skilled at foraging for himself, but the ranger had a bad feeling there wasn't much by way of game for him to hunt out here in the wastes.

"I want you to talk to someone," Leo said, beginning to pack up his things.

"Friend of yours?"

"More of an acquaintance," the necromancer said. "An outsider. Not native to Revery."

"So like us," Raven said.

"Yes and no. He's not from here, but he's not from where we're from, either."

"Aliens."

"Not all that far from the truth," Leo said. "Anyway. Old Bobby won't talk to me. Says he only wants to talk with interesting people. I figure a traveler from another world who has been raised from the dead might get his interest going."

"You must love that," Raven said.

"Irritates the living shit out of me, to be honest," Leo said. "I'm not interesting?"

Raven shrugged. He looked at Silence, and the wolf appeared to shrug back at him.

"The wolf doesn't find you interesting," Raven said.

Leo shrugged, resigned, and handed his pack to one of the skeletal servants.

"So if we get him talking, you want me to what, ask what's wrong with the world?" Raven said.

"You can ask him whatever you want," Leo said. "But it would be great if you could squeeze that one in. Maybe also how to fix it."

Raven shrugged, dusted off his pants, and hefted his own pack.

The necromancer led them up a rocky incline of black stone, marked by a natural, or at least seemingly natural, spiral walkway leading up to the top of the ridge. They made for an odd company, a necromancer, a half-living ranger, a wolf, and two silent, cheerful skeletons. If they were anywhere else in the world, Raven might have wondered what onlookers made of them; but here, in the middle of nowhere, they simply were what they were, a macabre menagerie heading for nowhere.

Raven soon heard a voice muttering to itself. Barely coherent, the voice was clearly engaging in a conversation with itself, answering its own questions, arguing against itself. When they got close enough to make out real words, Leo drew back his hood and called out.

"Bobby?" he said, his voice even and calm, almost soothing. "It's your old friend Mordecai the Unholy. I've brought company."

"Go away. You're boring," a scratchy, taut voice said.

Raven followed the voice to the source and found himself staring at an emaciated, green-skinned humanoid, glaring back at him with enormous yellow eyes. His head was slightly oversized, the skull possessing an alien shape to it. His limbs were spindly, unnaturally long for the creature's short, bare torso. A pair of batlike wings sprouted from his back, outstretched as if to absorb the scant, dry sunlight of this place. The creature wore only a ratty loincloth so grimy the ranger could barely make out its original color.

"Bobby, I'd like you to meet someone," Leo said. "His story is over, but he still walks."

The creature hopped down off his rocky perch and crept forward, staring at Raven with eyes the size of tangerines.

"You're not alive," Old Bobby said. "You're not dead though. What are you? Oh. Oh, Mordecai the Unholy, you continue to live up to your name. You made a revenant, didn't you, you cruel old man."

"I brought him back, yes," Leo said. "He still has a purpose in this world."

"No, no he doesn't," Old Bobby said, leaning in closer. His breath smelled like hot pavement. "You were complete, weren't you, dead but not dead one. You were complete, and this necromancer stole that from you."

Raven nodded, eyes darting at Leo, barely hiding his disdain.

"Those in the middle have a special place here, don't they Bobby?" Leo said. "They are privy to things others aren't. They get to peek behind the curtain."

"You be quiet, sorcerer," Old Bobby said. "I'm talking to the revenant. You've been outside this world twice, haven't you, unliving one. Once when you were born, and once when you died."

"I guess that's so," Raven said.

The creature leaned even closer, and Silence began to growl.

"Hush, dog," Old Bobby said. "The fey don't scare me. You have no power here."

"Fey?" Raven said.

Old Bobby pointed at Silence.

"You think that's just a dog?" the creature said. "He's a creature of pixie dust and chaos, and he knows what he is. Don't you, dog."

The wolf growled again but took a step back, huffing sullenly.

"What did you see on the other side?" Old Bobby asked. He backed away with a bouncing step and found a new perch on a knee-high rock. "Was it dark? Was it light? Did you go home?"

"Dark," Raven said. "But not in a bad way. It was peaceful."

"Is that what you wanted?"

"I—no," Raven said.

"Did you want Heaven? Yomi? Valhalla? Bulu? Lua-o-Milu? The Elysian Fields?"

Raven found himself taken aback by the terms. Words from his world, not Revery. The creature saw the look on his face and laughed.

"Yes, that's right, I know other worlds. I've been to many. I'll see others still. I am here in Revery only as long as it suits me."

"Good for you, then," Raven said.

"Good for me, yes. Not good for those who can't leave. Right, Mordecai the Unholy?"

"That's what we're trying to figure out, Bobby," Leo said. "To make things better for the folks who can't leave."

"Or who won't," Old Bobby said. He turned his attention back to Raven. "What about you? What do you want? To stay here? To live again, to feel your heart beating in your chest? Oblivion, as you hoped for but did not receive?"

"I don't know anymore," Raven said. "I wanted…"

He stopped himself, feeling stupid and lost. What am I doing out here in this wasteland, he thought. Being taunted by an alien and used by a necromancer. Everything's gone wrong.

"Go on," Bobby said, sitting down on his rock and swinging his legs like a child waiting for a story.

Raven fired a dirty look at Leo, then shrugged.

"I wanted to die doing something heroic," he said, finally. "I thought that would be the thing that made me feel complete. I never felt right in the other world, the one I'm from. And here I thought, well, I just want to do one thing right. Because I was tired of being me. And being someone else wasn't helping either."

"Revery gives you what you want, until it doesn't," Old Bobby said, his voice lower, more gravelly, more coherent than before.

Old Bobby whirled around and pointed at Leo with a long, clawed finger. Raven noticed that it had one more knuckle joint than a human finger would.

"Did you do this on purpose?" he said accusingly.

"I have no idea what you're talking about," Leo said, his expression one of genuine confusion.

"Revery can't resist a twice-tragic tale any more than it can resist great heroism," Old Bobby said. "Always the story, it's always the story it wants. You're a mean, clever, evil old man, Mordecai the Unholy. I am almost, almost in awe of your foresight."

"It wasn't foresight, Bobby," Leo said. "Maybe it's just fate."

The creature huffed and hopped away, wings fluttering to elevate him to a higher rock.

"He'll do, nonetheless," Bobby said. "The key is the right shape. A cruel jest, but you may yet save the waking dream. Now leave me, necromancer. I hope we never speak again."

"You always say that, Bobby," Leo said.

"And mean it, I always do," Old Bobby said. He leveled his eerie yellow eyes once more on Raven. "You exist outside the story now. Look for the flaw in the Maker's design. I am sorry this falls upon you, dead man."

"Yeah," Raven said, a gnawing feeling growing in his stomach. "Me too."

Chapter 16: The gateway to the soul, or something

Kit had to admit, while being eaten alive by a living, predatory doorframe wasn't on their list of experiences they had hoped to have in life, they were honestly having fun.

Not the predatory door part, if they were being honest. That was fairly unpleasant, punctuated by a horrible scraping sound as the creature's sharklike teeth grinded into Morgan's armor, or the terrible sloshing sound, followed by undignified yelping as the monster's massive, trunk-like tongue swatted the bard from his feet and sent him spiraling across the room.

No, the fight itself in all its disparate parts was not fun. But being among other adventurers again, people who wanted to be heroes, even if they were mostly not, that was what Kit had missed. Their friends were gone, disappeared or killed, leaving Kit here alone in this illogical world to fend for themselves. And Kit was pretty good at that if they allowed themself a moment of pride. A lone sellsword taking on bandits and dangerous beasts, surviving everything Revery threw at them, it wasn't a bad life. Kit was, if not happier in Revery, less miserable than they'd been back home.

But to be among companions again, even goofballs like these three, well, that was nice.

Kit's musing was cut short as a chair flew overhead, followed by Tobias, who had for at least the third time been thrown across the room by the creature's tongue, or whatever appendage it as using as a blunt weapon. The bard smirked at Kit as he climbed back to his feet, raising his sword, which had started singing at the start of the battle but been cut short by some sort of burst of anti-magic that exploded the moment Tamsin had reached for the doorknob. It wasn't a permanent effect—Tamsin fired a bolt of flame at the doorway a few seconds ago, which worked, if not effectively.

"Going to start singing again?" Kit asked, helping Tobias to his feet.

"It worked so well last time," he said.

"It's eating your friend," Kit said.

"I know," Tobias said, dusting himself off and raising his sword like a fencer. He took a step forward, then stopped. Morgan threw out a barrage of obscenities in the background. "I'm thinking, though. Is stabbing a door really effective?"

"Would someone get me out of here!" Morgan said, swing his hammer in vain trying to hit the door hard enough to unclench its jaws.

"Your friend is asking for help," Kit said.

"We're coming up with a plan!" Tobias yelled in Morgan's general direction.

"Tamsin! Don't let Tobias make the plan!" Morgan yelled.

The wizard, having been the first recipient of a bludgeoning attack by the tongue-thing before the bard, was leaning against the furthest wall, catching her breath. She waved at the cleric wordlessly.

"I think my sister is without a plan," Tobias said.

"Stabbing is the only idea I have," Kit said. "The downside to playing a warrior I guess."

"I'm going to reason with it," Tobias said.

"You're… going to reason with it."

"Maybe we hurt the door's feelings. I mean, I know if someone grabbed my doorknob while I wasn't looking I'd be upset."

Kit tilted their head at him.

"I can't tell if you mean for that to be innocent or filthy."

"That's my secret, Kit. I'm always filthy," Tobias said, and started walking off toward the door.

It'd be nice if he didn't get himself killed, Kit thought. I think I kind of like him a bit.

And then the idiot bard started to sing.

"You've lost… that lovin' feelin'…" Tobias began to croon.

"This is your plan?" Morgan yelled.

And then the door opened its mouth, dropped Morgan on the chamber floor, and started to sing back in a gorgeous baritone.

"Oh, that lovin' feelin'," the door sang.

And suddenly, Tobias and the door were doing an acapella rendition of the song, calling and answering each other with every other line. Then they started to intertwine into a harmony and Kit couldn't help but start laughing.

Tamsin helped Morgan to his feet and gave Kit a long, beleaguered stare.

"My brother," she said, shaking her head.

Tobias and the door were really starting to get into it now, moving from the Righteous Brothers to a hint of Elvis, even a dash of Hall and Oates.

"Every day, every single day, I find myself thinking, this is the weirdest thing I've ever seen," Morgan said.

"I think we can jump through the door when it hits a high note," Tamsin said.

"Yeah," Kit said. "Just have to time it right."

Tobias sheathed his sword and unslung his lute, doing a messy but workable version of the melody. He kicked out one foot, swaying his shoulders and swinging his hips like a Vegas musical act.

"I hate when he's right with these things," Tamsin said.

Kit listened to the lyrics, planning just the right moment, remembering how this was one of their father's favorite songs when they were growing up and how annoying he'd been singing it in the living room. But Kit still remembered all the lyrics, and knew just when to make their move.

"We gotta jump through on the whoa," Kit said.

"On the what?"

Rather than answer, Kit grabbed Tamsin's shoulder in one hand and Morgan's in the other, started running toward the door.

"And I can't go on," Tobias sang.

"Whoa-oh-oh-oh-oh," the door wailed, and Kit shoved all three of them through its open mouth, spilling onto the floor on the other side, Morgan's armor landing with the clang of a stack of dropped kitchen pans.

"I can't believe that worked," Tamsin said, brushing off her wizard robes and untangling them from around her legs.

Kit climbed to their feet and examined the room they were in.

Some sort of arcane, artificial light bathed the chamber in blue, revealing rows of books, a glass case with strange objects behind glass, and a door deeper into the tunnel. Tamsin began examining the books, looking interested, but unimpressed.

"What should we do about the bard?" Kit asked. "He can't sing forever."

"A, yes he can," Tamsin said. "And B, the way my brother works, we'll finish up in here and find him planning to start a band with the door and going on tour."

"You always said he could talk to a wall, but I never thought he'd sing to a door," Morgan said. "I wish I could enjoy the strangeness of this world more."

"So say we all," Kit said. They wandered over to the glass case to get a better look, and saw rings, medallions, and other objects the use or design not immediately obvious.

"Talismans or magic items, most likely," Tamsin said, joining kit by the case. "Is that a lamp?"

"Don't touch the lamp," Morgan said, his voice dropping an octave. "Never touch a magic lamp. Can we just get what we came for?"

"I'm looking for it," Tamsin said, a new edge to her voice.

Morgan began making his way through the next doorway, weapon in hand. Kit drew their sword and followed, waiting to see if Tamsin joined them, but the mage continued to examine the book collection in the first room. Morgan turned the corner, disappearing from sight, and then cursed under his breath.

"What?" Kit said, jogging to catch up.

This room was also filled with books, like the first, wall to wall shelves from floor to ceiling, but there were also cabinets of potions, bones, strange powders, all manner of spell components and alchemical inventions. Standing in the center of the room—well, Kit thought, more floating than standing—was a ghost, semi-transparent, a long, wild beard drifting around his chin.

The ghost turned to take them in, staring long and hard at both Morgan and Kit. Behind Tamsin caught up and stopped in her tracks.

"Hey, I found a book that might help—oh, come on," Tamsin said.

"Trespassers. You have bypassed the ooze of devouring, and made your way past the door that chews. You should not be here," the ghost said. "I have a single question for you."

"Okay," Morgan said reluctantly.

The ghost drifted in close, almost uncomfortably so, and whispered.

"Is the goblin still upstairs? I find him terribly annoying."

Kit looked at Morgan. Morgan turned to Tamsin. Tamsin looked back at Kit. Kit and Tamsin both looked to Morgan. Morgan sighed.

"Yes, Gristle the Second is still upstairs," he said.

"You did not dispatch the goblin?" the ghost asked.

"No…?" Morgan said.

The ghost wrinkled his nose.

"You did not scare the goblin away?" the ghost asked.

"He served us tea, and then he showed us how to get down here," Morgan said.

The ghost sighed.

"The Hawksmith Academy's hiring practices have always been hit or miss," he said. "I am not fond of their choice of caretakers, as he is unskilled and not particularly smart. Still, you didn't kill the goblin, you didn't dismantle the door, you didn't even kill the ooze of devouring. You have displayed a remarkable amount of restraint and mercy."

"Mercy, sure. Restraint, not so much," Tobias said, strolling in behind them casually, his lute still in hand.

"You're not dead," Kit said.

"The door needed a break. Apparently it's been so long since someone sang with him his pipes were a little rusty," Tobias said. "I promised we'd do a bit of Jackson Browne on the way back."

"How does the door know Jackson Browne?" Morgan said. He returned his attention to the ghost. "Do you know Jackson Browne?"

"I do not, but I am not a singing door, and thus I am unfamiliar with the great troubadours of distant lands," the ghost said.

Morgan was clearly waiting for Tobias to say something sarcastic, but the bard simply shrugged.

"What? Jackson Browne is, in fact, a great troubadour from a distant land, the man is not wrong," he said.

The ghost, fortunately, interrupted before the cleric and bard could devolve the conversation any further.

"So you have come here, in this hidden place, to what? Steal the treasures secreted here? To find words of power? To plunder what the academy has left behind?"

Tamsin pushed her brother aside, brushed past Morgan, and stared directly into the ghost's eyes.

"We want to bring back a fallen friend," Tamsin said. "Everything else here can rot if we can do that one thing."

The ghost raised an eyebrow, nodding approvingly.

"Did this friend fall as a hero?" he asked.

"He died saving us," Tamsin said.

"And do you all care for him?"

"So very much," Tamsin said.

"He was one of my best friends," Morgan added.

Tobias smirked.

"He was a better person than I am," Tobias said.

When the ghost looked at Kit, they shook their head.

"I'm new here," Kit said.

"A resurrection is a hard thing," the ghost said. "My last question is the most important. Does this fallen hero want to come back?"

Kit watched uncomfortably as the trio of adventurers seemed to have a silent, bitter conversation using nothing but their eyes. Tamsin looked furious, her mouth a hard, decisive line. Morgan looked sad, an old, desperate cast to his face. Tobias was resigned, glancing at his feet as often as his friends.

"What happens if he doesn't want to come back," Tobias said, not facing the ghost when he said it.

The spirit lifted his hands in a nebulous gesture.

"It's a terrible thing, to bring someone back who does not want to return," the ghost said, his aged face sad, almost wistful. "But the punishment for such a thing will simply be what you lose in the one you bring back. They will know why they are here, and who made it so, and respond as they see fit."

"Tamsin," Morgan said softly.

"He deserves better than to be slaughtered in some pit in a world that treats us like playthings, Morgan," Tamsin said. "He wants to die a hero's death? He should get to decide when that happens, not some game we're just pawns in."

Tobias leaned in closer to Kit. It felt conspiratorial at first, but they saw a pleading cast to his expression.

"Are we being selfish if we bring him back?" Tobias said.

"I don't know," Kit said. "I wish I did."

"Me too," Tobias said. "Me too."

The ghost clasped his spectral hands together and nodded.

"If you've decided, then," he said. "This is a just request of the academy, made with love. I will show you to the resurrection circle, and the spells you require. I assume you are able to cast the spell yourself? I am not."

"We have a priest and a wizard both," Tamsin said. "I hope that is enough."

"It is," the ghost said. "If you are certain, follow me."

Chapter 17: The twenty-sided room

The air had taken on a particular chill Eriko wasn't thrilled about as they neared the monastery. She was sure it had something to with elevation. They'd been making their way up a steep, if walkable, rocky incline But also there was a sense of change in the air that winter was on its way. They hadn't faced a winter in Revery yet, and for every idyllic, fantasy part of this world they'd encountered, it was balanced by something ferocious and excessive. Eriko was not ready to deal with a bitter, magical winter. She didn't even like February back home.

Hark led them around a craggy bend in the road, which was less of a road and more of a trail with aspirations. As they turned a corner and stepped out from behind a tall granite outcropping, the monastery itself finally came into view.

And the minute she saw it, Eriko started laughing.

"I don't understand the joke," Hark said. "What's funny?"

"The roof," Eriko said.

"It's a twenty-sided die," Cordelia said, fighting back a groan.

The building itself was a top-heavy stone structure, a narrow central building with smaller additions built on in ways that were both geometric and illogical. Walkways ran from the main tower to other, smaller buildings, which did not have doors on the ground level, at least not from Eriko's vantage point. The field around the monastery was overgrown, tall, yellowing grass waving eerily in the quiet breeze. The central tower was capped by something like a geodesic dome, evoking, as Cordelia said, a twenty sided die, though it appeared to be made of some sort of glass, triangular windows glinting in the sun.

"The dome?" Hark said. "It's strange—I've seen more than one Maker's church, and this is the only place I've encountered a dome like that. Why is it funny?"

"It means something else where we came from," Eriko said. "It's not actually funny. Just caught me off-guard."

"Hark, to be completely honest, seeing that shape makes me wonder if the gods of Revery have a very strange sense of humor," Cordelia said.

"Or they know more about where we came from than we realize," Eriko said. "Do you think there's anyone here?"

Hark gestured out over the sloppy field the tower stood in.

"I've passed here a few times, and this was always pristine," he said. "I've never seen it in such disarray. But I've never been inside. I don't know if this means anything."

Cordelia slipped her axe from her belt and held it low at her side.

"I wonder if the bastards we met in the Tomb of the Maker have already been here," she said.

Hark drew both of his weapons and scanned the field. The clearing was a mess, but nothing moved, and the tree line just beyond the tower seemed peaceful. The quiet was starting to give Eriko a headache.

"Let's head in," she said.

"Wait—" Cordelia started to say, but Eriko was already off, ninja-running through the tall grass toward the main door.

Not bothering to look behind her to see if Hark and Cordelia followed, Eriko dropped down low beside the entrance, a tall, double door with sturdy iron horizontal bands. She pulled her lockpicks out and scooted closer to get to work.

But the moment she touched the door, it creaked and swung slowly open, revealing a dark interior.

"Oh, for shit's sake," she muttered, standing up to her full height and drawing both daggers. Cordelia and Hark, giving up on stealth, trotted up behind her.

"Smell that?" Hark asked, tightening his grips on his axes.

"Smell what," Eriko said.

"Blood," Cordelia said, and Eriko caught an expression on her face that said she wasn't happy for whatever superior senses her barbarian abilities had given her at this moment. "I'll go first."

"Let me," Eriko said. "Rogues go first, you know the rules."

Before Cordelia could stop her, Eriko darted inside.

She got no more than a few steps inside before her breath caught in her throat at the sight of it all.

The temple had been desecrated. Beautiful, complex art, geometric sculptures, and paintings in hypnotic patterns had been smashed, slashed, burned. Books were scattered everywhere like obscene confetti, pages torn out and thrown aside. Handsome tables and chairs of dark wood were smashed and strewn about.

And then there were the bodies.

Men and women in deep blue robes, somewhere between monk and priest, lay like broken dolls everywhere. And they hadn't simply been run through, Eriko immediately noticed. Their bodies showed signs of slower deaths, hacked and split by torturous blows, their blood turned to glue in the pages of the discarded books. The geodesic dome was designed to refract and redirect the sunlight above, illuminating the entire main chamber with golden light in every corner. The room was almost too well lit, revealing things Eriko wished she could not see.

This was a place made for reading, she understood immediately. A place for secrets to be uncovered, for words to be seen at all times of day.

Behind her, Cordelia let out a sharp gasp in surprise. Hark began to mutter something like a prayer.

Eriko walked deeper into the main chamber, stepping over a corpse that Cordelia knelt down beside, examining the wounds.

"These people didn't fight back," Cordelia said. "They were torn to shreds… for what?"

"Knowledge," Eriko said, cocking her head.

She left Cordelia and Hark examining the bodies and began walking further inside, following a soft rasping sound.

"Where are you," Eriko said, placing one foot silently in front of the other. The rasping sound become clearer to her with each step. Inhale, exhale, the ragged breathing of a survivor.

She found him in a small side chamber, a reading alcove now turned into an abattoir. An older man, bald on top with wild, graying hair on the sides and back of his head, he sat at a desk, face down, each hand pinned to the desktop with a dagger.

Eriko made not a sound as she approached the desk, wincing at the man's labored breathing. She reached for one of the daggers, hesitating to pull it free.

The man sat up and gasped as though drowning.

"Holy shit!" Eriko yelled, stumbling back and almost falling over as the adrenaline hit her system. The priest looked at her with wild eyes, imploring.

"You mustn't let them go, they can't go," he said. "If they awaken the last Maker, all will be lost, he must remain asleep!"

Cordelia came charging in, Hark close at her heels.

"What the hell is going on?" Cordelia asked. "Tell me you didn't do this!"

"I didn't do anything!" Eriko said. She watched in horror as the priest tried to pull his hand free of the dagger, and nearly wretched. "Help him, I can't do it, I'll throw up."

Hark walked right up to the priest, steadied the man's right hand flat against the desk, and pulled the dagger free. With a swift, practiced motion, he wound a cloth around the hand to staunch the bleeding. Cordelia mimicked the orc's method on the other hand, but wasn't quite as smooth. Blood dripped onto the table thick as maple syrup.

"Who did this to you," Cordelia said softly as she bandaged the man's palm. He studied her face as if looking for someone to recognize within.

"They thought they could take the Maker's place," he said, his face twitching with pain. "They misunderstood. All the Makers misunderstood. To be the Maker is not to remake the world in your image. It is to keep it safe, to keep it strong. They were not worthy to become the new Maker, and the old Maker needs to stay interred. We are only safe if he stays dead."

"It's okay," Eriko said, joining Cordelia at the man's side. "We stopped them. They went to the Tomb of the Maker but we stopped them."

"No," the priest said. "No, you did not. If they opened the door, then the Maker is free, and if the Maker is free, we are just dust and starlight."

"If they opened the door?" Eriko asked. "What door?"

"The tomb," the priest said, leaning back in his chair, his eyes growing dim, his voice soft. "It wasn't a crypt. It was a prison."

The priest sank bank in his chair, exhaling as consciousness left him. Eriko and Cordelia exchanged a long, worried look.

"A prison for what?" Eriko asked.

Chapter 18: The right things, the wrong reasons

The ghost led the party into a large, mostly empty chamber, lit with soft blue light from small, arcane lanterns. The walls, Tamsin noticed, were adorned with religious iconography. Theana, the Lady of Light Morgan drew his magic from, was prominently displayed, but so were the other gods of Revery: god of storms, a goddess of nature; the trickster figure, forever smiling, eyes gleaming with mischief; a god of secret knowledge, whom an old woman had told Tamsin about during their time protecting their small village.

Central to the chamber, though, were three figures, women in robes—one in white, one in black, and one in gray.

"The three sisters," Kit said. "Life, death, and what lies between. I guess we're in the right place."

The ghost nodded approvingly.

"If you seek to bring someone back from the grave, it is best to petition the sisters. They hold sway over the living and the dead. To bring someone back to life without their blessing is to risk calamity."

Tamsin stopped short as she took in the floor itself. Runes were carved into the stone, careful, delicate etchings, forming a wide circle perhaps ten feet across.

"What's this?" she asked, pointing at the floor.

"A revivification circle," the ghost said. "It's similar to a summoning circle, but it opens a door to the dead, not to somewhere… worse, which most summoning circles do."

"A summoning circle," Tamsin said suspiciously.

"You do not have your friend's body, I presume," the ghost said.

"We don't," Morgan said sharply, as though to cut Tamsin off from answering.

"Then the circle is needed. Otherwise you may raise him and he will awaken wherever his body is," the ghost said. "Imagine the nightmare of finding yourself in your own grave, or at the bottom of a cliff…"

"I have a question," Tobias said, interrupting. "Who are you, exactly? You're down here alone, in the basement, what, as a tour guide? Just in case a bunch of adventurers come along and need help resurrecting someone?"

The ghost shook his head.

"I am a caretaker. Voluntarily bound to Hawksmith. The academy was my home in life, and I asked to watch over it in death. And this I will do until the castle no longer stands."

"Who were you before, then?" Tobias said. Tamsin found herself feeling nearly scandalized by the blunt rudeness of her brother's question. It felt almost obscene to ask a ghost who he was in life.

The ghost pondered it for a moment, stroking his spectral mustache thoughtfully.

"I can't say I rightly remember, exactly," he said. "It's been… centuries, I believe. I have memories of being among the living, but my time has passed. I exist strictly because I will myself to watch over the Academy. Is that so strange?"

Tobias shrugged.

"I guess I just hope that someday I love anything enough to want to watch over it forever," he said. "Do you remember your name?"

It was the ghost's turn to shrug then.

"I remember many names. Some are mine. Some were given to me. Some may just be fragments of memories."

"That's disconcerting," Tobias said.

"And how many names do you have, bard?" the ghost asked. "Names are simply words we wrap around ourselves for a time. They are not meant to be forever."

"I'm pretty okay with that," Kit said. Tobias smiled at them and began to make a circuit of the room, looking at the religious iconography in closer detail.

The ghost drifted to a small altar and gestured to a book there. Morgan and Tamsin walked over together, Tamsin examining the book with the gentle care of an archivist.

"I can't read this," she said, the symbology within its pages unlike anything she'd encountered in her studies.

"Strange," Morgan said. "I can."

"It's the language of the divine," the ghost said. "The chosen of the gods can read these words, and no others."

"So are the pages blank if I even look at them?" Tobias said. Kit let out a quick cough of a laugh.

"This is part prayer, part spell," the ghost said. "The priest must speak it, imploring the guardians of death and life to release this hero back to this world. Is there one among you who cared for him?"

"Yes," Tamsin and Morgan said simultaneously.

"That's good," the ghost said. "The invocation can be done without love, but it helps if the fallen hears a voice they would want to hear."

Tamsin caught Morgan looking at her strangely.

"What is it, Morgan," she asked, a sinking feeling in her guts as she spoke.

"Are we making the right decision, bringing him back?" Morgan said.

"I can't believe we're having this conversation right now," Tamsin said. "He shouldn't have died here. We're bringing him back."

"We've talked about this," Morgan said imploringly. "Revery gives us what we want. Are we being selfish? Isn't this what he wanted?"

"Morgan," Tamsin said, struggling to keep the anger from her voice. "We're in a game. If Jack was sitting at the table across from us, would you cast the spell to bring his character back to life, or not?"

"We'd ask him," Tobias said softly. "We can't ask him now."

"All the more reason to bring him back," Tamsin said. "I know I sound irrational. I know I sound selfish. But this game killed him, for what, to move the plot along? You tell me Jack was suicidal. I believe you. I really do. But he didn't commit suicide. He was stabbed through the guts by some asshole from the same world we came from, some selfish piece of shit who took our friend away. And you know what, the two of you? If I'm wrong, I'll take all responsibility. I swear to you I will. This will be my fault. But he was killed by this game, not because he chose to die, and I won't take the risk that we're reading too much into his history when the thing that killed him was another human being. He was murdered. Murdered. By a person, and by whatever makes this evil game keep going."

"I don't think I'm being unreasonable wanting to respect his wishes," Morgan said.

"Then don't bring him back," Tamsin said. "I can't cast the goddamned spell anyway. You hold the key here."

A heavy silence hung between them, Morgan's armor rasping as he struggled to find a comfortable way to stand.

"I wish I didn't know him as well as I do," Morgan said.

"Better than I do," Tamsin said. "Maybe better than I ever will. If I'm wrong, Morgan, I'm wrong. I'm sorry. I just don't want to see Revery take someone away from us. Blame me if you have to. Tell him it was my selfishness that brought him back. Let him never forgive me."

Morgan's face contorted with confusion, regret, tears welling up in his eyes as he visibly wavered back and forth, as if begging Tamsin to change her mind.

"Nah," Tobias said, interrupting. "I'll do it."

Morgan turned to him with his mouth hanging open. Tamsin felt a well of rage bubble up inside her.

"What?" she said, her tone too sharp for her to control.

"I'll do it," Tobias said, brushing past both of them toward the revivification circle. "Jack loved the two of you more than anything in the world. I'm just his girlfriend's asshole brother. He can hate me for the rest of his life and I can live with that. You shouldn't have to."

"Toby, you can't," Morgan said. "Right? It has to be me."

It was the ghost's turn to interrupt now.

"In Revery, there is as much magic in words and story as there is in the divine, or the arcane," he said. "The bard can cast the necessary spell, if he wishes."

Tamsin put a hand on Tobias' shoulder. Her brother turned around and winked at her.

"I got this, Tam. It'll be fine. Whatever happens. I promise."

And then Tobias looked up at the iconography of the three sisters and put his hands on his hips.

"Okay, ladies," he said. "How do we do this dance?"

Chapter 19: No god ever liked me, anyway

Now I've fucking done it, Tobias thought to himself, staring up at the three stone faces before him. I don't know how to cast a resurrection spell. Always stepping up to the stage unprepared, my whole stupid life.

On the right, a serene face, delicate, a soft smile carved into the stone, hands open. Our Lady of Hope, Tobias recognized. The goddess to whom all life is sacred. She seemed like a good bet in this case. Bringing someone back from beyond. But it also felt a little on the unnatural side. Maybe not her thing. Right?

On the left, a stern face, grim, beautiful in a dangerous way, fists clenched as if in frustration. She Who Waits. The goddess of death, of the void, of a nihilistic end. Also not a great option, he thought. Except, of course, that her iconography had a necromantic feel, skulls and decay. Maybe she was more comfortable with bringing the dead back to life. She might even find a special joy in an unwilling resurrection.

Well, that's uncomfortably dark, Tobias thought. Even for me.

In the center, the Mother of Graves. Funny that they called her the mother, as all three sisters looked to be of an age with each other, but that's immortal fictional goddesses for you, he supposed. There was, if were even possible, a kindness to the way her eyes were carved, as if she were conveying forgiveness. Or absolution.

"I think you're the one," he said out loud. The rest of the party was silent behind him, the dim, blue-green glow of the ghost flickering as the spirit observed.

Tobias took another step forward, staring into those stone-carved eyes.

"I can't say I'm a religious person," he said. "Probably not the best time to admit that, I guess. But back home, a lot of people who believed really hard in something divine also believed that people like me and Morgan and Kit shouldn't exist, so I guess I kind of knew that no god ever liked me anyway, otherwise why would the people that god loved hate us. But I don't know. You seem like a good sort. I read a little bit about you, back when we lived in Moderate Expectations. I thought it was really strange that there was a goddess who just thought death was precious, the way life was. You don't make a lot of sense, you know. I suppose a good marketing team could fix that."

Tobias rubbed his forehead, felt a trickle of sweat run down his back.

"Okay, look. I think if anyone in this room will do the right thing, it's you," he said. "Our friend, maybe he doesn't want to come back. And your sister over there on the right seems like she'd try to do the right thing and bring him back no matter what. And your sister on the left, well, I can't figure her out, and that's saying a lot because let me tell you, a lifetime of self-loathing? Nihilism is kind of my jam. But she scares me a little. You, though, you seem like you're no bullshit. And that's what I need right now, right? Because a lot of people love our friend and want him to come back to life, and a lot of people love Jack and don't want to force him to come back to a world that…"

Tobias' voice caught in his throat. He coughed a few times, sniffed, rubbed the back of his neck.

"I mean you know, right? It's not unreasonable to not want to be here anymore. It's a hard world. It's a cold world. We're all so fucking tired by the end of it, it's unfair to ask for any more than someone's already given," he said. "So I guess I'm asking you, as a… whatever you are, a goddess, a divine arbiter, a random number generator. I'm asking you to help me make the right decision here. Don't let me hurt my friend. Is that a lot to ask? It might be a lot to ask. Maybe hurting him is the only way to bring someone back. I just want to try to show him the respect this kind of a decision should have."

Tobias turned his attention to the goddess' hands. One was palm up, as if reaching toward him. He hadn't noticed that before, but for some reason he couldn't call to mind how her hands were held before. Folded? In her pockets? He had no memory of it. On a whim, he reached up and placed his open hand in hers.

He felt fingers close around his hand. Warm, strong, not stone but flesh, gentle but firm. The carving in the wall was looking at him. A single tear fell from the left eye and splashed on the floor at his feet.

And then the room began to glow with a pale white light.

"What did you do," Tamsin said.

Tobias turned to see the revivification circle slowly beginning to glow, the arcing light working its way from where the tear hit the ground in both directions to converge on the other side of the circle. Runes on the floor also began to glow, forming phrases Tobias could not read, yet somehow understood. They read like poetry, about loss, remembrance, death, rebirth. Once the outer circle was complete, an inner circle also began to form. Morgan was watching Tobias from the exact opposite side of the circle, his expression one of near panic, as though they'd made the single greatest mistake of their lives.

Tobias felt another hand grab his, not the one he still left in the grip of the Mother of Graves. Kit's long fingers closed around his, somewhere between offering comfort and seeking it from him. Tobias found himself suddenly very grateful for the human touch.

"I've been here for so long," Kit said. "And I've never seen anything like this."

The circle pulsed, glowed brighter, and then a cylinder of light broke through the ceiling, nearly blinding them as it consumed the center of the runes. For a moment, Tobias could see nothing, hear nothing, felt only Kit gripping one hand, and the Mother of Graves holding the other. The goddess' hand squeezed his just then, a noticeable tightening of her grip, and then let go, allowing Tobias' arm to drop to his side. He reached over and placed his free hand on Kit's shoulder, seeking comfort himself, to feel something he knew for certain was real and true.

The light faded, leaving an afterimage in his vision. Tobias blinked until the blind spots faded. And when they did, his heart sank.

The circle was empty.

Tamsin yelled out a sharp "No!" Her voice echoed in the

darkening chamber uncomfortably. Morgan let out a single, gut-wrenching sob, of relief or sadness Tobias could not tell. Kit squeezed his hand and said softly, "What happened?"

"I don't know," Tobias said. He looked at his sister, her eyes seeming to bruise with grief. "I don't know what went wrong."

"Nothing went wrong," the ghost said, shattering the tension with his almost clinical tone of voice. "If the spell failed, it simply would have failed. Your casting was successful. The goddess granted your appeal."

"Then where is he?" Tamsin said. Tobias could hear a sharpness in her voice she was barely restraining, as if on the verge of a panic attack. "Did he come back wherever his body is? Oh my god, is he at the bottom of that tomb all alone right now?"

Morgan placed a big hand on Tamsin's shoulder and she seemed to almost try to shake it off, but instead she leaned in, letting the cleric envelop her in his arms.

"I cannot tell you exactly what went wrong," the ghost said, drifting around the circle almost as though he were a crime scene investigator, examining the evidence. "But in all my centuries here, I know of only one reason why this spell would be successfully cast, but the intended soul was not restored."

"What stopped it before," Morgan said, his voice an octave lower than normal, worry palpable in the resonance.

"It means he's already been brought back by someone else," the ghost said. "Your friend is on this plane of existence, not the world beyond. He is already here."

Chapter 20: Give them something to believe in

Asptooth put the finishing touches on an armored skeleton, adjusting the helmet just so, and stepped back to admire his own handiwork. It would do, he thought, and said so to the imp perched on his shoulder.

The imp, Bloodstain, made a wavering hand gesture as if to say: meh.

"Everyone's a critic," Asptooth said. "Anyway. These are just for backup."

Asptooth looked up and down the corridor of the catacombs he now stood in, dozens of little alcoves now inhabited by inert, but battle-ready, skeletons. They weren't all made up of parts from the same person, so some were slightly off-kilter, arms too long or two short, bits and pieces held together with wire or twine. He shrugged and meandered down the hall to the room he'd set up as his lab. There, a larger body, one with some flesh still on it, was laid out on a stone slab, greenish chemicals being pumped into dead muscle through oversized syringes.

"What about this one," he asked the imp. This time, Bloodstain gave a pair of thumbs-up.

Asptooth threw a sheet over the body, dimmed some of the lights to the lab, leaving the room in an eerie, reddish glow, and went searching for Valamir.

They'd been in this new base of operations for a few weeks now, and it was coming along nicely, as far as Asptooth was concerned. He didn't much care about décor, but for his work he was strangely meticulous and tidy, and so the lab, though grim, was clean and neat. The corridors of the catacombs were appropriately dry, no pooling water to attract bugs or other pests, or to foster disease to grow. It was peaceful down here, Asptooth thought, and he rather enjoyed it, a place to play at being a mad scientist and necromancer in peace. It had been years, years since he'd been able to set up shop, with Dom, or Blaggard, constantly forcing the party to move forward on his weird quest for power.

What was the point of becoming of some old god-wizard when you could have a lab and build monsters in peace? This was power. The power to enjoy yourself in a good day's work.

Asptooth found himself annoyingly lost in the catacombs, taking one wrong turn, then another, kicking a loose brick in annoyance as he found he'd turned the same corner three times. Bloostain laughed at him, and Asptooth swatted the imp irritably.

"New living arrangements. I can't help if I'm a creature of habit," he said.

He listened, trying to get his bearings. He could hear respectful chanting above him, and began to follow the sound to where it was loudest. Eventually, he came across the stairs that lead up into the building above the catacombs. He tread carefully, listening intently to the chanting, the cacophony of human voices he had grown accustomed to hearing on an almost daily basis now.

He found Valamir standing just outside the secret door to the catacombs. The corridor was lined with a deep red carpet, and light filtered in through stained glass windows. There was a not-unpleasant scent of incense in the air.

And most unusually, Valamir was dressed all in white.

The cleric was looking out from a side-door into the main hall of the church they'd restored. It was the perfect dual-purpose building, really—the strange catacombs below for Asptooth's experiments, a sturdy house of worship for Valamir to run his scam above. The building was in good shape when they bought it, so hiring some unskilled laborers to polish up the pews, buying some replacement windows, and a bit of pious décor and they were all set.

And, of course, there was the wardrobe shift for Valamir. Gone were his black armor and vestments of a god of destruction and death he had claimed to follow the entire time they'd been in Revery.

Now he wore a tabard of white with the icon of a scale emblazoned upon it. He'd shaved his face, cut his hair, made himself look quite respectable, and now he sold himself as priest of a god of justice and balance.

"How goes your work, old friend," Valamir said, noticing the wizard stumbling out from the secret doorway.

"Good, good," Asptooth said. "The catacombs were filled with bones. We'll have an undead army if we need it. I'm cooking up a few surprises as well."

"Not surprises for me, I hope," Valamir said with a smirk.

"Oh, you'll know about them as soon as I'm sure they'll work," Asptooth said. "I just don't want to get your hopes up."

"I'm sure you'll do your usual wonderful work," Valamir said. He gestured out at the gathered worshippers, chanting at the direction of a young deacon at the head of the hall. "This is remarkable, isn't it?"

"It's a room full of fools," Asptooth said, perhaps too bluntly, but Valamir laughed nonetheless.

"True enough," the cleric said. "But it's remarkable still, how easily we swayed people to a god they know so little about, all for the chance to feel like their anger, their resentment, their hate is all justified."

"Especially because the working folk of Revery are free, or freer than they are in our own world," Asptooth said. "Revery may look like medieval Europe but the laws, the leadership, it's fantasy, isn't it? No real world society like this actually cares for its own sick like they do here, or…"

"There's always resentment, though," said Valamir. "Even if Revery is kinder than the real world to its people, there is still inequity. There is still anger. We just had to foment it, to ferment it, to get things cooking…"

"And now you've got a revolution if you want it," Asptooth said.

"And there's so much profit in war," Valamir said. "Revery's been unnaturally stable for too long. It needs blood in the streets. This world needs conflict. And conflict is going to make us very rich."

Chapter 21: The edge of the world

Raven stood on a vast expanse of ash-colored sand and stared out into a void of cloud-shaped nothing.

The cloud ran as far as he could see in either direction, and stood so tall he could not see the sky above it. It was a roiling, angry storm, but it stayed in place, as if it knew it was not allowed to progress any closer.

So this is the edge of the world, he thought. This is where Revery ends. A finite line in reality, and beyond it, oblivion.

"This is where the world ends," Leo said.

"Has it always been like this?" Raven asked, leaning down to scratch Silence behind the ears.

"I don't know," Leo said, leaning on his staff tiredly. "Nobody talks about it, not anyone from Revery originally, so maybe it's not something they can see. Or maybe it's new, a tear in the seam."

"Do you know for sure there's nothing beyond it?"

I've seen it swallow up creatures, undead who walked too close, that sort of thing," Leo said. "Nothing ever comes back."

"But there could be something on the other side," Raven said.

"There might," Leo said, shrugging. "I'm not sure I'm so willing to walk through and find out."

"I could walk through," Raven said.

"If anyone could, I think it's you," Leo said. "You exist outside of Revery's framework in a way no one else does."

"I'll do it," Raven said.

"I'm not going to force you to," Leo said.

"I know. I'll do it," the ranger said. "You've told me this cloud is growing stronger, eating up more territory. That it might grow strong enough to consume real town soon."

"If it continues unchecked, yes."

"Then I don't see how I have a choice," Raven said. I'll walk through, see what's on the other side. What's the worst thing that can happen. I die? Done that already. Didn't stick."

Raven started walking toward the wall of clouds. Leo scuffled after him to keep up. Silence trotted at his side.

"No, buddy," Raven said. "I don't think you can come with me on this one. It's not fair to you."

The wolf whined and nosed Raven's hand. The ranger laughed. The sound felt strange in his throat. It had been a long time since he'd found humor in anything.

"I appreciate it, I really do," he said. "But I need you to stay here, okay? Go look after the others. Go find Tamsin and Eriko and Morgan. They'll need you. Okay?"

Again, Silence issued a high-pitched cry, not taking his eyes off the ranger.

"People keep saying this place isn't real," Raven said. "But you're real, aren't you. I don't know exactly what you are, but you're real. I can't… You're better than I deserve, you know that? You're a better friend than I have ever deserved."

Raven knelt down, placed his forehead against the wolf's, scratched under his chin, and then started walking toward the edge of the world. He turned back to Leo and shook his head.

"It's the Great Nothing, isn't it," he said. "We thought we were playing Dungeons & Dragons, and it turns out we were in *The Neverending Story*."

"I guess so," Leo said. "It's disappointing, isn't it? We always thought we had agency here, but…"

"But we're playing someone else's game," Raven said. "Make sure the wolf makes it safely back to my friends, okay? I don't care about what happens to me. Just make sure he's not alone if I don't come back."

"I will," Leo said. "I promise."

Raven nodded, locked eyes with Silence one more time, and thought about how tired he was. Of saying goodbye, of trying to be happy, of trying to be someone worthwhile. Maybe oblivion does wait on the other side of the clouds, he thought. Or maybe it's our way home. I don't know which one I hope to find there.

The ranger nodded, then turned, walking boldly toward the wall of gray, knowing that there was only one way to do this, to face it boldly, to not hesitate. To see a thing through. I just want to see one thing through, he thought.

And then the worst pain he'd ever felt in his entire life spasmed in his chest.

His knees buckled, and he fell to the ground, unable to take a breath; the air caught in his lungs, clamping down on them like a vice. He heard a horrible sound and knew it was his own voice, choking and gasping. The pain in his chest became rhythmic, repeating, the thunder of blood running through his ears deafening him.

His face pressed into the gray sand beneath him, digging into his cheek and forehead. He wanted to scream in pain, but nothing came out, his entire chest seizing up with shock. What is that noise, he thought, a clanging bell in his blood stream, and then he realized, he was hearing his heartbeat, the rhythm having been silenced for all these weeks. His body was noisy, loud, messy, but somehow his again, not at the behest of some other power.

He nearly retched as head spun, thoughts swimming by in sharper clarity than they'd had before. He tried to stand up but only got up to his knees, breathing deeply and realizing how much richer the air tasted now.

The ranger turned to the necromancer and snarled.

"You piece of shit," he said.

"This isn't me," Leo said. "I didn't do this. I—oh, for fuck's sake."

"Things were so quiet for just a few minutes," Raven said. "Just a few minutes and then you had to go and bring me back, you selfish…"

The necromancer made a few quick arcane gestures in the air around him, leaving a trail of sigils glowing and fading. He sighed.

"Well, you can probably thank your friends for this," he said. "Someone tried to resurrect you."

"Someone tried to what now?"

"To bring you back from the dead," Leo said.

"Only you already did it," Raven said.

"Kind of, sort of, but not really," Leo said. "Just enough to screw up their spell."

He exhaled and threw his arms up in defeat.

"They're probably really pissed right now," Leo said.

"Or they're heartbroken," the ranger said. "I still can't remember my name."

"That, that is my fault," Leo said. "That's part of the cost of the spell I cast. We just need to… huh."

"We just need to what, you creepy old bastard," the ranger said.

"Look," Leo said.

The gray wall of clouds, the impenetrable void that had been so close Raven could almost touch it, had receded away from them by a hundred yards or more. It seemed to be pulling back further still, revealing more barren, twisted landscape, skeletal trees and rocky outcroppings, the partial skeleton of a giant reptile.

"I'm going to pretend I care what that means," Raven said.

"I'm not sure," Leo said. "But I wonder if it means that whatever just happened to you means you have more story to tell, and Revery is making sure that story happens."

"So if the tear in reality is on the other side of the fog, or smoke, or whatever, and it's now pulling away from me, and finding that tear is how the spell you have over me is completed, am I stuck never remembering my name?" Raven said.

"I'll, ah, have to get back to you on that," Leo said. "And just because the world briefly stopped shrinking because you have a sequel to tell with your life doesn't mean the tear's not still out there."

Raven struggled back to his feet, a hand gently on Silence's shoulder. He closed his eyes a moment, steadying himself.

"Well, we know the tear isn't out that way," the ranger said, resigned, irritable, but somehow newly determined. "I say we keep walking until we find it."

Raven took one unsteady step forward, then another, picking up his pace and hearing Leo doing the same behind. The cloud wall continued to pull back, a few feet at a time, and then Raven saw a skull.

A giant skull, twenty feet tall, a portcullis where its mouth should be. Springing back from the skull, a castle appeared, decrepit, grimy, ancient, forgotten.

"You've got to be kidding me," the ranger said.

"I honestly didn't see this coming," Leo said.

Raven continued walking, straight toward the mouth of the skull-castle. Leo called out to him.

"What are you doing?"

"We just found a castle in the middle of a wasteland," the ranger said. "Don't you want to see what's inside?"

Epilogue: Redrawing the lines

The old wizard nearly laughed when he watched the borders of Revery expand. The image, swirling around in his crystal ball, showed the dead ranger and the annoying necromancer together in the Endless Badlands, a place the wizard's scrying rarely took him anymore. It used to be prime real estate for adventurers, a place filled with tombs and barrows, but as Revery contracted, it so went those places of mystery. The wizard had hoped someone would find a way to push back into those gray sands again. He'd put so much work into designing the lore there, after all. It seemed like a waste of, well, a perfectly good wasteland.

He'd assumed the ranger's story was over, and while he'd been quite impressed by its finale—heroic sacrifices are fantastic story devices, after all—it meant there was one less adventurer left in Revery, to fill its reserves with wonder, to create conflict and violence and hope.

There were so few heroes anymore, the wizard thought. So few roads back into Revery. So few players to run the gauntlet of this violent delight.

The wizard turned his attention to the broken party now, first to the rogue and the barbarian. Lost among the stacks of a temple of knowledge, desecrated by the murder hobos who had, somehow, stumbled onto the usurper's path. The wizard had never enjoyed observing that group. He liked to see bloodshed as much as anyone, but there was no art to it. Just greed. Locusts, preying upon themselves. He was glad they were scattered and gone, not so much because of the destruction they wrought, but because they were so boring.

And the others, in the bowels of the academy abandoned by those Hawksmith cowards. He'd make them pay for the cries of pain Revery wailed as their magic left the world. This splinter group had his interest, now, with internal strife, a goal both heroic and selfish, their doubt growing. They'd picked up a straggler, the warrior from a party torn asunder just a few years back. The wizard missed that party. They could be stupid, but they fought a good fight, and their blood and struggle gave Revery something to live for.

The wizard went back to the ranger, not looking at the player but rather at the transforming edge of Revery itself. Something had happened to him that changed the game. He wanted to know if it was something the necromancer did, or perhaps his friends, meddling with the leftovers of the Hawksmith Academy's arcane tricks. But something strange had happened, something new, and Revery, while infinitely entertaining, was not a place where "new" things happened.

And then he saw the skull-shaped castle, newly revealed by the clouds.

The wizard bolted out of his chair, nearly tripping in the process. "No," he said.

He watched in horror as the ranger, trailed by the necromancer, began walking directly toward the skull's mouth. He slammed his fist on his desk, nearly knocking over the crystal ball, as the ranger attempted to open the portcullis.

He'd found one of the few places no one should dare to tread. A place not meant to be found.

The wizard began to pace, to talk to himself to question his next move. Something must be done.

Revery had long tested every adventurer who set foot in it. But it had been lifetimes, the wizard realized, an acidic pit growing in his stomach, lifetimes since it had, instead, tested him.

Also by Mathew Phillion

The Dungeon Crawlers Novella Series (Digital)

The Player's Guide to Dungeon Crawling (Book I)
The Dungeoneer's Bestiary (Book II)
The Ghoul Slayer's Guidebook (Book III)
The Tomb of the Maker (Book IV)
Splitting the Party (Book V)
Lost In Revery: Tales of the Dungeon Crawlers Vol. 1 (Collecting Books 1-3) (Also available in paperback)

The Indestructibles Series:

The Indestructibles (Book 1)
The Indestructibles: Breakout (Book 2)
The Entropy of Everything (The Indestructibles Book 3)
Like a Comet (The Indestructibles Book 4)
The Crimson Child (the Indestructibles Book 5)
Doc Silence: The Cost of Magic

Tales from the Indestructiverse:

Echo and the Sea
Poseidon's Scar (Echo and the Sea Book 2)

The Indestructibles One-Shots (digital shorts)

Roll for Initiative
The Soloist
Gifted
Blood & Bone
The Monsters We Make
Krampus in the City

About the Author

Matthew Phillion is a writer, actor, and film director based in Salem, Massachusetts and the author of the Indestructibles Young Adult superhero adventure series, the spinoff series Echo and the Sea and its sequels, and the pop fantasy Dungeon Crawlers adventure series.

www.ingramcontent.com/pod-product-compliance
Lightning Source LLC
Chambersburg PA
CBHW051139130726
47988CB00005B/1906

Every star is a Moon

SNEHA SHUKLA

Copyright©2023 Sneha Shukla
All rights reserved including the rights to produce this book or portions
and illustrations thereof in any form whatsoever. For any information,
address the publisher.
Characters, events, incidents and illustrations are either the products of
the poet's imagination or used in a fictitious manner. Any resemblance
to actual people, living or dead, or actual events is purely coincidental.

Cover design and illustrations by Insha Siddiqui
Instagram: _dexterous.insha_

ISBN-
Printed in India

First print edition 2023

Instagram: snehashukla_10

For

Annapurna Shukla

(my dearest grandmother)

EVERY STAR IS A MOON

~ 5 ~

The moon is special,
not because of its beauty
or luminosity
or brilliancy
but because we humans have made it
for we have ignored
that there are stars in the sky too,
they appear at night too,
they spread light too,
they are at a great height too,
the moon is definitely special
but for me,
"every star is a moon".

-everything matters

People say,
I'm an eccentric
dotty
and offbeat girl
I agree,
whatever I do,
is myself not clear to me
sometimes I'm out of the tune,
sometimes I'm within the tune,
sometimes I'm the tune.

Mermaids and unicorns are imaginations
for they are the creatures
that do not exist in reality
yet fill us with serenity
so make sure,
if thou canst speak
anything good
at least imagine
something exceptional.

-imaginations

You have a pure heart,
that's enough on your part.

A place where humanity is my work,
happiness is my cabin,
kindness is my chief,
and love is my salary.

-a place which cannot exist

ENTER
PASSWORD
1abc 2def 3ghi
4jkl 5mno 6pqr
7stu 8vwx 9yz
*+ 0 #

I wish like the mobile phones,
human beings too had
their own alphanumeric passwords
so that they can quickly
sense,
reject,
and neglect anyone
whom they feel
can ruin them.

-my happiness is important to me

Problem solving ability
PENCIL

Though being unequal at my sides,
I'm a scalene
a triangle,
a shape,
a whole concept

though being incomplete in my appearance,
I'm an arc
a curve,
a half moon,
a whole beauty

though being lost in my distorted life,
I'm a human,
a creation,
a story,
a whole book.

Circumstances could have been so much at ease
if twelve-hour long days
were as simple as

half a dozen mornings
and half a dozen evenings

half a dozen beginnings
and half a dozen endings

half a dozen greetings
and half a dozen goodbyes

with a little
or no space for
afternoons,
phases,
and conversations.

-short episodes

I have been one step away from so many things,

one step away
from expressing my anger

one step away
from taking my stand

one step away
from following my mind

one step away
from leaving your side

one step away
from making a right choice.

I was a sharp pinch
with strength in my bones,
thunder in my sound,
and leadership in my actions

these trembling fingers
will never realize
what they were
before they fell in love with iron rods

and at the end,
the amount of calcium
love
and trust
was destined to collapse
in front of the iron rods
which never knew
how it felt
to bear the pain of dominance.

-a hate story

Slowly and gradually,
the sun looked bigger than everything

the idea of being the loneliest,
the proud of being the boldest,
the feel of being the warmest,
the illusion of being the brightest,
the oddity of being the rarest.

-you cannot compete the sun

The snow and feathers
fell on the same ground
somewhere from the sky
with their appearances almost being similar
delicate,
light,
and white
except for the fact,
that snow came from a country of coldness
while feathers knew
how the warmth of bird's love felt like
except for the fact,
that melting is the ultimate end of the snow
while feathers die by getting crushed
under the feet of inhumane folks

It's quite enticing,
how the one who carried coldness
eventually succumbs to the warmth of temperature

and the one who carried warmth of love
eventually succumbs to coldness
and heartlessness.

-pains

Stop saying,
that gentlemen do not exist

I have seen men
leaving women in wretchedness
and I have also seen men
loving those same women
despite that same wretchedness.

-for all the men out there

"*Wake up! Sleeping folks*"

Eyes ain't the only place
where the sleep resides
sometimes,
there's a state of
sleep and indolence
in mouth and ears too
which keeps them unconscious
unobservant
and unaware
of the truth outside
and stops them
from listening to the right thing
and speaking for the right side.

-wake up! Sleeping folks

Me mourning over you everyday
is letting them wonder
if "you are the most priceless"
or "the most heartless person alive"

me mourning over you everyday
is letting them wonder
if *"it is the divinity in me which is not ready to leave you"*
or *"the divinity in you which keeps me attached to you"*

me mourning over you everyday
is letting them wonder
if *"it was me who left your side"*
or *"you were someone else's best choice"*

me mourning over you everyday
is letting them wonder
if *"it was my unbreakable ego which came in between"*
or *"your pointless insecurities which weren't even an issue
to me"*.

Each time my heart
worries about anything,
my brain cuts it to half
by reassurance
hope
and wit
and here's why I understood
why the heart has "four chambers"
and the brain has "two equal halves".

-four divided by two

Dedication has never been limitless
for I've always
limited,
controlled,
and stopped myself
from enjoying so many crucial moments

what was limitless
was the amount of
madness
it inculcated in me
which always compelled me
to stay "limited"
and remain "connected"
to my ambition.

-that madness was necessary

In a world where
everyone just "pretends",
my mum always wanted me
to be the one
who genuinely "comprehends".

To prove my chastity,
I would be unquestionable

to prove my innocency,
I would be unanswerable

to prove my rationality,
I would be unfathomable

to prove my rigidity,
I would be unbreakable.

I never had same folks by my side
especially at contrasting situations

all those who skindered
when I was subjected to
opprobrium and obloquy
were caught stealing eyes
when I received
venerations and plaudits.

My heart knows,
how many bonds
I would have broken
if it wasn't for the word "friendship"

my mouth knows,
how many bad words
I would have spoken
if it wasn't for the word "upbringing"

my brain knows,
how many people
I would have forgotten
if it wasn't for the word "memory".

Inside her was a scenic beauty
worth appreciating
mosses of harmony,
butterflies of comeliness,
mountains of acumen,
and trees of spontaneity
but unfortunately there was no one to
explore,
apprehend,
and analyze them
so eventually all that scenic beauty
turned into wildlife
destroyed by brutes,
one by one
according to their moods.

-undiscovered

Plethora of pains and perturbations
seek their mentions
in my poetries
but my hands
being captivated by trammels of criticisms,
always feared penning them down
so whatever you get to read
is just one-tenth of what
my hands are allowed to write.

-I'm sorry

Things could have been different,
if you had understood better
that not all insomniacs
need lullabies
and not all complaints
need apologies
things could have been different,
if you had understood better
that I did not ask for
lullabies or apologies
when I explained to you my problems.

-I was never understood

It has been one hundred ninety-one days since you left us

one hundred ninety-one days,
still not able to comprehend
what was our fault

one hundred ninety-one days,
still not able to comprehend
where did it all go wrong

one hundred ninety-one days,
still not able to comprehend
why you're still our constant thought.

-your home is waiting

WRONG
WAY
22646

You were always deaf to my opinions,
I expressed my heart out
but you kept disregarding
and it took me sometime to realize,
that it wasn't your fault
for you were an addict
who was so much engrossed in his earphones
that he became deaf to everything around him
except for what he himself chose to listen
your playlists were
designed by others
which continuously played songs,
songs of inhumanity
audacity
fatuity
and obscurity
so you were always
deaf to me
you were on the wrong path
with those few fellows who controlled you
controlled how you thought,
how you spoke,
what you felt,
and what you listened to
so you were always deaf to the one
who tried her level best
to make you walk on the right path.

-you kept ignoring me

Twinkling like flowers,
blooming like stones,
shining like darkness,
dancing like statue,
I was attempting everything
in every impossible
I was attempting everything
without letting anyone know

my circumstances were harsh and different
but my willpower stood
still,
firm,
and irresistible.

May be in some opposite world
I'm having *"them all"* I lost here
but definitely not the things
I earned here,
my individuality
my truthfulness
my unboundedness.

BOOK OF
Sufferings
BOOK OF sufferings

I won't complain
I won't utter a single word
I won't prove my point
I won't even cry

I would instead write
write a whole notable book.

-book of sufferings

All these rules of language can help me to deliver my
thoughts
but unluckily, they cannot provide me the support I need

these conjunctions will never be able to join
my broken heart

these adjectives will never be able to describe
my shattered soul

these tenses will never be able to track
my declining time

these interjections will never be able to feel
my deepest sorrows

these verbs will never be able to find
my serious faults

these pronouns will never be able to know
my destroyer.

-who is my destroyer?

Her half-opened eyes,
were not the sign of enlightenment
her black eyelids,
were not the sign of beauty
her shades,
were not meant to protect them
but to tuck them away
from the rest of the world.

-hidden

You are a flower
radiant,
firm,
vibrant,
which augments the beauty of the tree of your life
so be that flower
which is noticed by everyone
one that is the brightest,
the strongest,
the merriest,
but place yourself
in such a position
that it's difficult for them
to break you,
manipulate you,
or defame you
for the flowers on top of the tree
are often hard to pluck.

-being on the top

Validation is unnecessary
and infinite
a human creation,
a never ending fight,
a thirst for approval,
that compels you to die
a harsh veracity,
that no one can deny
people are crazy,
they have gone wild
unaware of the fact,
that they need no proof
of their best life.

Individuality is rare
and exquisite
it is accessible to everyone
yet only a few can enjoy
it is like,
one wired earphone
dutifully playing songs
when the other one
is not working right
it is like,
being the light
when others have lost their sight
a sense of who you are
a matter of utmost delight.

My existence was roaming around like a reclusive acapella
until it got completed by your harmonic background music.

-rhythmic love

All these personalities inside my head would've kept fighting if I wouldn't have committed them to writing.

-parts of me

Oaths were taken
but honesty was never sustained

sermons were delivered
but concentration was never maintained

folks were invited
but values were never ingrained

and all the odious crimes they committed
hid behind their saintly identity
and proved it on a daily basis
that despite the truth being present in abundance in this
atmosphere,
truthfulness can never be inhaled
and falseness can never be exhaled.

-breathing and surviving

Each time I run out of stimulus to write,
I remember of the
ignominies I have been subjected to,
mistakes I have perpetrated,
aims I have decided,
plans I have to accomplish,
people I have to answer.

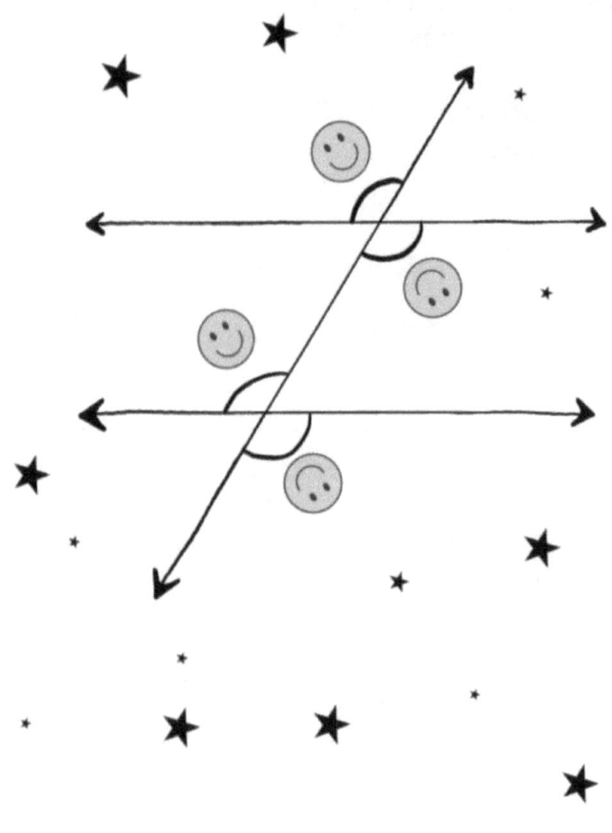

The parallel lines
never really met
but at least had a few angles equal
when cut by a transversal line

the same way,
I'm too waiting for a "transversal line of hope"
to pass through me
and all those who failed to understand me
so that,
a few of my sides or angles
can resonate with theirs
and even though
I'm not destined to meet them,
I can at least equate them
by either being
vertically opposite
or corresponding
or alternate.

-*I'm ready to make every possible effort*

I have seen caged birds existing in human bodies
dutifully applying vermilion on their foreheads,
cooking scrumptious meals,
nurturing their little ones,
relinquishing their dreams,
and most often
frenetically getting beaten by their spouses
they could have been anything
they could have got any position
but all they got
was a mansion
which is now their reality
a small world,
where they contribute altruistically
yet go unnoticed.

-incarcerated

My heart palpitates
and after every six consecutive thuds,
it says,
"it"
"shouldn't"
"have"
"ended"
"that"
"way"
till the whole seventy-two beats complete,
every minute,
the process repeats
and repeats
and repeats.

-heartbreak

Whenever I take off those rings,
my fingers feel liberated
for I'm no longer attached
with the societal rules of promises and fake relations

whenever I cry,
my eyes feel unrestricted
for I'm no longer attached
with the trauma that has been bottled up for so long

whenever I sigh,
my trachea feels alleviated
for I'm no longer attached
with the pain of not breathing enough for survival

and this is what happens dear
when you taste "freedom".

-azaad
Urdu ; noun

The light of heaven was watching the brutality of
the darkling sky
the bright rays of the sun always hid
the depression behind.

-beware

My imaginations are just strings,
I add to them
my own gemstones of
notion,
proclivity,
grief,
events,
and lexicon
and they become beautiful necklaces of poetry
adding beauty to those
who wear them
who read them.

-my poetries are carcanets

You said,
you will die without me
but instead left me
dying without you

you said,
you will die for me
but instead left me
dying for you

you are
my destroyer
my saboteur
my ravager
and I will never forgive you.

-I hate you

With happy faces
but broken hearts

with healing wounds
but ever lasting scars

with rainbow minds
but dull auras

with peer groups
yet no one closer

with excellent academics
yet roaming around like losers

with everything settled
yet unsettled

they are going through a tough time,
they are bearing the pain of teenage life.

-hard years

Healing is not a phase,
it's a sudden change
when "forever and ever"
changes to "forever and never"

an instant acceptance
when you're asked,
"will you still love them?"
and you reply,
"forever"
an instant rejection
when you're asked,
"will you still go back to them?"
and you reply,
"never".

-self respect screams

I was perplexed
if the world was against us
or you were on the side of the world

I was perplexed
if it was "the world versus me"
or "my world versus me".

-you were my world

Right below your eyebrows,
right above your eyelids,
right there
inside your forehead
is where the depression resides
and hangs
like a weight
which prevents your eyes to see
how beautiful this world actually is.

-exact location of depression

Absence equates to unimportant presence,
silence equates to unheard voice,
ineptness equates to unappreciated talents,
fadedness equates to unrecognized rainbows.

and everything in this world
which goes unimportant,
unheard,
unappreciated,
or unrecognized,
equates to "nothingness".

-*step up*

Not all lads
bragging about their plastic toy gun today
would be serving their country
by being a soldier tomorrow
some would be
terrorists,
thieves,
or shooters

not all lads
holding a paper and pen today
would be writing poetries tomorrow
some would be writing
a threat letter,
a hate speech,
or a suicide note

dreams are never wrong
paths are often.

Was allowed to sit
wherever I see flowers
was taught to fly
whenever I sense lust

was brought up like a butterfly
I wish you knew me more
I wish you knew me more.

My hometown is a smiling face of that little kid
whose cleft chin symbolizes the depth of its pious soil
whose cheek bones symbolize the beauty of its natural
vegetation
whose dimples symbolize the ethereal glory of its sunsets

my hometown is a smiling face of that little kid
who is evolving to become a mature adult
and keep up with this materialistic and mature world
created by cities and modernity.

-innocency of my hometown

Each night,
he came towards her
lecherously,
lasciviously,
inebriated,
like a compulsion
pulled her hair,
like hailstorms uprooting the trees
scratched her skin,
as if she were a moist field

and she mistook it for love
every action of his abuse

he was so obsessed with colours
that he eventually decided
to place them on her body
the red scratches
the blue pinches
the white blisters

and she was so obsessed with him
that she gave illogical excuses
when she was asked about them.

-abuse isn't obsession

I have always over lined
redrawn
and re sketched my palm lines,
my destiny never worked in my favour.

Delicately in my hands,
I hold a colour palette
ingeniously on a white paper,
I begin drawing myself
in a different way
purple hair,
red eyebrows,
orange eyes,
black lips,
and blue skin
for if I'm loving myself
this way,
I would admire myself
in any colour
any shade
anyway.

-colours on me

My heart is the only place
where I can make you go through
heaven
or purgatory
or hell
but unfortunately
inside this same heart,
you are reborn
over and over again.

Peace can never be the mother of any masterpiece
masterpieces are born when emotions coincide with emotions

masterpieces are born
with pieces of
chaos
troubles
and grief

masterpieces are born
when oceans compete with intrepid seas

masterpieces are indeed
masters of pieces of sufferings.

Destruction was prewritten
since you took no prescription

and while inhaling coincidence,
you dissolved excessive pills of
emotions and interpretations.

-have some understanding

The soul moving towards the sky
might be as light as an aerographene
as diminutive as a quark
but the soul moving upwards is
inflated
enlarged
and multiplied
due to the fear of judgment,
excitement of transmigration,
and trauma of past life
and if somehow
during this period,
my soul is having a chance to recall anything,
it wouldn't recollect
moments of joy,
or mirth,
or rejoice,
it would instead recall
all the debilitating,
enfeebling,
and excruciating moments of this life
so that the same mistakes
aren't repeated twice
and I'm able to deal with them
better in my another life.

-*way to heaven*

Being an insecure teen, I hated listening to a few words
as if they said something personal about me

I hated the word "stout"
as I was made to feel insecure about my own body

I hated the word "black"
as I was made to feel ugly about my skin colour

I hated the word "love"
as I was made to feel unlucky about my relationships

and now that I'm grown up
into a fully matured adult
and writing beautiful poetries out of all this
I regret,
that instead of hating these above mentioned innocent
words,
I should have hated
the names of those folks which served as perfect antonyms
to their habits
I should've hated them for having sweet names
yet not having any actions resonating the same
I should've hated them
for making me feel bad about myself.

-there's nothing wrong with you

I wonder if it was an island in the midst of a blue ocean
or a patch of cloud in the midst of a blue sky
I wonder if it was just an illusion
or some serious issue with my eyesight.

I never worried about my furious self
I always worried about the things
it mostly turned into,

the apologizes,
even though I barely did any mistake

the tears,
even though I barely did wrong to anyone

the panic attacks,
even though I barely deserved them

the sudden goodbyes,
even though I barely wanted to part ways.

May all your curiosities
get the reputation of questions

may all your uncertainties
get the reputation of decisions

may all your insecurities
get the reputation of inhibitions.

"You will never realize"
 my mum always said to me
 how we raised you,
 protected you,
 and nurtured you
 like flowers
 until
 you will start your new life
 in some another home
 with some other people
 and have your first child, a daughter.

-being the first child

I heard your voice
for the first and last time
you were yelling at me
but both my heart and mind
did not care
for the heart loved you
and the mind was slowly drowning
in the ocean of your saccharine voice
I went numb,
and ignored all the harsh things
you said to me
but deep down
both my heart and mind knew
that it is the first and last time
my ears are hearing your voice.

-improper conversations

The careless youth that had "dark future"
was living in the "present moment".

The deep roar after a little scream
was indeed a great deal
on the part of that small lioness
who was made to feel quite useless.

-it's never too early

My incomplete self
will forever cherish your incompleteness
just like
the midnight appreciates the half-moon
just like
that midnight
which has lost some parts of it
and aspiring for something brighter
finds its happiness in
that half-moon
which too has lost some parts of it
and evolving everyday to get better.

-incompleteness completes incompleteness

Strangers at the windows
might be superstitious fears

strangers at the doors
might be hopeless beggars

strangers in our hearts
might be passionate lovers

strangers in our memories
might be the best teachers.

I had everything
an unstable person would've wished for
guidance,
path,
residual strength,
and therapist
but what help a lighthouse could have done
to a sinking ship
and before anyone could come to save me,
I already drowned
in the deep ocean of shame
I already drowned
before realizing
that there might be many more ships
trying to survive in the same ocean as mine
I already drowned
before realizing
that I might be at much better condition
than the other ships.

-you're not alone

Learn to heal yourself before something else trounces you,

already damaged cities
suffer the most during wars

already shrunken plants
suffer the most during downpours

already torn books
suffer the most during reshuffling

already scraped skin
suffer the most during abrasion.

Have sweetness
and you will be shown everywhere

have sourness
and you will be kept in despair

have sweetness
and you will be treated right

have sourness
and you will be thrown out of sight

certainly because of their natures,
beverages are seen at gatherings
and served with delight
while acids are kept in laboratories
under strict precision
and dim light.

-try to be sweet sometimes

The morning was served in a silver plate appreciation
the night was just an old fashioned breakfast table
and yet after this injustice,
they both were inseparable.

-connections

You kept my picture inside the circular frame of your wallet
and little did I know
that you tossed it every week
like a coin
with "she" being on the other side
and little did she know
that it was "me" on the other side.

-poor girls

Now that we both do not exist
in each other's lives,
I wonder what will I do
if someday,
somehow,
this universe places me
right before you again
I wonder what my response will be
if I have to face you again,
may be I will faint
may be I will cry
or may be I will die
right there.

The flickering lamp
was a brutal fight
between two children
"brightness" and "darkness"

the flickering lamp
was a toxic relation
between two individuals
"sufferer" and "abuser"

the flickering lamp
was a bemusing indecision
between two conditions
"right" and "wrong".

Neither do you provide me any wherewithal
nor do you own any superpowers
still I'm pouring selfless love
on someone who is just like others
indeed,
some relations are like
undecipherable inscriptions
which are
arcane,
cryptic,
deep,
mystic,
and inscrutable
they cannot be comprehended
they cannot be pigeonholed
they are enigmatic yet enthralling
and so is
my admiration for you
it lies there in my heart
still and unplumbed
and I cannot attach any reason
for its presence within me
I just cannot.

-love is an inscription

When cardboard boxes
appear to be books

wooden sticks
appear to be quills

discard mounds
appear to be sceneries

fireflies
appear to be night lamps

dye-based inks
appear to be tears

is when you should congratulate yourself
for entering the world of poetry.

-newborn

You yelled at me
and told me to leave
but believe me,
whenever I write your name
with flower petals
and destroy it immediately
out of the fear of anybody reading it,
the excitement remains the same
for deep down
I still hope
that out there,
somewhere,
you might also be writing
my name
with flower petals.

I could be that innocuous dry leaf
fallen from some desolate tree

you might be mistaking me with some noxious snake
just because I have fallen at some dark place

I appear to have a curved hood
but believe me, I'm just a part of wood.

-please try to understand me

Out of the treasure box and the grave,
one was given a boon
to hold the jewels
and one was given a bane
to hold the dead remains
one became the reason for
someone's changed life
and one became the evidence for
someone's ended life

I imagine,
if the grave was a treasure box
or the treasure box was just a grave

I imagine,
a broken soul inside the grave
deciding to change itself into
shiny
esteemed
and valuable jewels

I imagine,
bane getting converted into boon

I imagine,
a grave getting converted into a treasure box.

-change yourself beyond imagination

It is true
that wounds heal
but when they're fresh
and new,
they fill us with insecurities
they make us feel
unlovable,
untouchable,
unapproachable,
our minds get concentrated
at those specific points,
we tend to think
that the whole world is
gossiping about them
not realizing that
we have the whole of ourselves
to offer to this world.

Something black and white
is my poetry
written on a white paper
with a black pen
something black and white
is my piano
containing the white
and black keys
something very pleasurable
strikes my heart
when my fingers
are working on them.

-colour palettes

Who's name?
Who's identity?
Who's soul?
Who's voice?

I'm just a grain of sand
introducing myself as an artist.

-we want exposure!

He was walking towards him
who was standing at the edge of a balcony
with no balustrade
his eyebrow flash,
deviousness in walk,
and unsteady breathing
raised her suspicion
she too started following him
as if she sensed something very heinous
she thought,
that he might push him
or frighten him from behind
but all he did
was touch his feet in formality,
seek his elder brother's blessings
and walk back as fast as he could

it wasn't the coldness in her heart
which made her think this way,
it was the coldness which blood relations
generally hold for each other
which gets the warmth of respect
only during festivals and gatherings.

-fake bonds

I cannot question
her kindness

I cannot question
her innocence

she wiped my tears
when she was herself crying incessantly
I cannot imagine a form of love
more pure than this.

-I'm ready to worship my mum

Before loving me,
you must learn
loving a broken flower vase
gather my broken pieces,
assemble me,
caress me,
and put flowers in my life again
and the rest of the task
to make your place beautiful
will be mine.

-waiting

Come fly with us

There's no such difference
between flowers and birds

birds have wings
flowers have leaves

birds originate by breaking the egg shells
flowers originate by breaking the seeds

they both coordinate with the bees,
birds give them space to construct the hive
flowers give them nectar to make honey

flowers and birds
might differ from each other
in terms of
appearance
place
and mobility
but their abilities to perform similar tasks
despite being at different places
is what ties them up
in a bond of similarity.

-make it happen

On the road of hope,
I stand alone
with open arms
and a constant thought
that you too will come back
just like these returning winds
which come back to me
and bring with them
some fine dust particles
causing my eyes to bleed

I hope,
that you too
will bring
the particles of
regret,
repent,
and sorrow
with you
and make my eyes bleed again.

-bleed tears

I regret
because I committed mistakes

I committed mistakes
because I was ignorant

I was ignorant
because I was brainwashed

I was brainwashed
because I was innocent

I was innocent
because I was a child.

-I was just a child

Yesterday,
I was writing
in a candle light

today,
I am writing
under a study lamp

tomorrow,
I might be writing
in an LED furnished room

what makes a big difference
is neither the writing place
nor the source of light

it was the light within me
which grew brighter
and brighter
and brighter
it was the light within me
which never blew out
and I kept writing.

-I will never quit

We are always a bit more attached
to the trees beside our balconies
even though we know
that the same trees
can be found at any faraway forest or ground

and the trees around us
are too a bit more attached
to the birds making nests on their branches
even though they know
that there are many more birds flying hopelessly in the sky
and trying to find a home for themselves

Just because everything around us is present in abundance,
it doesn't mean that they can provide us
with the same warmth

and you cannot give someone a reason
to stay away from you
just because humans are present in abundance
and humans have options.

-stay close

Your wounds should begin to itch
before you try to hurt others

your legs should begin to tremble
before you take a wrong way

your hands should begin to get numb
before you sign on fraud agreements

your heart should begin to turn concrete
before you decide to forgive your destroyers

"something" bad should happen to you
 before you go for "anything" worse.

 -something is better than anything

There was something very exceptional
about our last meet
since you looked extremely beautiful
the last time
I saw you.

-yes you

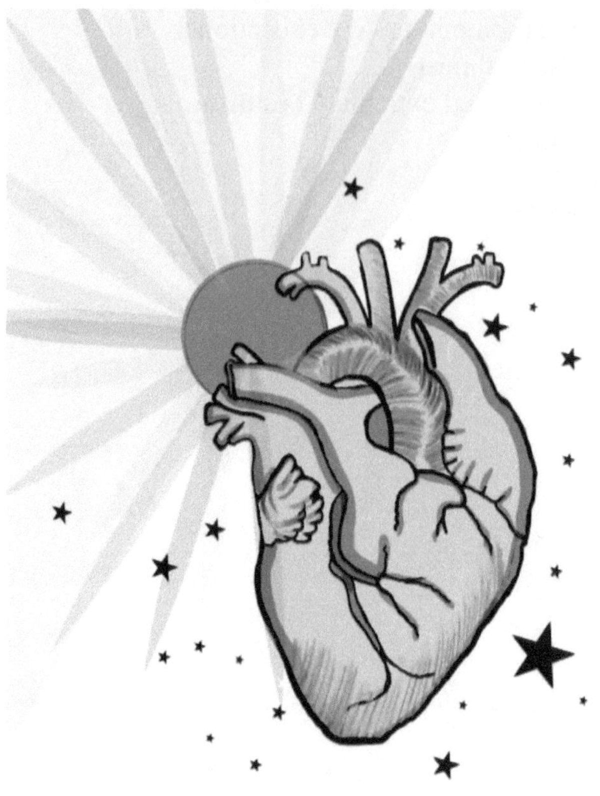

People have a sun within them
which they call "heart".

~ 125 ~

You're that favorite song
which doesn't give me same chills anymore
for when I got addicted to you,
I listened to you
and thought about you
every second
every minute
every hour
and every day of my life
and now that the phase of infatuation
has come to an end,
even your constant thought in my mind
is like any other normal thought.

-there's nothing special about you

My soul knows
how innocent I was
to be unable to distinguish between
good and bad
to be unable to distinguish between
birds and bats

between
those with feathery wings
and those with perplexing webbed wings
between
those associated with bright mornings
and those associated with dark evenings.

-I was mistaken

I kept falling for you
like the autumn leaves fall for the stones

despite knowing,
that my presence or absence
will cause no impact on you

despite knowing,
that the stones keep lying still on the ground
even if the seasons change
and new leaves grow at their place

despite knowing,
that my gathered sweet pinkish appearance too
won't be sufficient to allure your heartless pieces

despite knowing,
that even the deadliest winds
heaviest downpours
and fiercest heat
will rouse no sympathy from your side

and just like me,
the autumn leaves kept falling
for those who never really cared about them
but they indeed taught
the meaning of true admiration
which gradually breaks down
due to changing seasons
but can never be forgotten
or removed
or killed.

-one sided

Your conversations with me
were like the songs of my favorite playlist
played on loop
for when I was engrossed in them,
I barely realized
that the songs are changing
and so are the topics of our conversations.

When I was born,
I cried
and it makes no difference
for my eyes are still moist
on my each birthday
when I was born,
I had a bunch of people
talking about me
and it makes no difference
for people still make
different opinions about me
when I was born,
my mother fondled me with her love
and it makes no difference
for she is still there by my side
in all situations

hence I'm evolving everyday
with a few constants by my side
since birth
and probably this is how
the life actually works.

-happy birthday to me

All I ever wanted
was to turn my course
and kiss your feet
with my shapeless
yet purest admiration

all I ever wished
was to appreciate you
like rivers do to the mountains

but I couldn't keep up
with your mountainous ego
of being the highest
the greatest
the strongest

hopefully,
the only advantage
I have over you is that
besides being "emotionless",
you are "motionless" too
and with this strength by my side,
I will show you
how conquering the world looks like.

-*moving towards the ocean*

Dear moon,
I still admire you
and it won't be obscure to say
that I love you to the farthest galaxy and back,
you were indeed far from me
since the very beginning
since the beginning of this world
since the beginning of my existence
it was my childish fantasy
and unconditional inclination
which made me think
that you will come to meet me someday
that someday you'll also start admiring me back
I cry every single day
because of your absence in my life
even though I know that you will never talk back to me
I curse you for being this way
but at the end of the day
I have to appreciate you
for behaving like a gentleman.

-first letter to the moon

Dear moon,
these stars are making
all possible efforts
to separate you from me
they know the caliber of your enchantress
they know the intensity of my admiration
they're envious of you
they're envious of me
do not stay with them
they do not want to see us together
come to me,
I will heal your craters
accept you
and appreciate you
in all possible ways
or else someday
all these shrewd stars
whom you think are your close friends
will combine together
and destroy you.

-second letter to the moon

Dear moon,
I'm ready to gather courage
and move out alone
I hope that the first one to notice me right from the top
will be you
I hope that the first one to give me a recognition
will be you
I hope that the first one to make me feel special
will be you.

-third letter to the moon

I was the strength
the toughness
the powerhouse
but instead of charging myself,
I charged others with
love,
care,
and loyalty
not realizing that
before filling them up,
I too need to get the power
from somewhere else
which I never really received
and now the powerhouse herself
has ran out of power.

-please save me

There was a fruitless pleasure of opposite directions
which had the habit of bewildering the companions
with some tricky repetitions

those who got stuck in their infinite loop,
got the unforgettable lessons
while those who were calculative
earned the unforgettable reputation.

-this is life

I asked the sky,
why do we often feel the urge to cry
when we see our beloved ones
why do we often
behave this way
even if we know
that there might not be
slightest prospects of our union

to which the sky replies,
"I'm too no exception dear"
being far from the ground
I'm too having no hope of our union
but whenever the dark clouds of my emotions
cannot resist,
I fall down

and soon after this conversation,
it began to rain.

-*monsoon days*

Inside us,
there are some specific breeds

birds of colours,
(talent)
birds of papers,
(memory)

birds of divisions,
(intelligence)
birds of multiplications,
(over thinking)

birds of weapons,
(manipulation)
birds of chiffons,
(compassion)

birds of eternity,
(addictions)
birds of ephemerality,
(habits)

birds of monarchy,
(self-reliance)
birds of democracy,
(dependence)

birds of awareness,
(self-care)
birds of ignorance,
(self-doubt)

and the speciality of these birds is,
they can fly only inside a human body.

-being a human

Meanwhile,
the sea disappeared in a small boat

not realizing that
it had much potential
than the cunning boat
which changed its directions
after every second

not realizing that
it was the only one
giving surface and support
to that heartless piece of wood

not realizing their worth,
not realizing their importance,
there are so many important seas
that get disappeared in small boats
just because they aren't aware
of the importance
of their own existence.

-never destroy yourself for others

I learnt
to never get duped by tears
since it will eventually lead
to my own destruction
and if I let those tears
enter my dry heart,
it will be easier for them
to destroy me
and my heart
being as delicate as a paper
cannot even tolerate
something as acidic as
"tears".

You do not really have to seek topics
to influence you to write poetries
your inspiration can be anything,
ants or bees
butterflies or trees
heat or breeze
paws or feet.

-believe me

People could have entered a dark room
without lighting a candle
if they weren't always dominated by
the nyctophobia of darkness,
the scoptophobia of being stared at,
the claustrophobia of compact spaces,
the haphephobia of a sudden touch.

-scary

I only saw
a white tinge in the sky
and I thought
that I got the glimpse of the moon

you only gave me
slight tinges of
interest,
care,
and hope
and out of my habit
I always ignored
the dark clouds of
doubt,
hate,
and jealousy
just to console myself for once
that I have got the glimpse of your love

but your love was the moon
I never really saw.

-*what shall I do now?*

As a perfect response to "the flowers"
who are proud of their origin and beauty,
"the iron flowers" must be born

someone has to tell them
how it feels to melt in high temperatures
someone has to tell them
how it feels to be brave and rigid

someone has to tell those egoistic pieces
how their death comes just by withering away
and there is nothing much special about being
attractive or aromatic.

-be like iron flowers

Some personalities are like flowers
some grow naturally
and grounded
and some are the plastic ones
which humans create
by themselves

some are the way they are
and some just imitate the original ones

some are adjustable
even under the harshest sun
and some instantly melt
under the same sun

some shape their own growth
and some are shaped by some external force

some fall down
but sprout again
from fallen seeds
to continue their natural legacy
and some are mercilessly thrown away
once they become
moist and dusty

some take time to evolve and grow
and some can be easily seen at any random home

and this is why dear,
because of them being present in abundance
at a cheap rate
and desirable style,
the plastic ones are cherished
and the real ones mostly go unnoticed.

-real and fake

Them hurting us each time
in a different way
are what we call "memories"

it is insane how my sleep during nights
often breaks
not due to the bad weather outside
or the sauntering nocturnal animals
or the inappropriate room lights
but due to instant recollection of everything in my brain
due to sudden recollection of
each and every word
each and every sentence
people said to me
in some way
or the other.

-overthinking

I admired
how you showed your love
by putting your hand
on my head
combing my entangled hair,
parting them on either side,
and placing pearls on them
as if placing stars in an empty dark universe
indeed,
you formed a new universe
by showering me
with your selfless love
or else
everything was just
entangled,
hopeless,
and dark.

-*galaxies in my head*

Clean thresholds
hardly meant "clarity of opinions"

ironed bedsheets
hardly meant "understanding between individuals"

beautiful paintings
hardly meant "creativity in minds"

strong furnitures
hardly meant "strong backings"

effective lightings
hardly meant "bright futures"

and silent homes
hardly meant "peaceful homes".

Embrace your dim light,
acknowledge your gauziness,
cherish your movements,
adore your incompleteness.

-you're an aesthete in yourself

I never believed in
hiding my next step from the world
for I have seen "the sun"
which rises every morn,
raises temperature every noon,
and sets dutifully every evening

and if the world wouldn't knew
the sun's next step,
it would have been difficult
to cope with its presence
all day long
in the sky

and if the world won't know
my next step,
it will be difficult for it
to cope with my presence as well.

-don't underestimate me

I found that reason
by the side of a discrete lake
I found that reason
sitting alone,
bogged down,
and hopeless
left alone by those few fellows
it thought will remain with it forever

I kept my hand on its shoulder
and assured it of my presence behind

the reason was you,
the reason I've been searching for
since years
the reason,
why I always remained an annoyance for you
the reason,
why I kept myself away from you for so long
the reason,
why you deserved it
the reason,
"of your pathetic life"

the reason of your destruction
was you,
only you.

-the reason was you

Millions of unheard stories
hidden behind a few places,
scream
and invite me
to observe them thoroughly
and write poetries about them

the streets,
apart from being mere walking paths,
serving as complete,
concrete,
and concurrent proves of
torn letters,
crushed flowers,
broken ties,
and last goodbyes

the museums,
apart from being the displayer of rich cultures,
serving as absolute,
appropriate,
and accurate showcase of
collapsing empires,
running time,
unimportant jewels,
and intelligent kings

the amusement parks,
apart from being the most admired corners of mirth
serving as perfect,
powerful,
and peak results of
scientific excellence,

human wit,
profitable business,
and tireless teamwork

the gardens,
apart from being heavenly therapeutic corners,
serving as endless,
exceptional,
and exciting spaces of
tea time,
red roses,
soil contours,
and loneliness

the study rooms,
apart from being the comfort of the sophomores,
serving as depressed,
detached,
and demotivated portrayals of
broken hearts,
silent conversations,
hidden talents,
and unseen hardworks.

-stories behind

Absence be gentle
at least for once,
I want to experience
a kind of love
full of self praise
where I'm my best choice,
my best place,
and my best decision

at least for once,
I do not want to get caught in an addictive infatuation
which revolves around you
where you are the first thought
which comes to my mind
immediately after I arise from sleep

at least for once,
I want to dedicate and live
instead of destroy and end
my life for you

I have made up my mind
to stay away from you
I hope,
that I do not go for the kind of love
I never really want to experience.

-betrothed to absence

"Happy endings" are not a great deal
   if women start admiring men's eyes
   not for their toughness
   or deepness
   or sharpness
   but for the way
   they look at other maidens

   if men start admiring women's eyes
   not for their seductiveness
   or delicateness
   or mysteriousness
   but for the way
   they are able to see through the intensions of their suitors.

-parakh
Hindi; noun;

eye reading

A pigeon that wants to fly back
is not in love anymore

it wants to return
to its old shattered nest
which smells the same as its companion

it wants to remove everything
which reminds her of the past

it wants to rebuild its life
on that same corner again

it wants to work on itself
and the only one
to motivate her
is that little squirrel
which keeps rummaging for nuts and seeds
for survival
and competency.

-lessons

Presume a life like cotton wools
which are kept inside the iron box
neither being able to scream
nor being able to breathe
or escape
until picked up by someone
to wipe the wounds
until the parts of them
are taken
and thrown away
one by one,
and despite all this contribution,
still losing the reputation of "being a healer"
to the antiseptics
which have got chemicals mixed within them.

-unfair

Not every source of light
can be "a ray of hope"

not every source of sound
can be "a call of positivity"

thunderstorms are clever,
they bring with them
"light"
which gives us a glimpse of daylight
"sound"
which feels good to listen just for few minutes

thunderstorms are excellent teachers,
they teach us
to never believe these dark clouds
which feel good
only at the beginning of a deadly downpour
they teach us
to never get exited over
happiness lasting for a short span of time.

The lightning struck me
on a bright sunny day
and destroyed the civilization of colours
within me
which existed over the years
perpetual,
preserved,
protected.

-sudden drastic change

Everyone said,
I was the one who moved on
I was the one who broke those bonds
there were my faults,
my culpabilities,
I should be held responsible
but how do I explain?
I was actually the one who was
betrayed
battered
and abused
and even after all this,
whenever my eyes notice any shooting star,
their names are still the ones
which come to my tongue
instantaneously
their well being is still
on top of my wish list.

-broken friendships

After crossing zillions of galaxies,
I found a "palindrome world"
where everything was
organized,
linear,
and satisfied
then eventually
I woke up
in a world where there is
manipulation,
hate,
and disgust
I saw a dream of a world
where perfectness was reality
I saw a dream of perfect world
in a real world
where perfectness is a mere dream.

-I wish I could sleep more

What if,
that mic turns off
in the midst of my speech

what if,
the audience begin to laugh
at a fault which isn't even mine

what if,
I faint or collapse right there
due to this embarrassing situation

all these apprehensions
which keep revolving in my head
are capable to explain
that an artist's biggest fear
is not "rejection"
but "disrespect".

The blue crayon
always goes out of the limit
whenever I draw the sky on a white paper
it always goes out of the page
and out of the lines
sometimes,
even turning those white clouds blue
around their edges

the sky definitely has limits
but colours don't
the sky definitely has limits
but an artist's hands don't

there's little or no difference
between an artist holding a colour
and a king holding his sword
since they both showcase
how going out of the limits
is often the first step towards
"Conquering".

-conquer the clouds

I must turn back this clock
to write some more poems
I must allow myself
to make some more mistakes.

-running out of ideas

Either break into several pieces
and choose to lie still on the ground
until parts of you are picked up and thrown

or choose to grow at regular intervals
even though you're uprooted till your core

either be a glass
or grass
the choice is yours.

People around us are letters,
some are torn
some are incomplete
some are unread
some are burnt
some are misplaced
some are vanished

people around us are emotions
sometimes misunderstood
sometimes over expressed
sometimes buried

the universe has written letters
and now,
it is the duty of us letters
to reach our correct addresses
and destinations.

-letters of universe

The rope to reach the top
is within you,
behind you,
something which you call
"backbone".

-self sufficient

I will never fail
in conveying my emotions
to all of you
for if someday
I'm died
as "poetry",
I will be reincarnated
as "music".

-I love you all

EVERY STAR IS A MOON

Sneha Shukla is a 19 year old contemporary poet and writer. In her debut book, "every star is a moon", she has tried to cover every possible topic through her thought provocative poetries which will surely resonate with the experiences of the readers being a sensitive human she has always kept mental and emotional well being of her closed ones as a top priority. She is an extrovert who has always expressed herself to the fullest. Ever since she was a child, she always felt a strong connection with music, she can sing songs in *Hindi, Punjabi, Sanskrit, Arabic, English, French and Italian.*
If not studying or writing poetries, one can easily find her mimicking her favorite anime characters.

EVERY STAR IS A MOON

EVERY STAR IS A MOON